The Dark Age
Survivors Of The Pulse

By

Jeff W. Horton

Jeff. W. Horton

This is a work of fiction. Names, characters, places, and incidents are products of the author's imagination or are used fictitiously and are not to be construed as real. Any resemblance to actual events, locations, organizations, or person, living or dead, is entirely coincidental.

World Castle Publishing
Pensacola, Florida

Copyright © Jeff W. Horton 2011
ISBN: 9781937085049
Library of Congress Catalogue Number 2011928105

First Edition World Castle Publishing July 15, 2011
http://www.worldcastlepublishing.com

Cover Artist: Spittyfish Designs
Editor: Beth Price

Dedication

For my family, and my God...

Dedication

For my family, and my God...

Jeff. W. Horton

Prologue

It has been five-hundred years since the Pulse bathed the earth in a brilliant flash, instantly ending the Golden Age of humanity. At the speed of light, it destroyed modern technology all over the planet, ushering in the Great Collapse, and the conclusion of ten-thousand years of civilization. There had been no time to prepare, for the end came without warning. The cause of the cataclysm remained a mystery however, until one night people looked to the skies during the time of the Great Collapse, and found a new, beautiful, heavenly light there. Scientists soon uncovered the painful truth behind the fantastic lights; the Pulse was not alone when it struck the earth. The appearance of the powerful electromagnetic pulse had coincided with the arrival of a significant coronal mass ejection from the sun, trapping the power of the Pulse in the earth's magnetic field, creating a brilliant, nightly light show, similar to the aurora borealis in appearance, which came to be known as The Effect.

The terrible consequence of the Effect kept the people of the Golden Age from re-building the most advanced civilization in human history. Gradually, over the course of time, more and more of the accumulated knowledge that existed during the Golden Age began to fade from human memory. The abrupt loss of all modern technology had been a shock to the world's collective system, a catastrophe from which it was unable to recover. The subsequent descent into the darkness that began during the Great Collapse continued well into the period known as the Dark Age. After several hundred years, the rapid decline of civilization eventually leveled off, leaving humanity at a level of technology comparable to life during the Middle Ages, a time when illiteracy was the rule instead of the exception, and the world was ruled by the sword, and by the bow.

The Holy Christian Church, which has existed since the time of Christ, has now survived two dark ages. The unified Church has been the only light of hope for the people of the Dark Age, maintaining a continual presence in Rome, which serves as the nerve center of the Church, and a beacon of hope to Christian pilgrims from all over the world.

The Warrior Clan, founded during The Great Collapse by a group of ex-soldiers and civilians, maintains enclaves scattered throughout the Outlands. Shunning contact with the outside world since its inception, members of the Warrior Clan are disciplined fighters, constantly striving to perfect their martial skill. They are recognized and feared throughout the known lands as fierce and accomplished warriors.

Urbas inhabit the crumbling meros, all that remains of the great urban metropolises that once dotted the surface of the Earth. Living together in packs of twenty or more, they are the descendants of the few men and women that remained in the great cities during the Great Collapse. They survive by preying on outsiders and on each other, with allegiance to no one other than their pack, and themselves. The balance of humanity clusters in small, scattered villages, working mostly as farmers.

The Dark Age is a harsh and unforgiving time. The Golden Age and the Ancients are now largely remembered only in bedtime stories for small children. Just as the light always burns brightest in the darkness however, hope remains as some cling stubbornly to their faith, praying that one day the light of civilization will return. For among the many stories passed down from generation to generation over the centuries there exists an ancient prophecy, dating from the time of the Great Collapse. The prophecy holds that one day a sign would appear from God, announcing to believers that the time had come to find and activate the Great Oracle of Knowledge, giving the world the opportunity to emerge from the great darkness, into a glorious new Golden Age.

Chapter 1
Pilgrims

Somewhere ages and ages hence:
Two roads diverged in a wood, and I-
I took the one less traveled by,
And that has made all the difference.
Robert Frost, "The Road Not Taken"

Ferrell made his way through the dilapidated ruins of the once great metropolitan area, mindful of the many dangerous inhabitants that now called it home. He scanned the ruins as he walked down the wide ancient road, which passed through the middle of a number of tall, crumbling buildings, overgrown with ivy and rust. Outside two of the larger buildings, where the grass that sprouted through the concrete was the tallest, he saw something that worried him. A hundred yards in front of them stood a small herd of whitetail deer, that had stopped to feed on some of the poison ivy and poison sumac that grew out of the cracks in the road. Ferrell hesitated because he knew what it meant…trouble. The deer were a favorite food source for the large predators that roamed the overgrown ruins in the mero. It was only a matter of time now.

He was preparing to turn the group back the way they came in an effort to try to find a way around the herd when he saw something out of the corner of his eye. The movement was subtle yet familiar. Crouching low in the grass, their massive sinews tensing as they prepared to attack the herd, was a pride of lions, emerging from the edge of a dark alley between the two buildings to his right. Ferrell turned to face the people with him, pointing toward the big cats. "Slowly," he whispered, "everyone back away, slowly, no quick movements."

The three lions launched their attack with lightning speed, quickly moving to flank and encircle the herd. Two of the male lions, a mature, large cat, and a much younger, smaller one, chased after a part of the herd that had split off from the rest and was now running in their direction. The remnant of the herd separated, some to Ferrell's left and some to his right, but this time the lions did not follow the deer. Instead, they were now racing toward him and his companions. They had encountered human beings before, Ferrell surmised, and had probably discovered that people made for an easier meal than the much swifter and more agile whitetail deer. Two of the men travelling with him panicked and ran before Ferrell was able to stop them. I told them to stay close to me! How can I protect them unless they stay together? With a solitary movement, he drew his sword from its scabbard, sliced at the neck of the smaller beast, and then watched as it dropped lifeless to the ground. The second lion circled him for several moments, letting out a ferocious growl as it charged. The cat lunged at his throat with its massive claws outstretched, and its enormous canines positioned to close around Ferrell's neck. Just as the beast sunk its claws into his sides, Ferrell buried his katana sword into its chest, though the momentum of the now dead animal's carcass knocked him to the ground. He withdrew the blade from the animal and turned his attention back to the rest of the pride, breathing a sigh of relief when he saw the remaining lions devouring one of the deer that had been unfortunate enough to be at the rear of the herd.

Leading the group away from the feast and down a different path, he took a moment to catch his breath and check himself out as soon as they were clear. There were several puncture marks followed by deep scores where the big cat had nearly ended his life. Were it not for the thick and incredibly tough armor that he wore, the lion would surely have torn him apart with its powerful claws alone. Ferrell looked up briefly to survey their position. He soon regained his bearings and led the group around the ferocious animals.

Permitting himself to relax for a moment now that the immediate danger had passed, he paused to take in his surroundings. The crumbling structures on all sides reminded him of why he disliked the mero so much, regardless of how often he brought pilgrims through it. The ominous ruins of the ancient city stood as cold and foreboding relics of a strange and long-dead civilization. There was something unnatural about the place that made his skin crawl, and despite his regular treks through the long-deserted metropolitan area, he never could get used to it. The endless rows of buildings, clearly built to accommodate a vast number of people, now stood empty and desolate. As the travelers passed through the section of the mero where some of the tallest and most exotic structures stood, Ferrell tried to imagine what the city might have looked like when it was still in its prime, during the height of the Golden Age. Traveling through the mero alone so frequently had given him plenty of time to reflect on the disparity between what had once been, and what now was. Clearly the Ancients had achieved an incredibly advanced civilization, while the peoples of The Dark Age lived in such a primitive, feudal manner. It left him longing for something better for humanity. Perhaps, one day, we will tear down this graveyard, build a new civilization, and bring about an end to the Dark Age, as well as the death and decay all around us!

If the lion ruled the mero, then his four-legged subjects were the rat, the deer, and the dog, along with the many other descendants of zoo animals who, like the lions, had escaped their confinement hundreds of years earlier during the time of the Great Collapse.

Like most meros, however, the ruins were also home to packs of urba, people said to be descended from the Ancients that had built and once inhabited the now-deserted meros. The urba, who lived like bandits, robbed and killed anyone adventurous and foolish enough to venture into their territory unprepared. The ancient city Ferrell and his companions were traversing happened to be home to the only ocean port in the territory, resulting in a considerable amount of human traffic through that particular mero, despite the danger. The port to the Great Waters was the only reason so many risked the dangerous crossing through the mero. Most travelers were pilgrims or priests on their way to Rome, or settlers leaving for distant lands seeking a more hospitable place to live and raise their families. Few ships made such dangerous trips however, and fewer still were captained by men competent and honest enough to be trusted to carry them safely across the troubled waters.

Since the only way to get from the Outlands to the Great Waters was through the ruins, the urbas in this mero fared better than most. Even well-armed pilgrims fell victim to the vicious attacks of the urbas, who would then take anything and everything of value. Only a pilgrim of substantial means, who could afford to hire a warrior like Ferrell, could expect to have a better-than-average chance of completing the dangerous journey in relative safety. Though he often helped wealthy pilgrims get safely through the meros, he also offered free escort to those most in need, since he knew most of them would never survive without his protection. It had always seemed odd to Ferrell that they would risk their lives in such an endeavor. Even for those that made it to the port, navigating by ship was a dangerous enough business in itself, at least as dangerous as passing through the mero, by even the bravest man's reckoning.

The group of pilgrims accompanying him through the mero on this trip was a typical assortment of men and women; consisting of three couples, one who had brought along their five year-old son, and three men and two women, each traveling alone. They were on their way to meet their ship, which was docked where the Great Waters began on the eastern side of the mero. Once there, if everything went as he hoped it would, he would be escorting a different group of pilgrims from the ship to the Outlands. Some would be travelling to local villages; others would make long treks through the Outlands to distant territories. Ferrell had long ago considered the absurdity that just as many people seemed to be heading into the Outlands as there were people trying to get out. Most of them were either just restless or desperate he had concluded, hoping that their next home would be better than their last.

They had made excellent time and were now well over halfway through the mero. The thought occurred to Ferrell that maybe, just maybe, this would be the first time he made it all the way through the mero with at least one group of pilgrims without any challenge from the troublesome urba.

A sound from behind him caught Ferrell's attention. He turned, drawing the sword out of his scabbard as he did so, swinging the blade as if decapitating an invisible enemy. Although he did not see anything, he could hear a number of soft steps in the shadows to his left and to his right.

"Urba! Everyone, get behind me. Those of you with weapons, get them out. Do it now!"

Urbas emerged from alleys behind them, as many as twenty in all. Placing himself between the urba and the pilgrims, Ferrell ran toward the urba, sword in hand. He became a blur to the pilgrims as the only discernable feature became the flash of his blade. One of the urba stabbed at him with a sword, which nearly found its intended target. Ferrell sidestepped the attack at the last second, causing the urba's sword to stab his companion instead of Ferrell. The clansman then struck the second urba on the head with the hilt of his sword, rendering the urba unconscious. Ferrell looked up to find himself suddenly surrounded. He looked hard at the urba standing closest to him.

"Just so you know, you urba punk, " he said, pointing a finger at the big man standing in front of him, "I'm taking you out first!" A flash of fear fell on the urba he had singled out, while the others around him relaxed. Ferrell took a step forward, before suddenly stepping back, away from the frightened and intimated urba. He then delivered a powerful back kick to the solar plexus of the urba behind him instead, knocking him back six feet and onto the ground. The other urba rushed in and with Ferrell suddenly gone, they ran clumsily into one another, with two of the urba accidentally stabbing other members of their pack.

When the remaining urba attacked, Ferrell's blade sprang into action. Within seconds, the urba lay in a heap on the ground.

Ferrell had already dispatched most of the urba when he noticed that one of the pilgrims was in trouble. In a moment of folly, the naive man had left the others, dropping his guard in a misplaced attempt to try to talk with one of the urba, to try to reason with him. The attempt failed of course, as the pilgrim was knocked unconscious from behind, snatched up by two of the urba's companions, and dragged toward one of the tall buildings nearby. Ferrell knew what gruesome fate awaited the man if they reached the building with him. If he was lucky, they would kill him quickly before robbing him, taking whatever they could find on his corpse. Trying to reason with an urba! Ferrell decided to focus on helping the others instead of going after the hapless pilgrim. He had given explicit instructions to the group before they started through the meros that if attacked, they were supposed to stay by his side and just as important, they were to say nothing, and stay together. The man would get what he deserved for his foolishness in not following his instructions.

"Get to the ship," Ferrell told the others, "I will take care of the urba. Now go!" Ferrell took out two more of the urba before he noticed that most of the pilgrims were still there, standing motionless and staring at Ferrell. "What are you waiting on? I told you to head for the ship!"

"We will not leave without our companion, Mr. Young."

Unbelievable. Ferrell shook his head as he assessed the situation. He dispatched the remaining urba until they were all down. Even before the last one hit the ground, Ferrell was already sprinting after the man that was taken. He caught up to them just as the urba were dragging the terrified man across the threshold and into one of the buildings. When they saw Ferrell running at a full clip toward them however, they immediately dropped the pilgrim out of fear, and ran deep inside the bowels of the building in a panic. They had seen what Ferrell had done to the other members of their pack, and decided that they had had enough.

"Is everyone okay?" he asked, looking the group over for signs of injury after retrieving the man."Is anyone missing?" he asked, counting even as he did so.

"We all appear to be okay, and I believe that everyone is still here, Mr. Young," answered one of the women,"thanks to you. We owe you our lives."

"Hmm!" Ferrell grunted as he sheathed his blade and started walking toward the dock." Then maybe you will learn to listen next time, hmm?"

Ferrell and the pilgrims saw no further urba. Furthermore, he knew it was unlikely that he would have any additional trouble on the way back through the mero. It would be some time before the urbas he had just taken out were replaced by urbas from other packs. Since a pack typically roamed a specific part of a mero, and he had just dispatched most of the pack that patrolled the section they had passed through, the return journey would be quieter.

As they neared the dock, the pilgrims began to breathe easier, sensing the danger had passed. It was common knowledge that the urba stayed away from the docks, having learned long ago that messing with the armed crews that worked the ships was far more trouble than it was worth. When they finally made it to the ship, the pilgrims thanked Ferrell once more for all he had done. A crewmember greeted them as they approached and asked about payment for their passage. Visibly pleased with what they offered, he nodded his head, and pointed toward the gangplank, which they would need to cross to board the vessel.

Ferrell lingered at the dock for a while, taking the opportunity to sit down, rest for a few moments, and relax while waiting to see whether anyone disembarking from one of the ships would require his services on the return trip. Since he had to walk back through the mero to get to the Outlands anyway, he figured he might as well be paid for his trouble. He looked up at the sun, which was now sitting high in the sky, and determined that based on its position directly overhead, that it must be close to noon. If he left soon, he might make it back through the mero before nightfall.

"Mr. Young?" Ferrell quickly looked down, having been blinded momentarily after looking up at the sun. After looking away for a few seconds, he turned back around to find a tall, elderly man with a kind face and dressed in black clothing, standing before him.

"Yes?" Ferrell answered roughly.

"You come highly recommended by some of the men that just boarded this ship. They tell me that you handled yourself quite well on the way here, when your group was attacked by wild beasts, and then by urba. They said you are an exceptional warrior, and that they had never seen anything like you before. I was hoping you might be willing to help me get back through the mero."

Within a few moments, Ferrell was able to see clearly again. He recognized by the man's clothing that he was a priest.

"Sure," he answered, "I'll take you."

Jeff. W. Horton

Chapter 2
The Expedition

It was still early morning, and fog lingered several feet above the ground all around him. The sun had risen thirty minutes earlier and was beginning to cause the fog to dissipate, at last enabling Alex to make out some of the taller structures, confirming for the first time that he was indeed nearing the mero. It had taken him longer than he had anticipated to reach it however, and he was now running behind schedule. He preferred entering the meros just before dawn, before most urba, and animals as well for that matter, began moving around. The delay meant that with the sun already up, he would have to be particularly careful when entering the mero.

After searching for the artifact for many years, Alex felt certain that he was close, and that he would find it this time. He had to. The priest told him that finding the ancient relic was of paramount importance to them, that finding it could mean the end of the Dark Age. But how?

Alex missed Hannah. He had been spending far too much time away from her in recent months and it was beginning to weigh on him. It was unfair to both of them, especially since they had only had each other since her mother died. I'll make it up to her. She is the main reason I'm doing all of this anyway.

Alex was confident he had come close to finding the artifact the last time he was in the mero. He had seen something under a fallen bookcase, just out of his reach. It had to be the one he had been looking for; it had all of the markings. The Church would already have it in their possession had he been given only a few moments longer, and not been forced to abandon his search at the last moment. Several urbas had unexpectedly entered the ancient structure to get out of the downpour of rain, nearly tripping over him in the process. It was his own fault though; in his zeal to find the artifact he had become reckless, a mistake that nearly cost him his life. Alex had promised the priest that he would have it with him when he returned, however, and Alex was nothing if not a man of his word.

He cursed under his breath as he neared the edge of the mero. He dropped to the ground and peered through the top of the tall grass. Several hundred yards from his position, there was a large group of urba, apparently an entire pack, positioned directly between him and the mero. He looked around for options. He would prefer to go around them to ensure that his presence went undetected. He could not go right, however, because his way was blocked by the river, while a number of collapsed buildings blocked him on the left. He considered trying to wait them out, but the pack appeared to be settled in for the long haul. He could try to swing around the collapsed buildings to his left, but it would cost him at least a day, maybe two, to do so. After a few moments of deliberation, he finally decided that he could make it by the urbas. He would have to use great stealth however, as being caught meant certain death.

Alex slowly made his way through the tall grass, crawling carefully on his belly to avoid detection. He had been able to evade the urbas for many years as he made his way in and out of the meros on expeditions. Nevertheless, as dangerous as they were, it was not the urbas that worried him the most, nor was it the myriad of creatures that roamed the meros. It was the deteriorated condition of the buildings, which dated from before the Great Collapse, that posed the greatest threat. After nearly being killed on more than one occasion by collapsing buildings over the years, he had learned to exercise extreme caution when moving around inside of them.

He made his way toward the building behind them, while several of the urbas sat around arguing with one another. Though focused on avoiding detection as he made his way past them, Alex was still able to discern the topic of discussion, something about one of the urba women. As it heated up, one of them abruptly struck the other with a haymaker to the jaw, knocking him to the ground. It was a welcome turn of events for Alex, as the pack focused on the altercation. As he made his way past the pack, he looked back only to feel his heart race. All of the urba were looking in his direction. One of the bigger urba, apparently the leader, pointed toward him.

"Hey, you! What do you think you're doing?"

Alex froze. At any moment, they would surround him and it would all be over.

"Take it easy, Skye, it's just me. Take a look at what I found!" The voice came from in front of Alex. She was so close that she had nearly stepped on Alex's hand as she walked by. Alex looked back long enough to see that the urba woman was carrying something in her hand; it looked like an ancient knife.

"Hey, that looks nice. Bring it here so I can take a look at it..."

Alex quietly took in a deep breath and continued crawling on the ground, until at last he cleared the tall grass and was well out of view of the urba pack. He arrived at the building, opened the door, and began searching for the fallen bookcases.

***

The wind whistled as it passed through the trees in the nearby woods. The young girl heard a branch snap nearby and a pack of wolves howling in the distance. An owl called out in a nearby tree. The sights and sounds around the remote village of the Outlands where she lived might have frightened other children her age, but they did not bother Hannah in the least. Even at the tender age of twelve, Hannah was as brave and courageous as anyone in her village. She had been born and raised in the Outlands after all, and she had spent so many days and nights alone when her father was gone that the sights and sounds from the woods brought her comfort. She was armed and she knew how to use the weapons that she had both on her person and in the house. She used them frequently while hunting, even when her father was at home. Though she would never say anything to him about it, she was such an accomplished hunter that she suspected she had surpassed her father's hunting prowess some time ago.

Hannah sat down in the chair sitting in front of the old cabin that she called home. The full moon shone intermittently through the clouds that sped along through the night sky. Every now and then, the clouds would clear just enough that she could clearly see the wave of beautiful lights that floated in the night sky. She knew it only as, "The Effect." The lights were usually still easy to see, especially on a moonless night, but the bright light of the full moon had washed out the colors in the Effect, making it nearly impossible to see. She had heard stories that long ago, a much brighter and more brilliant Effect had dominated the night sky. It had been considerably brighter and more vivid then, during the time following the Great Collapse. According to some of the stories she had heard, the luminescence of the Effect had been intense enough that the moon itself paled in comparison, though she had a hard time imagining how that was possible.

17

Hannah watched the trees bending slightly as the cool wind blew through them. Temperatures were already starting to drop and she feared that the wind would bring with it much colder temperatures. Her thoughts drifted toward her father. He had been gone several weeks and was late getting back. She had been through this many times in the past, wondering whether her father was going to make it back alive from his latest expedition. She recalled how, when she was much younger, she would often lie awake in her bed, terrified of the night, and wondering whether her father would ever return home. Even when some of the neighbors would stop to check in on her to make certain she was doing okay; it provided her with little comfort. Her father had been her only world for many years, ever since she had died. Her fear of something happening to her father had often made its way into her nightmares, when she grew fearful that she would never see him again. Had animals attacked him on his way to the mero? Had he been caught and killed by urbas after getting there? Despite her fears however, he had returned safely from his expeditions, gradually allaying her fears. Over time, she had learned that her father was very good at what he did. He was able to get in and out of the meros easily because he had taken stealth to an entirely new level. She knew that he was good enough that he could walk through the middle of a pack of urba undetected.

She heard the great owl in the nearby tree call out once more. It had taken up residence in the woods outside their house soon after her father had left on his current expedition. Most likely, it had come across some resident mice on a nightly patrol, and had taken advantage of the easy meals.

She reached down for the ancient firearm that she had tucked away under the left side of her belt, and felt a sense of relief at finding the cold metal of the revolver securely fastened on one hip, while she wore her sharpened bowie knife on the other. Her father had allowed her to use the firearm once, so Hannah knew the awesome power it possessed. Alex had come across the unusual weapon in one of the ancient houses he had been in during his search. When he first discovered it, her father had been unaware that it was a weapon. It often happened that way with the countless artifacts that he came across on his trips. Sometimes he would literally stumble across such objects by accident while looking for something else entirely, and the firearm was no different. Having spent some time studying it, he set out to discover what it was and how it functioned. Her father had seen people killed handling ancient artifacts before so he exercised caution in handling the firearm. After learning how it operated, he soon found the weapon made an incredibly loud noise, much like thunder, when used. After recovering from the intense ringing in his ears, he noticed a large hole that he had not seen before, in the wall opposite where he was standing. Thankfully, he had not been home with her when he tested it. When he emerged from their home with the firearm, he also brought with it a small box with strange lettering on it. He pronounced the lettering as b-u-l-l-e-t-s, and told her that he had found the box in a drawer next to where he found the weapon. The box contained small objects that fit perfectly into the small chambers inside the weapon. Without them, it appeared the firearm did nothing, and once they were gone, there would be no more. After months of constant pleading, Hannah had finally been able to convince her father that showing her how to use the strange contraption was the right thing to do.

Hannah closed the door and went back inside the cabin, where she warmed herself by the fireplace. It was late fall and the nights had been growing steadily colder. She didn't mind the cold so much however, as long as she had a nice warm fire.

She laid the weapon down on the table by the bed and walked over to rummage lazily through some of her things. After several minutes of searching, she found what she was looking for. Her father had brought them back from an expedition when she was still only a little girl. None of the other children in the village had even seen a photograph before, much less ever had one of their own. She gently held one of them in her hand. It was her favorite, a photograph of a man, a woman, and a young girl. It often reminded her of her own family, of how happy she had been as a little girl, when she was still alive. Hannah felt the familiar sadness return, as she recalled her father trying to explain to her what had happened to her mother. She was still too young to understand sickness and disease at the time, though her father had tried his best to explain it to her. They had both taken her mother's death hard. Grief had weighed so heavily on them both that it was several months before he left for his next expedition.

Hannah continued staring at the picture, focusing her attention for a moment on the man. The picture always brought her comfort when her father was away. She missed him. Many times, she had pleaded with him to let her go, but the response had always been the same.

"I must go Hannah, please try to understand that I have no choice," he told her. "You know how much I hate leaving you here all alone sweetheart, but I must work if we are to survive. Besides, you know how important my work is."

"Then let me come with you Daddy, please!"

"No Hannah, I can't. I know that you don't like me leaving you here at the house when I go away, and I don't like it either, even with our neighbors checking in on you every day, but I cannot, I will not take you with me, no matter how much I would like to. It's far too dangerous in the meros for a little girl like you, even more dangerous than staying here alone."

It was not staying in the house alone that bothered her so much; she just despised being there without him. She wanted to go with him on his expeditions, regardless of the risk. She was not afraid of urbas, lions, or any other creature for that matter, not if it meant that she could be with her father. He had never taken her with him and she had always resented it. Nevertheless, she knew that it was dangerous enough for her father to travel alone in a mero with only himself to worry about, much less having to worry about looking after a little girl as well. Besides, she knew that he already carried heavy guilt about leaving her alone, and she did not want to do anything to add to it.

She was no longer a little girl, however, and she had insisted that she accompany him on his next trip. Her persistence and determination had apparently made quite an impression on her reluctant father, for despite the considerable reservations and the endless debates; he had finally relented, promising that he would take her with him on his next expedition. He had only one condition to which she immediately and eagerly agreed; she would obey his every instruction on the trip without question.

Hannah looked once more at the faded picture of the family of three, trying to imagine what life would have been like for her had things turned out differently, had her mother lived. Tears began streaming down her cheeks once again as she thought of her mother. She began sobbing all the harder once she realized it was growing harder and harder to remember her mother's beautiful face. She sat staring at the picture for quite a while, until at last the tears dried, and her eyes started to grow heavy. Hannah yawned. It was getting late and she had plenty of chores to do around the cabin in the morning. She hoped that her father would surprise her and arrive back early in the morning before she awoke. He had already been gone for several weeks, and it was time for his return. He had always made it a point to be gone no more than a few weeks at a time.

She sat down on her bed exhausted and looked around the cabin one final time. The firearm was still lying on the table next to her. Having satisfied herself that everything was in its proper place, she reached into her box, took out her cross, and placed it on her chest. She had watched her mother follow the same ritual night after night, and when she was old enough, she adopted the custom as well. Within a few minutes, she fell fast asleep.

Hannah never heard the door open or the boards creaking when, an hour later, the tall man in the odd-looking hat walked quietly across the room, until he stood quietly over where she lay sleeping on the bed.

Jeff. W. Horton

Chapter 3
Kraken

Madgar surveyed the large, crowded room, careful not to draw unwanted attention to himself amidst the flurry of activity that surrounded him, especially since all of the men there were heavily armed with knives and crude swords.

He noticed that some of the men, the ones of superior rank and status, wore a second, peculiar-looking weapon, made mostly of metal and unlike any he had ever seen before, tucked under their belts. They were clearly very old, worn down by the gradual passage of time. The weapons were ancient artifacts, forged centuries earlier by the ancient peoples, during the Golden Age. He had heard the stories growing up, as so many in his village had, the tales of various ancient weapons found by villagers and urbas alike, weapons which were often said to possess bizarre and extraordinary powers. Their deadly reputation was widespread enough that the artifacts were prized above all else throughout the known lands. While it was becoming uncommon to hear of a new discovery of an ancient weapon, based on the evidence all around him it was obvious to Madgar that it still happened.

According to the stories, the ancient weapons made deafening sounds when used, much like the thunder that ushered in the spring rains. Fire was said to emanate from the mouth of the device when used, causing it to appear even more fearsome in appearance, as it destroyed the enemies of the one who mastered it. The weapons varied greatly in shape and size, with some being small enough to fit in a man's hand, while others were said to be large enough that they required horses or even oxen to transport. While he waited to learn the reason for being summoned there, Madgar wondered whether the bizarre claims about the ancient weapons were contrived or factual. One thing was certain however, the weapons that he now saw before him were very real.

Madgar turned his attention back to the big man at the head of the table, having been told that he was the reason Madgar had been brought there. While he had never seen their leader before, Madgar had heard many tales of his exploits. The man had a reputation as a ferocious fighter, and as an exceptionally intelligent and cunning leader. He was also widely known to be a sadistic, cold-blooded murderer. Tales of his escalating cruelty had spread in recent years as a wildfire might spread throughout the villages of the Outlands and the meros, spreading considerable fear and uncertainty throughout the territory. Looking at him now, Madgar knew many of the stories about this man were true, indeed; perhaps they did not do him justice.

They called him Kraken. Standing well over six feet tall, he was a powerful and fierce-looking man in appearance. His body was covered in tattoos as well as scars, trophies from the many altercations that he had been in throughout the course of his life. A particularly nasty scar sat just above his left eyebrow, a souvenir from his younger days growing up in a mero. If the stories Madgar had heard about Kraken's childhood were true, perhaps it helped explain, at least in part, how Kraken had turned into the vile and pitiless human being he had become.

According to one version of the story, the one Madgar was most inclined to believe, Kraken was not born in a mero. Instead, he began his life in a small village in the Outlands, just outside of a large mero. The only child of a humble farmer and his wife, his life changed one tragic morning when Kraken was only seven, when his young parents decided on a brief excursion into the local mero. Planning to go no farther than the outskirts, it was a trip that they had made numerous times before. During their fateful last excursion however, the trio ventured deeper into the mero than they had intended to, and into the territory of a pride of hungry lions. The big cats had seen the defenseless family coming and had positioned themselves between the villagers and the way out of the mero. With their way home blocked by the beasts, the young parents were forced deeper and deeper into the mero, in a desperate effort to flee the hungry cats. The ferocious animals pursued them relentlessly throughout the streets and buildings of the mero. Realizing there was no escape for them, Kraken's parents opened a door that led into one of the ancient structures, and pushed the reluctant child through it before closing it behind him. They ran away from the building as quickly as possible, successfully leading the pride far away from the boy, sacrificing themselves to save their son. According to the story, the child watched as the lions fell upon his parents.

Despite the overwhelming odds against him, the boy from the Outlands was somehow able to survive, alone in the harsh and unforgiving environment of the mero. He managed to evade the dangerous predators and vicious urba packs that roamed the ruins, and learned to collect drinking water from the rain that fell from the sky. He ate rodents, and almost any other creature that could provide him enough nourishment to live on. He endured when most would have perished, growing and even thriving in the harsh environment.

Some years later, while still a teenager, Kraken killed his first human being. It was rumored to be an accident, according to the stories Madgar had heard. While walking home one day, the young man had a chance encounter with one of the meanest and biggest men in a pack of particularly nasty urbas. Coming upon the group unexpectedly, a knife slash from the leader of the group was his reward. In the ensuing chase onto the roof of a tall building, a single misstep caused the big man to fall to his death. Kraken raced back down the stairs to have a closer look at the dead body. When the other urbas in the pack arrived and found Kraken standing over their former leader, they assumed that the teenage boy had managed to kill him in combat. In accordance with their custom, they made him their new leader.

Leading a group of cutthroats and thieves was something that Kraken discovered he was surprisingly good at doing. An ambitious, resourceful, and industrious young man, he proved to be an equally effective killer. He soon grew to become one of the most feared and vicious urbas in the entire mero. Over the course of the years following his ascension to pack leader, his notoriety continued to grow among the various packs of urbas. At twenty years of age, through a violent campaign of intimidation and warfare against competing factions of urba, he successfully unified all the of the urba packs in the mero under his leadership. Kraken was not content to stop there, however. Unlike any before him, Kraken led the urba from his mero in attacks against other meros. One by one, the urba packs in each mero were given a choice, join Kraken with him as their leader, or die. At the age of twenty-five, he had successfully unified the urba packs from the neighboring meros in the area. By the time he reached thirty years of age, he had expanded his sphere of influence to all of the meros in the territory, nearly a hundred in all. Kraken continued building and organizing an army of urba, which became exponentially more powerful as it grew.

Madgar had learned from one of the elders in his village about what happened next. With most of the meros in the known lands under his control, Kraken soon began looking for new opportunities for his emerging and bloodthirsty empire. He launched a new campaign, this time against the villages in the Outlands surrounding the meros that he now controlled. He began by sending out raiding parties, taking whatever food or resources he wanted from any village they came across. The young men were enslaved, murdered, or in some cases conscripted into Kraken's army. The women were frequently taken captive and were kept as slaves or on rare occasions, as wives or concubines. Of course, first choice always went to Kraken, followed by his closest lieutenants in order of rank. Kraken's appetite for women was second only to his lust for cruelty and power, and his growing vision of a heartless new world, united under him as its absolute and merciless ruler. He would crush the weak, kill the innocent, and destroy anyone or anything that stood in his way.

In addition to his ruthlessness and his evil lust for power, one other thing stood out about Kraken; he had an extremely hot and violent temper. Any man unfortunate enough to be around him when he entered into one of his fits of rage would likely be subjected to a slow and painful death. He would murder another human being without even the slightest hesitation. Human life meant little to Kraken. The longer he remained in power and the larger his empire grew, the more unpredictable, paranoid, and evil he became.

Madgar had heard all of this and more about Kraken, whose campaign of terror continued to grow, threatening a world that had already endured five-hundred years of darkness, threatening to unleash upon it an even crueler fate. Had he been aware of its existence, Madgar would doubtless have referred to the world as Kraken sought to remake it, as Hell on earth.

Madgar contemplated why Kraken had summoned him to the stronghold, because it was certainly not his style. When news came that Kraken's men were approaching his village, Madgar had done everything that he could to prepare. They had few weapons and only a hundred fighting men, nothing that could come close to being enough to stand up to Kraken. He had expected Kraken's hordes to descend, armed to the teeth. When his men arrived at Madgar's village however, it turned out to be only a small contingent, carrying a simple message from Kraken. Madgar was ordered to accompany them to the stronghold, where Kraken would speak with him.

"You, come here." Kraken was pointing at Madgar, who walked over to the table where Kraken was sitting, and bowed. With a wave of their leader's hand, all of the men in the room left, except for three dangerous looking men, which Madgar took to be Kraken's personal bodyguards. Kraken spoke in between bites of cheese, fruit, and bits of meat.

"Your name is hmm… Madgar," he said with a wave of his hand, "and you are the leader of your village?"

Madgar nodded. "Yes, Lord Kraken."

"I am told that you are well respected by many of the other villages in the Outlands, is this true?"

"I suppose it is. Why do you ask?" Kraken looked Madgar over as a predator might assess its prey. Madgar took notice and it made him even more nervous. It reminded him of a cat toying with a mouse just before the kill.

"I have plans for extending the "protection" of my vast empire to include the entire Outland territory, along with the meros and all of the surrounding lands, including of course, your own quaint little village. I will take your village under my wing and care for all of the people in it, as I have many others over the past several years. I will protect them and I will provide for them. As long as all of my demands are met, all will be well. Do not worry, Madgar; you will be permitted to continue in your current capacity, as governor of my new little province."

Madgar breathed a sigh of relief. Given his reputation, it could have been much worse.

"Now, of course, you and your family will be required to come and live here, in the village just outside of this stronghold, with me."

Madgar swallowed hard and felt his heart skip several beats. Kraken noticed the concern written on Madgar's face and smiled.

"It will help ensure that you maintain order, and that you remember where your loyalties lie."

Madgar started to reply but Kraken continued his rant, as if oblivious to Madgar's presence. It was apparent that he had given this speech many times before.

"Of course, this tiny little region is only the beginning. I am expanding my sphere of influence, bringing an entirely new order, my order, to the entire world."

"Impossible!" The words had issued from his mouth before he was able to stop them; he now feared for his life. Few ever challenged Kraken and lived to tell the tale.

Kraken leaned in and narrowed his gaze at Madgar, focusing on him with a cold stare of unnerving intensity. "That is why I will do it, little man, because people believe it's impossible. But then, there has never been anyone quite like me before, now has there?" Kraken sat back and relaxed his facial muscles. Madgar sensed that his near brush with death had past. "There is no need to fear me, Madgar, for I will be a generous sovereign, requiring only half of all the produce and livestock from your farms. I will also "borrow" some of your young women and young men from time to time of course, to use as I see fit. The young men will serve me in various capacities, sometimes as my personal servants, sometimes in my army. The villages will provide me with whatever I want, whenever I want it, in return for my generous protection. In addition, I will expect my orders to be obeyed immediately and without question. Furthermore, I demand reverence from those who serve me. Of course, I will not deny any who wish to pay me the homage I deserve. They can even worship me if they desire, for I will be their gracious and powerful sovereign."

Oh I understand, Madgar thought to himself, you are completely insane.

"Yes, of course Lord Kraken, I understand," Madgar told him instead.

Kraken made a waving motion toward the door, indicating that it was time for Madgar to depart. As he was leaving, Kraken said, "Oh, and Madgar, there is one more thing I need to tell you. I want you to keep me apprised of any rumors of discontent in the villages under your control, and of anything unusual or out-of-place that you feel that I should know about. I require all of my regional governors to keep me well informed of what is happening in their respective domains." Kraken waved his hand, once more signaling for Madgar to go.

As he turned to leave however, Kraken glimpsed the smirk and tightened lip on Madgar's face, which revealed his contempt for the urba leader. Just as the village elder reached the door, Kraken added, "You know Madgar; if you object to anything I have said to you, please, feel free to let me know at any time. I would be more than happy to pay a visit to your home and discuss the matter with your wife and children, personally." Kraken's tone had become sharp and his voice cold, even for him. "I understand that your wife is an attractive woman. To tell you the truth, I wouldn't mind having a look for myself. Perhaps after she and I spend some quality time together, she would be able to persuade you to follow my instructions. Oh and how I would hate to see your two lovely daughters dragged from your home, and pressed into my imperial brothel, or perhaps given as female servants to my men." Madgar shot a hot, angry glance back at Kraken, whose eyes remained hard, focused, and menacing.

The two men glared at one another for several moments, engaged in a brief but intense battle of the wills, which Madgar inevitably lost.

"That will not be necessary, Lord Kraken," Madgar answered, lowering his eyes in a gesture of subservience. "I will do as you say, and keep you well informed," he said, looking at the ground. "I will do whatever you ask only please, don't harm my family."

"I know that you will, Madgar, I know that you will," said Kraken. "Now you may go; I will call for you again when I have need of you. Remember to bring your family to live here, in this stronghold, within one week."

"Yes, Lord Kraken," Madgar heard himself reply, scarcely believing how sheepishly the words had come out of his mouth.

Chapter 4
Vatican City

Darius tripped over a floorboard in front of the doorway, causing him to stumble out of the house on one leg, nearly falling flat on his face just outside of the front door. Without another moment of hesitation, he quickly made his way down the walkway leading up to the aged building, racing haphazardly down the crowded street and toward the Papal Palace.

"How is this possible?" he asked himself. "I don't believe it! I have lived in Vatican City for over a year now, without getting even a look at the Holy Father. Now I am going to be late for my first meeting with him! What am I supposed to say when I show up late for a meeting with Pope John Paul V? Aarrgghh!"

Darius ran as fast and as furiously as he could, dashing down ancient roads, in front of carriages and angry passengers, occasionally even bumping into other priests, in his frantic dash to make it to the meeting with the pope.

Running past several of the larger buildings, he turned a sharp corner without slowing down. His recklessness caused him to run headlong into an older priest with enough force that the papers the elderly priest had been carrying flew ten feet into the air. "I'm so sorry Brother, please forgive me! I'm late for my first meeting with the Holy Father!" The older priest cast Darius an irritated glance, shook his head, and began picking up the papers scattered on the ground all around him. When he looked back up, the young priest had already disappeared in the distance.

Darius slowed to a steady jog as he approached the Papal Palace, where the pope would be waiting to meet with him. By the time he reached the doorway, his heart was pounding like a jackhammer. He entered the building and slowed to a fast walk down the corridor, still sweating profusely. After several minutes, he gradually began to catch his breath and allowed himself to relax some.

Darius was curious as to why he had been summoned to the Papal Palace to meet with the Holy Father. What could the pope possibly want with him, such a young and lowly priest? No explanation had been offered, only the message that the pope wished to speak with him, in person, about a dangerous mission that he would ask him to undertake. He had never met or even seen the pope before, so Darius had no idea what to expect. He was resolved that no matter what the mission was that the pope had in mind for him, he would be more than happy to undertake it in service to the Lord, and for the sake of the Church.

Upon arriving at the designated meeting room inside the Papal Palace, Darius was relieved to find the door still closed. He had explicit instructions to wait outside should he arrive to find the doors shut, so he sat in a chair outside the doors and waited. He heard muffled voices coming from inside and assumed that the pope was still in a previous meeting. Thankful that he had not arrived late only to find the pontiff waiting, Darius was at last able to relax and calm his nerves.

He did not know what the mission would be or why he had been the one chosen to go, but based on the sense of urgency that had been impressed upon him, he knew that it must be something important.

As he waited, his thoughts drifted to Brother Mark, a close friend of his from seminary who had died in service to the Lord the previous month, and to Brother Phillip, Darius' cousin, martyred a year earlier. Darius feared that at the rate that missionaries were dying in the field, it could soon become difficult if not impossible to continue their missionary work abroad.

Darius considered the possibility that he might be sent overseas, just as Brother Mark and Brother Phillip had been. He knew how dangerous life was in most parts of the world, and that if he was sent overseas, he might never return. While he liked to believe he was prepared to die in service to the Lord, Darius knew that deep down, he was still scared at the prospect of dying. After all, he was still young, and he had so much to offer. Following some thoughtful reflection, Darius concluded that a person could never really know whether they are truly prepared to die, until death's cold touch is actually upon them.

After resting for a while, Darius began roaming the corridor outside of the meeting room, perusing the many pictures hanging on the wall. He paused for a few moments to admire one of them, a picture of the Lord Jesus Christ, as he was dying on the cross. Darius had seen paintings like it a hundred times. Still, something about the painting, placed in that corridor at the Papal Palace, with him facing what was likely going to be a dangerous mission, gave him a sense of perspective, and moved him deeply. The Son of God laid down his life for the Church, dying a most painful and humiliating death on the cross, for Darius and for everyone else that would ever call on his name. If the mission the pope had summoned him for was to end in his own death, what a privilege it would be for him, a dead dog, to follow in humility the example of his Lord and to die in his name! After all my Lord and Savior Jesus Christ has done for me, how dare I feel fear, even if it should lead to my earthly death?

Darius had grieved for days upon learning that Brother Mark and Brother Phillip had died fulfilling the Lord's Great Commission, "...to go into the entire world and preach the gospel, baptizing them in the name of the Father, and of the Son, and of the Holy Spirit..." While he sat waiting for the pontiff, he began to wonder how many of God's children knew who the Lord Jesus Christ was after centuries of living in the darkness. Even if it cost him his life, Darius resolved in his heart that he would do everything possible to spread the Good News of Jesus Christ all over the world.

Passing the time waiting for the Holy Father, Darius noticed another painting on the wall that he recognized. The work had been commissioned centuries earlier, with a number of replicas appearing afterwards. He remembered seeing one of the replicas in the local parish where he grew up. The painting, which he recalled had been completed a hundred years or so after the Great Collapse, was a scene from the famous Re-Unification Conference, held during the early years of the Dark Age. The conference was a unified gathering of what was left of both protestant and Roman Catholic clergy, where they signed a joint resolution to restore all Christian denominations back to a single church body, the Holy Christian Church. The differences that had separated them for centuries no longer seemed so important, given the suffering and death that followed the collapse of civilization. Both sides had made major concessions in order to come back together under the umbrella of the Holy Christian Church, in many ways returning to the structure of the early Church. No longer were there Catholics and Protestants, now there were only Christians. Darius appreciated the irony; that it took something as horrific as the collapse of civilization, to bring about the restoration of the church universal.

The door in front of Darius suddenly swung open and Cardinal Daniels stood in the doorway. He emerged from the inner chambers, closing the door behind him. A tall man, the cardinal towered above almost everyone else at the Vatican. He was a thoughtful and kindly man, well into his seventies at a time when it was rare to find anyone alive past fifty. Darius had liked the cardinal from the day that he first met him; the warm smile and easy mannerisms made him an easy person to talk with.

As he emerged from the inner chambers, the cardinal wore a disconcerting look on his brow. In all of the years that he had known Cardinal Daniels, Darius could not recall having ever seen such a solemn look on his face. Lost deep in thought, the cardinal did not seem to notice Darius's presence as he stepped out into the corridor. When he finally looked up and noticed Darius standing in the hallway, the solemnity fled away and the familiar smile took its place. He smiled warmly and reached out to shake Darius' hand. Despite his attempts to conceal whatever troubled him, the kind man still appeared preoccupied.

"Darius, could I please have a moment of your time, before you go in to speak with the Holy Father?" he asked, before placing his arm behind Darius' shoulders and escorting him to a large office. He paused for a few moments before finally settling on the words he would share with him. The cardinal motioned to a chair and asked him to sit down.

"Darius, as you well know, the church has struggled to remain caretakers of our Lord's Gospel, and to share His comfort with all people." Darius nodded in acknowledgement. "There is something else, "he added letting out a heavy sigh, "something that is not as well known. We have also been working to preserve some remnant of man's history, his knowledge, his legacy, as part of the larger objective of one-day restoring civilization to the world. You see Darius, throughout the centuries, ever since the time of the Great Collapse; certain knowledge has been passed down from pope to pope, a plan believed to have been given to the Church by God himself. Popes have been entrusted with this information throughout the Dark Age, with the exception of a select few. It was the desire of the pope at the time of the Great Collapse, his Holiness Pope Matthew, that this knowledge be limited to a small group of clergy. Each succeeding pope has honored that request."

Cardinal Daniels paused to gather his thoughts. "The time following the Great Collapse was a period of tremendous chaos and turmoil. The foundations of the Church itself were shaken as many died. Confusion and chaos reigned. Pope Matthew had a dream, a dream that he believed was a vision given to him by God. In the dream, he saw what he believed was a future time, when the world would be at a crossroads. After centuries of darkness and suffering, there would come a time when the darkness would end, and the world would have an opportunity to emerge from the darkness into a time of great prosperity, peace, and the re-birth of civilization. He saw a future so wonderful that the Golden Age would pale in comparison. According to this prophecy, the Lord went ahead before the Great Collapse to provide a means to hasten the re-birth of civilization and to provide a means for the world to re-emerge from the Dark Age. The way out of the darkness would require something called the Great Oracle however, which, according to the prophecy, holds all of the knowledge of the Ancients. Pope Matthew learned in the vision that a sign would one day be given to the Church, a sign that would announce to the world that the time was right to seek out the Great Oracle, and access its immense knowledge in order to restore civilization to the world. In the vision, the Church was instructed to wait until the sign appeared. If the people disobeyed the Lord, and attempted to find and activate the Great Oracle before the sign was given, all would be lost, and the opportunity for a new Golden Age would be gone for a thousand years. Worse yet, if the Oracle fell into the wrong hands, instead of a new Golden Age, there would be a time of pain and suffering that exceeded that of the Great Collapse and the Dark Age combined."

Darius was preparing to ask him a question when Daniels raised a hand, motioning for him to hold his question.

"The Holy Father has selected you Darius, as one of a select few priests that will seek out and attempt to find the Great Oracle. He believes that the sign will soon appear, and he greatly fears the Oracle falling into the wrong hands.

"When do I leave, Your Eminence?" asked Darius, already rising to leave.

"Peace Darius, peace! Wait a few moments and allow me to finish, please."

"Yes, of course your Eminence, please forgive me." Cardinal Daniels looked on Darius and offered a warm, sincere smile, admiring the enthusiastic priest, even while finding his impatience a little irritating. He felt certain that the Holy Father had chosen wisely in selecting the young priest.

"As I was about to say, there is a problem that we must address. No person, no man, woman, or child alive today, knows where the Great

Oracle is located. Nevertheless, we have learned of a book which, once we have found it, should lead us to it. We have had someone searching for this important book for some time, and we have every reason to believe that he is close to locating it. We recently sent another priest, Brother Sebastian, to find this man and to ascertain whether the man has indeed found the book we seek."

With a puzzled look on his face, Darius asked, "But Cardinal Daniels, why me? What have I done to merit the attention of the Holy Father, and to undertake an important mission like this? What if I fail in this mission? It would mean a time even worse than the Dark Age, and it would be my fault! What if..." Once more, the cardinal gestured to Darius.

"Peace Darius, peace!" the cardinal repeated. "Save your questions for now, Darius. I will do my best to answer them after your meeting with the Holy Father is over. Now go on in and meet with his Holiness, he is waiting for you. After you have finished, we will speak again."

"Yes, Cardinal Daniels."

"And Darius?"

"Yes?"

"I hope that you will pardon me my envy. I wish that I were thirty years younger, and that it was I who had the privilege to seek out and to find the Great Oracle."

Darius looked at the cardinal and smiled. As Darius rose and went in to speak with the pontiff, Cardinal Daniels contemplated the whole affair, and as he did so, he could not help wondering about what the future held.

Chapter 5
Exhausted

Ferrell was exhausted from his long journey. The walk from the mero to the village was a long one, and though he still had the body of a younger man, it had taken its toll. He was not as young as he once was, and it was some distance on foot from the edge of the Great Waters on the other side of the mero, to the village where he lived. He had attempted using horses for the journey through the meros years earlier, but the endeavor had ended in disaster when, during an urba attack, two pilgrims had fallen off their horses and perished. One woman had died when thrown from her horse, and one of the men had been crushed underneath his horse after it was killed during an urba attack. Given the nature of the threats he so often faced, he found it was easier just to travel through the meros on foot. Besides, he was much more effective on the ground when problems invariably arose.

Tired as he was from the journey, Ferrell was thankful he had been able to bring something home to eat, in addition to the payment of several sacks of wheat, corn, and a cow that he had received as payment from the pilgrims.

He had started venturing into the meros years earlier to help search for unfortunate children that had strayed from nearby villages into the dangerous and forbidding ruins of the meros. Soon after, he began escorting pilgrims that needed safe passage through the large ancient city and to the ships destined for the Great Waters. Few individuals could wander into that particular mero with any hope of ever coming back out alive, or at least not without paying a heavy price for it first. Even with a warrior like Ferrell to protect them, only half survived the journey through the meros on their pilgrimage to the Great Waters.

Christians. He had to admit that while he had learned a few things about the Christian pilgrims after years of providing them protection through the meros, he simply could not understand what it was that compelled so many of them to risk their lives and the lives of their families on these ridiculous pilgrimages. He could understand people needing a source of comfort. It was, after all, a harsh and unforgiving world that they all shared. He had always been perplexed however, as to why the pilgrims were so willing, seemingly even anxious to die because of their faith. Why would they risk their lives, even their children's lives, just to reach the Great Waters? They must be sick in the head. He then looked up to find that he had arrived back at his small house.

His legs aching and his head throbbing, Ferrell patted the front of his home, smiled, and opened the door and walked inside. Collapsing into his favorite chair, he felt great relief to get off his feet. He closed his eyes for a few moments, and would undoubtedly have drifted immediately off to sleep, were it not for the constant complaints coming from his stomach. He opened his eyes, sighed, and decided that he would eat, drink, bathe, and rest tonight, for tomorrow he would go back to his training.

Fortunately, he had come across a wild boar as he passed through the woods on his way home. He had killed it with a single stroke, ensuring that he would have enough meat to carry him through the next few days. He would eat most of the meat and then trade the rest, along with the sacks of seeds, to some of the farmers, in return for some of their harvest and some bread. After returning from his last trip into the mero, he had traded with some of the vine growers for some wine. Though water was plentiful in his village because the well ran deep and tapped into an underground river, he enjoyed the relaxation that accompanied an occasional flask of wine, particularly after a long, hard day.

After resting for a short while, Ferrell grudgingly got up from his comfortable chair, walked over to the table where he had put the dead animal, and carried it out the door with him. He then walked around the cabin to the back, where a table sat some fifty feet behind the house, with a knife laying on top of it. The table was not so much a table really, as much as it was a collection of boards, nailed together just enough to make them sturdy. The gap in between the boards made cleaning the animal much easier, not to mention the cleanup afterwards.

"Aarrgghh." Ferrell looked down and noticed the empty bucket sitting beside the table. He had forgotten water. Exhausted though he was, he left the dead animal on the table and walked down to the river. He considered drawing the water from the village well before thinking better of it, deciding instead to abide by the rules set forth by the village elders, permitting them to take only drinking water from the well. All other water must come from the river. It was an ancient rule, dating back well over a hundred years. It had been established during a severe drought in order to protect the village, and it was still applicable. It was not far to the closest river, less than a mile away, but he was barely able to stand as it was, without having to walk another mile to the river and then another mile back again. He had no choice; however, if he wanted to eat, so after uttering a few unkind words in the direction of the bucket, Ferrell reached down and grabbed it without breaking his stride, and began walking toward the stream. "That's alright," he muttered aloud to himself, "I needed some water anyway. A hot bath will be refreshing after spending so much time in the mero."

Water was nearly impossible to find anywhere in the meros and the precious little water that was there was carefully hidden and zealously guarded by the urba. Nothing inside the meros was valued more highly than water, including human life. Any water pilgrims needed for drinking on the trips through the mero they had to take with them, and bathing was something that had to wait for until they reached the Great Waters, or until they returned to their village. Despite the pain and exhaustion that racked his body, Ferrell decided the meal and the hot bath would be worth the walk. He would have much-needed sustenance and the bath would make him feel more refreshed.

As he approached the river, Ferrell came to realize that he was not going to be alone. One of his neighbor's, Ariel Sherwood, was already there. He watched her as she knelt down to fill several containers with water. Ariel, he thought to himself. How old is she now, nineteen, twenty years old, or more maybe? He struggled with what to say to her. Ferrell had never been good with people, even less so when it came to women. He knew more ways of killing a man with his bare hands than he could count anymore, even more so if he were armed with a sword, and he had defiantly stared death in the face more times than he cared to admit. When he was trying to talk with a beautiful woman like her, he became a virtual statue. He was about to turn and walk back to his cabin when she spoke to him.

"Hello, Mr. Young" Ariel said to him. "It has been some time since we last saw you in the village, we were beginning to worry." Ferrell looked at Ariel and smiled. He found himself taken aback by her stunning beauty. She had grown into an attractive young woman over the last few years, a fact that had not gone entirely unnoticed by the warrior. The little girl that first greeted him when he had first entered the village was no longer little, nor was she just a girl. With long dark hair and the most beautiful blue eyes he had ever seen, it was surprising to him that she had not yet married. In addition to her exterior beauty, he also knew her to have a magnificent spirit. He had always admired her quiet demeanor, and her concern for others, even as a child. It was a trait all too rare throughout the Dark Age. Was her father searching for potential suitors for her? He must be, thought Ferrell. If only things were different. He filled his bucket with water and smiled back at her.

"Hello Ariel. I appreciate your concern, but there was no need for you, or your family, to be concerned for me. I may be getting a little older, but I can still take care of myself."

"Oh, I don't know about that Mr. Young, I think maybe what you need is someone to look after you, perhaps someone with a more delicate touch, perhaps? After all, these are dangerous times we live in, and you just might need someone to protect you!" They laughed together.

"You might be right about that, Ariel."

"I think I know what you need Mr. Young. That house of yours desperately needs a woman's touch, and some color!" Ferrell's eyes opened wide as he looked at her and nodded his head, in a not-so-subtle effort to flirt back with her.

Even though he knew better, Ferrell cared for Ariel and for her family. When he had first arrived at the village, her family had been the first in the village to welcome him. They had treated him with great kindness, despite his often ill-mannered demeanor. They offered him food, shelter, and friendship. He might not be the most gregarious and friendly man at times, but Ferrell was honorable, and deeply loyal. There were few people he had ever called friend over the course of his life, but the few that had earned his trust and friendship, had found in him the truest of friends, someone they could count on, who would risk his own life to save theirs. He admired her parents for daring to raise a family in such perilous times, but he constantly feared for their safety. He had built his home near them in part for that reason, though he never would have revealed this detail to them. It was far too dangerous for others to know the level of affection that he held for Ariel and her family; his enemies might learn of their importance to him, and then kill the family just to get to him. Even as a child, he had been taught to avoid forming friendships outside of the Clan, mostly because of the danger it posed for others, and the vulnerability they in turn caused for the clansmen. It was also the reason why he had wandered the Outlands alone for so long, roaming from village to village ever since leaving the enclave.

"Will you be home for long this time, Mr. Young?" she asked him with a certain hope and eagerness in her eyes. While he had been aware of the special affection that she held for him for quite some time, it was his growing fondness for her, which had surprised him the most. Ferrell had done everything he could to keep to himself and to avoid entanglements with her or anyone else in the village. He now feared the time was rapidly approaching when he would once again have to abandon the place that he had called home. He had already stayed there longer than he had at any other village and soon, it would be time for him to leave. Attachments were something that men in his line of work could ill-afford.

"I will be home for only a short while," he finally replied, "just until I have rested and attended to a few errands.

They both grew quiet as they walked back up the path together toward the village. The day was almost over and the sun was starting to slip down behind the horizon.

"Mr. Young..."

"Ariel, I think that it's about time that you start calling me Ferrell." They both smiled.

"Ferrell," she continued, "I've been meaning to ask you something. I know that you've spent a considerable amount of time in the meros, especially the one nearest to us. What are they like; will you please tell me about them? Are they full of wondrous, amazing things, like the stories I've heard about them?"

Ferrell furrowed his brow. "The meros are dangerous places, Ariel. I strongly suggest that you avoid them. They are full of dangerous, deteriorating buildings, murderous urba and dangerous animals, all of which would kill you without hesitation."

"What do you think happened to the people that built them long ago?"

"I don't know."

"I wonder why we don't know more about them," she added.

Ferrell grunted. Hungry and exhausted from the trip, he quickly found himself tiring of the pointless questions.

"Women! Only women have time to think and talk about such things! I worry about what I am going to eat today, and you worry about the people who built the meros over five-hundred years ago!"

Ferrell immediately regretted what he had done as Ariel frowned and dropped her head in shame. He had not intended to be harsh with her. He sighed.

"I'm sorry, Ariel," he said gently. I haven't eaten, the journey back was long and tiring, and you know that I have lived and worked alone for a long time now. I'm afraid that sometimes, well, I'm not so good with people anymore." Ariel perked up. Ferrell looked in the direction of the mero before adding, "It has long been my hope, Ariel, that one day, maybe, just maybe, we will build a new world, one with new and even greater meros that will exceed even those of the Golden Age."

"That would be truly amazing," she said smiling at Ferrell. Ariel looked in the direction of the mero, before turning to face Ferrell, who smiled and nodded.

"As to the Ancients," he began, "I have no idea what happened to them. Maybe they fled the mero before some young, beautiful woman came along, wanting to take care of them, and asking them all sorts of questions that they couldn't possibly answer!" he replied, smiling warmly at her.

Ariel hit him playfully on the arm. "You just wait Mr....I mean Ferrell. I will make you eat those words some day!"

As they continued walking silently back toward the village, he wondered what she meant by her last comment. His thoughts then drifted to some of the incredible sights he had seen in the meros. Will there ever again be a world like that of the Golden Age? His thoughts were interrupted by a loud shriek.

"The village!" screamed Ariel, pointing up ahead of their current position.

Ferrell looked up ahead and soon recognized the reason for her outburst. Smoke rose from behind the trees, from where they both knew the village was located.

They picked up the pace as Ferrell focused his full attention on the village. Based on the noise and commotion coming from the direction of the community, whatever was happening, it had only just started.

"Stay behind me, Ariel," he said as the outskirts of the village came into view. A few minutes later, they arrived at his house, which sat between them, and whatever was happening in the village. "Get inside," Ferrell instructed. He set the water down inside the house and turned to leave. Do not leave here under any circumstances Ariel, not until I say it is safe. Understand?"

Ariel started to say something, but the stern look he gave her convinced her it was useless.

"Okay," she answered, "I understand." Ferrell walked out and closed the door behind him, his hand resting on the hilt of his sword.

He ran into the center of the village and toward the sound of the commotion. He soon found the source of the smoke. Several bandits on horseback carried torches and were going from house to house, setting them on fire. While the villagers focused on putting out the fires, other bandits on the ground had started sacking the village. Some of the men had already taken several young women and some of the younger boys as prisoners. Most likely taking them to the slave market.

Ferrell drew his sword and struck at one of the bandits on horseback, cutting into the bandit's side. The man fell behind Ferrell, who advanced toward a group of three bandits who were trying to lead a group of young women, bound with ropes and chains, out of the village. Two of the bandits drew their swords, while the third managed the prisoners. The fight was short-lived however, as Ferrell dispatched the two men with only two strokes of his sword. He then advanced toward the third attacker, who turned and faced Ferrell with his sword drawn. The warrior made short work of the third bandit, and cut the rope that ran through the chains on each of the women, effectively severing the rope that bound them together.

Ferrell was preparing to address the young women from the village when several of them suddenly gasped, and their eyes widened. Puzzling momentarily over what had solicited such a response, he soon had his answer. Just before turning to see what the women were looking at, he suddenly felt a sharp, searing pain in his right shoulder. He glanced down and saw the leading edge of the barbed arrow protruding from his shoulder. Ignoring the arrow, Ferrell turned and charged the archer on horseback, who by this time had already strung another arrow. He was preparing to let it fly when Ferrell's sudden and ferocious charge caused him to panic. The bandit archer dropped both the arrow and the bow before turning his horse to flee. Ferrell caught up to him just before he was out of range. He slashed at the bandit's back and then at his horse, causing the horse and rider to fall together, pinning the bandit underneath. With most of their fellows already dead, the bandits that remained turned and ran in the opposite direction, some on horseback, some on foot, abandoning whatever they had been carrying.

With the villagers now safe, Ferrell turned and stumbled back toward his house, looking down at the arrow sticking out of his shoulder. He was fortunate; it had missed his vital organs, passing instead through the muscle just inside of the shoulder. The pain was excruciating, but he would recover, provided he was able to remove the arrow and stop the bleeding. He would need to get the irons into the fire so that he could cauterize the wound.

"Ferrell!" Ariel rushed over to examine his wound just as he was opening the door to his home.

"Ariel, I'll be okay, but I need your help. I need you to do exactly what I say," he said calmly. "First, please start a fire. Second, take the long iron poker there by the fireplace, and place it in the fire once the embers are red-hot. Please hurry," he said calmly, not wanting her to panic. Ariel complied, hurrying quickly over to the fireplace where, despite her considerable anxiety, she worked quickly and methodically on starting a fire. A large, bright flame appeared within minutes. As soon as the flames had devoured most of the dry wood she had fed it, she waited and watched until she saw the familiar orange-red glow of the embers, and placed the iron in the fire.

Meanwhile, as Ariel prepared the iron, Ferrell searched for and found a small stick. After also finding a small piece of cloth, he wrapped the cloth firmly around the stick, took off his shirt, and walked over to his bed.

"Ariel, would you mind, assisting me?" He asked, taking a knife out from under his pillow.

"No, of course not, Ferrell! What can I do to help?"

"Once the iron is ready, I need you to take this knife and cut the part of the arrow that is sticking out of the back. You can then pull the remaining shaft of the arrow out from the front of my body. You will then need to act quickly, taking the hot iron and placing it on the entry and exit points of the wound. This will close the wounds and stop the bleeding. It's not bleeding badly now, but it will the instant you remove the arrow."

He then walked over to a chair in the living room next to the fireplace, carrying the cloth and stick with him. He looked in the fireplace and saw that the iron was getting hot.

"What do you need me to do now?" she asked.

"Get the other knife lying there on the table, the sharp one, and bring it over here. In that box over there are a several pieces of cloth. You will need to use the knife, and tear them into strips wide enough to use as bandages after we have cauterized the wound."

Ariel picked up the knife and prepared the bandages. When she had everything ready, he looked over at her.

"Thank you for helping me, Ariel; you're doing a wonderful job."

"I told you that you needed someone to take care of you!" she said smiling. Ferrell started to laugh but the pain soon put a stop to it.

"Okay. Ariel, are you ready?" Ariel nodded her head. "Now then, carefully cut the shaft of the arrow as close to my back as you can. Remember, once you pull the arrow out the front, you need to apply the iron as quickly as you can, understand?"

"I understand," she said, gritting her teeth.

"Good, go ahead and cut the shaft."

Ariel went to work, holding the arrow as steady as she could while she worked the sharp blade back and forth until finally the last four six inches of the arrow containing the red feathers fell to the floor. Ariel then walked in front of Ferrell, who took the stick with the cloth wrapped around it and placed it in his mouth, biting down hard. Ariel positioned the poker in such a way that she could easily reach it. She placed one hand on Ferrell's shoulder and the other she wrapped firmly around the black shaft of the arrow. She looked at Ferrell, pleading with her eyes that he would take this responsibility away, but instead he closed his eyes.

"Okay, here we go. One...two...three!" With a firm yet smooth pull, the arrow came out easily. Ariel wasted no time reaching for the red-hot poker, taking the glowing end of the iron and laying it across the edges of the wound, which by now was bleeding profusely. Ferrell started to scream, but the blackness overtook him before he could get it out.

***

The loud knock at the door woke Ferrell. It took only a few seconds for the pain to rouse him to full consciousness. He looked down at his now bandaged shoulder. It looked as if she had taken one of the cloths and folded it several times, before placing it over the wound. She had then used the remaining bandages to secure the folded bandage in place. It was exceptional work, considering it must have been the first time she had ever treated such an injury. Ferrell smiled when the thought occurred to him that she would make a fine healer. The knocking continued as he looked over at Ariel, who was still asleep in the chair where she fell asleep watching over him the night before. What does she see in a man like me? Ferrell finally made it out of bed and began walking toward the door. He opened it to find several of the young women he had rescued from certain death and slavery, the day before.

45

Each of the women held in her arms baskets of food, wine, and gifts. The oldest, a young woman in her early twenties, stepped forward, and presented an armful of fresh vegetables and fruit to Ferrell, before setting them on the table.

"Mr. Young, we hope you will accept these small tokens of our appreciation for what you did for us yesterday, suffering such injury, and risking your own life in order to save ours. We can never fully repay you for what you have done. The whole village has been talking about you, and about what you did for us, thank you."

"You're welcome. All of this, however," he said, pointing at their gifts, "is totally unnecessary."

"Please accept them, Mr. Young. Everyone in the village wanted so much to do something to thank you for what you did. They will be disappointed, possibly even offended, if you do not accept them."

Ferrell sighed. "Very well, in that case I will accept them, but it really is unnecessary. After all, I live here too."

"Thank you Mr. Young, we owe you our lives."

"Nonsense. Please tell everyone in the village that I am grateful for their gifts."

After Ferrell accepted the baskets, the girls smiled and left.

"Ferrell, who was that?" Ariel asked as she walked up behind him. "You need to get back in bed, mister."

"It was two of the girls I rescued yesterday. They and some of the other villagers wanted to show their appreciation by bringing me these," he said, pointing toward the table.

"Ferrell, you need to rest for at least another week or two. You need time to heal inside."

He smiled, closed his eyes, and nodded.

"I know, you're right, I do. But Ariel, you don't have to stay here with me, I can take care of myself now." She shot him an odd look of rejection mixed with flirtation.

"Do you want me to leave?" she asked.

"No, I don't," he replied, looking into her eyes. "I enjoy your company. It's just..." Ferrell hesitated, "well, shouldn't you be spending your time with someone closer to your own age?"

"You're close enough for me, Ferrell. That is, as long as you are okay with it."

"Well I..."

"Good, it's settled. Now then, it looks like you have plenty of vegetables and fruit. Now all you need is some meat. My father and my

46

brothers were supposed to go hunting today, I'll see if they found anything. If they have, I'll see if they have any venison they can spare."

It took several months for Ferrell to fully recover from the wound, and he was already preparing for new trips through the meros. He had suffered no lack of necessities during his convalescence however. Grateful villagers continued to show up at his door bringing food, water, and anything else he needed. He also had no shortage of company, since Ariel had been there by his side during most of his recovery.

The clansman finished wrapping the last cut of venison from the deer he had brought down that morning. Since he had recovered so well, she had reluctantly gone back to her father's house to assist with harvesting some of the corn in the fields, leaving Ferrell alone. Ferrell took the leftovers and threw the remaining parts that he would not eat down the back hill, where hungry birds quickly set upon them. After preparing wood for a fire, he grabbed his torch and walked to the center square of the village, where he took some fire from the community torch, before returning home to cook his meal. When it was done, he grabbed his bottle, his cup, and his meal, and sat at the table. It was the best meal he had eaten in a very long time. After drinking several large glasses of wine, he lay down in his bed feeling warm and relaxed. After a short while, he fell into a deep and restful sleep.

Had he not been so exhausted from his recent exploits, perhaps Ferrell would have reacted when the door to his home creaked open, and a dark, strangely dressed, and well-armed figure, peered into the small house. Realizing that Ferrell was in bed and appeared to be fast asleep, the intruder crept inside, crossing the floor to where Ferrell lay in bed, with his hand resting on his sword. The intruder slowly raised his sword over the motionless Ferrell, poised to strike.

Chapter 6
The Book

A board let out a loud creaking sound and Hannah's eyes popped open. Terror ripped through her when she realized there was a stranger standing over her. She tried screaming, but with the man's hand firmly covering her mouth, all she let out was a weak and muffled whimper. She struggled to get free but the man had a firm grip on her right arm, which he kept pinned to the bed while his other hand covered her mouth. Without a moment's hesitation, she bit into the man's hand, causing him to jerk it away and release his grip on her arm. The girl jumped out of bed and leapt for the door, but the strange man made it there first. He stood in the doorway, blocking her only way of escape. She studied him for several moments now that she was on her feet and completely awake, attempting to assess the situation. The intruder was a tall, older man, dressed in black, with dark gray hair and a moustache.

"That was not necessary, my child," he said, holding his injured hand and wincing in pain. "You have nothing to fear from me, my dear, I assure you. I am sorry if I startled you, but my mission is of the utmost importance, and it cannot wait, not even for a single night. Now then, please tell me where your father is. He was supposed to meet me by the ruins just outside of your village this morning. I waited all day until nightfall, before deciding I could wait no longer. I thought this might be his home based on its location as he described it to me some time ago. Now I ask you again, where is your father? Are you Alex Montgomery's daughter?"

Hannah thought about screaming before deciding it was unlikely that doing would bring any assistance anyway; they were too far away from their nearest neighbor. She also considered making a run for the door but with the man now standing between her and the only way out, she doubted she could make it. It crossed her mind that she could attempt to overpower the man and escape, but she felt that this too was unlikely to succeed. She decided not to do anything until she found out what the stranger wanted, hoping that in the meantime, an opportunity to escape might present itself. She sat in a chair, never taking her eyes off the trespasser, not even for a second.

"Now, then, that's better. As I said, I am very sorry that I frightened you, and I promise you that I am quite harmless. Please, tell me now, are you Alex's daughter?" Hannah hesitated for a few moments before deciding she might as well find out what it was that the man wanted.

"Yes," she answered with a sneer.

"Wonderful! Perhaps I had better take a moment to explain why I am here. My name is Sebastian, Brother Sebastian, and I have come here from a faraway place called Rome, on an urgent mission. Your father has been doing some important work for the Church, helping us to locate a very special artifact. The object that we seek is very old, extremely rare, and of great importance to us. When he last spoke with one of my colleagues, your father told him that he was getting very close to finding it. When the news reached us, we decided to visit your father immediately. Where is he now, child, has he gone back to the mero?"

Hannah stared at the man and said nothing.

"Now see here young lady, you must be able to see by now that I am no threat!" Still no response. "Okay, we can sit here all night and stare at one another, or we can try to have a conversation. Who knows, you might even find out that I'm not such a dangerous man."

She considered screaming again, making a run at the door, or even reaching for the ancient weapon, but by now, Hannah was growing more curious about the man and his intentions, despite her better judgment.

"I haven't seen him since he left here several weeks ago," she finally answered. "He should already be back by now."

"Hmmm, that's not good..." he said, catching himself after glancing over at the girl and noticing the fear and concern on her face.

"I mean-, I'm sure that he is fine. We've worked together for some time your father and I, he is an extremely capable man. He knows what he is doing and he can certainly take care of himself, I assure you. How long has he been gone then?" he asked.

"About three weeks, maybe four."

"How long does he normally stay gone for?" asked Sebastian.

"He never stays gone for more than 2 weeks; I have been getting worried."

Brother Sebastian walked over to the wooden chair against the back wall and sat down. He stared at the window for a while, considering what the girl had told him. Her father's delay could mean that he had found what he was looking for, or it could mean evil had befallen him, perhaps at the hands of the urba, or worse. If something had happened to Alex, all would be lost and their struggle would be in vain. He had been the best man for the job, and he had been getting close to finding it, closer then any had ever been before. They had no backup plan and they were running out of time. The priest tossed this thought around for some time, examining the precariousness of their situation. The search, the sacrifice, the future; were they all doomed now to failure and darkness? Had all been lost? Would the people of The Dark Age be forced to endure even greater suffering than what they had already endured? After struggling briefly with panic and great despondency, he took a deep breath and began to relax, as he considered who held the world in his hands, the one who was, and always would be, in control. They would find their way out of the Dark Age, if it was his will. He then dropped to his knees as Hannah watched. "Forgive me oh God, my Lord, and my Savior, for indulging, if only for a moment, in such useless despair! Please take away my fear and my worry, and restore to me a greater, stronger faith in its place!" Whatever happened, he would do as he had always done; he would continue placing his trust in God. Sebastian rose and sat back down in a chair.

Hannah, who had observed the man and his odd behavior with intense interest, found herself baffled by the man's actions. The intruder, who seemed more and more like a harmless old man, had invaded her home, terrified her by standing over her bed with his hand over her mouth in the middle of the night, told her that he knew her father, and had just finished talking to someone who wasn't there while on his knees. She found herself bewildered by it all.

"Who were you talking to just now?" she asked with an inquisitive look, her anger now gone. "Are you sick?" she asked him, thinking he might have developed an illness, which might explain the odd behavior.

"Why, I was talking to God, my dear. I asked him to forgive me for my despair and for my lack of faith."

Hannah looked at him even more puzzled. "Who is God?"

"Who is God? You mean, your father never told you, about him?" The gentle man looked at her first with surprise, then with sadness. His eyes watered up, as he looked upon the young girl, living in such a dangerous world, with no knowledge whatsoever of God.

51

"I sometimes forget what life is like for so many of God's precious children, without the word of God, without the Church, without civilization. I spend so much of my time surrounded by God's people that I sometimes forget how many live with no knowledge of God! At least during the Golden Age, people had the opportunity to learn about God, though for some inexplicable reason they often chose to reject him. 'Who is God, you ask?' Why, my dear child, God created you, the world, and everything that is in it."

Hannah shook her head in defiance. "That's not possible! How could anyone make the whole world? Besides, I wasn't made, I was born. My father told me all about it!"

Sebastian blushed briefly. "I tell you what, how about I tell you all about God in the morning, while we wait for your father to return, how does that sound to you?"

"No, my father has forbidden me to allow any strangers in the house, especially when he has gone away."

"I assure you if your father knew that I was the stranger, he would make an exception."

Hannah thought about that for a moment. If this was the man her father had worked for all this time, he would want her to take him in. Still, she also knew that he could be lying. "I don't know, I doubt he would approve," she repeated.

"If you decide to let me stay, I promise I will take up little room, and perhaps I can repay you for your trouble?"

"Okay," she said after thinking it over for a couple of minutes. "We do not have much left to eat," she told him, "but you are welcome to some of what we have."

The priest, touched by her generosity and unselfishness, looked at Hannah with a warm, sincere smile. "That is kind and charitable of you my dear, but perhaps I can help both of us. Please, excuse me for just a moment," the clergyman said, before walking out the front door.

After a few minutes, he returned, carrying a sack in his hand.

"I came well-prepared for my journey my dear, and God has blessed me on my travels." He reached into his sack and pulled out a loaf of bread, some cooked meat and a bottle of wine. Hannah's eyes widened, at what looked like a feast to her. "Would you mind if I joined you for dinner tonight?"

Hannah did not even have to respond, the wide smile on her face answered for her. She had been truthful with Sebastian. She had not eaten anything since the day before because the food was running low, and she had been rationing what little she had left in case she ran out completely. She brought out the tin cups and plates, and placed them on the table.

"Would you please permit me the privilege to thank the Lord for this food?" Sebastian asked as they sat down to eat.

"Sure, that's okay, I guess," she answered, wearing a puzzled expression.

The priest bowed his head and began speaking. "Most merciful and Holy Father, we thank you for blessing us with this food tonight. We ask Lord, that you prosper the mission of this wonderful young woman's father, and that you will bless the cause that has brought me to this land. We ask in the name of our Lord Jesus Christ, one God, now and forever, Amen."

After they had filled their empty stomachs, Hannah decided she wanted to learn more about this man, and what it was that her father had been looking for. He had mentioned to her several times that he was looking for something important, but he had never told her what it was.

Brother Sebastian was much older than her father, his hair gray and thinning. She felt certain that he was the oldest person she had ever met. Now that she had spent some time with him, he seemed a kind and thoughtful man. Perhaps they would have gotten off to a better start, had he simply knocked on the door and introduced himself to begin with.

"I'm sorry if I hurt you," she said, watching him rub the hand she had bitten, the one he had used to cover her mouth, "but you deserved it. You scared me!" she told him, feeling equal measures of remorse and satisfaction; remorse at hurting him and satisfaction that she had given an intruder something to remember her by.

"It's a good thing I didn't hear you coming though!" she added matter-of-factly, "because I might have used the ancient weapon my dad found instead! How was I supposed to know who you were?" Sebastian noticed her looking down at his hand and then back at his face.

"I understand perfectly, my dear," he said. "I certainly did have it coming, sneaking into your home in the middle of the night like that, and waking you from what looked to be such a very pleasant and restful sleep."

Hannah smiled. She was beginning to think that if she were to spend enough time around this man, she would end up liking him.

"Why did you say your name was "Brother Sebastian?" she asked him.

He chuckled and replied, "Because," he answered, "I have many brothers, many Christian brothers," he added. "You see, I am a priest, my dear. Do you know what a priest is?"

Hannah looked at him blankly. "Sure, I…um…no, I have no idea."

Brother Sebastian laughed again. He had always adored children. He missed the wonderful time he had teaching children at the school back in Vatican City.

"No? Okay, um…you know, I don't believe you ever told me what your name is."

"My name is Hannah," she answered.

"It is wonderful to make your acquaintance Miss Hannah! As I said earlier, I am Brother Sebastian, a priest of the Holy Christian Church, and like all Christian priests I serve the Lord Jesus Christ, my Savior and my King!"

"Who is Jesus Christ, is he the King of Rome?" she asked, imagining a man sitting in a great palace, and Brother Sebastian bringing him food and drink. Sebastian laughed again.

"Well yes he is, of a sort, but he is really much more than that." The priest thought for a moment before continuing. "I tell you what. Let's see if we can get some sleep tonight, and then, as I said earlier, I will tell you all about him in the morning, while we wait for your father to return. Would that be okay with you Hannah?"

A disappointed look came over her face for a moment. She had been bored ever since her father left and she felt that Brother Sebastian probably had many interesting stories he could tell her. Nevertheless, he was right; it was time to go to back to sleep. She yawned and suddenly felt very tired. It had been a long day and she was exhausted.

"You can sleep in my bed, Brother Sebastian. I like to sleep in Dad's bed when he's gone anyway."

"I would never think to impose on you in such a manner. I insist that I sleep on the floor next to the fire, while you rest comfortably in your bed." She yawned again.

"Okay…whatever you say. Good Night, Brother Sebastian," she said, climbing back into bed.

"Good night child," he responded. He lay down next to the fire and tried to get comfortable. He smiled when, just a couple of minutes later, he heard Hannah snoring.

The next morning, Hannah awoke to find that Brother Sebastian had already risen, prepared breakfast, and left a plate of food for her sitting on the table. While she ate, she tried to imagine how much food they must have in Rome.

She finished her meal and went outside looking for the priest. She found him just outside of the cabin, sitting on a stump, watching with great interest a colony of ants busy at work. Every few seconds he would look up and scan the horizon. Probably looking around for signs of Dad, she thought to herself. She walked over to him and touched him on the shoulder, startling him.

"I'm sorry Brother Sebastian; I didn't mean to startle you."

The priest smiled back and shaking his head said to her, "Think nothing of it child. It is a sign of the times that we have lived in for so long, I'm sad to say. Did you see the plate I prepared for you on the table?"

Hannah nodded. "Yes, thank you. Where did you get all of this food anyway?"

He just laughed. "God has been good to me."

"So, will you tell me more about God now," she asked.

"Well, I suppose that when your father arrives, we shall both know it. Let's see, where should I begin? Believe it or not, once upon a time, long ago, during the Golden Age, the world was full of the knowledge of God. Nearly everyone knew about the Lord, although not everyone trusted in him. In fact, it would have been difficult to find many households anywhere in this part of the world that did not have a copy of the Holy Bible."

"What is the Holy Bible?"

"The Bible is the book that contains the most Holy word of our Lord. It was written by many different men over the course of several thousand years."

"If there were so many Bibles everywhere, why is it that I have never seen one? Not that I could read it if I had one."

"You don't know how to read, Hannah?"

"No, not really. In fact, I don't know anyone that can read, except for my father of course."

"You mean he never taught you…?" The priest started but Hannah cut him off.

"He promised me that he would, but he never seems to have enough time to. I can read just a little, but not much."

"I'm sorry, child. Would you like to know something, Hannah? The world wasn't always like this you know. During the Golden Age, nearly everyone could read and write, but then came the Great Collapse, starting the rapid descent into the darkness. After the Great Collapse, people were no longer concerned about trying to learn or teach others how to read and write, because they were too busy just trying to survive the great calamity that had befallen humanity. Unfortunately, most of the knowledge of the Golden Age was lost during that time. People began to burn books just to stay warm during the cold winter months that followed, and knowledge of our Lord, as well as civilization, began to fade in the collective memory of mankind."

"So how do you know so much about God, if all of the books were burned I mean?" she asked.

"Oh to be sure, not all books were burned, and not all knowledge of God passed away. Would you like to know something else, Hannah?"

"Sure."

"This is actually the second Dark Age our world has known, not the first. A long, long, time ago, well before the beginning of the Golden Age, there was another Dark Age, a time when the world suffered through a time of darkness similar to our own, when the light of civilization and knowledge nearly disappeared from the world. That period, once commonly known as "the Dark Ages," followed the collapse of another great civilization, called the Roman Empire. During that time of upheaval, the Christian Church served three vital roles. First, it preserved knowledge of the Lord and enabled the Church to spread. Second, it helped maintain order during a period of great chaos. Third, the Church helped to preserve knowledge of the civilizations that existed before the fall of the Roman Empire. Without the Church, knowledge gained over thousands of years would have been lost."

"Wow. How do you know all of this?"

"Because in Rome, where I live now, God has preserved much knowledge about himself and our past, despite the considerable chaos and confusion that reigned during the time of the Great Collapse. Given the great chaos that followed the fall of civilization however, even the Church struggled, at least for a time. Now, the Lord has once again started growing his Church. We have once more slowly started building parishes across the world."

"Is God all-powerful, Brother?" she asked. "If he is, why did he allow the Golden Age to collapse in the first place? Doesn't he care about people anymore?"

"Those are great questions my dear," answered Sebastian, with more than a little admiration for her curiosity and intelligence. "Perhaps it was because he has given mankind something called free will, the

freedom which God gives us that allows us to make decisions on our
own, such as the decision to follow him or to reject him. Unfortunately,
by the time of the Golden Age, humanity had chosen to trust in
technology rather than God. Some believe that everything that has
happened has been part of God's plan for humanity, to stop man from
destroying himself and the world, in order that he might give others the
chance to be born, to love, to choose him, until the Day of Judgment. The
truth is, we don't really know why God does many of the things that he
does, but we trust him anyway."

"So God has allowed mankind to suffer for so long because of this
free will? Maybe we should give it back to him, so that he can make the
world a better place to live!"

Brother Sebastian chuckled.

"Who is this Jesus Christ you mentioned?" asked Hannah.

"That is a wonderful question, but not an easy one to answer. He is
the Son of God. He suffered and died to save us from our sins."

"So he is dead, then?"

"Well, he died, but God raised him from the dead, just as he will
one day raise us from the dead as well."

As he was considering launching into a discussion about the Holy
Trinity, he noticed a figure in the distance coming down the path. His
focus shifted from his conversation with Hannah to the man coming
toward him. Hannah turned around to see what he was looking at.
When she saw the familiar figure in the distance, a big smile appeared on
her face. She jumped up from where she had been sitting in the grass
listening to the priest, and ran toward the man now approaching them.

"Daddy, Daddy!"

Hannah jumped into her father's arms, adding to the heavy weight
of the pack he carried on his back, and knocking him to the ground.
Brother Sebastian noticed that Alex didn't seem to mind it in the least.
The pair lay on the ground, locked in a long, warm father-daughter
embrace for some time, with both laughing, and crying for joy.

Brother Sebastian had a million questions for Alex, but they could
wait. After all, what was the point of restoring civilization, the love of
family, like the love of God, was not the most important consideration?

It was a while before the pair once again took notice of the priest.
The man stared at Sebastian for some time before asking, "Brother?
Brother Sebastian, is that you?"

The priest smiled and answered, "Hello Alex, and welcome back."
Alex rushed over and embraced his old friend.

"It's good to see you again, Brother. It has been a long time!'

"It is good to see you again as well, Alex," answered Sebastian.

"I see that you have met my daughter, Hannah, as well!"

"Indeed. I have had the great pleasure of making her acquaintance while I waited for you. You have a bright and lovely daughter, Alex. You must be very proud of her."

"I am, Brother, I am."

"Forgive me if I seem blunt in asking this Alex but please, I must know, did you find it?"

Alex said nothing. He stooped down to the ground, taking off his pack as he did so. After a few moments of rummaging through the brown sack, he pulled out several ancient books.

"Alex, please! Did you find it or didn't you?"

Alex seemed surprised by the uncharacteristic impatience of his friend; he had never seen him like that before. He thought about it for a few moments before saying anything.

"They know about it now, don't they Brother Sebastian?" he asked. "They have learned of its existence, haven't they?"

The old man hung his head in sadness and frowned.

"Yes Alex, they know. We don't know how they found out about it, but they did. He has men searching everywhere for it. If you have the artifact however, it still may not be too late; there may still be time. The sign has not yet appeared, but I am convinced that it soon will, and so is the Holy Father."

"Who is the Hol…?" Hannah was interrupted by her father.

"Not now Hannah. I'm sorry, honey but this is extremely important."

He turned back to the priest. "How much time do we have?"

"For now, they know only that it exists, so they have only part of the puzzle. We do not have much time, however, before they uncover enough of the rest to pose a problem for our mission. Now tell me Alex, please tell me, I implore you. Do you have it?"

Alex looked at the two books he pulled out of his sack and handed one of them to Brother Sebastian. "This is the one I saw the last time I was in the mero. I believe this is it, but I wasn't sure."

The priest took the book from Alex and looked through it for what seemed to Alex and Hannah as an eternity. After some time, he raised his eyebrows and a broad smile consumed the face of the kind priest.

"Yes Alex…..I believe this is it, the key to restoring civilization, and ending the Dark Age."

Chapter 7
Brother Ramos

Kraken bellowed in rage upon hearing the knock on the door. "Who dares to interrupt me?"

Angry, Kraken grabbed his favorite knife from underneath the pillow, and climbed out of bed. "I warn you, if I do not like what I hear, you will know it only for the last few moments of your life!"

He opened the door to find one of his top lieutenants, Mansa, standing there. The fact that he was his top man mattered little to Kraken at times like this, and Mansa knew it. He was all too aware that each time he disturbed Kraken; he placed his life in the hands of a hot-tempered, dangerous lunatic. He was mad, yes, but he was also a fierce and powerful leader with a bold vision, and the best fighter that Mansa had ever seen. Perhaps he would one day challenge Kraken's hold on leadership, but it would not be anytime soon, in part due to the likelihood that he would never survive such a challenge. Besides, why not wait for Kraken to complete his conquest? He could always take him out after he had finished building his empire. Maybe, just maybe, that is when Mansa would make his move.

The movement was nothing more than a blur. In the blink of an eye, Kraken had the knife at the throat of his most loyal man.

"Mansa," he said in a low growl, "I will give you fifteen seconds to draw your last breath, and tell me why you interrupted my entertainment," he told him, nodding toward his bed, "before I relieve you of your responsibilities, permanently."

Mansa swallowed hard and slowly kneeled down before Kraken. "Forgive me my lord, for disturbing your rest. We have word of something of great importance that I believe you will want to hear. I was afraid to wait, because of the significance of this news."

"Breath your last my friend, and tell me what could possibly be so important," said Kraken.

"Your empire, my lord. We might have found a means to complete the conquest of all of the known lands, much sooner than we ever thought possible."

Kraken paused, thought about what he had just heard, and motioned for his female slaves to leave. "Tell me," he said after watching the last of them walk out, "what have you learned?"

***

The men waiting outside of the small house were growing increasingly impatient. The man banged on the door again for the third time, this time even louder than before. "Okay, knock it down," the man in charge ordered.

Two of the men took the large stone by the wooden handles that were tied around it, and prepared to bash the door in. The door suddenly swung open, and Madgar appeared in the doorway.

"What is going on here? Why do you disturb me at this hour?"

"We have orders from Lord Kraken. Come with us. Now"

"Very well, give me a chance to….."

"We said, now!" One of them grabbed hold of Madgar's collar and jerked him out into the street. "Now move it. Lord Kraken wants to see you immediately."

Madgar complied, closing the door behind him, wondering what Kraken wanted this time. He walked with the men down the path to Kraken's lair. Madgar hated living in this awful place. He missed his village, he missed the woods, and he missed the quiet. He had never even been in a mero before, at least not up to the time that he first arrived at the small mero that Kraken had turned into his stronghold. Madgar began listing in his mind anything and everything that could be important enough to prompt Kraken to summon him in the middle of the night. Madgar knew that the lives of everyone in his family depended on his response.

When they finally arrived at Kraken's compound, Madgar was led in through the largest of the three main rooms leading into the lair. This fact alone worried him, as he knew all too well that Kraken preferred torturing prisoners in the first, larger room, so that when provincial governors were brought in to see Kraken, they were forced to walk past those being tortured. The torture was intended to serve as a warning to those brought in to see Kraken; of what could happen to them should they ever cross him. Madgar had to admit that it had proven an effective means of psychological intimidation. By keeping his governors terrified of him, Kraken was able to ensure that they remained obedient.

Madgar and the others passed by several occupied cages, where the unfortunates were kept between sessions of torture. All too soon, however, Madgar realized why he had been brought to Kraken's favorite room in the stronghold.

"Brother Ramos, is that you?"

Madgar had spotted his friend lying in a heap on the floor of the cage, but he had barely recognized him. The priest had been badly beaten and was covered in blood; his hair matted. "What have they done to you, Brother?" Madgar asked, in tears at the site of his friend's pitiful state. A loud roar of laughter suddenly erupted from behind him, as Kraken, who had been watching, could no longer contain himself.

"What have they done to you...Brother?" Kraken mocked. Madgar wheeled around, trying to restrain himself but unable to hold back his daring tongue.

"Kraken, this time you go too far. This is a man of God, a priest in the Church! You dare to mock God?"

In the brief time it took for Madgar to recognize the change in Kraken's expression from arrogance and mocking to one of violent, explosive anger, Kraken had already pounced on him, blade in hand. Ever so slowly, he brought the blade along Madgar's throat, pressing it deeply enough into the flesh that blood began to flow freely, but not deep enough to sever an artery.

No, Kraken thought to himself, I must not kill him, at least not yet.

"Yes, Madgar, I do dare! Gone too far, have I? Gone too far?" he roared. "I don't know this God you speak of, but I will tell you who has gone too far. I know about your little secret now. Our mutual friend here, your Brother Ramos, just confided to me that you two have been collaborating lately. It took a few weeks to break the priest; he is strong, I will give him that. He lasted longer than most. Nevertheless, I have become particularly skilled at finding out what I want to know, and I assure you Madgar, I will learn everything I want to know about this plan of yours."

"Kraken please, I don't know what you're talking about!"

"Really? That's too bad. You see Madgar, I had hoped that you and I could remain friends, but now I'm starting to think you don't like me. You are forcing me to take actions that I didn't want to take, my friend!"

He nodded toward one of his henchmen and said, "Bring her in."

They brought in Madgar's oldest daughter, Braca, who had turned eighteen the previous year. Madgar could see she had been treated roughly, probably beaten, but otherwise, she looked okay.

"Now, so far," Kraken continued, "I've only allowed the men to rough her up a little. I've not allowed them to have their fun, at least not yet." Madgar bristled at Kraken's last remark. He knew he must be careful at this point because Kraken was, if anything, wildly unpredictable.

"The priest tells me that you have certain knowledge that he and others like him have shared with you, something about a book they are looking for, a book that supposedly holds the key to some great power of the Ancients. He told my men that once the priests have this book; it will 'change the world.'" Kraken leaned over close to Madgar. "Well, the problem is, I don't want my world changed," he roared. "I like it just as it is. Your Brother Ramos here said that these priests are looking for a book that will lead them to something called the 'Oracle', which was mentioned in some ridiculous prophecy of theirs. Now, you will tell me everything I want to know Madgar, and you will tell me now. I will warn you that as the priest has discovered, my patience is thin."

Madgar sighed. "What do you want to know?"

Kraken bent over and leaned into Madgar's face, only inches away.

"I want to know what is going on with these priests. What is this book they are looking for, what is this Oracle he was going on about?" He thought for a few moments and added, "You know, Madgar, until your Brother Ramos joined us here, I had believed that priests of that ancient religion had long since died out. I guess I was wrong. Now tell me Madgar, what is so important about this book he told me about, that he would give up his life to protect it?"

"All I know is that it supposedly contains the location where the Great Oracle is hidden. The Oracle is said to be extremely powerful, containing all of the knowledge and technology of the Ancients, knowledge that has been lost for five centuries, since the Great Collapse. It is said that this knowledge can bring mankind back from the brink of destruction, and out of the darkness."

"Out of the darkness? But I like the darkness!" crowed Kraken. "I will not permit them to find this place. I will not permit them to ruin the plans I have been making. If anyone is going to have this knowledge, this power, be certain that it will be me. With it, I will learn the secrets of the Ancients, and with it, I will conquer the rest of the world, crushing anyone who dares to oppose me! Now, tell me Madgar, where is this book to be found, and who is looking for it, other than this priest?"

"From what Brother Ramos and the others told me, they believe the book to be located in one of five meros, scattered around the world. They have been searching for this book for a long time. Some years ago, the Church started sending experts out into the various meros, and from what I am told, they are getting close to finding it."

"Is that so?" asked Kraken. "Well then, we will have to do something about that, won't we? If I can't handle a few pathetic priests, I certainly don't deserve to rule the world now, do I?"

"There is one other thing," remarked Madgar, with a slight smirk on his face this time. "They have enlisted the help of the Warrior Clan." For the first time Madgar saw something on Kraken's face he had never seen before... fear.

"The Warrior Clan? How can that be? They keep to themselves, they always have! They don't concern themselves with the affairs of the meros and the Outlands."

Kraken began pacing the room, assessing how the news might affect his plans.

"No matter," he said at length. "We will find this ancient knowledge and with it, we will build new and powerful weapons. Once we have them, even the Warrior Clan will be unable to stop us! Now Madgar, tell me, how do we find this book?"

Chapter 8
An Old Friend

The sword's rush to Ferrell's throat was met by a flash of light and the sound of steel clanging in the night. Ferrell's own sword appeared from beside him, clashing with the attacker's blade just inches above his neck. The ringing sound of steel on steel was so loud that it filled the cabin and left a ringing in his ears. After blocking the attackers sword, Ferrell countered by cutting at the stranger's mid-section. As Ferrell had correctly anticipated, the attacker easily blocked the blow. Nevertheless, it had given Ferrell the time he needed to rise to his feet and meet the enemy, this time from a much stronger fighting position.

He tried making out the attacker's identity, but it was still too dark. It was impossible to find enough light to see anything more than just vague shapes and shadows. He knew that his only chance was to rely on his other senses, particularly his sense of hearing. It was difficult to follow his attacker's movements, but he forced himself to rely as much on his hearing as he did on his sight.

Whoever he was, the intruder was clearly a skilled fighter, well trained in the fighting arts. The two men matched blow for blow, attacking and defending the head, the torso, and even the legs. It was Ferrell who finally broke the stalemate, delivering a solid back-kick to the attacker's midsection while he was standing close to the door. The kick landed solidly against the attacker's solar plexus, knocking him backwards and through the door. The consummate fighter, Ferrell followed his attacker outside, pressing his attack in order to keep the pressure on the enemy. All of his years of experience told him that his kick should have severely injured or killed the attacker. It should at least have knocked him out, unless of course he was wearing some kind of protective armor. The attacker executed a smooth and graceful roll once he finally landed on the ground, immediately coming back up into a defensive stance. He was wearing armor. This posed a particular problem for Ferrell, because he knew that only clansmen wore the type of armor that was so effective, flexible, and so easily concealable. While urbas sometimes wore armor, it was much clumsier, and would never allow the type of maneuverability that the unwelcome visitor clearly possessed. His attacker was either an outcast from the Clan or worse yet, had attacked Ferrell at the behest of the Clan.

Suddenly, as if the enemy knew what he was thinking, the attacker backed up several steps, and slowly laid his sword on the ground. Ferrell reluctantly accepted the challenge of hand-to-hand combat, still fuming at having a peaceful and much-needed rest so rudely interrupted. A man should not poke a stick at a tiger, unless of course, he wishes to be eaten. He was going to make certain that if he did not kill the man, he would definitely make him pay dearly for disturbing his sleep. Still, Ferrell was mindful that he had to be extremely careful. While the attacker was wearing armor, he was not. His armor was still hanging up inside his home, and Ferrell felt confident that the attacker would not allow him the opportunity to go back to get it.

The assailant came at him with a flying sidekick to Ferrell's Solar Plexus. Ferrell dodged the attack, moving off to the side, and followed the attacker to the ground, landing a powerful sidekick of his own just as his attacker turned back to face him.

The blow once again knocked the attacker down to the ground with substantial force; Ferrell was now able to get a long enough look to see that the attacker was masked, something uncharacteristic of a clansman, former or otherwise. Regardless of what the intruder was up to, Ferrell was beginning to tire of the game and decided to close for the kill. As the man rose to his feet, Ferrell could see that he was now beginning to slow. He saw an opening and delivered another kick, this time a powerful roundhouse kick to a weak spot in the armor. His adversary was able to block the blow, but only barely. The masked intruder hugged his side with his elbow, an instinctive reaction meant to protect the ribs. It appeared his attacker had been injured, most likely some broken ribs.

It was time to end it. Ferrell was preparing to deliver one final and deadly kick followed by a strike to the attacker's throat, when the attacker suddenly backed off and bowed low to the ground.

"Enough! Enough, please...you win, old friend!" the attacker exclaimed, with a trace of laughter. Ferrell's adrenaline was still pumping at maximum capacity however, so he was still in fighting mode. He had to struggle to muster the self-control needed to withhold the final blow, at least long enough to process what he had just heard.

"Old Friend?" he asked as he started to calm. That voice, I recognize it. He felt something gnawing at him, telling him that it was indeed a voice from his distant past, though part of him refused to accept it. It had been so long ago, so long since he had been at the enclave, since he had taught at the school.

The attacker was still on the ground, resting on his knees. Ferrell knew not to relax even for a second, until the attacker's identity was revealed, until he knew why he had been attacked. The man motioned to Ferrell to give him just a moment to rest. He held his side and grunted in pain, breathing heavily. When he saw Ferrell studying him, he laughed and started clapping his hands in applause.

"That was impressive, Ferrell. You have actually improved your skills since the last time we last saw one another, remarkable. It is clear to me now that your years as a wanderer have given you the time and the experience you needed to sharpen your abilities, and to hone the skills that you learned at the enclave. Where have you been practicing?"

"In the meros, where the urba and beasts have served as my instructors for the last few years."

The stranger laughed and answered, "I bet they have, how gracious of them, eh?"

Ferrell just grunted. If the visitor didn't soon reveal his identity and state his reason for attacking him, Ferrell was resolved that he would beat the information out of him.

"You have become much more efficient in your movements Ferrell. Your timing has improved, and you are considerably faster. Though in some ways your technique has lost much of its elegance, it has grown in terms of power and effectiveness, a worthy trade-off in our line of work, I would say. I knew or rather, we knew, that you were the right man for the job, that's why I came to find you of course. That is why he sent me."

"What are you carrying on so about?" asked Ferrell. "Who are you?"

Ferrell was growing increasingly curious, though still highly annoyed at being attacked in his own home, at night, while he was asleep. He started to assess the situation as his mind began playing back the attack. Had the intruder ever really intended to kill him, or had he only been testing him? Ferrell continued, "Tell me who you are, and why you attacked me in my own home, in the middle of the night, or I promise I will beat it out of you. It's clear to me that you are, or at least you were, in the Clan at some point, though attacking people as they sleep is not the Clan way, unless of course things have changed since I left. I should kill you now for this intrusion. Again, I suggest that you quickly tell me who you are and what you are doing here."

"Now Ferrell, take it easy. What would the others think if they learned that you had killed your old teacher again?"

Impossible, Ferrell thought to himself. He is dead. I should know, I killed him. I watched him die. He started to reach over and remove the man's mask when the attacker saved him the trouble. The man reached up and felt for the edge. It was a clear night under a half-moon, so there was just enough natural light combined with the torch lit out front that Ferrell could see clearly, as the man removed his mask.

"Hello, Ferrell." This time, Ferrell fell to his knees and bowed to the ground.

"Teacher!" he exclaimed. He had correctly identified the voice, but it was a voice from the grave. The attacker was none other than his friend and former mentor, David-Michael, the same teacher that he had murdered while he was still with the Clan. It was the death of his former teacher that had led to his self-imposed exile.

"I thought you were dead, teacher, I thought I had killed you!" It felt like a dream, surreal and vivid, yet impossible.

"Oh believe me old friend, there were more than a few days after our little skirmish that I wished that I were dead. My injuries were severe to be sure, and it was a long and painful recovery, as I am sure you might imagine."

"But how did you survive?"

"As you know, the Clan still has knowledge of many of the ancient medicines. They were able to heal me back to much if not all of my former strength. As soon as the elders realized that I was going to survive, they dispatched search parties to locate you, to let you know I was alive, but they were unable to find you."

"I am so sorry for what happened, teacher, for what I did," Ferrell said to the man, bowing his head in deep shame. "I dishonored myself, and the Clan."

"There is no need for you to apologize to me Ferrell, my dear friend, no need at all. It was as much my fault as it was yours. I pushed you too hard, more than anyone could bear. I knew what I was doing, and I should have known better."

The two sat on the ground together, facing each other for several minutes saying nothing. David-Michael noticed how Ferrell continued staring at him in disbelief. "Well, make up your mind Ferrell, whether I am a figment of your imagination, a dream, or a ghost. No matter what you decide, however, I assure you that I am real." Ferrell reached out and hugged his fellow clansman.

"I felt badly, losing my temper like that. It was arrogant, reckless, and inexcusable of me to attack my teacher."

David-Michael looked at Ferrell, noticing the anguish and guilt that had filled him for so long. "Listen Ferrell, I was pushing you way too hard, driving you to the breaking point time and time again. I recognized your potential and I was determined to push you to your limit, and beyond it. Add to that the fact that I was intentionally provoking you as well, and any man would have done exactly what you did, no matter how well disciplined. It was not your fault. Neither I, nor any of the other elders blame you, Ferrell. You are a powerful, and naturally gifted warrior my friend and former student. We have always known that."

"Thank you Teacher."

David-Michael nodded.

"But Teacher, how did you find me, and if you are not angry with me, then why did you attack me? I don't understand."

"Well, as to the latter part of your question, I had to test you. I had to know whether you had maintained your skills, or abandoned your training. I had to make certain that you would be ready."

"Well?" Ferrell asked him. How did I do?"

Rubbing his side and laughing, David-Michael answered, "I guess you have provided me with that answer at least! As to the first part of your question, finding you was certainly no easy matter. We sent teams out looking for you years ago, but none could find you. It seems that you have not stayed in one place this long before, Ferrell. We were always just a step behind you. You moved around so frequently and kept such a low profile that for the longest time, I thought that you had died, and that we were chasing a ghost."

Ferrell sighed. "The thought of your death on my hands weighed heavily on me, Teacher. I avoided any contact with the Clan, preferring to be alone as much as possible. Which brings me to my next question, why were you looking for me? Did the Clan send you to bring me back to answer for my crime?"

"Ha!" exclaimed David-Michael, "hardly. Nothing could be further from the truth. We have been looking for you because we need you, Clansman Ferrell; the Clan needs you."

"Me? Why me? It's been years since I was at the Main Enclave."

"Because you were the best we had ever seen, and the need was just too great to risk it to anyone else."

Ferrell sighed. "I am no longer the man I once was. I am no longer worthy to be called a clansman. My life has lacked meaning, purpose. These days I am only a paid guide and bodyguard, helping Christian pilgrims through the meros, protecting a bunch of religious zealots from packs of urba and beasts, and guiding them to the Great Waters. I am nothing more than a guide, a hired body guard."

"I see. Well then, you are by far the most skilled bodyguard I have ever known, and the most honorable. Now, how about inviting your poor, wounded, former teacher inside your home, so we can talk about why I'm here?"

The two stood, embraced, and walked inside the cabin. Ferrell lit a lamp, and they both sat down at the table.

"You see Ferrell; it is about a bunch of religious zealots that I wish to speak. Some years after you left, the Warrior Clan began discussing an alliance with the Holy Christian Church."

"What? An alliance you say?" asked Ferrell. He stared out the window and up at the night sky. He watched as the moon disappeared behind one bank of clouds before reappearing a short time later. He turned away from the window and turned his attention back to David-Michael.

"In the five-hundred years of its existence, the Clan formed no alliances," he said, more to himself than to David-Michael. He was growing increasingly concerned. "Whatever the circumstance, whatever the cause for this alliance, it must be serious indeed."

"It is Ferrell," replied his friend, "it is of historic importance, and it is why I am here. As you said, in as many years, the Clan has never maintained relations of any kind with any group outside of the Clan. You know that when civilization began falling apart during the Great Collapse and into the Dark Age, the Clan isolated itself, shielding members from the outside chaos. In the beginning, the Clan was concerned with just surviving the Great Collapse, offering hope to many and preserving what it could of civilization. Sometime within the first hundred years however, after the worst of the Great Collapse was over, the primary mission of the Clan expanded beyond the preservation of life, to include the eventual rekindling of civilization." David-Michael looked at Ferrell and asked, "Do you know why the mission shifted?" Ferrell shifted in his seat and shook his head. "Because our ancestors had the foresight to recognize that one day, mankind would once again rise from the ashes of its own demise. The same technology that had once brought men to the edge of the sky would one-day rise again, and a new civilization would emerge from the darkness. Though the dream of the founders would have to wait another four-hundred years to be realized, that day has now arrived Ferrell. It is here, now."

"What are you talking about? What does any of that have to do with the Christian Church?" he asked.

"They have been looking for something Ferrell, something of great importance." David-Michael now shifted in his seat as a dark foreboding came over his brow. "We don't have much time Ferrell, we must move quickly, before it's too late."

"What do you mean?"

His former mentor turned to him and answered, "You no doubt have heard of the rising urba threat?"

Ferrell nodded. "I have heard that the urba have started to unite under the banner of a single leader, a particularly nasty urba from what I'm told, and a vicious fighter. It is said that he enjoys having enemies and friends alike tortured for his own amusement."

"Yes, that is true. His name is Kraken. He is exceptionally intelligent for an urba, and a natural leader, but he is as evil as any man that has ever taken a breath. He values no life other than his own. He is a ruthless man, who thinks and feels nothing for those who lay down their lives for him and his cause. His goal is the antithesis of the mission of the Clan. Where we seek to preserve life he seeks to destroy it. Whereas we seek to restore civilization, he seeks to do everything he can to preserve the darkness. He believes that it is his right, his destiny, to rule the world. He is a twisted, evil man."

Ferrell smiled. "Tell me Teacher, you like him then?" Ferrell burst out in laughter. David-Michael however did not so much as crack a smile.

"You think this is funny do you? Follow the man after one of his conquests, and you will find nothing but mutilated corpses. I know this because I've seen it for myself. Not just the corpses of warriors mind you, or even just the corpses of men. No, you will find the twisted, mutilated corpses of women, children, even infants. He is truly a monster. You laugh only because you do not grasp the importance of what I am telling you Ferrell. This man, this Kraken, like the mythological creature of old, threatens to reach out with his tentacles, and destroy everything that we have been working for, destroying what little hope we have left for rebuilding civilization. We believe Kraken will attempt to destroy the Clan as soon as he is strong enough. If he succeeds, humanity will be plunged into darkness greater than any it has ever known. If he succeeds in his twisted dream of conquest, all hope is lost. We must stop him, my friend, or die trying."

Chapter 9
The Sign

How beautiful they are. He continued gazing in wonder at the heavens above him. "How majestic, how incredible is God's creation!" he said aloud to himself, since he was alone on the balcony.

Pope John Paul V had always held a special place in his heart for the beauty of God's creation. Stars were so plentiful that they blanketed the night sky the way sand covers the seashore. He could easily make out all of the visible constellations, Gemini the Twins, Pisces the Fish, Orion's Belt. On nights like this, he thought, it seems I could reach out and touch the sky.

His thoughts drifted to the time of the Golden Age when, according to what he had read in some of the books from that time, there were so many man-made lights on Earth that it was impossible to see many of the magnificent heavenly lights that God had placed in the heavens. As he once more looked up at the dazzling beauty above him, one thought came into his mind. At least something good has come out of the Dark Age. Almost directly above him, he saw the beautiful waves of light they called the Effect, which while still beautiful, had grown increasingly faint throughout his lifetime.

The priest walked along the balcony outside of his quarters, still a bit restless after waking from yet another disturbing dream. He reflected that dreams must be the lot of men with great responsibility like him. He never thought of the great responsibility he carried on his shoulders as a burden. On the contrary, he had always considered it a great privilege to serve the Lord, the same Savior that had carried the sin of all men for all time on his shoulders.

The pontiff had always tried to follow his Lord and Savior as faithfully and completely as he could. His patron saint, St. Francis of Assisi, had rejected his family's considerable wealth and taken instead vows of poverty, so he had done the same. When his predecessor had appointed him as Cardinal of the Outlands, he had experienced no small amount of apprehension about the honor bestowed upon him. He had held little interest in politics, longing only to serve. The pope chuckled to himself as he recalled how one of the senior cardinals had chastised him once, when he confided something to him after a Sunday service.

"So let me get this straight Henry, you are saying that you question whether His Holiness did the right thing in appointing you as a cardinal? You feel that you could do more good as a local parish priest, where you could serve the poor more directly, instead of having to deal with Church politics. Do I understand you correctly?" the senior cardinal asked.

"Exactly" Henry replied. The cardinal paused in his walk and stopped to look the young man square in his eyes.

"Tell me something, Henry, who exactly do you think you are? Are you so much better than the rest of us? Where do you think we came from, if not serving as local parish priests ourselves?" Henry had blushed and said nothing. "You have much to learn yet, Henry, so I strongly suggest you learn this lesson--that we can each serve God in many different ways, not the least of which is one of the greatest of all possible responsibilities, caring for his Church, and spreading the light of his Gospel throughout the whole world." Henry nodded. "The world is a cold, dark place these days young man, and these are difficult times that we live in. But always remember that the light shines the brightest in the deepest darkness."

The pope's face saddened at the thought of his old friend, who passed away later that same year, murdered at sea by pirates as he returned from a trip to a foreign monastery.

As he continued his casual stroll along the balcony of his home, his thoughts turned back to his restless sleep, and to the disturbing dream. Was it really just a dream, or was it a vision? It had seemed real enough to him, enough that he was surprised when he woke up. "Behold and remember," the voice had said to him, but what had it shown him? It was a struggle for him to recall the vision that had prompted him to take the late night stroll. He made it a point to never think too highly of himself, and while he also made it a point to teach and preach that not every dream or vision comes from God, he believed that perhaps this one had, there had been such vividness and detail.

The man once known as Henry allowed his mind to wander freely. He knew from experience that struggling to recall a memory only made it that much harder to recollect. His mind floated back to the stars, back to what they must have looked like before the Dark Age. Then it hit him like a bolt of lightning. He staggered back and sat in a chair as the full force of the incredible vision came flooding back into his mind.

"Behold and remember!" It was a loud, booming voice, like a voice of thunder echoing over the waters of a lake or sound. In the vision, he saw what looked like an explosion in the sky, and he heard the sound of it immediately following the blast. The flash in the sky had been almost as bright as the sound had been deafening. As he continued watching, airplanes suddenly began falling from the skies, exploding when they struck the ground. He looked on as multitudes of people walked down highways after climbing out of stationary automobiles.

"Behold and remember!" the voice said again. The vision continued, and Henry winced when he saw the terror that filled the streets, people fighting over scraps of food and water, sick, dehydrated, starving, and grieved over the deaths of loved ones.

Suddenly the vision had shifted scenes, and Henry had found himself inside a strange building, surrounded by an unusual gathering of people. He noticed a piece of paper lying on a desk in the building that read:

"The First Annual Reconciliatory Conference of Theologians and Scientists

Washington, DC, October 20th, 2025."

The vision progressed faster now, with brief flashes of the same location, but on different days. During one of the gatherings there appeared to be some intense discussions underway. There were drawings on a wall, featuring mountains, rivers, and the ocean. After another flash of light, he found himself standing among a number of strangely dressed people. All of them had a look of confusion on their faces as they looked up at the sky as night fell, and found that strange waves of light had suddenly appeared in the darkness above them. Although nearly every child of the Dark Age knew of the Effect, most believed it to be a natural phenomenon, something that had existed since the earth was new. The true nature of the Effect had long-since passed into antiquity for most of humanity. As he looked on the Effect as it was during the Great Collapse, Henry noticed it was much brighter, and more dramatic in the vision than he had ever seen it during the Dark Age.

Another flash of light, and he was suddenly back in Rome during the Dark Age. Once more, he looked up at the ribbon in the night sky, as he had known it for his entire life. He stood there, transfixed as something about the ribbon began to change. While almost imperceptible at first, it suddenly started to flicker and fade, before disappearing altogether. Then, one final time, he heard the voice cry out, "Behold and Remember."

John Paul V thought on the vision and concluded that the dream had truly been a vision from God. If he was correctly interpreting the dream, the sign of the prophecy would soon appear, and the Effect would be gone forever. One way or another, the world was about to undergo another metamorphosis, and the change would either usher in with it the dawning of new Golden Age, or the dawning of a Hell on Earth, with a vile urba named Kraken as its master.

He rang the bell and his attendant came to the door. "Yes, Your Holiness?"

"Please ask Cardinal Daniels and the young priest Darius to join me as soon as possible."

"Yes, Your Holiness."

Chapter 10
The Puzzle

"Tell us what the book says, Brother Sebastian!" Hannah was unable to contain herself any longer. Brother Sebastian had been thumbing through the book for two hours. He had said little and had hardly moved a muscle the entire time, though his facial expressions changed often. The aged priest looked up at Hannah, who offered him a glass of water.

"That was very thoughtful, Hannah, thank you my dear," he said.

"So, Brother Sebastian," began Alex, by now nearly as impatient as his daughter, "please tell me what is so important about this book, that you came here yourself to check on how my search was progressing? I looked through the book, but with the exception of the occasional word or phrase, the words were all gibberish, I didn't recognize more than a few words in the entire book!"

"That was by design, my dear Alex. The book was written entirely in a language that was ancient, even during the Golden Age, a language known as Latin. The language has been used by members of my religious order for thousands and thousands of years, but by few people outside the Church."

"But why? What is the purpose of writing a book so that no one can read it?" asked Hannah, quite perplexed by the clergyman's response to her father's comment.

"Why my dear Hannah, because this is a very special book."

"Like the Bible?"

"Oh my, no Hannah, it's nothing like that at all. The Bible is the Word of God, the most holy of all books!"

"Then what makes this book special, Brother?" she asked.

"What makes this book special, my dear, is that it can lead us to something extraordinary. It can lead us to something that can literally

77

change the world," Sebastian answered enthusiastically. "We must get this book to the Council Meeting at the Warrior Clan's Main Enclave, and we must leave tomorrow!"

"Wait a second, what are you talking about, Brother Sebastian?" asked Alex. "I just got back to Hannah, and I am not leaving her again. I only left her this last time because I knew how important this was to you, and to the Church. Besides, I am exhausted, Brother. I need some time to rest!"

The priest looked at them both with concern.

"Why do you need me anyway, Brother? I mean, you have the book. You can take this yourself and leave whenever you're ready."

"Alex, you don't understand. It is imperative that you come with me. You can bring Hannah; you should bring Hannah. I promise you that once we get to the Warrior Clan's Main Enclave, she will be safe there. The truth is that she will be much safer there than she is here."

Alex looked at Brother Sebastian and then at Hannah. He looked around at the village, at his home. Then he looked back at Brother Sebastian.

"I tell you what Brother. I need some rest. How about I go inside, get some sleep, and in the morning you can tell me what's going on, and I will decide then. Is that acceptable?"

Brother Sebastian considered what he was saying for several moments. "Of course, Alex, of course. I'm sorry if I've been pressing you too hard. You just don't understand the importance of it all, not yet anyway."

"Perhaps in the morning I will, Brother."

The priest smiled as Alex walked into his home, exhausted. Minutes after collapsing on his bed, he fell fast asleep.

While Hannah went about some of her daily chores around the home, Brother Sebastian sat back down, and proceeded to leaf through the book once more.

"Oraculum of Scientia" [The Oracle of Knowledge]

"Illa es tristis lacuna of ones quisnam testis denique dies of civilization, quod coming of obscurum. Is EST Annus 2025, quod mankind has pervenio zenith of suus technological factum. Is has constructum apparatus ut have portatus men ut Luna, ut plagiarius, quod ultra."

[These are the sad words of the ones who witnessed the final days of civilization, and the coming of the darkness. It is the Year 2025, and Man has reached the zenith of his technological achievements. He has built machines that have carried men to the moon, to the planets, and beyond.]

For the sake of history, and for posterity, we are calling ourselves, The Unity. Included in our number are some of the world's greatest theologians and scientists. As some of us would say, it must have been divine intervention that determined that in the year 2025, on the very day that catastrophe struck our planet; we would be gathered together at the exact time and place necessary to offer hope to some distant, future generation, like yours.

While gathered to discuss God and science, and how we might better work together to solve the many problems that faced us, we witnessed the event that we now call 'The 'Pulse'. After much discussion about what this event will mean, we have concluded that the world will rapidly descend into the darkness. Civilization will begin to collapse, chaos will run rampant, and all governments will fall.

As with the ancient Babel of Old, when the Lord God looked down upon the pride of man and scattered him across the Earth, so God will scatter man once more, by destroying his technology in a single stroke.

The Lord has always provided a way out for mankind in the past, however, and we believe that one day the Lord will visit us again, and remove the curse of the Pulse from the Earth. For while we were gathered together, we learned of the existence of the Great Oracle of Knowledge. We believe that this 'Oracle' could be the means through which one day; God will once again deliver his people.

In preparation for that day, we have developed this small book in the little time we had remaining. A number of copies of this book will be scattered across the globe in hopes that our Christian brothers will one day discover one of them.

To this end, we have provided you with a map that will lead you to something that we believe will enable you to restore the light of civilization after the years of darkness have ended. We invite you, we plead with you, Christian brothers, and all those of good conscience who value and appreciate the power of knowledge, to seek out The Oracle of Knowledge!

In the right hands, the Oracle of Knowledge can bring mankind back from the brink of extinction. In the wrong hands, however, it has the power to destroy the world, perhaps completely the next time. This was the dilemma that we struggled with the most; should we plainly disclose its location or should we take the chance that the Great Oracle will never be found? We elected to go the latter route, in order to ensure that the great power of the Oracle did not fall into evil hands.

It is because of this danger that we are taking such great pains to ensure that this awesome power falls into the right hands. Working with our brothers in the Christian Church, and the scientists here with us, we have created a map showing the location of the Oracle. This map has been divided into seven pieces, and will be transported to seven monasteries all over the world. Each piece of the map will have vital information about the location of the Oracle. Without all seven pieces, you will not be able to determine its location.

To find the map, you will have to solve seven riddles that will reveal the location of that respective piece of the map. Solve the riddles, find the monasteries where the pieces of the map are hidden, and find the key. Collect all seven pieces of the map, survive long enough to find the Oracle, and you will have access to great power and knowledge.

If you should find the Great Oracle of Knowledge, it is our great last hope, our fervent prayer, that you will use the knowledge more wisely than we did.

We wish you good luck, clear thinking, and pray that God will speed you on your way.

Remember to wait for the Lord's sign, so that you will know the proper time to act.

May God be with you.

The Unity"

***

"Well, was that all of it?" Alex asked the following morning, after Sebastian finished recounting what he had read. Alex was still half-asleep, but well-rested now.

"No, there is more, mostly the riddles pointing to the locations of the fragments of the map, and the mention of some key that is required to unlock the mysteries contained within the Oracle of Knowledge."

Hannah was sitting down outside with the two men, enjoying the fresh air. She loved listening to the birds sing, and the feeling of a cool breeze on autumn mornings. There would be few more days like it before winter set in.

"Brother?" she asked.

"Yes, Hannah."

"What is the Great Oracle of Knowledge?" Brother Sebastian sighed.

"Well, that is a good question, my dear, and one that I am afraid I do not have the answer to, at least not yet. While the Church has been able to preserve a considerable amount of our history and cultural legacy, we have had many struggles ourselves throughout these past five hundred years. The best I can say is that we believe that the Oracle may indeed be the answer to our prayers."

"So why do you need me, Brother?" asked Alex. "I mean you have some of the greatest minds in the world with you in Rome."

"It is regrettable, but true however, that our numbers have been greatly diminished Alex. We have spent almost a hundred years just looking for this book alone. While many in our order believed in its existence, to be perfectly frank with you, that number has been greatly diminished as well. Now, with the threat that has been rising from the urba over the past several years, we now find ourselves in a race to find the book, before they can become better organized."

"Are you worried they might pose a threat to the Church, Brother?" asked Hannah, who had given up listening to the birds and was now engrossed in the conversation the two men were having.

"Well yes dear, we are, and rightfully so, I'm afraid. We recently learned that Kraken, their leader, has said on more than one occasion that once he has finished uniting the urba packs, he intends to sail to Rome, and destroy all that is left of the Christian Church. It seems that he sees the Church as a threat."

"Do you believe that, Brother?" asked Alex.

"Yes, I'm afraid I do Alex, and there is more. We also have reason to believe that Kraken has not only learned about the book, but of the existence of the Oracle as well." Brother Sebastian grew extremely pale. "Alex, I don't have to tell you what will happen if that bloodthirsty madman finds the Oracle before we do."

Alex stared at the priest for a few minutes before excusing himself. He needed time to think and to consider all that he had heard. He decided to take a try to clear his head.

"I'm going to take a short walk, Brother. I'll be back in a few minutes."

Alex began walking toward the woods as he considered Sebastian's request for them to come with him. He knew that a trip to the Clan's Enclave would be a dangerous one. He also knew that Brother Sebastian was right however, and that Hannah would be much safer with the Clan than she would be at home. He was also beginning to understand just how important this quest to find the Oracle was. Kraken posed the greatest single threat since the Great Collapse. He strolled around the familiar meadow where his cabin was, took a well-traveled path through the woods and around the lake, before finally returning to the cabin.

"I will start packing, Brother," he said, before walking into the cabin and closing the door.

Chapter 11
The Mountains

The sun was already high overhead as the two men rode along side-by-side, down the long, winding, ancient road, that stretched for endless miles through the mountains. It was unseasonably warm and the sun was hot, but a cool breeze made the long ride considerably more comfortable for them and their horses. The two men rode without saying much, just as they had for the past several days. Each had much to consider on the long journey back to the Clan's Enclave.

Looking ahead Ferrell saw the carcass of a dead deer along the side of the road, and pointed it out to David-Michael, who nodded in acknowledgement. It had been a large animal, a fifteen to twenty-point buck. All around the carcass, he saw large, deep tracks. It was a big animal, most likely a large black bear. They were in bear country now, they would have to be careful and stay alert. Killing men and boars with swords was child's play; killing a bear that size with nothing but a sword, was another thing entirely. Bears were as unpredictable as they were fierce,

The two men continued on their trek to the Main Enclave. As they left the dead buck far behind them, Ferrell found himself longing to see the Main Enclave again after being away for so long. He had been certain when he left it that he would never see it again; it was the Clan's law, and it was his law. No clansman had ever been permitted to return to the Clan after once turning his back on it. It had been the law for hundreds of years. Now that he was on his way back however, Ferrell could not help but ponder whether he even wanted to go back to the old ways. After all, he had been on his own for a long time, and while he had missed his brothers, he had come to appreciate the considerable freedom that came with being a wanderer.

His thoughts also drifted to his traveling companion, his former mentor, and friend David-Michael, whom Ferrell had long thought to be dead and buried. Ferrell had loved his old friend, and had heaped upon himself far more punishment and guilt than anyone else ever could have, and he was ecstatic that David-Michael was still alive. Yet, he could not help but wonder what his life would have been like had he not struck his friend in anger. Would he have left and become a wanderer anyway, choosing the way of the nomad over the way of discipline, the way of the warrior?

He looked over at his former mentor and felt a sudden sense of loss. In the old days, he would never have bested his former instructor in a fair fight. Only dumb luck had enabled him to defeat David-Michael in combat on that fateful day so long ago. Ferrell had attacked his teacher in a fit of rage with the intent of killing him, but in an ironic twist of fate, someone watching the epic clash between the two men accidentally knocked over a pail of water in the large room where they battled. Ferrell did not hesitate when his mentor, who was closest to the pail, lost his footing and fell on the floor. He had been quick to strike, taking immediate advantage of David-Michael's misfortune, driving the sword deep into the torso of his friend. Perhaps it was destiny that in his haste, he had missed the man's heart by only fractions of an inch.

The two clansmen continued to ride at a brisk yet casual pace through the mountain pass. It would take them at least another day to complete the trek through the mountains and arrive at the Clan's Enclave.

While Ferrell prepared himself for his arrival at the gates of the Main Enclave, David-Michael's thoughts centered on the looming threat posed by Kraken, and what they could do to stop him. The Clan had been the most powerful military force since the time of the Great Collapse, and had been unchallenged for five-hundred years. This Kraken was a new kind of threat however, highly intelligent yet savagely ruthless, a raving maniac, yet also a brilliant and highly organized strategist. Without question, he was something they had never faced before, and David-Michael assumed he would be the topic of much discussion at the council. He feared that the discussion of the urba threat might be overshadowed by the other purpose for which they were holding this Council Meeting.

"One of us will need to circle back soon." David-Michael casually said to Ferrell, who looked back at him a bit puzzled.

"What do you mean?" he asked him. "Circle back... for what purpose?"

"Someone has been following us. I only discovered it yesterday myself, but I saw him again just an hour ago."

Ferrell looked behind them but saw no one. "Are you certain?" he asked.

"I am certain," David-Michael replied.

"Then I will take care of it." Ferrell told him. "I'll circle back when we stop for the night, find out who follows us and why, and then I'll take care of them."

After several more hours of riding, the two men stopped and made camp for the night. Making as if he was off gathering wood for a fire, Ferrell slipped away from the camp and took off in the direction from which they had just come. Who was following them and for what purpose? Had Kraken already learned that they planned to stop him, and so sent men to eliminate them? Or perhaps a bandit thought he would be able to take advantage of two lone travelers on a trek through sparsely inhabited mountains.

Ferrell made his way through the woods, watching for signs of movement. The tall pine trees in the woods were not particularly dense and offered him little cover, so Ferrell moved slowly and quietly. He would swing around wide through the woods, being certain that he gave himself plenty of room to come back in behind their pursuers. David-Michael had only noticed one person following them, and had been unable to determine whether there were any more without raising suspicion.

At last, Ferrell made it back to the road, having given himself plenty of room. As he approached the road, he saw a lone figure ahead that had dismounted from his horse only twenty or thirty yards ahead. He quietly drew his sword from its scabbard and prepared to strike. He would deliver only a crippling blow, not a killing one. He needed information before he killed the man. He needed to determine whether Kraken had sent him and learn what he could about the enemy. He would cut the hamstring on the back of the leg, crippling his pursuer without killing him. Slowly, he raised his sword into position. As he prepared to strike the blow, the person suddenly turned in his direction. The man turned out to be a woman, and one that he recognized.

"Ariel?" he exclaimed. "What are you doing here? I could have killed you just now had you not turned around when you did! You are supposed to be back at the village!" Before she even had a chance to answer his question he asked another. "Do you realize what you have done? Now we will have to backtrack to the village, the delay will cost us a week!"

Ariel's face was flush and tears began to stream down her face. His expression of anger and exasperation, born from his concern for her safety, soon softened.

"I 'm sorry, Ferrell. When I saw you ride out of the village with that man," she said, pointing ahead to where David-Michael waited for Ferrell, "without saying so much as a single goodbye to anyone, I was concerned for you, and I was afraid I would never see you again. Please don't take me back to the village; I want to go with you! I don't even know where you are going, or why, but I want to be with you."

Ferrell sighed. "I wanted to say goodbye, Ariel, you know how I feel about you."

"Actually, I don't. How do you feel about me Ferrell?"

The clansman just smiled before turning, and walking back toward David-Michael and the camp. "Come, we must hurry back to camp before it turns dark. These mountains are not without dangers."

Fifteen minutes later, they were back at the campsite where Ferrell had left his companion. The pair arrived to find David-Michael sitting in front of a fire. A large hare was attached to a stick that was slowly rotating over the flames. The clansman looked up at the pair with a brief flash of surprise followed by a smile.

"You could have waited until we made the Enclave," laughed David-Michael, motioning for the pair to join him as he sat on a fallen tree eating his dinner. Ferrell just flashed him a short look of irritation before sitting down on the ground nearby.

"Her name is Ariel, she followed us from the village," he said, not even looking in her direction.

"Ah, yes." David-Michael answered, before standing up to shake her hand. "I recall seeing her, while I waited for you the other day. Hello Ariel, my name is David-Michael. I am an old friend of Ferrell's."

"It's nice to meet you David-Michael."

He looked at Ferrell, this time with a more serious look. "Well?" Ferrell just shrugged.

"What can I do? To go back would delay us by at least a week. We would be late for the Council Meeting. It is too dangerous for her to go back on her own." He thought of the deer carcass he had seen back on the road.

86

"Very well," David-Michael said. He turned to face Ariel. "We are in a hurry, Ariel. Can you keep up?" She offered a sheepish nod. David-Michael turned back to Ferrell, who subsequently shrugged again. David-Michael shook his head, sat down in front of the fire, turned his attention back to the hare, and asked, "Is anyone hungry?" After some enthusiastic nods, he divided the hare and shared it with his companions.

Exhausted after a long day's ride, they finished the meal in relative quiet, with little subsequent conversation. Soon after, Ferrell threw some large sticks on the fire to help keep predators at bay, and lay down to get some rest. They would need to get an early start the next morning.

Ferrell dreamed that night of days long past, of the days of his youth, growing up at the Main Enclave. He had just slipped into a deep sleep when he was suddenly awakened by a loud shriek from Ariel. Two large black bears had come into the camp during the night and were now walking around them in a circle, held back only by the fire. "Aarrgghh" was the best response he could give.

In their haste, they had been careless. They should have cooked the hare away from their camp, and buried what remained. Since they had not taken the precautions, the smell had drawn the bears to their camp.

Ferrell was the first to strike. He lunged at the bear closest to Ariel, slicing at the neck. It was an accurate strike to be sure, but the thick hide on the bear made it difficult to kill with a single blow. The bear roared in pain but did not stop. Now it lunged at Ferrell with great ferocity. Ferrell leapt in the air, driving his sword into the back of the bear as he did so. That was a mistake. The bear kept going before stopping to turn on its tormentor, with Ferrell's sword still sticking out of its back.

David-Michael had already killed the other bear and was now watching Ferrell with some amusement. Laughing he said, "Ferrell, why don't you try smacking it around a little while you're at it. Will you please hurry up; I need my rest for tomorrow's journey!"

Ferrell pulled out his short sword as the bear lunged again. This time he waited until the last second, stepped aside at a forty-five degree angle, and plunged the short sword deep into the animal's neck, all the way to the hilt. This time the animal crashed to the ground and stopped moving.

"Well," David-Michael said as he continued to laugh, "look at the bright side. At least we will eat well for the remainder of our journey!" He looked over at Ariel, who was standing quietly by a large tree. "Ariel, are you okay, are you hurt?"

She just looked at the two men with her mouth open, and nodded.

Chapter 12
The Ocean

Darius saw only pitch black when he walked outside and onto the deck of the ship. A new moon meant the only light came from the stars, which were out in force that evening. Sharing a fondness for the night sky with the current Pontiff, he prided himself on his ability to identify most of the various constellations visible in the northern hemisphere. He considered himself a good enough astronomer that he felt he might even be able to navigate by the stars alone should the need ever arise.

He had brought a favorite book along with him to help him pass the time on the long voyage across the Atlantic. The book, entitled The Great Waters by Louis Franklin, would have made for a great read on the deck of the ship next to a lantern, while sailing under the night sky, but the captain refused to allow lamps out on deck.

"Too dangerous," the captain had told him, "pirates have become a bit of a problem lately. With it this dark outside, and a lamp on deck, they could see us coming from a hundred miles away."

Darius felt this was likely an exaggeration, but he really didn't mind, as the journey had already made him a little jittery. No need to upset the captain anymore, he thought to himself. We still have a long way to go yet.

"One more thing, young priest," the captain had said to him as they pulled away from the dock in Rome, "be careful to stay away from the edge. One careless slip and we would never be able to find you out here. I have enough problems without being responsible for your untimely death." Darius had nodded thoughtfully, suddenly a bit uncertain about what he had gotten himself into.

It was quiet out on the deck at night, except for the sound the ship made cutting through the waters. It was that same quiet and serenity, that went along with sailing on the ocean at night, that he had grown to love throughout the course of the journey. They had a good wind behind them so they were making good time, or at least that was what the captain had said the night before.

At only twenty-five years of age, Darius was still rather young for a priest, but he was widely regarded as one of the best and brightest minds among all of his contemporaries at the Vatican. He was one of the sharpest young men the cardinals had seen for quite some time. A local bishop had taken a keen interest in the young man at an early age, soon recognizing the exceptionally high level of intelligence he possessed, along with an even rarer trait–an equal portion of humility. "Quite an extraordinary combination, especially during these extraordinary times," the cardinal had remarked to Cardinal Daniels.

Darius took his time making his way over to the railing, since the visibility was unusually low on the deck of the ship without the benefit of a lantern or the moon. The misty spray of the ocean filled his nostrils as water lapped up the side of the boat, splashing his face. He stood there at the railing for some time, allowing his imagination to roam freely as he contemplated all of the wonderful creatures God had made that lived in the oceans, many of which at that very moment might be swimming beneath the ship. Darius knew that the oceans teemed with life, and just the thought of all the unseen life beneath him filled him with awe. The journey had already left him with a real appreciation for the sea.

When he learned that part of his mission would include traveling by ship, he felt no small measure of apprehension at the thought of being on the water with no recourse for so long. Would he have to spend the entire voyage hanging over the rail, facing seasickness day after day? He had known several priests that had traveled by sea before, and spent the entire voyage doing that very thing. He felt both surprise and relief when, after his first two days at sea, he found that he had suffered no ill effects whatsoever from the constant, rocking nature of travel by sea. I could really learn to like sailing. Yes, I believe I am going to enjoy this trip after all.

Something flashed in the distance, a brief light on the open water that had appeared and disappeared so quickly that he was unsure whether he had seen it or not. Darius stared intently into the darkness for what seemed like an eternity, trying to discern the source of the flash of light, wondering whether he had only imagined it. If the captain were correct, and Darius had every reason to believe that he was, light was visible over immense distances on the ocean, particularly when the seas were calm. After staring into the darkness for some time, he eventually gave up, finally ascribing the flash to an overactive imagination.

Darius stretched out on the deck and looked up at the stars. How beautiful they were, especially out on the water! He made out Taurus the Bull, the North Star, Orion's Belt. As he lay there gazing at the heavens, he found himself starting to grow drowsy. They had hit some rough seas the previous day and he had found it difficult to get any sleep the night before. The rough turbulent waves had dissipated throughout the morning however as the sun rose in the east. He had tried to catch up on lost sleep during the daylight, but the combination of the heat and the activity both above and below deck during the day would not allow him to sleep. Ever so slowly, without any conscious intention, the young man slipped into a deep and blissful sleep.

***

BOOM!

"Pirates, Captain, off of the starboard bow!" the First Mate hollered out.

"Get every man up here now," replied the captain. "Get those canons loaded and do it now. Well what are you waiting for man? Move!"

Darius sat straight up and looked around trying to assess the situation, despite the mental haze that still lingered in his mind. The sun had risen, so he concluded he must have fallen asleep while still out on the deck the night before. I'm lucky I didn't fall overboard last night!

BOOM!

Water splashed up on deck and soaked the back of Darius's neck.

"That one was much closer Captain. It gave our young priest there an unexpected bath," the First Mate said to the captain while smiling at Darius.

The Captain looked down to find Darius still half-asleep and confused by what was happening. "Someone get that man down below, now!" the captain barked. The First Mate grabbed Darius under his arm and rushed him down below deck.

"Well, okay then, so he has a few cannonballs left for us does he?" the Captain asked. "Well then, let's show him that we have a few of our own!"

"He's trying to force our surrender, not sink us, sir!" remarked one of the crew.

"Well then, that should work nicely to our advantage, eh Steward?"

"Fire cannons!" ordered the captain.

BOOM!

BOOM!

"We struck her on her port side Captain," said Steward.

"Let's give them another round, just to be on the safe side," the captain ordered.

BOOM!

"We've been hit Captain! Looks like only some minor damage though, starboard aft."

"Ready to fire, Captain."

"Very good Steward. Fire!"

BOOM!

BOOM!

"Direct hit, Captain!"

"Yes, yes I see. Can you tell how badly damaged she is, Steward?"

"We hurt her, Captain. It looks like she's taking on water."

"Take us sharp to port, Mr. Mincer! They seem to think we carry something too valuable to sink, or else we would already be at the bottom of the ocean. We're clearly outgunned, so let's see if we can make a run for it!"

The Captain of The Valiant walked over to the First Mate, who had since returned from down below and taken the wheel. "Now Mr. Mincer, find out how fast our friends can go. Hoist the mainsail; let's give them a run for their money, gents!"

As he poked his head above deck, it occurred to Darius that the flash of light he had seen the night before had not been his imagination after all. He now regretted not taking the information to the captain.

Darius stepped back up on the deck.

"What's happening, Captain?" he asked.

"It looks like they are pirates, lad. It's not often that we see them out here on the open ocean, but when we do, it's rarely pleasant."

"Did they give up?"

"Hardly. We hit them with a couple of volleys and got lucky, that's all. Now we're making our escape. It looks like there's a fog bank up ahead. We'll make a run for it and see if we can lose them in the fog."

"I will pray for your success, Captain. Perhaps God will grant my petition and give us both deliverance and safe passage."

"That would be much appreciated Brother. I am sure that the crew will agree as well. These are shark infested waters you see, and none of us want to end up as a tasty meal for them this morning!"

Darius looked out on the water to see if he could see any sharks. He had only a vague notion of what he should be looking for, as he had never seen a shark before and he had never really known anyone who had, but he had heard of them, and what they could do. He decided that he would again take the captain's word for it. He went back down below and as promised, began praying to God for deliverance and safe passage.

"Captain, they are still after us. We have a good lead but she's moving fast."

"How many cannonballs do we have left?"

"Only two, Captain."

"Only two? I told you to find some more at our last port!"

"We tried sir, but we were unable to procure any. They are getting harder and harder to come by."

"I know, I know," replied the captain, cursing under his breath.

"Do you think we can make the fog bank, Captain?" asked the first mate.

"Yes, I think so, Mr. Mincer. We are going to try it regardless. It sure beats letting these no good lazy bums get their greedy little paws all over my ship!"

The two ships were locked in a race for the fog bank ahead. One ship intent on getting into it, the other determined to stop them. As they approached the fog, it appeared they were going to make it. They slid into the fog bank just as the other ship came within firing range. To the surprise of the captain and the crew, the ship did not fire another round.

"Well either they are out of ammunition themselves, or they really want something that we have on board, and are afraid of sinking us," stated the captain.

"What could we possibly have that they would want?" asked the first mate.

"Maybe they think we're a supply ship," the captain said, turning to look toward the hatch where the priest had been a short time before. "Or perhaps it's not what they are after, but who. Either way, I don't intend to stick around long enough to ask, Mr. Mincer."

"Agreed, sir."

They remained in the fog bank for over an hour. They had not seen the pirate ship nor heard anything that might give away its position.

The captain stayed at the wheel while motioning to the first mate to prepare the canons. After waiting another few minutes, they slowly emerged from the fog. The pirate ship was nowhere to be seen.

"Alright Mr. Mincer, let's get back on course. Full speed ahead."

"Aye, Aye Captain."

As they distanced themselves from the fortuitous fog bank, Darius concluded that he may have been a bit hasty the night before. He really wasn't going to like sailing, and he suspected that he wasn't going to enjoy the trip so much after all.

Chapter 13
The Enclave

Hannah squirmed in her saddle. They had been riding through the mountains for days and were now riding down a long, winding mountain trail. The long trip had taken its toll and as much as she hated to admit it, she had saddle sores. Despite her discomfort, she was considerably more excited than irritated, because Brother Sebastian had just informed her that they should soon arrive at the Warrior Clan's legendary Main Enclave.

"Brother Sebastian, what do you know of the Warrior Clan?" she asked, shifting once more in her seat.

"And what should we expect when we arrive?" added her father, Alex.

Alex and the priest were riding in front of Hannah, no more than a few yards ahead of her.

"Well, why don't we start by you telling me what you know Alex?" the priest answered.

Alex thought about that for a moment.

"Well, let's see...I have heard that they have nothing to do with outsiders, that they keep mostly to themselves, and that they've spent most of the time since the Great Collapse developing and honing their fighting.

"All true, all true," replied the priest.

"I have also heard that they are known to kill strangers who show up at an enclave uninvited, especially at their Main Enclave," joked Alex, with a feigned attempt at severity. The priest responded with a nervous laugh, causing Alex's demeanor to suddenly change and take on a more serious appearance.

"That last part Brother, that's not actually true, is it?"

This time Brother Sebastian managed a smile. Hannah looked at them, trying to see what was happening. Brother Sebastian decided he should try to lighten the moment, lest they frighten the girl.

"No, Alex, no, of course not, at least not if you're invited, which of course, we are!"

He smiled warmly at Alex, but the mild humor seemed lost on him. Brother Sebastian decided he had better continue.

"The members of the Warrior Clan are a peculiar people, Alex. As you know, the founding of the Clan dates back to the end of the Golden Age, back to the time of the Great Collapse. Legend has it that while civilization fell apart, a group of men that considered themselves warriors founded the Clan. Perhaps they were members of one of the ancient armies I have read about, we honestly don't know. What little we do know of the time immediately following the Great Collapse remains shrouded in mystery, with more questions than answers. That is to be expected I suppose, given the circumstances...."

He paused for a moment before continuing, "Anyway, it is said that their immediate objective after the founding of the Clan was simply to isolate themselves from the chaos all around them, to survive the aftermath of the Great Collapse. At some point however, they decided to take on a new mission as well."

"And what is that, Brother?" This time Hannah asked the question.

He looked at them both and answered, "To do what they could to preserve knowledge, and to one day aid in the reemergence of civilization."

"Wow, that explains a lot," remarked Alex.

"What do you mean, Dad?" Hannah asked her father.

"What I said earlier is true honey. The Clan has nothing to do with outsiders, they never have. For them to have suddenly formed an alliance with the Church, well, it's completely out of character for them. From what Brother Sebastian just told us, it appears that they share a common interest with the Church, the desire to restore civilization, of bringing mankind into a new Golden Age."

"Exactly," agreed Sebastian.

"Okay Brother," said Alex, turning back to the priest, "so the Clan is working with the Church to preserve knowledge, to help usher in a new dawning of civilization. How long has this collaboration been going on between the Church and the Clan?"

The priest was silent, staring ahead as if hoping the question would go away if he ignored it.

"Brother?" After shrugging his shoulders, Sebastian looked at Alex.
"Oh, it's fairly recent."

"How recent, Brother, the past hundred years?"

"Well, no, not quite that long."

"How long then? The past twenty years or so?"

"Well no, not that long either I'm afraid."

Alex looked at the priest. "You mean...."

"Well what do you want me to say, Alex? Okay then, yes! This is going to be our first council meeting with them. We were only recently able to convince them that we shared a common goal, and a common threat."

"A common threat?"

"Why yes, Alex, a common threat."

"And what is the common threat, Brother?"

"Not what, but who. Why, Kraken of course. He's building a massive army that may well be powerful enough to challenge the Clan." It suddenly dawned on Alex that he should have taken a longer walk around the lake.

"We have arrived," announced Brother Sebastian rather pointedly, as he gestured down the hill to a number of large structures, surrounded by massive, fortified wall on all sides.

Hannah took in the incredible sight for a long time. The wall alone must have been at least thirty feet high, ten feet thick, and so long that it stretched into the distance as far as the eye could see. Men walked along the top of the walls, dressed in strange looking clothing.

"Many warriors in times past wore protective clothing called armor on the outside of their bodies when they were going into battle," her father explained. Hannah just nodded without looking back, unwilling to look away from the breathtaking site. She had never seen or imagined anything like it.

Suddenly a long, loud sound echoed throughout the countryside where they had stopped. When the horn stopped blowing, the small group suddenly found themselves surrounded by twelve unhappy looking men, dressed in the same armor as the men she had seen walking along the walls. Some of them brandished swords, some spears. Brother Sebastian was the first to speak.

"Greetings, men of the Warrior Clan, on behalf of the Holy Christian Church. My name is Brother Sebastian, and this is Alex Montgomery and his daughter Hannah. We have been invited to come here to attend the Council."

Hannah watched as the men scrutinized the three intruders for what seemed an eternity, before eventually handing something to the priest. At the same time, two of the clansmen men drew their swords and held them high above their heads. Her eyes opened wide as it began to dawn on her what they planned to do if they did not receive the proper response from Brother Sebastian. Her father pulled up close to her as he muttered what he could remember of the Lord's Prayer, something that Sebastian had taught him. She watched as the priest drew a small picture and handed it back to the man. Hannah could barely make out the markings on the paper, a cross, like the one that he wore around his neck, and two swords beside it, one short, and one long. When they had looked over the picture, the guards asked them to get down off their horses, and after a brief search for weapons, the men stood aside, allowing them to continue toward the enclave. Alex let out a huge sigh of relief.

They climbed back on to their horses and continued on their way. Brother Sebastian smiled once more and looking at Alex asked, "What's the matter Alex, where's your faith?"

Hannah looked back to see that the men had now closed ranks behind them. Perhaps it was a safeguard in case they had been followed, perhaps they didn't trust strangers, she could not tell. One thing was certain however, these were very serious men, an observation that her father had also made.

"Wow that was an interesting experience. These folks don't mess around do they?" asked Alex. "Did you see the looks on their faces?"

"Don't be too quick to judge them Alex. Their way of life has kept them alive since the Great Collapse. That's no small feat by any measure."

Alex nodded his head as they arrived at a second checkpoint. This time they were at a gate in the massive wall with another twelve men stationed outside. Sebastian was handed something to draw on as the he and the clansmen repeated the same exercise as before, and once again, upon recognizing the proper response, the guards allowed them to continue. Once they were inside the gates, Alex started breathing again.

"This is all really just a little too intense for me," he said as they passed through the massive gate and rode into the enclave.

Chapter 14
The Coming Storm

Kraken stood on the roof of a large building overlooking the mero. From where he stood, he could see everything that was happening below. Watching the battles take place had once filled him with excitement. Recently however, they had started to bore him. It looked as if yet another battle would be easily won that day, and he would soon have plenty of enemy prisoners, which he could use to light up his compound after he returned home. He felt great delight at the prospect of passing time torturing information from some of the captured enemy, especially those that refused to join his growing army, but Kraken knew that the good days were not going to last forever. The other meros had already started surrendering before his armies even arrived. Where at first, the battles were hard-fought and they had gained ground only inch by inch, it was getting much easier as his fame, and his army, grew. Soon, all of the meros would be under his control, under his absolute rule. What had seemed a nearly impossible task to him at one time, conquering all of the meros from Great Sea to Great Sea, now seemed not only possible, but also inevitable. It would take time to be sure, but he knew it would happen; it was his destiny.

Nevertheless, Kraken was also troubled. He had been thinking about what the priest, Ramos, had divulged when tortured, the existence of the ancient book, and the Oracle, that the Church was now seeking. He also did not like what Madgar had told him about the Clan's dealings with the Church. He had already planned to destroy the Church, and eventually the Clan as well, but he was not ready, at least not yet. The Church offered the first of the only two threats that could challenge his growing empire; hope. As long as the people had hope, he knew his victory could never be complete. Kraken smiled as he continued watching his army plow through the weakening urba resistance below.

The Clan; they offered the second threat to his empire, the only group with an organized military capable of offering him any real resistance. As long as the Clan was around to challenge him, his future empire was in jeopardy. Kraken had never concerned himself about them before, because he thought that they would stay out of his way, as long as he left them alone. Oh, he had made plans for dealing with the Clan as well, but he needed to wait until he had completed his conquests, because he would need to muster the full strength of his growing army in order to destroy the Clan. Though he had no direct experience with them himself, he had heard the endless stories about their skill as warriors, and he had seen evidence of their handiwork. One of the meros where he had sent spies in preparation for an invasion had been located near one of the Clan enclaves. When his spies had arrived, they found urba bodies hacked up all over the mero. The clansmen had left only a few urba alive, and only because it was the Clan's policy to always leave a few survivors alive so they could tell the tale of the slaughter as a warning to others. Kraken's spies learned that the urba packs in the mero had been foolish enough to join forces to launch an attack against the Clan enclave. Based on the information his men had gathered, the Clan had made short work of the powerful urba packs, which had lived in that mero.

Too bad they stand in my way. They would make a nice addition to my empire. Perhaps I would have even made them my personal guard. Now they are in my way however, so I will crush them. I will grab them by the neck and I will crush them like the stray dogs they are.

Kraken turned when he heard footsteps approaching from behind him. Collins, Kraken's top general, approached him. "Sir, we have taken the mero. All of the packs here have surrendered, and have sworn an oath of allegiance to you, and to your empire."

"Hail, Kraken," he added. The others joined in, "Hail Kraken. Hail Kraken. Hail Kraken." The large, vicious urba smiled broadly. He so loved being a tyrant. After soaking up the adulation for a while, Kraken finally tired of it and held up his hand. The chanting stopped as Kraken turned to face Collins.

"Find Mansa, and bring him to me."

Kraken then left the battlefield and went back to his tent, with his escort by his side. He ordered a slave to pour him some wine and sat down on his makeshift throne. After a minute, the slave returned with wine in hand, poured the wine into a different, much more common cup, and tasted the wine. Kraken waited a couple of minutes until he was

100

satisfied that the slave was not going to collapse dead on the floor from poison. He ordered the slave to leave. Kraken drank deeply of the wine as he pondered his next moves. About that time, Mansa arrived at the entrance of his tent.

"My Lord, you wished to see me?" Mansa looked a bit squeamish as he walked in, which was exactly the way Kraken liked it. He knew the more he kept them in a constant state of fear, the more inclined they would be to obey his every command without question.

"Yes, come in my friend," he said to Mansa, adopting a soft, gentle tone with his top lieutenant. Sometimes hard, sometimes soft. "I want to discuss our plans going forward. All meros, as well as the Outlands, are cowering before me now, and surrendering before my armies even arrive. I do not need to be present at these pathetic little skirmishes any more. I will let Collins handle these operations from now on as we continue marching toward the Great Western Sea. I would now like to turn my attention to those pathetic religious freaks, and this supposed alliance with the so-called 'Warrior Clan," he said as mockingly as he could muster at the moment. "What do you suggest we do next to address this situation?"

Mansa cleared his throat as he considered what they had learned from the priest, and from Madgar. "My Lord, let us review what we know at the moment."

Kraken nodded in approval and said "Go on."

"We know that there is a book that seems to be of great importance to the Church. We also know they have been seeking this book for a long time, searching for it in various meros scattered across the known lands. According to the priest, there is supposed to be more than one copy of this book. That means if we can find just one of these books, we might be able to learn more about this Oracle for ourselves. Our men have been out looking for the book for some time now, based on information garnered from the priest, and from Madgar, but all efforts to locate any of the books have failed."

Kraken looked at Mansa and laughed. "You see Mansa that is why I am the master. Why should we bother looking for this book ourselves, if those fools are already so close to finding it? No, we'll let them do all of the work."

"Yes, my lord."

Kraken stood and began pacing. "Our spies watching the Clan's Main Enclave reported some unusual activity there yesterday.

Something is happening in that precious enclave of theirs, some kind of gathering."

"For what purpose, my Lord?" asked Mansa.

"That's what I want you to find out. I want you to find a way of infiltrating this little gathering of theirs, find out more about this Oracle they've been looking for, and bring word back to me. If this thing is so important to them, perhaps it is something that should be important to us as well. We'll let them find out where it is hidden, so we can then take it for ourselves, and then use it to crush all of them under our feet. We will destroy these pathetic little priests, but only after we have crushed the mighty Warrior Clan. No one will be able to oppose me once I have it, I will be unstoppable. I will rule as it suits me to rule, and I will crush all who stand in my way." Kraken looked at Mansa and smiled. "First, there is one final matter first that I want to take care of. I want to talk to that old man, the one with the ship. Find him for me."

"I was talking to him a short while ago, Lord Kraken, when you called for me. He is here, in the stronghold."

"Excellent, bring him to me–now."

"As you wish, Lord Kraken."

Mansa left and returned a short time later at the door with an old man.

"You wished to speak with me, Kraken?" he asked.

Kraken did not care for the man's tone, or his attitude. He snarled at the man for his lack of respect. Had he not needed the old man's ships, he would have had him killed without even a second thought for not kneeling or bowing before him. Better yet, he would have killed him himself. Kraken dismissed the thought of killing the old man, at least for the time being. Now is the time for business, he thought to himself.

"Your name is Marsh?"

"That's Captain Marsh, Lord Kraken."

The nerve of the weak old fool, thought Kraken. Ships or no ships he might kill him where he stood anyway.

"Captain Marsh," mocked Kraken, "you have ships that float on the water?"

"I do."

"How many?" asked Kraken.

"Why do you want to know?" he asked.

Kraken began to rise from his throne, causing Mansa to take several swift steps back, away from the old man.

"Why, you ask–why?" His voice was deep and loud.

Kraken moved so fast that Marsh's facial expression had no time to change, because the captain had no time to react to Kraken's sudden leap in his direction. The man moves like a big cat!

Kraken grabbed the old man by the back of the head and held him tight. He moved slowly because he was savoring the moment. He brought a large bowie knife to the man's throat, and in a seesaw fashion, pressed it against his neck with just enough pressure that blood began trickling down from his neck. Kraken was careful however, that the blade did not penetrate deep enough that it severed the man's windpipe, or his carotid artery. But he did press the blade hard enough that he made his point.

Kraken looked over at Mansa and said to him, "Do you see what happens, Mansa, when I try to be nice to these pathetic idiots. They mistake my kindness for weakness." He looked down at the old man, who now wore a look of absolute terror on his face as the full extent of his peril had become more evident, causing Kraken to grin from ear to ear. "Why do I want to know how many ships you have? Because I want your ships for my empire, you old fool. I need them to expand my empire beyond the borders of these lands. Would it be okay with you, Captain, if I take your ships, for the good of my empire?"

The man nodded his head very slowly and carefully, as more blood flowed down his neck

"That's good news for you then Captain Marsh. One more thing, if you ever neglect to pay me the proper homage again, I will slice you open, slowly mind you, from end to end, and I will tie you to a tree so I can watch the beasts of the field eat you alive. Do we understand each other now?" he asked. The man, even more terrified and shaking, nodded once more as Kraken let him go and sat back down. "You see Mansa, it always pays to negotiate!"

"Now then, as I was saying, Marsh, your ships belong to my empire now. We will use them when we raid and conquer foreign lands, or whenever and however we see fit. And don't worry, as long as you remain obedient to me and follow my every command, you will be richly rewarded." Kraken waved him away and Marsh quickly turned to leave.

"One last thing, Marsh. I understand that one of your ships recently attacked a ship transporting some of those Christian religious freaks last week, but that you lost them in some fog. Do you have any idea where they were headed?"

"Why yes, Lord Kraken," he answered, bowing his head in subservience this time. "It looked as if they were heading somewhere near here."

Kraken waved Marsh off to leave and stared absently after him. When Mansa returned, Kraken spoke. "They must have found the book Mansa. They will be leaving soon to search for the ancient artifact so we must be ready. I want you to gather up some of our best men, and have them ready to leave out soon. Also, make certain we have some of our most trusted men on each of Marsh's ships, and ensure that one of those ships stays in port at all times as my personal transport. Also, send in General Collins."

Mansa left and soon after General Collins came in before Kraken

"Lord Kraken" he said, bowing before Kraken.

"General Collins. I want you to pick out fifty of your finest men. I want you to train them, to prepare them, to make them ready to become members of my new Imperial Guard. They will remain by my side at all times as my personal guard. I want this done immediately."

"Yes, Lord Kraken, it will be done. I will see to it personally."

Kraken dismissed Collins, left the throne room, and walked into the room which housed his concubines. He would soon take one of them as a wife. He wanted an heir that would one day rule in his place after he was gone, preserving his legacy, and his grip on the people of all the known lands. There was one lovely young woman in particular that he had recently taken into his harem, named Jessica. She was feisty and full of spirit, something he enjoyed immensely. He had already started on breaking her, but she would take some work. How he relished the challenge! Perhaps, once she was broken, he would take her as his wife.

That would be some time off in the future, but not too far. He had much that he wanted to teach his offspring. Of course, the first lesson would be to teach them who was in charge. Kraken looked around at the beautiful concubines and smiled.

Chapter 15
The Council Meeting

"This Council is now in session," Alex heard the small, white-haired clansman announce. Clansman High Elder Lord Sarkoth, the leader of the Warrior Clan, was well advanced in years, yet despite his many years of life; Sarkoth looked to be in better shape than Alex. Even when compared to graying men like Brother Sebastian, the Clan elder was very old, ancient even. No one seemed to know just how old Lord Sarkoth actually was, not even Ferrell. Some speculated he was nearing a hundred years old, others said he was well past a hundred already, though that seemed to Alex to be an exaggeration. Whatever his age, there were few that had lived as long as he had. His hair had turned completely white, and he wore it in topknot fashion, as a gesture of respect to the ancient Samurai Warriors, that had vanished long before the beginning of the Golden Age. A small man, with a powerful and commanding presence, it was evident that all of the clansmen held him in very high regard. Each warrior bowed deeply when approaching the revered leader, who now sat at the head of the large, oval table that stood in the Main Gathering Room of the Great Hall. Alex looked on in amazement at the curious mix of warriors and clergy that sat or stood around the large wooden table that occupied the centermost part of the meeting hall.

Lord Sarkoth continued, "I would like to begin this Council of the Warrior Clan by welcoming, for the very first time, our Christian brothers from the Holy Christian Church." He gestured toward Brother Sebastian, Darius, and the others. Lord Sarkoth continued, "I would also like to take a moment to welcome back our long lost clansman brother, who was lost to us for so long, Clansman Ferrell Young."

Ferrell looked around at the gathering, looked down, and grunted. He then stood, and offered a deep bow of great respect to Lord Sarkoth.

105

"Thank you, High Elder Lord Sarkoth. I have been away for far too long."

Lord Sarkoth continued, looking at Ferrell as he spoke, and said, "If what I have heard already at this gathering is true, I fear that we will have great need of many skilled warriors like you, Clansman Ferrell." Turning back to the rest in attendance, he said, "We have a great many things of a serious and urgent nature to discuss, my friends. First, I would like to ask that everyone please be seated, so that we may begin." Everyone sat down and a great, palpable silence fell over the large gathering as they waited for Sarkoth to begin. The aged elder took a few moments as he gathered his thoughts in preparation.

"Some of you may be wondering what this meeting is all about, and why we have invited our Christian brothers here today. I would like to begin by telling you about a chance meeting between a young priest and a young warrior that took place almost fifty years ago." The old man's countenance lightened and a warm smile found his face. "You see, the young priest was seeking to establish a new parish for the Church near where the young warrior had been hard at work establishing a new enclave for the Clan. Now the young priest was unaware of the new enclave, which had only recently been completed. His only desire was to serve his God by spreading his word among a people that he felt desperately needed to hear it. The young warrior however, was well aware of the intrusion of the young priest into the area where the warrior had labored for so long to establish the new enclave. Already having difficulty recruiting enough young warriors to help build and grow the enclave for the Clan, he was furious at the unwelcomed competition for the hearts and minds of the local inhabitants. 'What does religion have to do with the warrior?' the young clansman asked himself.

"One day, not long after his arrival, the priest was busy talking to a small child while walking down a very narrow path. Not looking where he was going, he inadvertently walked into the young, brash, hotheaded warrior. When the clansman saw who it was that had almost knocked him to the ground, he flew into a rage. He drew his sword from his scabbard and it flew to the neck of the young priest. Now, most men would have jumped back in vain, trying to escape the blade; the young priest, however, did not even flinch. Instead, he stood looking the warrior squarely in the eyes, with a great sense of peace that completely confounded the young warrior. Even when the warrior caused his blade to draw blood from the neck of the priest, his demeanor did not change. Even after the warrior sheathed his sword, and struck the priest with a measured punch to the solar plexus that knocked the priest to the ground, the clergyman never lost his composure. Instead, he chose to maintain a quiet yet determined calm that during the brief moments of their encounter, had caused the attitude of the warrior toward the priest to change dramatically. He knelt down at the feet of the holy man, and out of his respect for the priest's incredible discipline and courage, he begged his forgiveness.

"Soon after this first encounter, the priest and the warrior became the closest of friends, while the enclave and the monastery each grew and prospered." A sad look fell on the elder's face as he added, "I am sad to say that the warrior has not seen his old friend since the priest left to take a new position with the Church many years ago. Nevertheless, they have been in touch a number of times over the years through various people," he said, as he again motioned toward the priests. He looked around at those listening attentively to everything the elder warrior said.

"As you may have guessed by now, I was that young warrior. The young priest, who has since been my dearest friend, is Henry, now known to most as Pope John Paul the V." The crowd buzzed with excitement as he continued. "Throughout the time of the Dark Age, the Christian Church and the Warrior Clan have existed side by side, with little or no dealings between the two. The Warrior Clan offers hope and rescue to promising young men and women from the ravages of this world, to build and shape their character through the discipline of the Clan. The Christian Church also offers hope and rescue for humanity, both young and old alike. The Church of course offers hope not only for this life, but also for the life that will come.

"What these two groups did not know however, was that they had something else in common. Both shared a mission, since The Great Collapse, to preserve as much human knowledge and culture as possible from the days of the Golden Age. They also shared a dream that one day, humanity would emerge from the ashes and deep darkness, ushering in a new Golden Age of prosperity."

He paused for a minute to take a drink of water, and to give everyone a chance to digest everything he had said. Conversations erupted throughout the Main Gathering Hall. After several minutes, he motioned to a couple of warriors, who then sounded a bell, signaling for everyone in the room to come to order. Once again, the room grew silent.

"Several years ago leaders of the Church and leaders of the Clan decided, through a dialogue started by Henry and myself many years ago, to hold a conference to see how we might work together in this effort. While this conference has been planned for some time, another, more urgent matter has since come to light that we must also discuss while we are all gathered together."

The Elder motioned to the young priest Darius. "First, I would like Brother Darius to tell you about an opportunity that we have to bring about our common dream of a new dawning of civilization. Brother Darius."

"Thank you, Clansman High Elder Lord Sarkoth. First of all, I would like to thank you and the rest of the Warrior Clan, on behalf of His Holiness the Pope, and of the Holy Christian Church, for your invitation, and for hosting this Council."

The Elder nodded warmly.

"For many years now, the Church has been searching for a lost artifact, a book written during the time of The Great Collapse, which was said to hold clues on how to find The Great Oracle of Knowledge."

"Excuse me, Brother Darius," asked David-Michael, "What is this Oracle of Knowledge?"

"We don't know exactly what it is, but we believe it to be an artifact dating back to the Golden Age. According to some ancient documents, it contains much of the wisdom and power of the Golden Age, and is the key to bringing humanity back from the brink of extinction. We believe it to be our best chance of reigniting the fire of civilization. The Church has been aware of the Legend of the Oracle for at least three hundred years. Unfortunately, it was all but forgotten until knowledge of its existence was rediscovered a hundred years ago. The pope at that time, Pope Benedict III, decided to launch an effort to find the book, in hopes that through it we might find the Oracle of Knowledge. This search has continued up until the present." Brother Darius paused, trying to calm himself. "I am excited to tell you, that just a short while ago, today, while attending this conference, I learned that the book has been found!" Darius looked over at another priest. "Brother Sebastian, would you please tell us about the book?"

Brother Sebastian stood.

"Fellow priests, members of the Warrior Clan, I present to you what might well be the key to mankind's future, the book we have been searching for all of these years, The Unity.

Once again, the room buzzed with excitement as conversations spontaneously erupted. Once again, Sarkoth motioned and the bell was sounded.

"But what good is a book? Assuming we can believe anything these religious fanatics tell us, what can we possibly hope to gain from a mere book?" asked one of the warriors in the room.

Lord Sarkoth frowned when he recognized Bokra's voice. As his peer growing up, he had always been jealous of all of the attention given to Ferrell, who had also been next in line to become an elder at the time he left the Clan. Ever since being denied his place in line after Ferrell left, he had become a bitter man. While Bokra had always made a pretense that all was well in front of him, Sarkoth often suspected that when Bokra was around warriors closer to his own rank and opinions, it was a different story.

Darius responded. "This book can lead us to the Oracle, where we will have access to all of the knowledge of the Ancients. Once the sign is given, we can activate the Oracle and..."

Bokra interrupted Darius as he threw up his hands. "But how, priest? Does this book have a map showing the location of this so-called Oracle? How do we know that this Oracle even exists? Why are we wasting time talking about this anyway? This Council has far more important things to discuss!"

Lord Sarkoth rose to his feet. "Enough! That is enough from you, Bokra. You will show proper respect, or you will leave!"

"I beg your forgiveness, Lord Sarkoth. I meant no disrespect to you, or our guests."

"You will remain silent for the remainder of this Council Meeting, is that understood?"

"Yes, Lord Sarkoth."

Sarkoth thought he detected a brief smirk on Bokra's face that quickly faded. He would need to have a few words with Bokra, soon.

"So tell me Brother Darius," Sarkoth began, "what is in this book, and how can we use it to find the Great Oracle?"

Brother Darius replied, "Well, with your permission, Lord Sarkoth, I would like for Brother Sebastian to tell you. He has had more time to study it and can better answer your questions. Brother Sebastian, would you please?"

Brother Sebastian nodded and rose to address the council.

Jeff. W. Horton

Chapter 16
The Clues

Brother Sebastian cleared his throat and began.

"The Unity was written in Latin, a language that was dead long before the time of the Great Collapse. The authors used Latin to make it more difficult for anyone outside of the Church to read, fearing that the book could cause the Oracle to end up in the wrong hands."

"Brother Sebastian, may I ask a question?" Sebastian turned and looked at the warrior who had spoken, struggling to recall his name.

"Of course, err–Clansman Ferrell, please do."

"If the Oracle is as powerful as you say, whose hands are the right hands?"

"Clansman Ferrell," said Sebastian, with great respect for the wise words from the clansman, "you have asked the right question! Who is able to wield such knowledge and power, but God alone! We must trust however that this is all his doing. In fact, Brother Darius told me of a dream the Holy Father had only days before he sent him here, a vision he believed had been given to him by God, announcing that the end of the Dark Age has come. For the first time since The Great Collapse mankind now has a choice; emerge into a new Golden Age, or slide deeper into the darkness, into the abyss."

"What do you mean?" asked Sarkoth.

"We now believe that others have learned of the Oracle's existence and will seek to find and use it before we do," answered Brother Sebastian. "These men would seek to use the Oracle's power to do great and terrible things, plunging the world into a time of vast misery and suffering that would last for a thousand years."

Brother Sebastian looked over at Ferrell. "You demonstrate great wisdom my friend, asking me this question. It seems that power is dangerous even when it's in the best of hands. Nevertheless, I am sure

111

that you will agree that we cannot, we must not; allow it to fall into the hands of such dangerous men."

"You refer to the urba threat?" asked Sarkoth.

"Indeed, Lord Sarkoth, I am referring to Kraken and his growing urba army."

David-Michael stood to address the council. "We must not allow that to happen, brothers! I've personally seen the handiwork of this man's evil."

Ferrell put his hand on his old friend's shoulder. "Don't worry, old friend, we will not let that happen."

"Brother Darius mentioned that there were clues in the book Brother Sebastian, would you please explain?" asked Brother O'Reilly, from one of the Outland parishes.

"According to the information in the book, there is indeed a map."

Brother Sebastian tried not to look at Bokra, who stared icily at him from across the table. "This map was divided into seven pieces. The pieces have been taken to seven different monasteries scattered all over the world. The clues in this book will lead us to each piece of the map. According to the book, the members of The Unity believed that the monasteries might survive The Great Collapse, and offered the best hope that one day, the seven pieces of the map would be found and reunited. Once we have all seven pieces, the map will lead us directly to the Oracle. Based on what I've read so far, I believe that four of the monasteries are located somewhere here in the Known Lands, in what was once called the United States. I believe that the other three have been taken to monasteries beyond the Great Waters."

The old priest looked around the room, and then at the elder clansman. "Lord Sarkoth, I know that you have the full trust of the Holy Father," he said, as he looked at the men seated around the large table, and the guards standing at the doors, "but can everyone here be trusted to hear what is in this book?"

"Yes, Brother Sebastian. These men live and die by their honor. I trust each of them with my life." Something gnawed at Lord Sarkoth after he said that. He looked over at Bokra.

Brother Sebastian continued, "Very well then, Lord Sarkoth, I will continue. There are seven clues listed in the book, written in Latin, which will, I believe, tell us where the pieces of the map are located.

'Clue Number 1- Qua Valde Era lux lucis via.

Clue Number 2- Qua Barbatus Vir Sits.

Clue Number 3-Urbs of ventus.

Clue Number 4-Qua quietis miles militis sileo.
Clue Number 5- Qua Democracy Eram Prognatus.
Clue Number 6- Valde urbs of Crocus Vir.
Clue Number 7- Urbs of Silicis - Vir in Gero.'"

"But what does all of that mean, Brother Sebastian?" asked Sarkoth.

"I believe the seven clues refer to seven meros, where the Church had monasteries during the Great Collapse. At each monastery, we should find one piece of the map.

I have translated the clues from Latin," said Sebastian, "and here are their translations. The first clue, 'Qua Valde Era lux lucis via' means, Where the great lady lights the way. The second clue, 'Qua Barbatus Vir Sits' means, Where the bearded man sits, the third clue, 'Urbs of ventus', means, City of wind. The fourth clue 'Qua quietis miles militis sileo' means, Where the quiet soldiers rest.

I believe the following three clues point to meros that lie beyond the Great Seas. The fifth clue, 'Qua Democracy Eram Prognatus' means, Where democracy was born. The sixth clue, 'Valde urbs of Crocus Vir' means Great city of the yellow man. The seventh clue, 'Urbs of Silicis - Vir in Gero' means, The city of the rock-man in the bear.

It is my belief that while they were very concerned about the safety of the Oracle, the authors also did not want to make these riddles so difficult that someone finding them hundreds of years later could not solve them. I have read and re-read this book many times over the last week, as we traveled here from the village where Alex Montgomery, the man who found the book for us, lived. I'm convinced that the authors were anticipating that only the most determined individuals with the proper education and background, would spend the time and expense travelling all over the world just to collect all of the pieces of the map."

David-Michael motioned to speak. "Brother Sebastian, can you determine which meros the clues are talking about?"

"How will you find these meros?" asked Ferrell.

"Well…" Sebastian started as he began to laugh,"…one of the few advantages that someone my age has left is that I have been around for a long time, and I have learned a few things. While I still need to confer with some of my brothers here to be certain on a few key points, the book tells us which meros to look in. Ancient maps will help us find the meros."

"What do you propose we do, Brother Sebastian?" asked Lord Sarkoth.

"I believe that we should make preparations to seek and find the pieces of the map as quickly as possible."

"I agree," said Ferrell, looking at Brother Sebastian and then at Lord Sarkoth. He stood to address the Council. "Lord Sarkoth, I believe that we must make haste. Kraken and his men have heard about this book. From what I have heard about this man, he will do everything within his power to get his hands on the Oracle."

"Clansman Ferrell has made an important point, my friends," added David-Michael, looking at everyone seated at the table. "Surely this Kraken recognizes that the Clan as his only real obstacle to world conquest, and will attack us as soon as he feels he is ready. As you may have heard, the urba's power has grown considerably over the last few years. His army already outnumbers the Clan by a factor of ten, and it grows every day. Soon, his power will rival our own. If we do not act to stop him, we may well find ourselves unable to stop him."

"Then we must prepare to move against Kraken as quickly as possible," said Lord Sarkoth. "David-Michael, I want you to take some men and travel throughout the Outlands, visiting as many Enclaves as you can. We need to begin gathering our fellow Clansmen together as quickly as possible."

"Yes my lord, it will be done, with all haste."

"And we must also begin the search for the seven pieces of the map," said Sebastian. "I suspect we will find the sections of the map at monasteries located in the seven cities referenced in the riddles. We would like to seek out these pieces of the map, as quickly as possible."

"Would you like some company, Brother Sebastian?" asked Lord Sarkoth. "After all, Kraken may seek to find and kill you before you can locate the Oracle."

Brother Sebastian smiled. "Lord Sarkoth, I feel confident in speaking for all of the brothers gathered here when I say that we would welcome the company of however many clansmen as you feel should come with us."

"Good, it is settled. David-Michael, go to the enclaves, bring our men here to me. My Christian Brothers, may God go with you on your journeys. I will see to it that some of our finest warriors are selected to accompany each priest on his respective journey to find the map. Ferrell, I would like for you to assign a group of warriors to each priest, while you accompany Brother Darius."

"It will be done, Lord Sarkoth!"

"Lord Sarkoth, with your permission, I would like to review my interpretations of the riddles in this book with you and the others."

"Of course, Brother Sebastian."

After several days of discussion, all of the priests felt confident in Brother Sebastian's interpretations of the riddles. The council then determined that the group would split up as follows:

Clue Number 1- Where the Great Lady lights the way, was interpreted as referring to the mero once known as New York City. The council selected Brother Francis and Julius to find the first piece of the map.

Clue Number 2- Where the Bearded Man Sits, was interpreted as referring to the mero once known as Washington, DC. The council selected Ferrell and Brother Darius to go there.

Clue Number 3- City of Wind, was interpreted as referring to Chicago, IL. The council selected Alex, Brother Sebastian, and Wilijah to search there for the third piece of the map.

Clue Number 4- Where the quiet Soldiers Rest, was interpreted as referring to the mero once known as Arlington, VA. The council selected Brother O'Reilly and Sanjo to find the fourth piece of the map.

Clue Number 5-Where Democracy Was Born, was interpreted as referring to Athens, Greece. The council selected Brother Wayne and Norris to journey by sea to search for the fifth piece of the map.

Clue Number 6- Great City of the Yellow Man, was interpreted as referring to the mero once known as Hong Kong, China. The council selected Brother Dan and Monasa to cross the Great Waters in search for the sixth piece of the map.

Clue Number 7- The city of the Rock-Man in the Bear, was interpreted as referring to the mero once known as St. Petersburg, Russia. The council selected Brother Benedict and Yoshi Monasa to find this final piece of the map.

As the groups prepared to leave the Main Enclave, Sarkoth shared a few final words. "I urge you to make great haste on your journey. Remember what is at stake, my friends, and look to your God for guidance. In the meantime, I will make plans for dealing with Kraken's army."

After many prayers and words of encouragement, the eight groups said their final goodbyes to their families and friends, before heading off in separate directions; seven groups looking for the map, the last looking for help from the many Clan enclaves scattered throughout the Outlands.

Chapter 17
The Healer

She paced impatiently outside of the large green and red building that stood in the center of the vast complex, shuffling back and forth, and kicking at the dirt as she did so. She had the troublesome habit of occasionally biting at her lip when her impatience got the better of her, and it had already started to bleed. Years had gone by since she had seen him last, and she had so many questions to ask, as well as a few things to say to him.

After waiting all morning until the sun was high in the sky, the main doors of the Great Hall flung open at last, and people began making their way out of the central building, which served as the unofficial center of the Main Enclave. A long line of clergy and clansmen carried their conversations outside, as they discussed and debated various weighty matters, which meant little to Tara at the moment. Gradually they made their way out of the building and through the main gate to where she had been waiting. Many of the passers-by gave her curious glances as they made their way past her, due in large part to the way she stared intensely at them as they approached. After several minutes, she saw Lord Sarkoth approaching and bowed.

"Lord Sarkoth."

"Good day to you, Tara. It's nice to see you this morning."

"And you as well, Lord Sarkoth."

"So how goes your training?" the aged master asked her.

"Oh, it's going very well, sir!" Tara answered proudly, "Why just the other day Clansman Masters and I were sparring, when I used a new move with the long sword that I..."

"I meant with your training as a healer, young one," he said raising his eyebrows, in a pseudo-stern manner.

117

"Oh, that's going fine also, sir, thank you for asking," Tara answered, looking down at the ground.

The old man took a long breath as they walked together over to where several tables and benches sat under a thatched roof. High Elder Lord Sarkoth furrowed his brow as he searched for the right words.

"I know, Tara, that you have the heart and spirit of a great warrior, and that you yearn for battle, the way others yearn for the comfort of the enclave. But it has been our way since ancient times that the women serve as healers, teachers, and the like, not as warriors."

"I know, Lord Sarkoth, I know, and I want to learn the ancient healing arts, I do! It's just that..."

"...you would prefer holding two swords in your hands, throwing punches, kicks, and knives, or perhaps pulling a bow and letting an arrow fly, is that it?"

"Yes, sir, that's it exactly. Please, Lord Sarkoth, allow me to continue my martial training, I beg you!"

Lord Sarkoth stared blankly past the giant walls that surrounded the enclave, and off into the blue, cloudless sky above

"You know, Tara, you have already been training under one of the best clansmen in the enclave, despite the fact that you were supposed to be focusing your time and energy on your training as a healer."

The young woman stared at the leader of the Warrior Clan with a blank look on her face.

"How did you know, I..."

"No, I am afraid there is only one thing left I can do..."

"But Lord Sarkoth, I have continued my training as a healer. I promise, I..."

"There is only one punishment that fits the crime."

"Please, no..."

"...and that is to put you under the best clansman warrior I have ever met." He smiled as he pointed toward the entrance of the Great Hall, just as Ferrell emerged.

Tara looked at Ferrell and then back at Sarkoth, who nodded his head in affirmation.

"Ferrell!" she yelled, before running over and grabbing him around the neck. Ferrell, however, jerked back to examine the young woman who had called his name before wrapping her arms around him. After looking her over for a moment, a smile appeared on his face.

"Tara? Tara, is that you?" he asked, wrapping each hand around an arm.

"It's me big brother! Where have you been all of this time! Do you know how worried I have been about you, just taking off like that? Mom has been sick with grief since the day you left! Why have you waited so long to come back?"

"Whoa, slow down, Tara. I'm sorry. I have been…busy."

"Doing what?" she asked, still irate. Lord Sarkoth walked up as Ferrell's face began turning red.

"Ferrell, your sister has become quite the young warrior since you left."

"Tara, a warrior? She should be learning the art of healing, not the art of war!" he exclaimed, looking at his little sister with irritation. "What are you doing, Tara? Have you been causing trouble while I was gone?"

"Just following in your steps, big brother. You left a big reputation behind when you took off."

"But you're a girl, Tara. You can't fight!" he said.

"Why can't I fight, just because I'm a girl?" she asked rhetorically.

Sarkoth just shook his head and sat back down, anticipating what was about to happen. Tara suddenly stepped out into the open area.

"Come on, Ferrell. Let me show you some of what I have learned."

"No, Tara, you're my sister, and you're a girl!"

"I'm a woman," she answered defiantly, "and I can fight. Come on out here with me, unless of course, you're afraid to be humiliated by a woman."

Ferrell crossed his arms in anger. "Okay, little sister. I'll go around with you, just so I can teach you a lesson. I'll show you where your place is!"

Sarkoth, who had been watching the drama as it unfolded, looked up at the blue sky, rolled his eyes, and sighed.

Ferrell walked out into the open area where his sister stood waiting. The moment Ferrell set his foot down in the open area, Tara ran immediately toward her older brother, and jumping high into the air, she pulled both knees to her chest, with the heels of both feet pointing toward her brother. Surprised by the suddenness and ferocity of the attack from his little sister, he sidestepped the attack just as one of her heels struck his right shoulder, spinning him and knocking him to the ground.

"So what did you think of that, big brother? Still think I can't fight?"

"I think you need to learn your place," he replied.

Tara didn't even bother responding to her brother's remark. She threw a roundhouse kick to her brother's midsection, striking the middle of his armor and knocking him back several feet, before following it up with a back kick. Ferrell was prepared this time however, as he moved up the back of her leg, and placed his foot behind Tara's supporting ankle while pushing against her shoulder, knocking her to the ground face down in the dirt. She arose, angry and embarrassed, with a sword in each hand.

"Enough!" Sarkoth stepped in between them, ending the brief altercation.

"Sit, there" he said to Tara, giving her a stern look.

"And you Ferrell, you should know better. Have you learned nothing since you left us?"

"Forgive me, Lord Sarkoth," answered Ferrell. Sarkoth narrowed his eyes and fixed his stare at Ferrell for a moment, before turning to Tara.

"As for you, young lady, have we not been through this before? You know that many of the clansmen object to your training. You must learn to control your temper, allowing the unpleasant remarks made by others to flow over you, just as water flows over stones in a brook. If you cannot do this, you will cease your martial studies, do you understand?"

"Yes, Lord Sarkoth, and I apologize for my behavior." she said. Sarkoth looked intently in her eyes for a moment, before looking down at the ground and shaking his head.

"You each have baggage that you have carried for some time. I suggest that you spend some time together talking, not fighting, as brother and sister. Perhaps that way, you can unload some of this baggage together, hmm?"

"Yes, Lord Sarkoth," replied Ferrell.

"Yes, sir," said Tara.

Ferrell and Tara stood there for a moment as the elder Clan leader walked back into the Great Hall. After a few minutes, the siblings slowly drew closer to one another, before finally holding one another in a long, warm embrace.

Chapter 18
The Spy

His first impressions were twofold. First, Kraken appeared to be one of the most intelligent barbarians he had ever encountered. Second, based on what little he had seen since he had entered Kraken's lair, he was also by far, the cruelest human being he had ever seen. He had been in the middle of torturing a Christian priest when Bokra had arrived at the compound a few hours earlier. Not known for having a weak stomach, what Bokra had seen made him nauseous. He watched as Kraken took a blade and slowly peeled back one layer of skin at a time on the man, causing the priest to scream. Kraken wore a broad, cruel smile, so large and so unnatural on his face that Bokra thought for a moment that Kraken might not even be a man.

Bokra was thinking better of his decision to meet with Kraken, and was turning to leave when he saw Mansa immediately behind him, blocking his way.

"Come on in my friend, come in! Please forgive my poor manners. I'm afraid I was a little preoccupied when you came in; I apologize for being so rude." Kaken motioned for him to sit down. "Your name is Bokra?"

"It is."

He was supposed to tell Kraken everything he had learned at the Council Meeting. Bokra had sought out Kraken, and now he was regretting that decision. He had acted impulsively, planning to betray his old Master, and the Clan as a whole. He had heard of Kraken's depravity, but he had written it off as mere exaggeration. Now that he had seen it firsthand, Bokra feared he was in trouble. He had come too far however to turn back now. He would have to tell them everything, well almost everything. As badly as he wanted revenge on the Clan for the many wrongs done to him in the past, he could not betray his brothers to this …animal.

"So, Mansa tells me that you wanted to meet with me, that you have some sort of information for me regarding the Council Meeting at the Warrior Clan Enclave that you thought would interest me? Please, tell me, what information do you have for me? I would like to have been there so I could have heard it for myself but then, hmm, for some reason they didn't invite me!" Kraken laughed while eyeing Bokra with suspicion. "Tell me something first Bokra; is it true that all members of the Clan must swear an oath of loyalty to the Clan, vowing to endure a slow and painful death before breaking the oath?"

Bokra snarled slightly at Kraken's remark. "It is true," he answered.

Kraken smiled as he feigned surprise saying, "Well, I'm shocked that you're here talking with me then, Bokra, what about your precious oath? Coming here to me, telling me what was discussed during your Council Meeting… would your esteemed Lord Sarkoth approve?"

"I am breaking no oath. No Clansman will be harmed by what I will tell you; a few priests perhaps but no Clansman, and my oath is to the Clan, not to the Christians. I came here to tell you about what they now seek, this Oracle. If you are more concerned about me breaking my oath, then perhaps I should be on my way."

Bokra stood up and prepared to leave.

"Now, don't be so hasty, Clansman! You should have known when you came here that I would have to test you. You and I should be friends… after all, I have never caused any trouble for the Clan, now have I? No, I have nothing but respect for your Clan."

Bokra began to relax a little, and Kraken seized on the opportunity. "Tell me what they discussed at the Council Meeting; why are the priests meeting with them, and what does all of this have to do with the Oracle?"

"The Council Meeting was called so that the Clan, and the Christian Church, could join forces on some ridiculous quest to go looking for a fantasy, some mythological, legendary ancient artifact called the Oracle, which will supposedly save the world from the darkness. One of them found a book, which they say will tell them how to locate this artifact. Supposedly, this book, coincidentally written in a language that only these fanatical priests can read, says there is a map, divided into seven pieces. They plan to find the pieces of this map, and then use them to find the Oracle."

"I have heard of this book, and of this Oracle. Bokra, I want you to tell me everything that you know, leave nothing out, do you understand me?"

"At the Council Meeting, the decision was made that the priests would travel to the seven meros mentioned in this book in search of this map. Some of these meros are located in distant lands, beyond the Great Waters.

"And the Clan?" asked Kraken, "What is their role?"

"The Clan will send escorts to protect the priests."

"I want to know more about these plans, Bokra. I need more information," growled Kraken.

"I was in only part of the Council Meeting Kraken, not all of it. "

"Then you must go back and spy out more information for me clansman, and do it quickly, if you wish to live," growled Kraken.

"You do not frighten me, Kraken! I came here to share this with you for my own reasons, but make no mistake, I don't work for you!" Of course, he and Kraken both knew that this was only half-true.

"Oh, I wasn't talking about me, Bokra, my friend. No, I was referring to your precious Lord Sarkoth, and your fellow clansmen. Why, I doubt that they would allow you to live, what with that warrior code of ethics and all that you so-called "warriors" live by, if they knew what you've told me. I expect that once they learn you have given me the Oracle, and brought about the destruction of their precious Clan, they will kill you on the spot." He leaned in closer to Bokra at the end to add emphasis as Bokra lowered his head in shame.

"Now then, you will bring me more information on their plans, and you will do so immediately, is that clear?"

"Yes," Bokra replied, with considerably less defiance than before.

"Now get out of my sight, you impetuous little worm, before I kill you myself." Bokra turned and left the room, just as Mansa returned.

"What news do you have for me, Mansa?"

"It is as he said, Lord Kraken. Our scouts report that they have been making arrangements to leave the Clan's Main Enclave." Mansa stood in front of Kraken, waiting for additional orders.

"I want you to send some of our men to the enclave immediately, to follow each expedition," said Kraken. "Tell our men to follow them to the map, and once they have it, to kill everyone. Tell the men that if any of the priests or clansmen escapes with the map, their lives will be forfeit. Tell them that they will suffer a slow and painful death, because that pleasure will be mine alone."

"Yes, Lord Kraken. I will take care of it immediately."

As Mansa prepared to leave the room Kraken added, "Be certain to choose only our stealthiest men, Mansa. Those cursed Clansmen are well trained, and they can sense and smell trouble coming a mile away. As an added measure of precaution, I want each of our men to have one of the ancient weapons. We cannot leave anything to chance with this endeavor."

"Yes my Lord. I will see to it personally."

Mansa left the room, wondering to himself what could be so important about the Oracle. What kind of power did it possess? Perhaps, Mansa thought to himself, when the time comes, I will be the one that ends up benefiting from the Oracle's great power. He must be cautious however, as Kraken seemed to have the ability to read men's minds. When the time came, Mansa decided, he would be ready.

Chapter 19
The First Map

Valde Era Lux Lucis Via (Where the Great Lady Lights the Way)

Julius looked over at Brother Francis. The priest had obviously never done much horseback riding before, and he was now paying a price for it on the journey to the mero. He had been told that the mero they were travelling to was one of the largest meros in the known lands; there were certain to be dangers at every turn. If they acted with great stealth as they approached the mero, and with haste, perhaps their presence would be undetected by the inhabitants of the mero. In addition to their safety, the clansman was also concerned about their ability to locate the monastery in the midst of such a large mero; it could take days, perhaps even weeks to find it. It was not the danger to his own life that bothered Julius. As a clansman, he was well trained and prepared to die. He wondered how he was supposed to keep the priest alive against such difficult odds.

Julius estimated that the trip would take them at least several more days. Though not as aged as Lord Sarkoth or even Brother Sebastian, Julius determine that Brother Francis was easily old enough to be his father. He would therefore show an even greater respect to Brother Francis than he would have otherwise, not only because he was associated with the Church, an entity that Lord Sarkoth had deemed a friend to the Clan, and not just because he was a priest, but because he was his elder. Julius was a proud, traditional man, and a proud warrior. He respected the code, he breathed the code, and he lived by it.

"Brother Francis, we have made excellent progress today. Perhaps we should stop here for the night to camp." He almost laughed aloud when he saw the expression of relief on the face of Brother Francis.

"Very good my son, if you feel that is best, of course." Brother Francis got off the horse. "I am grateful, my young friend, and I thank you for your kind mercies," he said to Julius while rubbing his posterior. "We are both grateful to you my son," he added. Both of them burst out laughing.

After they had rested for a short while, Brother Francis noticed the faces of the warriors that had accompanied them on the journey. They appeared to be a solemn lot, a very serious group of men. He turned to face his companion.

"Clansman Julius, may we talk for a few moments?"

The warrior turned to Brother Francis, and sat down on the ground next to him at the fire.

"Yes, Brother Francis, what can I do for you?"

"I am curious about something, about the Warrior Clan. I know that the Holy Father has a relationship with Lord Sarkoth, but other than the short time I was at the Enclave, and our time together on this trip, I have spent little time with clansmen, so I know next to nothing about you. Don't get me wrong, you are an impressive group of people; fiercely loyal, dedicated, and as committed to rebuilding civilization as we are. What I am curious about is your religious beliefs. Do you believe in God? Do you have any religion at all?"

"I suppose we are like any group of people... no two members believe exactly the same thing. There are a number of clansmen that worship the Christian God, and certainly Lord Sarkoth does nothing to discourage this practice. Some clansmen find peace in the creative arts, learning the ancient art of calligraphy, or writing poetry, while others prefer to simply meditate. Since the time of The Great Collapse and the founding of the Clan, we have all been focused on perfecting our fighting skills in order to survive, and to help teach others how to survive. As you know, we also value and understand the need for civilization to once again flourish and thrive in our world. Throughout this Dark Age, we have done what we could to preserve knowledge of the ancient ways."

"That is incredible. Do you maintain libraries? Are warriors taught to read and write as well?" asked Francis.

"We have books Brother, and everyone learns the basics of how to read and write. Extensive reading however, is a luxury that we can ill-afford during these difficult and trying days. We have collected books when possible and practical to do so, but most were burned during the Great Collapse or since by urbas, who care nothing whatsoever for learning or knowledge. They seek only to prey on others, to take what they want from whomever they want. They are a vicious, unprincipled lot."

"But they are human beings, Julius. You talk about them as if they are animals, not men."

"They may have been men once, long ago, Brother, but now, they are nothing but murderers, thieves, and worse. They hold no value for life, no morals."

"Perhaps that is only because they do not know God, and his great love for them."

Julius was starting to get agitated with the priest. "Well, I can tell you what would happen to you Brother, if you decided to go and tell them about your God. They would take you, strip your clothes off of you, and kill you for fun!"

"If that is God's will for me Julius, then so be it. It is one of our primary callings."

"Then it is my hope that you are not called to do so during this trip Brother, for it is my duty to keep you alive, even at the cost of my life, and the lives of those that travel with us."

The priest frowned. To put his own life at risk was one thing; to put the lives of the young warriors that traveled with him at risk was something altogether different.

"Don't fret my young friend. Unless God directs me otherwise, it is fully my intent to complete our objective and find the map."

"Good, I'm glad to hear it, Brother," answered Julius. He had been a bit harsh with the priest, and despite Francis' naïveté, he liked the priest. "Forgive me Brother, I did not mean to snap at you, but you do not know these urba the way I do. I have seen them murder innocent men, women, and children, with no hesitation whatsoever. They may indeed be human beings, and perhaps one day they will learn of this God of yours, and become better people for it. Until then however, I will kill any urba who crosses paths with me." He then turned without saying another word and lay down to sleep. He dreamed of battle that night.

Early the next morning, several of the clansmen woke up and immediately set off in search of firewood while others went looking for game. A short time later, there was a blazing fire started, with several hares cooking over it. Brother Francis awoke to the tantalizing aroma of breakfast. He stood up and walked toward the fire, where Julius stood cooking a hare.

"Good Morning, Brother Francis."

"Good Morning, Clansman Julius."

"Would you care for some breakfast?"

"Yes, thank you my dear friend, you are a saint"

Julius handed him some rabbit meat, for which Francis bowed his head, gave thanks, and then quickly consumed. They had not eaten since the morning of the day before, and he was famished.

"So how much further do we have to go, Brother?" asked Julius.

"I would say we have another two days journey. We should begin to see the mero late tomorrow."

"But how is that possible," asked Julius, "if we are still another day out?"

"This mero has many very tall buildings in it that were built during the Golden Age. Some of them are so tall they touch the sky. They should be visible from some distance out."

"Truly, the Ancients were a remarkable people," remarked the warrior.

"Yes, they were," the priest replied, "but keep in mind they had their faults. Just look around you and you will see their legacy."

"Tell me something, Brother, what else do you know about this Oracle, and why is it so important that we find it?"

"I tell you what," Brother Francis replied, "how about we get started, and then I will tell you what I know on the way," he said, as he worked to finish his breakfast before collecting his things.

"Very good, I will tell the rest to get packed up and ready to go."

Julius went around to the other men, informing them that it was time to break camp. Brother Francis watched Julius as he spoke to the men, each of whom seemed to have great respect for him. The clansman seemed to consider each man his equal, though he outranked them all. Francis had been told that Julius was almost an elder himself, and that he had long been one of the most dependable and trustworthy of all the clansmen, among a group who were themselves, dependable and trustworthy. Brother Francis decided that he liked this man, Julius, and his respect for the Clan as a whole grew daily. He began praying that all of the Clan would convert to Christianity one day. Perhaps once they had found the Oracle, he would make it his mission to serve among the Clan as a missionary, if the Church permitted him to do so. He was pondering this when he noticed a tense expression on the face of his traveling companion.

"What's wrong, Julius?" he asked.

"One of our men is missing, Brother. He was on watch early this morning. One of our men thinks he saw the missing clansman, Chung, leave camp to investigate something earlier, but he's not certain. We are forming a search party now to look for him."

"What can I do to help?" asked Brother Francis.

"I appreciate the offer, Brother, but you would be the most help to us by remaining here with several of my men while we search. We could move more quickly and cover more ground without you. If you came with us I would be concerned for your safety, which would hamper my search effort."

"Very well, replied Brother Francis. I will stay here as you request. If you need more help in the search, please do not hesitate to ask." Julius nodded as he and the others left the camp and spread out, looking for their missing brother.

They had been gone for no more than an hour when Brother Francis saw them returning to camp. Each man wore a sad, angry look as they drew closer. When they arrived back at the camp, he saw the reason why. One of the larger men was carrying a man's body slung over his shoulder.

"Is he…" Francis started to ask.

One of the men replied. "Yes, Brother, he is dead. He was murdered no more than six hours ago. It looks like he took at least four of the attackers with him before he was killed however. They overwhelmed him with sheer numbers."

"But who?" Francis started to ask.

Julius came over to tell him the rest.

"The dead attackers looked like urbas, Brother, but there was something different about them. They were wearing some strange markings on their clothing. We took this from one of the dead attackers before we left to bring Chung's body back to camp. Each of them was wearing this same design on their clothing. Have you ever seen anything like this?" he asked, holding out the patch of cloth for the priest to examine.

Francis looked over the insignia and shook his head.

"No, I haven't. Any idea who they were and what they were doing here? We are not even close to the mero yet."

Julius shook his head and grimaced.

"No Brother, I don't know for sure, but I have my suspicions. If they bear out, we must be extremely cautious on our way to the mero, and doubly so as we return, if we return, from the mero."

Francis gave Julius a perplexed look. "What do you mean Julius, what are you thinking?"

Julius thought for a few moments whether he should give Brother Francis a straight answer, before deciding he had to trust the priest.

"We have had a spy among the urbas that follow Kraken for some time. Not too long ago, we learned that Kraken's army is becoming better organized. There are rumors among Kraken's men that he recently formed an elite personal guard that reports directly to Kraken and are not part of his regular army."

Brother Francis said, "So you believe these men are part of that elite guard, and that they are following us, waiting for us to find the missing piece to the map before attacking us?"

"Yes Brother, I do. If they are members of his elite guard, they are likely among his best and most trusted warriors, which would explain why they were able to overpower Chung, and why there were only four or five attackers dead. Chung was an exceptional fighter, even for a clansman. If they are Kraken's men, they will wait and attack us on our return trip."

"So you think they know about the map, and about the Oracle?" asked the priest. Brother Francis was growing concerned.

"It doesn't matter whether they do or not, Brother, they will not get the map from us. I give you my word."

"I am grateful for that Julius. I don't need to tell you how bad it would be if Kraken gets his hands on the Oracle. Based on what we understand, the Oracle would grant him access to tremendous knowledge and power. With the Oracle's power, he would plunge the world into such a time of misery and suffering that it would make the Dark Age look appealing!"

"Yes, Brother, I understand."

"Why do you think they killed Clansman Chung?" asked Francis. "What did they have to gain from it?"

"I can only surmise that Clansman Chung came across their camp by surprise, and that they killed him to try to conceal their presence," answered Julius. "I suppose it never occurred to them that we might discover the bodies. They are a stupid lot, these urba," he said in a low growl.

The clansmen buried their brother Chung, and Brother Francis conducted a brief service afterwards in his honor. Soon after the funeral was over, the group broke camp and continued their march toward the mero.

The expedition for most of the day was uneventful, at least until one of the men that had been scouting ahead reported to Julius.

"I saw it, I saw the mero! It is the largest mero that I have ever seen! I could see buildings that were so tall they touched the sky!"

Julius spoke with the scouts, who showed him the direction from which they had come. Soon, they were all able to see some of the taller buildings of the Mero. Julius thought the scout had been exaggerating, but he soon saw that he had not been. It was indeed an incredible site, larger than he had ever imagined. The Clan still had some of the old records at the Enclave from the time of the Golden Age, so he had known that some of the meros were impressive. As he gazed at the mero in wonder, he found himself wondering what it had been like before the Great Collapse, and how remarkable it must have been! Julius and Francis led the group as they continued on their way.

"Brother, you promised that you would tell me more about the Oracle," Julius said to Francis, as they climbed down a hill.

"Indeed I did," answered the priest. Well, let's see, where should I begin? To start with, we don't really know all that much. What we do know is that the Christian brothers alive at the time that were members of the Unity believed that the Oracle held great promise for rebuilding civilization. According to the prophecy, the Oracle contains all of the knowledge of the Ancients, and will provide whoever finds it with access to its vast and wondrous technology," said Francis.

"If that is the case, then why has the Church waited for five hundred years to act? Why did they not go looking the Oracle centuries ago?" asked Julius.

"That is a good question," the priest answered. "According to stories I have heard, the Church was given instructions to wait until a sign appeared before trying to activate the Oracle. If it were activated before the sign was given, the Oracle would be lost to us forever."

"What is this sign, Brother?" asked Julius.

"According to the prophecy, the Oracle would not yield up its knowledge until the Lord gave a sign, announcing to the world that the curse of the Dark Age had been lifted."

"And what makes you think that the curse has been lifted?" asked Julius. "Has this sign appeared?"

"Yes, apparently so, that is why Darius was sent to the Council Meeting. The Holy Father had a dream, a vision that the sign would soon appear. He believed it was a vision from God, revealing to him that the curse would soon be removed, and that it was time to seek and find the Great Oracle."

131

Julius nodded his head and continued riding, until at last they arrived at the edge of the enormous mero. Julius raised his right hand, signaling that they were stopping.

"We will make camp here for the night, and enter the mero in the morning. I don't believe I need to tell everyone how dangerous it will be here tonight. We will stand guard in two-man shifts. If you see anything unusual, let the other know, and wake us if necessary, but remember what happened to Chung, and do not underestimate these men of Kraken's. Some of his best warriors are following us now. We will have to fight tomorrow, brothers, and we will have to fight again once we leave to go home. But remember who and what we are, for we are not ordinary men, we are Clansmen!" he yelled, and all the men chanted "Clansmen!"

After setting up camp, they all lay down except for Julius and one other, trying to get some sleep before their watch. To Brother Francis, it appeared that the clansmen fell quickly to sleep. He suspected that years of training and danger had prepared the clansmen for situations like these, and that the need for rest before fighting had enabled the men to develop the ability to sleep, even the night before an important battle. The same could not be said for Francis however. Try as he might, he tossed and turned for hours, trying in vain to take his mind off the danger, and off the mission. Finally, he uttered a short but sincere prayer to the Lord, pleading for rest, before falling into a deep and restful sleep shortly thereafter.

The next morning they broke camp and headed into the mero, with everyone keeping a vigilant lookout for danger.

"Okay Brother, we are here. Now what?" asked Julius.

"Well, I don't know exactly where it is, but I believe I know how to find it. The words in the clue say "Qua Valde Era lux lucis via" which means "Where the Great Lady lights the way." There is supposed to be a large statue that rises out of the water somewhere near here. If we can find the water, and head in the direction of the statue, we should be close to the monastery. Why don't you ask your men to fan out and search for the water, and for the statue?"

"What does this statue look like Brother, how will we know it when we find it? I have seen many statues in the various meros I have been in."

"Oh don't worry Julius, this one is different. It was bigger than almost any other statue from the days before the Great Collapse. It is big, really big, and looks like a woman wearing a crown and holding a great torch."

"Very well," replied Julius. He gave the order to his men and they began searching. After only a few moments, one of the men spotted it. "I can see it!" he yelled.

The warriors were rushing toward the clansman when they spotted something out of the corners or their eyes. A large pack of urbas rushed toward them at a rapid clip.

"Everyone, gather around me! Protect the priest at all costs, even at the cost of your very lives!"

"Yes sir!" the Clansmen replied, moving quickly in obedience to the commands of their leader. As for himself, after selecting several of his best men to surround the priest, Julius decided he would be most effective leading the battle against the urba. From his estimation, there were no more than thirty urba attacking. It was typical of a pack of urba. They generally were not able to function well in a large group. If the pack grew beyond twenty or thirty men, they just fell apart or splintered.

Julius took a position out in front, sword drawn. He had just enough time to check his armor one last time to ensure it was properly fastened.

"Okay, men, I will personally take all watches on the trip back for the man who takes out the most urba, are you up for the challenge?" he asked them jokingly.

One of the men replied "That is quite generous of you sir. I certainly appreciate the opportunity to get more sleep!"

Julius replied. "You will have to earn that sleep first, clansman. Believe me; I have no plans to make it easy for you!"

Conversation ceased as the first wave of urba arrived and launched their attack. A few of them had slowed to a stop as they approached the group. Francis wondered to himself whether the urba had ever seen clansmen in battle before, and had recognized their unique armor.

Since Julius was out front, he was the first to meet the charge. With a single sweep of his blade, he sliced upward killing one urba and then sliced down taking out a second.

"Okay gentlemen," he said, "that is two for me!"

Cameron, one of the younger clansmen, met the attack of an urba's blade. Like most urba, he carried a knife and an urban hatchet, the favorite weapons of most urba. Urbas liked to make an impression on their victims that instilled the maximum fear. This had the added benefit of making their butchery all the simpler. These "victims" however, were not pilgrims seeking passage to other lands, these were clansmen, and the urba quickly learned the difference.

The urba attacked with a hatchet to his head. Cameron easily sidestepped to the left, allowing the hatchet swing to pass by his right shoulder. He countered with a slice of his blade to the back of the urba's neck. Another urba attacked Cameron before he could recover, knocking the blade from his hands with a powerful stroke from his hatchet. Cameron turned to face the new attacker; barely moving back enough as the knife in the urba's other hand missed his throat by a mere inch. Cameron countered with an elbow strike to the urba's ribs, causing him to yell in pain. He followed up with a kick to the groin, and then a single blow to the back of the urba's neck.

"Looks like we are tied Master Julius," he yelled out, drawing a smile from his leader.

After seeing the ease with which the warriors had dispatched their companions, the rest of the urba backed away, and when the clansmen moved in their direction, they scurried off. It occurred to Julius that that this pack seemed to possess more common sense than most of the urba thugs he had run across. Typically, they would not run off until at least half of their number had been dispatched. Perhaps the pack had run into clansmen before, maybe a local enclave.

After taking a brief assessment to ensure everyone was alive and unhurt, the clansmen hastily packed up as quickly as they could. What seemed like mere moments later, they had already mounted their horses and were putting some distance between themselves and the site of their recent battle. Though none of the clansmen said anything to him, it was obvious to Brother Francis that something was troubling them, something unspoken, yet something that everyone else seem to already know.

"Clansman Julius, what's going on?" he asked. "Why is everyone in such a hurry to leave?"

Saying nothing, Julius turned to look back in the direction from which they had come. The other clansmen stopped as well. All of them had the same hard look on their faces, an expression that Brother Francis had not seen on any of the clansmen during the entire journey, a look of solemnity, and fear.

Francis followed suit and looking behind him, tried to discern what they were waiting for. Then he saw something coming out of the shadows, a black silhouette that rapidly covered the ground where they had stood only minutes before. He squinted as he struggled to make out what the strange shape was. Finally, to his horror, he understood why they were afraid. The black shadow wasn't a shadow at all, but a swarm of rats that had swiftly covered the carnage they left behind. Brother Francis made the sign of the cross and recited the Lord's Prayer. By the time he had done so five times, he looked up to find that they had arrived at a section of the mero which looked old even by ancient standards.

Julius was the first to speak. "Some of the structures in this area looked considerably different from the others. Perhaps what we seek is somewhere nearby."

"Perhaps it is," replied Brother Francis, "I certainly hope so."

They rode on passing building after building, carefully examining each structure. Eventually, they came to a building with symbols similar to what he had seen on the book. The structure was much darker and smaller than the surrounding ones. A rusted fence about four-feet high surrounded most of it, except for where it lay tilted or completely flat on the ground, having long-ago surrendered to the effects of time and the elements. Broken shards of glass surrounded the inside window frames of most of the windows.

"This has to be it!" Brother Francis exclaimed. They dismounted their horses and walked toward the building. Just before they reached the steps that led up to an entrance, the clansman that led the group stepped on something covered in dirt and grime. His foot slipped, causing it to slide across its metal surface.

"Hold on a minute, what is that?" He walked over to where the clansman had nearly fallen, and saw the letters "e-r-y." Using his foot, he began to clear some of the grime off the metal sign to reveal the words, "Sacred Lord Monastery."

"Here, look at this Julius! We're here, this is it, we've arrived at the monastery!"

"That's great news, Brother! So what exactly are we looking for now that we're here?" asked Julius.

"I don't know exactly," replied the priest. "The clues were not specific as to what to expect. I would say to look for anything that looks out of place."

"Do as he says," ordered Julius, "and make it fast."

The men spread out searching the ancient monastery for anything unusual. Francis began his search on the main level of the monastery, focusing primarily in the chapel area. He looked all around inside the chapel, carefully scrutinizing the paintings that still hung on the walls, searching through the debris that was scattered throughout the inside. Finally, he came to the altar. Kneeling in reverence to the Lord, Francis offered a prayer asking the Lord to bless and guide his mission. After concluding his prayer, he opened his eyes to find himself looking at something unusual on the floor. A closer examination revealed it was the sign of The Unity. He felt around on the floor, and found that the wooden board on which the symbol was engraved was loose. After removing the rotting board, he found it. The map, made of some type of dark, ancient cloth, had been placed inside of a strange, clear material. It was in remarkable condition to date back to the days of the Great Collapse. It must be the clear material that preserved the map for long.

"I found it. I have the map!" he yelled out to the clansmen. The others rushed into the chapel and joined him at the front of the altar. Once the initial excitement, celebration, and relief about finding the map were over, Julius walked over to Francis.

"It would be best if we stay here overnight, inside of the monastery. The day has grown long, and it is far too dangerous now to risk leaving at night. Many creatures that live in the meros hunt at night. Now that we have the map, it is too great a risk to leave before dawn."

Chapter 20
The Second Map

Qua Barbatus Vir Sits (Where the Bearded Man Sits)

Ferrell rode in front of Brother Darius, with ten Clan Warriors surrounding them, two in front, two behind, and three on each side of them. Notwithstanding the seriousness of his mission, he felt like a babysitter, since in addition to protecting Brother Darius, he was now also going to have to watch out for Ariel. She had insisted on coming with him, unwilling even for a moment to consider staying behind, and he worried whether he would ever be able to protect her when trouble came, which it would. Ferrell grunted.

Ariel rode up beside him, clearly hoping to strike up a conversation with him.

"Are you doing okay, Ferrell? You look like you're not feeling so well. Is the wound from that arrow still troubling you?"

Ferrell just grunted again.

"You're still angry with me for coming, aren't you? Well what was I supposed to do? I couldn't sit by and wait to see if you were going to come back to me or not!"

Ferrell grunted for a third time.

"Is that all you are going to do until we get to the mero, just keep grunting at me when I try to talk with you or ask you a question? Because if you're going to be like that, I will just go and talk with Brother Darius!"

Ariel pulled back on the reins slightly until the horse had slowed enough and she found herself alongside Brother Darius. She looked ahead and cast a sharp and rebuking glance back at Ferrell, who had looked her way.

"So, Brother Darius, I understand that you actually spent some time with Pope John Paul V, is that true?"

Darius nodded in reply.

"Tell me, Brother, what is he like?" she asked.

"Well, let me see, I only spoke with him a few times, but he seemed to be one of the most caring and compassionate men I have ever met. He might be one of the best popes the Church has ever had."

"He sounds like a remarkable man," she added.

"He is indeed extraordinary, Ariel. I believe that the Lord chose him for just this time. The Holy Father had a remarkable vision from God just before he sent me here for this Council meeting, always a rarity, especially so during the Dark Age. The Pope believes the dream was a sign from the Lord, a sign that the prophecy is about to be fulfilled, and the end of the Dark Age has finally come. It is his fervent belief that if we are successful in our endeavor to find the Oracle, that it will usher in a new age of wonder, the rebirth of civilization, and a new age that will surpass even the Golden Age of the Ancients!"

"What happens if we are not successful, what if we don't find the Oracle?"

Darius looked down and frowned, saying nothing. "Brother Darius?" she asked again. Darius turned and cast a solemn glance at Ariel.

"Then the world will experience a time of misery and suffering unlike anything it has ever known, and civilization will not reappear for another thousand years," he answered gravely.

Ferrell raised his hand, signaling for the others to stop, and slowed his horse down to a trot. Something didn't feel right. He turned around and rode to the rear of the procession, looking intently back in the direction from which they had just come, but saw nothing but trees and countryside. Nevertheless, he could not shake the uneasy feeling that someone was following them. He carefully surveyed the surrounding landscape, searching for anything that looked out of place. Ferrell had first suspected they were being followed a week or so into their journey, yet each time he looked behind him, he saw no one. The other clansmen turned as well, looking in the same direction as Ferrell, puzzled at the reason for the delay. One of them rode back to where Ferrell sat, nearly motionless, atop his horse.

"What is it, Ferrell? What did you see?"

Ferrell looked around one last time. "Nothing Lloyd," he said. "That's what worries me." Ferrell rode back to the front of the party, looking behind them one last time as they went, and stopped beside Darius.

"It is getting late, Brother Darius. There is a clearing, and a lake, not far from here where I think we should stop. We can rest once we arrive there and then setup camp for the night."

"That sounds good to me, Clansman Ferrell. What is it like, this mero we are going to?" asked Darius.

"I have been in this mero many times before," said Ferrell, "it is a dangerous place. There are vicious packs of urba there, many big cats, wild dogs, and rats. I can guide us, but we will have to be careful." He studied Darius face and recognized the look.

"Does that frighten you, Brother Darius?"

"Of course, it would frighten any sane man."

"Hmm, good," Ferrell replied. "Fear sharpens the senses, preparing them for combat. It will keep you alive."

"What about you, and your men, Clansman Ferrell, aren't you afraid?"

A wry smile appeared on Ferrell's face. "As you said, Brother Darius, such a place would frighten any sane man." He looked at the other clansmen travelling with him. Darius noticed that Ferrell didn't bother to try to hide the pride he felt for his men. "These are some of the best fighters in the Clan, Brother Darius; they are all prepared to die if necessary, in service to this mission, to the Clan, and to Master Sarkoth."

They rode on for another hour without saying much more, before coming to a clearing. A beautiful lake spanning the horizon spread out before them.

"We have arrived at the clearing I mentioned," said Ferrell. "We will camp here for the night. Be certain to boil any water before drinking it, Brother. We will leave out at first light, and should arrive at the edge of the mero by midday tomorrow."

Ferrell and the other clansmen then dismounted their horses and set about to work on setting up the camp, before settling down for the night.

The following morning, Brother Darius awoke to a loud and embarrassing growl coming from his stomach. He climbed out from under his blanket, and walked over to Ferrell, who was attending to some fish over a fire.

"Smells delicious," exclaimed Darius.

"Brother Darius, good morning, I was just about to wake you. Lloyd and some of the others caught these this morning. Eat up, Brother. We need to get started soon." Darius gladly obliged, barely taking time to chew as he devoured his meal.

Barely thirty minutes later, they broke camp, and started out on the last leg of their journey to the mero. Once again, Ferrell took the lead, this time accompanied by Darius, followed by Ariel and the rest of clansmen. They travelled for several more hours before coming to a wide river. About that time, Ariel rode up and joined the two men. Once again, she cast an annoyed look at Ferrell, before turning to talk with the priest.

"So, Brother Darius, how will we know where to look for the map?"

"Well, let me see. When the Unity hid the pieces of the map centuries ago, they chose Christian monasteries that were in existence at the time. We are looking for a specific monastery, in the mero once called Washington, DC. It was an old monastery even then, that once belonged to a group of Franciscan brothers. We should find the monastery just inside the mero. If we have correctly interpreted the clues in the book, the map should be there waiting for us, as it has been for five centuries."

"Then the wait is over Brother, and we will soon have the map, for we have arrived at the mero where the bearded man sits," announced Ferrell.

They were still a fifteen minute ride from the mero, yet off in the distance they could make out an unusual stone structure, standing tall as if reaching for the sky, rising high above all of the others like a towering stone tree, much taller than every other structure in the area. Scattered throughout the mero were enormous buildings made almost entirely of granite. All of them had fallen into a state of disrepair, yet they still stood out to Darius as beautiful monuments to a forgotten past."

"What magnificent structures! Even in the condition they are in, they are magnificent. I have never seen anything like these, even in Rome!"

"We should be safe as long as we do not go far beyond the bearded man," said Ferrell. "Once we move past him, we will run into urba. Several prides of lions also hunt in this mero." He looked over at one of the warriors. "Jonathan, come here."

One of the warriors rode up next to Ferrell.

"Yes, my lord?"

"I want you to stay here and guard the priest, with your life if necessary. I will be back shortly."

"Yes, my lord. But where…"

Jonathan was about to ask Ferrell where he was going, but was interrupted.

"Just where do you think you are going, mister?" asked Ariel.

"You must stay here, Ariel, I will be back soon."

"I am coming with you," she said stubbornly.

"No, you will not, not this time. You would put us both at risk, Ariel. I must do this alone." Ferrell rode off and this time, Ariel did not follow.

After riding ahead of the others, he scanned the area, looking for animal tracks, and for signs of urba. After riding ahead for a considerable distance into the mero, and with no signs of trouble in the vicinity, Ferrell turned to rejoin the others. He was no more then a few hundred yards from them when he felt something strike him from his left side, knocking him off his horse, and he suddenly found himself looking up from the ground. Ferrell turned to see a pride of lions circling around him. A large, young male stood facing him nearby, probably the one that had knocked him off his horse. Ferrell looked down to see that the claws of the giant cat had cut deeply into the leather armor he was wearing. Had it not been for his armor, he would have been disemboweled by the animal's initial attack.

"Lord Ferrell!" exclaimed two of the warriors in unison.

Several of the warriors rushed to Ferrell's aid, while the remainder stayed with Darius and Ariel.

Ferrell had already drawn his sword by the time the others arrived. The lions continued circling the warrior, expecting to make an easy meal of the human being they had already taken to the ground once. There was one fact that the pride had not taken into account however; the next time, Ferrell would be ready. One of the females came at him next, charging at Ferrell as she instinctively leapt for his throat. Ferrell cut through the air even as he sidestepped the great cats lunge. With a single stroke of his sword, Ferrell sliced through the cat's carotid arteries, crippling and then killing it. "One cat down and five to go," he said to the other clansmen.

Sergei and Lloyd arrived at Ferrell's side.

"It's about time you showed up," said Ferrell. "I was beginning to think that I was going to have all of the fun myself. You better hurry if you want to catch up."

"No worries" replied Sergei, as the male that had initially attacked Ferrell lunged at him. Sergei met the attack by jumping into the air as the great cat lunged beneath him. Then, as it was turning to launch another attack, Sergei thrust his sword through the back of the great beast's neck. It collapsed to the ground with a thud.

"Well then, looks like we are tied, Lord Ferrell!"

Ferrell grunted, and then smiled.

"What's that on your face, my old friend," said Sergei. "Wait, could it be a smile?"

Ferrell laughed. "You should pay more attention to what's going on around you, and a little less interest in my facial expressions!" Ferrell said, pointing behind Sergei. Two lions were now pacing behind Sergei, poised to attack.

"Hey, what about me?" quipped Lloyd, who feigned a move toward another of the male lions, trying to goad it into attacking him. Just moments later Lloyd was struck by one of the females and knocked to the ground. Ferrell was at his side in a moment, just in time to drive his sword into the back of the cat. With a turning of his sword, he had driven it deep into the heart of the ferocious feline, who roared one final time before lying still at his feet.

"I had her just where she wanted me," joked Lloyd, rising unhurt from the ground.

"That may be true brother, but I am now ahead two to nothing!" laughed Ferrell, as he moved to cover Lloyd until he had retrieved his sword.

"I'm not worried," countered Lloyd, there are still two left!"

"Sorry Lloyd," said Sergei, as he dispatched another female. "I guess that Ferrell and I are tied!"

The two waited for the remaining male to attack, but breathed a sigh of relief as they watched the only remaining beast turn and run away, before disappearing into the tall grass of a clearing.

After determining that the danger had passed, the three men sat down on the ground, taking a moment to relax. After resting for several minutes, the three collected their horses and walked back to join the others. Exhausted from the battle, they failed to notice the three men sitting on horseback off in the distance, carefully observing the entire encounter unfold from afar.

After searching for the monastery for another hour, Ariel grew bored, and decided to strike up a conversation with Brother Darius.

"Brother Darius, may I ask you a question?"

Darius had been lost in thought as they made their way through the mero; so much so in fact that he had been unaware that Ariel had been riding silently beside him for some time.

"Certainly," he answered.

"What is the Church all about anyway, and what makes Christians so different from everyone else?"

Darius was surprised by the question. In Rome, everyone followed the Lord and worshipped regularly. Throughout the Dark Age however, many outside of Rome, and other clusters of religious orders scattered across the planet, had never heard the Gospel.

"What is the Church? That really is a good question; with a bit of a long answer I'm afraid. Would you like for me to share it with you, understanding that it might take a while?"

Ariel looked at him and nodded enthusiastically. "I would," she answered. "It's not like I have anything else to do."

"You both should be looking for this monastery. It will be dark in a few hours, and we must be out of the mero by then," injected Ferrell, irritated with their idle chatter.

Darius frowned. "This won't take but a moment, Clansman Ferrell, please."

Ferrell simply grimaced in response.

Darius continued. "Well, in the beginning, the Lord God made the Earth, the sky, and the stars, even the sun and the moon, and of course, people."

"He made people? I had no idea!"

"Yes, Ariel, he did. He created men and women, and he gave them the freedom to choose whether to obey him or disobey him; something we call free will. Unfortunately, the first human beings chose to disobey him, allowing sin to enter the world. God, in his loving mercy however, provided a way out for mankind. He loved us so much that he sent His only Son, Jesus Christ, to die for us."

Ariel decided to interrupt Brother Darius. "How did people disobey God?"

"They were deceived," answered Darius.

"By what?"

"By the serpent in the Garden of Eden."

"By a snake?"

"After a fashion, yes. Satan appeared in the form of a snake. He tricked them into disobeying God, causing mankind to fall into sin."

"Who is this Satan, Brother Darius? Is he the enemy of God?"

"I suppose in a manner of speaking, he is. He was originally a beautiful angel named Lucifer, created by God. He was a splendid and powerful creature, so much so in fact that he became arrogant, thinking himself equal to God. He then rebelled against God, and was punished as a result."

"So he is not equal to God?"

143

"No, he is merely another creature, though an extremely powerful one. He does wreak havoc on humanity, but in the end, he will be punished for all eternity, as will everyone who rebels against God. That is why Jesus Christ laid down his life, in order to provide humanity a way back to fellowship with God.

"But Brother Darius, why did he have to do that. Could God not find some other way to save man? Why did his Son have to die?"

"That is a good question Ariel. Perhaps because mankind's sin of disobedience was so great, that it required a tremendous act of obedience, the willingness of his Son to die on the Cross."

Ariel thought about what he said for several minutes, and asked him.

"If it was Jesus Christ who died for our sins, is that where the word "Christian" came from? They are people that follow Christ?"

Brother Darius nodded his head.

"What does someone have to do to become a Christian?" she asked.

"Well, many, many years ago the Church had a long formula of what you had to do to be a Christian. The Great Collapse, however, caused the Church to re-think what was actually necessary to become a follower of Christ. Finally, the Church went back to basics, back to the words of our Lord that are in scripture, that you must believe in the Lord Jesus Christ, 'That he died on the cross for our sins, and that God raised from the dead on the third day, and that he reigns forever with the Father and the Holy Spirit.'"

"Who are the Father and the Holy Spirit, Brother?" she asked.

"The Father, the Son, and the Holy Spirit, all make up God; together they are referred to as the Trinity."

"Is there anything preventing me from becoming a Christian, Brother?"

"Nothing, if you have the desire in your heart to become one."

"I do, Brother, I do."

"Very well, my child. We need to find some water." He yelled ahead at Ferrell. "We need a body of water, Clansman Ferrell."

Ferrell shrugged his shoulders.

"There is the river that we passed coming into the mero. It is late anyway; we should leave the mero and return at first light. Will that do, Brother Darius?"

"That will do nicely, Clansman Ferrell, thank you."

Ferrell then turned his horse, and led the expedition out of the mero. When they arrived at the river, Brother Darius took Ariel down to

144

the water's edge, where they both waded in until they were knee deep. Brother Darius had Ariel get down on her knees, poured water over her head, and made the sign of the Cross.

"Ariel, I baptize you in the name of the Father, the Son, and the Holy Spirit. Welcome into the Lord's family!"

The following morning, they broke camp and left once more for the mero. Darius and Ariel discussed God, the Church, the Bible, and what it meant to be a Christian, for most of the trip back. Ferrell glanced back on occasion at the pair, engaged in various discussions about the Christian religion. Her newfound faith seemed to make Ariel happy, something that had not gone unnoticed by Ferrell. The experience had given her something that he had not experienced for some time; hope.

Finally, they arrived back at the mero. Time seemed to fly by as they rode through the mero, looking for the monastery where they would find the map that would change the world.

At the priest's suggestion, Ferrell rode toward the giant stone monument, exploring the long stretch of land opposite where they had run out of daylight the day before. There were less of the large granite buildings on that side, but based on his conversations with some of the other priests at the enclave, Darius felt confident that the monastery must be there. After searching all morning, they came within view of a building that vaguely reminded Darius of buildings he had seen in Vatican City.

"There, Clansman Ferrell. I can't be certain, but I believe that must be what we are looking for."

The caravan turned toward the ancient structure. As they drew closer, they could see the words etched in stone, Benedictine Monastery.

Everyone dismounted from their horses and made their way into the monastery, hopeful that the map would be inside, yet filled with uncertainty and doubt that they would find an intact artifact that had survived The Great Collapse, and the five-hundred years that followed. They would search until they found it, however, because failure was not an option.

"Okay Brother Darius, where will we find the map?" asked Ferrell.

Darius threw up his hands and answered, "I don't know exactly where it is Ferrell, but I do believe that it is here, somewhere. Let's spread out and see if we can locate something that gives us a clue."

The old monastery had been abandoned some time ago. Cobwebs and dust filled the ancient structure.

"What are we looking for, Brother?" asked Ferrell.

"I suspect there will be something that stands out, possibly some kind of chest, or safe. They would probably have kept it somewhere they knew it would be safe."

Ferrell and two clansmen searched downstairs, while Darius searched around the Sanctuary, then the study, and finally a small library. Brother Darius was starting to lose hope, wondering whether they had misinterpreted some of the clues. He was almost ready to give up the search when he saw it.

"Ferrell, everyone, come here," Darius shouted.

"What is it Brother Darius?" Ferrell asked when he arrived. "Is everything okay? Have you found something?"

"Yes, I believe I have. I came across this room and on the door was this symbol of a Cross and some circles, do you recognize these markings?"

Ferrell studied them for a moment. "Yes, these look like the symbols I saw on the book at the Council Meeting."

"Exactly the same," said Darius. "Now if I am not mistaken, we will find....ah, here it is!" He held up another copy of the book that Alex had found.

"But Brother," Ferrell exclaimed, throwing his hands up in the air, "we already have that book! What good is that going to do us?"

Brother Darius opened the book, looked through it, and smiled. He held up his hand and in it, was a piece of cloth. It was aged but still in reasonably good condition.

"Clansman Ferrell, I present to you a piece of the map that will lead us to the Great Oracle of Knowledge!" Ferrell sat down and breathed a deep sigh of relief. Darius gently unfolded the map on an old wooden desk, taking great care not to damage it any further. Ferrell stood and walked over to the desk, curious to see what they had gone through so much trouble to find. He also began to wonder whether perhaps, that old, ragged piece of cloth, might really be part of the key that would truly enable them to rebuild civilization, something he had dreamed of since childhood.

Having found the map, and anxious to return to the enclave, they departed the monastery a short time later. Within just a few hours, they were back in the Outland Territory, where they proceeded to set up camp. Ferrell sent two of the clansmen out to search for food, and two to search for fresh water. After the men left, he walked over to where Ariel sat, propped up against a pine tall pine tree.

"Ariel?"

"Ferrell! It's all so incredible, isn't it? Who would have thought that in the mero so close to where I grew up, we would find a piece of a map that could save the world!"

"Um, Ariel, that's what I wanted to talk with you about. The village is not far from here. I think I should take you back to your family on our way back to the enclave."

"Absolutely not, Ferrell Young, and this time, I mean it!" Ferrell recognized the familiar, determined look in her face. He would have to drag her kicking and screaming back to the village. Even then, she would probably just follow them back through the mountains once more. "I am not going to miss out on an opportunity like this, no matter what you say or do."

"It's a dangerous journey back, and I don't just mean the lions and the bears. Kraken has sent men to follow us. They have been following us since the enclave. Now that we are heading back, they will assume that we have the map, and they will try to take it from us. I don't want you to get hurt, Ariel, I...care about you."

I care about you. Ariel had nearly decided that Clansman Ferrell Young was incapable of saying those four words.

"And I care for you as well, Ferrell. That's why I want to come with you, because my place is with you."

The two groups of men that Ferrell had sent out returned at nearly the same time a few minutes later. One pair carried a freshly killed deer, more than enough to feed them all, and the other carried two skins of fresh water. After some conversation and another meal consisting primarily of venison, water, and some wine, they all fell asleep, dreaming of the enclave, and the Oracle.

***

The attack came in the middle of the night. Lloyd, who had been on watch when it came, was the first clansman to fall. Three attacked him simultaneously, one from the front, another from the rear, and a third from the side, attempting to kill him before he could alert the others. The attacker from behind had grabbed him by his hair and silenced Lloyd's short but effective alarm to the others with his blade, but it was at the cost of his own life.

At the sound of Lloyd's alarm, Ferrell and the others leapt into action. Ferrell quickly determined there were fifteen to twenty attackers. He kicked one in the groin and struck him with his sword, stopping the attacker in his tracks. Another came in from his side, stabbing with a sword. Ferrell stepped off to the left, striking the attacker's sword with his own. He followed up with an elbow to the attackers head, stunning him long enough to bring his own sword around for a fatal strike. Another urba came at him from behind. Sensing the attack, he reacted with just enough time to move slightly off to the right. Even with his evasive movement, he was still struck on his shoulder with the blade. His armor absorbed the blunt of the stroke, but enough penetrated his armor that he felt a searing pain and then a flow of blood. He had been wounded, but it was not deep. He threw a back kick to his attacker that landed squarely in the area above the groin. The kick itself had probably been enough to kill his attacker, but Ferrell took no chances and finished the job with a thrust of his sword.

When the fight was over, the clansman found that he had lost three men in the fight, an unacceptable loss for the Clan. Ferrell would take measures when he returned to the enclave, to increase the intensity of their training regimen to help ensure that it never happened again.

Two hours later, Ferrell and his men then said their goodbyes to Lloyd and the others, burying them in a nearby field. The clansmen and the priest then broke camp the following morning, and continued their journey back to the Enclave.

Chapter 21
The Road Back

Julius and the rest in the group gathered everything together and began the long journey back to the enclave. Weaving their way back through the mero's tall buildings, they looked around in wonder at the impressive mero. Even after five-hundred years, the buildings that reached into the sky remained a testament to the wonders and technology of the Golden Age. As his horse made its way through the ruins of the mero, Julius wondered whether their mission would be successful, whether the various expeditions would be able to retrieve the maps, and even with a complete map in-hand, whether they would ever be able to locate the Oracle.

The journey would take them several days, and they still had to make it out of the mero alive. With the rat infestation, the many packs of urba, and all of the assorted beasts that called the vast mero home, he wondered whether they would ever make it back to the enclave with their piece of the map.

As they approached the edge of the mero, the scout returned from patrolling ahead and pulled up alongside Julius. "Riders ahead sir, and they are not ours. I counted maybe thirty or more."

"Yes, I can see them," answered Julius.

As the riders drew closer, the clansmen gathered around Brother Francis once more, placing him behind them this time, with themselves between Francis and the unknown riders.

As they drew closer, Julius discerned that they were wearing uniforms, the same kind of uniforms the men who killed Chung had worn, men the clansmen suspected were with Kraken's elite guard. The riders stopped when they were only a hundred yards away.

"Clansmen, may I approach?" asked the leader.

"Come forward, rider," answered Julius.

The man rode forward alone, meeting Julius in the middle.

"I am Kronos, of the Kraken Empire. On behalf of Lord Kraken, I demand that you give us the map."

"You demand that we give you the map, you say? Well now, I will have to give that some thought. Hmmm…no, I guess we won't be doing that today, but thanks for asking. You sound as if you are not accustomed to being denied what you want, urba scum. I suggest you get used to the idea, if you want to live."

The rider pulled something out from under his cloak. He pointed it into the air and–"BOOM."

"I warn you clansmen, all of my men are armed with ancient weapons just like this!" the man boasted, hoping the threat would frighten the fierce-looking clansmen into compliance. "Now give me the map, or suffer the consequences."

Julius looked back in feigned horror. "Oh," he said, "you mean with weapons like this?"

From under his own cloak, Julius produced a firearm of his own. Unlike the one held by the rider, however, the one Julius produced was much newer, and looked well maintained. With shock and fear written all over his face, the Kraken guardsman was clearly horrified at the prospect of facing clansmen armed with ancient weapons. Saying nothing, Kronos turned and re-joined his companions.

Julius yelled back at his men. "Quickly, I want three men to take the priest and find cover, now!"

His men complied and rushed Francis back to a building they had recently passed, and waited just inside the building. The riders charged with the weapons in their hands, even as the clansmen produced their own.

While the clan viewed firearms with disdain, they always had them in their arsenal of weapons to use in the event the need arose. Unlike the riders however, the clansmen had practiced on them enough to be deadly accurate.

The riders began firing at the clansmen, who then returned fire, killing twenty-five of the riders before they even reached the group. Only five remained, while only one clansman had been fatally wounded during the attack. Once the enemy was within striking range, the clansmen stowed their firearms, and took out their swords, by far their preferred weapon for close-in fighting. One of the riders knocked Julius off his horse during the attack. Julius responded by taking his sword, and attacking the horse of the rider that had attacked him. The horse fell, landing on top of the rider. A quick slice with his blade finished the job.

Julius looked around and found that the other clansmen had made short work of what remained of Kraken's "elite" guard. While he was grateful that their firearm training had come in useful for once, the revelation that their enemy had firearms as well, and knew how to use them, represented a fundamental shift in the status quo. He needed to get back to the enclave and report the finding to Lord Sarkoth as quickly as possible.

Brother Francis held another brief service for their fallen companion followed by the clansman's burial. The priest was beginning to wonder how many more funerals he would have to hold before this was all over.

Chapter 22
The Third Map

Clue Number 3- Urbs of Ventus (City of Wind)

Alex was thankful that he had decided to leave Hannah at the Enclave. He knew that she would be safer with the Clan than she ever would have been traveling with them to the mero. Alex had never been this far from home on any of his expeditions, and while it had been only a few days since he left the enclave, he missed Hannah already. He had been gone away from home for longer periods of time in the past, but he had never felt as scared that he might never see Hannah again as he was now. Perhaps it was the dangers that he knew they would inevitably run into, or maybe it was because he had promised himself on his last expedition that it would be just that, his last.

How did I ever let Brother Sebastian talk me into this?

They had been riding for days and it was getting colder by the hour. While they had brought heavier clothing in case they ran into cold weather, it was getting much colder than he had prepared for. Alex was beginning to question whether they would even make it to the mero, much less find the map.

"Brother Sebastian, how much further is it to this mero again?"

"We should be there within a few more days, Alex," he said.

They had seen little but wilderness for days as they traveled, though they passed a mero from time to time.

"I was thinking, Brother. From what you have old us, this is a large mero. How will we find the map once we get there?"

"That is a fair question Alex, but this monastery is actually not inside of the mero. I know because a long time ago, as a young monk, I once visited it. Then, as now, the trip was a bit dangerous, but God never promised that life as a priest would be easy!"

"But why did you visit this monastery Brother, if it was abandoned long ago?"

Brother Sebastian turned and looking surprised, said, "Oh no Alex. This monastery was never abandoned. It remains an active monastery. It serves as a central location for brothers traveling across the known lands."

"Brother Sebastian, Alex." Wilijah, the clansman leader for their expedition, had come up from behind them and pulled his horse up next to theirs. "It will be dark soon," he said, pointing toward the setting sun, now sitting low on the horizon off to the southwest. "I wanted to let you know that we will be stopping up ahead for the night."

"Thank you, Clansman Wilijah," answered Sebastian. "We will be ready to make camp." Wilijah rode on ahead to inform the other clansmen.

"Brother Sebastian, you know that I spent a lot of time looking for that book."

"Yes, of course Alex, and I know that we would not be where we are now without your help."

"No, Brother, I was more than happy to do it, but that's not what I meant--I needed the work and I am happy to do anything I can for the Church," he said. "What I was trying to say, is that while I was searching for that book, I came across a number of others over the last few years that had not been destroyed. Many of them were written during or even before the time of the Golden Age. As you know, there have not been many books written since the Great Collapse, and certainly very few can be found in libraries anymore."

"Yes, Alex, I am aware of that sad fact."

"Some of the books I read, well Brother Sebastian, as fantastic as life was during the Golden Age, it seemed that there were plenty of bad times back then as well. There were wars, great and terrible wars. There were evil men then as now, men like Kraken, who murdered millions of people. Do you suppose that things were really so much better during the Golden Age? Even if we are able to find the maps, and the Oracle, what's to say that things will be any better? Do you think it's possible that we are better off now, even during the Dark Age, than they were then?"

Brother Sebastian considered the question Alex had asked him for some time.

"Alex, you may well be correct in saying that if we find the Oracle and civilization does return to the world, that things may end up being no better than they are today. Who knows, perhaps they will even be worse than they already are!"

Alex nodded. "Exactly."

"Well then, let me answer your question with a question. What if Hannah was very sick, on the verge of death, and new breakthroughs in medicines that come about because of the Oracle save her life. Would that not make finding the Oracle worth it?"

"Yes Brother, I suppose it would," answered Alex.

"Now then, suppose we do nothing and Kraken, or someone like him, conquers and enslaves the world, wouldn't that be a worse state of affairs than what we have today?" continued Brother Sebastian.

"Yes, that would be true as well," answered Alex. "Of course you're right, Brother Sebastian. I know that you're right. What troubles me, is that despite all of the wondrous technology they possessed, and all of their vast knowledge, the Ancients were still really no different than us. They treated one another just as badly, and they were still just as lost."

"An astute observation, Alex. It does seem that most people alive during the Golden Age placed too much faith in their technology, more than they did in God. Perhaps, if we are given another chance, we will do better next time, use the technology and knowledge to improve humanity's lot, until the Lord's return. Mankind has lived with war, death, and suffering since man's fall back in the Garden of Eden. We will not have peace and joy in this world; we will always live with sin. Nevertheless, let us at least strive to enlighten humanity with knowledge, to preserve the body through medicine, and to build the best world we can while we are here on the Earth."

"I couldn't agree more," Alex replied. Sebastian paused for a moment, seemingly wanting to say something, but unsure how to proceed. "What is it, Brother?"

"Well, Alex, there's something else I've been wanting to discuss with you. You are a Christian, aren't you? You know the fundamentals of Christianity, what being a Christian is all about, don't you?"

"You know I am, and that I do, Brother Sebastian."

"Your daughter, Hannah, she is a wonderful young lady, with an extremely sharp mind. Shouldn't you start teaching her about your faith, about God, before it's too late?" admonished Brother Sebastian.

"Yeah, I know, I know," Alex answered somewhat sheepishly, "it's just that I have been gone from home so much--"

"You cannot let that stop you, Alex, especially when this is all over!"

"Yes, Brother, again I know you're right."

About that time, Wilijah rode up and announced that they were stopping to make camp for the night. Many of the clansmen began setting up tents, while others went to work building a large fire to ward off any animals that might be tempted to wander into the camp looking for an easy meal, while others disappeared into the woods hunting for dinner. One of the warriors was fortunate enough to stumble upon a wild boar in the nearby woods, enabling all of them to enjoy some fresh pork for dinner, a luxury Brother Sebastian had not had for some time.

Wilijah, who was sitting next to Sebastian at the large fire enjoying his meal, took a break from his dinner to speak to the priest.

"Brother Sebastian, I believe there is another Clan enclave close by. Would you mind if we stop in on the way to the monastery? I would like to speak with some of my brothers about a certain matter while we are there."

"Of course, Clansman Wilijah, of course, that would be fine. I would enjoy meeting clansmen from another enclave. Please keep in mind however, the urgency of our mission. We should not tarry long."

"I understand perfectly, Brother. Thank you."

They finished their dinner, posted guards, and settled down for the night. The expedition would likely arrive at the enclave the following day. An exhausted Brother Sebastian, along with the clansmen, slept soundly that night.

It was late the next day when they arrived at the gates of the local Clan enclave. After some brief introductions, they were led into the Great Hall, where the High Elder of the enclave greeted them. After they had all been seated at the large, rectangular table, the High Elder stood.

"Welcome travelers--clansmen, and friends of the Warrior Clan. Welcome to our humble enclave. We seldom receive outsiders here, as I am sure you are now aware. Clansman Wilijah has shared much news with me, not the least of which is your mission, and the importance of its success. But please forgive me, where are my manners? I am Clansman High Elder William, leader of this enclave. And you are...?"

"I am Brother Sebastian, a priest in the Holy Christian Church, and this is Alex, the archaeologist that found the book left by The Unity."

"Well then, it is certainly my honor and my privilege to meet you both."

"We are honored you have received us, High Elder William."

William smiled and nodded to Sebastian. "Please, tell me something, Brother Sebastian, do you believe that this Oracle truly exists? Perhaps it is only a legend."

"No, High Elder William, it is no legend. We have known of the Oracle since the time of the Great Collapse. As to the likelihood of our success, I would put that at one-hundred percent. Remember, it's my job!" Both men laughed, enjoying a brief moment of levity.

"You realize of course, that if you are successful and the Oracle is found, that it will change a way of life that we have known for hundreds of years?"

"Yes, I do realize that, Lord William," answered Sebastian. "Still, is that not the way of things? Change is constant, some good, and some bad. What can we do?"

"That is true, my friend." William's countenance changed and his smile disappeared, replaced by a furrowed brow. "Brother, please tell me what you know of this Kraken, and this growing urba army of his."

Brother Sebastian's voice took on a more serious tone. "There is great fear that his power and sphere of influence are growing rapidly. There is also much concern that he has already learned of the Oracle's existence, and that he seeks it for himself."

"We have heard of this urba even here, and it is true, his influence is growing. As recently as last week, a nearby mero fell to his growing army. His army crushed the remaining resistance inside the mero within a day. They have also started attacking villages in this region as well. It is said that he takes the women and children as slaves and the young men as soldiers. Those who offer any resistance whatsoever are killed without hesitation."

Brother Sebastian sighed. "Sounds like him. If Kraken gets his hands on the Oracle, it will almost certainly extinguish our shared hope for a new Golden Age."

"Tell me Brother, what can my men and I do to help you in your quest?"

"I don't think that—"

"Perhaps we could take care of the men who are following you?" the elder added.

"Following us?" a perplexed Sebastian asked.

"It is true Brother," answered Wilijah. "We spotted them the day before yesterday; they have been trailing us for almost a week."

"But why trail us, why haven't they attacked?"

157

"Because Kraken has likely ordered them to wait until we leave the monastery and head back to the Main Enclave with the map," answered Wilijah. "Then, they will attack us, try to kill us, and take the map back to Kraken."

"If that is true, all of the expeditions are in jeopardy!" exclaimed Alex.

"Don't worry, Alex," answered William. "Our people are the best fighters in the world. Despite his growing numbers, the Warrior Clan will handle Kraken and his men."

"Lord William, are you aware that Lord Sarkoth has been asking for enclaves to send men to him at the Main Enclave?"

"Wilijah told me of this just a short while ago. I will be sending a number of men to Lord Sarkoth tomorrow morning. Now, in regards to the men following you, here is what we will do. Tomorrow morning, a short while after you leave here, I will dispatch fifty of my best warriors after you. They will come up behind Kraken's men, and they will deal with them. You will have no trouble on your return journey."

"Thank you, Elder William; we are in your debt."

"Nonsense, it is we who are in your debt. You are a brave man, Brother Sebastian, as are you, Alex Montgomery. May God bless you both on your journey."

"Are you a Christian then, Elder William?" asked Brother Sebastian, with a look of surprise.

"Having met you Brother Sebastian, I am seriously considering becoming one."

"It is my prayer that you not only consider it but that you will altogether do it! God bless you as well, Elder William!"

The priest, the archaeologist, and the visiting clansmen were then escorted out of the main hall and into a long hallway, where they were led to a large dining hall for dinner. The wearied travelers enjoyed their most fulfilling meal since leaving the Main Enclave, a meal that included venison, fresh vegetables, bread, and some wine, before being taken to their quarters.

The next morning, after thanking Elder William once again for his hospitality, they departed from the Enclave and resumed their journey to the monastery. Though Sebastian struggled to remember the specific location of the monastery after such a long time, some information gleaned from clansmen at the enclave helped to fill in some of the gaps.

By mid-afternoon, they came upon some ancient street signs, still standing after five centuries and still serving to point them in the right direction. Sebastian felt they were close, and after another hour of searching, they found the monastery. It was an old but well-kept wooden building, with a fence running the length and width of it, standing six high.

Sebastian and Alex knocked on the monastery door, flanked by the Clansmen. After a short wait, an elderly monk greeted them at the door.

"Hello, I am Brother Mark, can I help you?"

"Brother Mark, I am Brother Sebastian, do you remember me?"

"Ahhh...Brother Sebastian! Yes. It has been a long time!"

"And this is Alex; he is an archaeologist, a treasure hunter of sorts. He has been doing some important work for the Church over the last couple of years, and recently found something that we long feared was lost to us."

After a few moments, Brother Mark noticed the heavily armed clansmen standing behind Brother Sebastian.

"And who are all of these men with you?" he asked, noticeably concerned.

"Brother Mark, we have much to discuss. May we come in?"

"Why of course Brother, of course. Forgive my ill manners. These are difficult times that we live in! Please, come into our humble monastery!"

Sebastian and Alex spent an hour telling Brother Mark about the book, the council meeting, and about Kraken.

"You say that it's here somewhere, at this monastery? There's a piece of the map here that leads to the Oracle, and the Pope himself has had what he believes to be a vision from God, that the end of the Dark Age is at hand?" He looked at Brother Sebastian with disbelief. "Incredible. Well Brother Sebastian, as you know I have lived here most of my life, and I cannot recall ever seeing anything that looks like a map. Are you certain that it is here?"

"Brother Mark, we have studied the clues left in The Unity, and we are convinced that one of the pieces of that map is in this monastery."

"I suppose that if it was hidden well enough it's possible that it has gone unnoticed all these years. What do you think it will look like?

"We don't really know," answered Sebastian, "but there should be something here that will seem a little out of the ordinary."

Mark helped as they all looked around the familiar building that he had called home for so long.

"Brother Sebastian, if it is here, then why didn't someone tell us about it before now?"

"Because, in all likelihood, over the centuries the knowledge of its significance had all but faded away, until it was finally forgotten altogether. Remember, it has been five-hundred years."

Mark continued looking around, trying to be helpful. "Wait a minute, he said. You said something that seemed unusual, something "out of the ordinary?"

He walked over to a wall in one of the old studies. Sebastian and the others followed him. "I've always wondered what this painting was all about. It seemed, well, out of place. I sometimes thought about getting rid of it. It was so old however, that I couldn't do it. I'm not sure that this qualifies, but how about this?" he asked, pointing to a picture on the wall. The painting was a picture of a cross with spheres circling around another.

"This is it!" Alex exclaimed. He went over to the wall, took down the painting, and started looking it over. Less than a minute later he opened the back of the painting, allowing a small piece of cloth wrapped up in a clear material to fall out.

"Brother Mark, you're not just a priest, you are a saint!" declared Alex.

"I don't know anything about that, young man. But you can put a word into the ear of the Pope for me if you like."

"Brother Mark, with your permission, may we spend the night, and leave out the first thing in the morning?" asked Sebastian.

"Of course you may Brother Sebastian. You are certainly welcome to stay much longer, if you like. After all, we don't get many visitors these days."

"Thank you, Brother, but we must make haste to return the pieces of this map back to the Main Enclave."

"Of course, I understand, Brother Sebastian. Please, at least let me provide you and each of your men with a hot bath and a hot meal before you retire for the evening. How does that sound?"

"You'll get no arguments from me!" said Brother Sebastian.

"Nor me," added Alex.

The next morning, the men awoke to the exquisite smell of bacon and eggs cooking over a fire, something that none of them had seen for weeks. They all sat around a large table, enjoying conversation and sharing the meal. Sebastian looked up from his eggs long enough to notice that Wilijah seemed preoccupied.

"Is everything okay, Clansman Wilijah?" asked Sebastian.

"I am fine Brother, thank you," he replied.

"Concerned about the men that have been following us?"

"A little. Don't get me wrong, I have great confidence that my men and I can handle any trouble that may come our way. Still, I will rest easier after I get you and the map back to the Enclave."

"You have my thanks, Clansman Wilijah!"

"That is not necessary, Brother. It is my duty, my honor to be part of such a noble mission."

After finishing breakfast, Sebastian, Alex, and the clansmen bid farewell to William and the others at the monastery, and started on the long journey back to the Main Enclave. They had not gone far when they came upon the bodies. A number of men, wearing uniforms that no one recognized, lay strewn across the ground. There were at least twenty-five of them, and evidence that a couple of warriors from the local enclave had been killed. It appeared that indeed Elder William had not been exaggerating. They did take care of the threat, completely.

Chapter 23
The Fourth Map

Clue Number 4- Qua Quietis Miles Militis Sileo
(Where the Quiet Soldiers Rest)

The sun rose over the jagged mountains, radiating a warm, amber glow as it did so. The cicadas were still singing in the beginning of a new day as the sun ascended over the mountain peaks. Dawn had long been Sanjo's favorite time of day. He savored the unique smell found only in the early morning hours, like a fragrant reward to those willing to rise early enough to appreciate it. Sanjo rode alone, far ahead of the rest. He found he enjoyed riding by himself at times, though it wasn't because he did not appreciate the company of others. On the contrary, he cared deeply and profoundly for his Clan brothers and surprisingly, he had found himself enjoying the company of the priest as well. He enjoyed riding alone because he found in it a certain peace, a restfulness, a closeness to nature that only the occasional solitude of a ride alone provided.

Sanjo turned his thoughts to the elderly priest, Brother O'Reilly. He could not recall ever seeing a Christian priest, much less riding with one. He had heard of the Holy Christian Church, but he knew next to nothing about it. The Clan neither encouraged nor discouraged clan members concerning the Christian faith. They were permitted to learn more about the Christian faith if they chose to, and some in the Clan had decided to follow the Christ, particularly after learning about him after the arrival of the priests at the Council Meeting. On their journey to find the map, some of his brothers that followed Christ had tried talking with Sanjo about their faith, but he had shown little interest at the time, passing up on the opportunity to learn more about him and the Church. Perhaps I shall learn more about this Christ from the priest, if the opportunity presents itself.

Sanjo stopped at a clearing and peered into the distance. He thought that he had caught a glimpse of smoke rising above the trees, and a village off in the distance, but it was difficult to tell for sure. They had already traveled several days without finding fresh water and would have to find some soon or they would be in trouble, as their canteens were nearly empty. He rode further ahead to where he thought he had seen something, and found a village in the clearing at the bottom of a hill, less than a mile from his previous position. It was a small village, as most villages were during the Dark Age, with no more than a few hundred people in it. Sanjo rode back to the others, instructing them to hold their positions while he rode into the settlement.

He slowed his horse to a gentle trot and entered the village. At what appeared to be the center of the community, he found a large well. As with many other villages, this one had a large deep well that had been placed in the center of the village, providing easy access to the life-giving water for all who lived there.

As Sanjo looked around and carefully examined the activity within the village, it took him just seconds to determine that something did not look right. It occurred to him that the village appeared to be populated exclusively by elderly people and a few cripples. Scarcely a child could be found anywhere and there were no more than a few young women. He concluded that something must have happened to a significant portion of the village's population, and suspecting he knew what that something was. He decided to investigate. He rode along the various unpaved streets of the community, soon noticing the look of fear on the faces of nearly all of the villagers. People were unusually frightened of him, either avoiding his glance and looking away, or ducking into shelters out of view. Eventually, he came to an old man walking down the street that seemed different from the others. Sanjo noticed that the man had a large gash on the back of his head, which looked no more than a few days old.

"Excuse me friend, may I speak with you for just a moment?" The man stopped walking and turned to face Sanjo, who then dismounted his horse.

"What can I do for you stranger?" The old man looked him over for a minute. "I would venture by your attire that you are a member of the Warrior Clan."

"I am."

"Then I consider you a friend. Welcome to our village," said the man, extending his hand out to Sanjo.

"My name is Ben, Ben Wilkins."

"I'm Sanjo."

The men shook hands. The man had a firm and honest handshake, something that impressed Sanjo.

"I noticed as I rode into your village, Ben, that there were almost no women or children."

"Yeah, that," growled Ben. "We have Kraken and his goon squad to thank for that. They rode into the village a couple of days ago, took the young men as conscripts for Kraken's army, and the women and children as slaves. The few that dared resist them were either butchered, had their homes burned to the ground, or both-- mostly both. When I said something that one of them took offense at, he thumped me from behind, knocking me unconscious, and leaving me this little beauty as a keepsake," he said, pointing to the injury on his head. "I was out for two days."

The man looked at Sanjo and said to him with his voice cracking, almost sobbing.

"They took my daughter, and my grandson."

Sanjo wanted to offer words of comfort to the old man, but in the end said only, "I'm sorry, Ben."

"What will the Clan do about him, Sanjo? I know that the Warrior Clan will likely do as it has always done, and keep to itself. You must know by now however that this Kraken is something different. He already claims ownership of this village, and every other village throughout these lands. If the Clan does nothing, he will end up controlling what little is left remaining, and mark my words, he will turn his attention to the Clan next. He will not tolerate the existence of any threat to his complete domination of these lands." He paused for a moment, giving his words a chance to sink in. "Will Lord Sarkoth do anything to stop this madman?"

Sanjo looked at the man, shocked that he knew the name of Sarkoth.

"Tell me, Ben, how does a villager come to know so much about the Clan, and about Lord Sarkoth, for that matter?"

The man's look hardened and he took on an air that Sanjo recognized.

"I was once a member of a group that in many ways was not so different from the Clan. We trained and studied the martial way, led and taught by a former clansman that had left the Clan some years earlier. He had come to disagree with the Clan's lack of involvement with the affairs of those outside the clan, believing they had a greater responsibility to the world than just hiding away in their enclaves. He decided he would do all that he could to make a difference, so he formed The Protectors, hoping to provide some kind of law and order in the Outlands."

"What happened to the Protectors, and how did you come to end up here?"

Ben looked down at the ground, saddened by reliving the painful memories.

"I grew up here. It was not so bad really. It was a nice, quiet, peaceful place to raise a family, nestled here in the mountains, safe from the distant, rat-infested meros, and the vile urba. At least, that is what we thought. A few years ago, before he had grown so powerful, Kraken sent some of his men to attack our village, to take our young men, women, and children as slaves. He said that he would 'protect' our village, claimed ownership of it, and declared himself its sovereign. Well, we stopped his men in their tracks, even sending a few of them back to tell Kraken to steer clear, that this was our village, and this and every other village in these parts were under our protection.

"The next time, Kraken came in person, but this time instead of fifty men he brought over five-hundred. We didn't stand a chance. They attacked us in an open field a few miles from here. Only a few of us escaped to tell the tale; it was a slaughter. The next day I went back to the field where we had fought. The woods were full of my dead companions, hanging from almost every tree for miles."

"I am sorry for your Loss, Ben. It was a brave and noble thing that you and the others tried to do. Listen Ben..." he said, taking him aside, far away from the prying eyes and ears of others, "the Clan is well aware of Kraken, and we will deal with that vile creature when the time is right, trust me. Do not lose hope."

Sanjo climbed back onto his horse and shook Ben's hand again. He noticed a slight smile on the man's hardened face, reflecting a small glimmer of hope.

"Do you think I might bring a few friends into the village for water? We have brought our own food."

"That will not be a problem, Sanjo. You and the others are welcome to come and stay with us for as long as you like. I am certain that the others would welcome having clansmen in our village."

"Thank you for your hospitality, Ben. I'll be back later this afternoon."

Sanjo hurried back to the others and told everyone about the village, about Kraken, and about what had happened.

"Sanjo," began Brother O'Reilly after hearing Sanjo's recounting of the tale, "if we happen to come across Kraken's men on the way to the monastery, perhaps we can do something to save those poor children from that evil creature Kraken, and a life of complete misery?"

Sanjo looked at Brother O'Reilly with a tight smile that thinly concealed the considerable amount of anger underneath. "I was hoping you would say that. I'm glad you feel that way, Brother."

The group broke camp and made for the village, where they received an exceptionally warm welcome by the villagers. Sanjo surmised that Ben had spread the word that clansmen would soon be coming to their village. Sanjo knew they were hoping the clansmen would help them recover their children, their husbands, and their wives. Who can blame them?

O'Reilly watched and tried to listen as Sanjo asked Ben a question, but the priest couldn't make out what it was. The man then pointed off toward the east. Sanjo gave orders to several of the Clansmen, who immediately turned their horses and took off in the direction that Ben had pointed. The priest sat pondering what was happening when Sanjo suddenly turned and walked toward him.

"Brother, what direction is the Monastery from here?"

O'Reilly looked around, trying to get a fix on the position of the sun.

"I'm not certain, Clansman Sanjo, but by the Grace of God, I believe it is about five or six miles east from here."

Sanjo looked back at Brother O'Reilly, grinned, and said, "Brother, I was hoping you would say that, too."

It was only a few hours later that the two clansmen returned, found Sanjo at the table where he was eating dinner, and talked with him for several minutes, before taking a break themselves for some food and water. After a few minutes, Sanjo walked over to speak with Brother O'Reilly.

"Brother, they are no more than five or ten miles from here. My men spotted them some distance ahead. It looked like they were moving slowly. My men estimated there were no more than twenty-five, maybe thirty of Kraken's men."

"What will you do?" O'Reilly asked the clansman.

"I ask that you promise to stay here, Brother, while I take ten men with me late this evening, steal into their camp, and bring the villagers back home."

Brother O'Reilly looked warmly at Sanjo and said, "You know Sanjo, this is unlike the Clan. You folks have a reputation for staying out of the affairs of villages and meros alike."

"That may be Brother," answered Sanjo, "but it was never because we didn't care. Our people stayed isolated for so long because in the beginning, there was so little we could do. The world was falling apart; it was all the founders could do just to survive. Then, as the Clan grew stronger, we became focused on developing our skills, and working toward one-day restoring civilization for all humanity. Once again, however, everything is changing. The clan is moving in a new direction now, under the leadership of High Elder Lord Sarkoth. With the alliance with the Church, preparing for war against Kraken, and now this quest, it is time we changed. It is time for the Clan to make its move, and to once again become involved with the destiny of this world."

O'Reilly mused over what that meant, as Sanjo walked back to the others, and led them to a good spot to make camp just outside the village. The sun had set and without its warmth, the temperature had already started to plummet. After setting up the tents and starting a couple of large fires, they sat down to enjoy a satisfying meal, before lying down to get a few hours of sleep. O'Reilly climbed into his tent and lay down, pulled the blanket up close, and let his mind wander. His thoughts turned to the villagers, to the monastery, and then to the Oracle. Humanity stood at a crossroads, and everyone knew it. They would succeed at finding the Oracle; they must succeed. Surely, God would not have brought all this to pass for nothing! A few minutes later, O'Reilly succumbed to exhaustion, and fell fast asleep.

The priest awoke to no small commotion the next morning. He opened his tent and as things gradually came into focus, he noticed that the sun was already well above the horizon, and realized he had overslept. He struggled to shake off the lingering drowsiness so he could make out what was happening. Within just a few minutes, he had his answer; Sanjo and his men had returned with the former captives from the village in tow, just as he had promised. Brother O'Reilly found himself overwhelmed with emotion as the villagers scooped up their children and grandchildren into their arms, tears of joy flowing freely down their weathered cheeks. He watched as Sanjo returned with the last of the captives in his arms, a little girl who was no more than five years old. Sanjo set the child on the ground, and O'Reilly teared up as she leapt toward her mother, flying into her mother's arms while smiling from ear to ear. The priest smiled when he noticed that the proud clansman warrior was himself fighting to hold back the tears. All who bore witness to the scene could not help but be moved. Frightened mothers snatched up their children and held them tight. Husbands and wives embraced as they were reunited. Grandparents rejoiced and welcomed their families home.

Sanjo looked over at Brother O'Reilly, nodding his head as if to say, "this is what we are fighting for Brother–this!"

Chapter 24
Recruiting

David-Michael and his five traveling companions had been running their horses too hard, so they decided to stop to give them a rest. Desperate as they were to rally as many of their clansmen brothers as they possibly could, the horses were completely exhausted. If they rode them any harder, it would kill them.

He looked in his bag and retrieved a big red apple. Walking back around to the front of his horse, he rubbed the stallion on the neck, and held out the apple so he could enjoy his reward. "That's it boy. You have more then earned this, my old friend, considering everything I have put you through these past few weeks."

They had been resting for no more than an hour, enjoying a snack and a short rest, when Samuel, one of the scouts rode back into camp.

"Lord David-Michael, the local enclave is near, less than a half-day's ride."

"Very well Samuel, thank you," answered David-Michael.

The scout bowed respectfully and proceeded to look after his horse as well.

David-Michael said to the others, "Samuel tells me the enclave is less than a half-day's journey." He looked off into the distance to see the sun already starting to disappear behind the horizon. "The day is almost spent…we will camp here tonight."

The men retrieved their packs from their horses and began to setup camp. They put up their tents, and Samuel helped David-Michael build a fire while several of the other men went off to hunt for food.

"How many of our enclaves would you say we have been to now?" Samuel asked as they worked on the fire.

"I don't know for sure; fifty, maybe fifty-five. I would prefer that we had been to twice that number, or even more."

"How many more enclaves are left?"

"It's hard to say, if I remember correctly there should be at least five times as many scattered throughout the Outlands. We must get Lord Sarkoth's message to as many clan members as we possibly can, Samuel. We have at least another twenty-five enclaves within a week's ride from home, twice that number within two weeks ride."

Samuel frowned. Another clansman sitting with them exchanged glances with David-Michael briefly, before speaking up.

"I understand your disappointment, believe me," said Jake. "No one wants to go home more than I, Samuel. When you are feeling homesick and wanting desperately to go home, take great comfort knowing that if we are successful, we will leave our children, and our children's children, a magnificent future. Just try to imagine a second Golden Age, even greater than the first!"

Samuel nodded his head and smiled. "For our children," he replied.

"For our children," echoed David-Michael.

The next morning, he and the others rode up to the enclave and tied their horses up just outside the entrance. They knocked on the door and waited. A few moments later, the door opened. A large and surly clansman warrior filled the doorway; David-Michael greeted his clansman brother.

"Greetings Brother, we are here from the Main Enclave, on an urgent mission from High Elder Lord Sarkoth. The guard motioned for them to wait, disappearing for several minutes before finally returning.

"I am to take you to the Main Hall, where Elder Edgar will meet with you. If you will please come with me, I will show you to the Main Hall."

The group walked into the enclave and down a long hallway, to a huge room furnished with a large, oval table. Around the inside of the Main Hall were assorted paintings, calligraphy, and various other works of art. David-Michael walked around the room, admiring the beautiful artwork, while they waited for the enclave's elder. He took out the letter from Lord Sarkoth, imprinted with the seal of the Clansman High Elder, and held it in his hand.

A few minutes, the enclave's elder came in and introduced himself.

"I am Elder Edgar. I understand that you are David-Michael, here from the Main Enclave with a message from Lord Sarkoth himself?"

"We are, Lord Edgar." He presented the scroll to the elder, who took it, and invited David-Michael to sit. After a couple of minutes, the elder looked up at David-Michael with a look of uneasiness, before re-reading part of the document, and placing it to the side.

"Just answer me one thing, David-Michael. Is this true? Do you know for certain that this thing, this Oracle, even exists? Have you seen it?"

"No, Lord Edgar, I have not seen it. Regardless of whether I have seen it or not however, these three things are certain. First, the Church has known of its existence for many years–as we understand it, their knowledge of the Oracle goes back to the time of the Great Collapse. Second, if it does exist, then it is certain to be the hope that we have been waiting for."

"And the third," asked Lord Edgar?

"If we do not prepare soon, Kraken will most certainly destroy us anyway."

Lord Edgar sat quietly for several minutes.

"You know something, clansman? I've spent the past twenty years building up this enclave, offering these young men a chance for survival, and now I am sending them to fight in a battle that may well lead to their untimely deaths."

"Perhaps Lord Edgar, you are instead giving them a second chance, a chance that their children may benefit as civilization returns, and the world becomes a much better, safer place, and you are sparing their children from the servitude and misery they would certainly face, should Kraken succeed."

After several more minutes of silent deliberation, the elder let out a heavy sigh.

"My men and I will depart at first light. Thank you for bringing us this news, David-Michael. Had you not done so, within the next year, maybe two, Kraken's army would have likely have been upon us anyway. This way, as you said, we have a chance, together."

"Then I take my leave Lord Edgar. I have a few more enclaves that I must visit before nightfall."

"Safe journey to you then, Clansman David-Michael."

"And to you as well, Lord Edgar."

"Please give my best to Lord Sarkoth when you see him."

"It will be done, Lord Edgar."

David-Michael, Samuel, and the rest left Lord Edgar and the small enclave, and started out for the next. The sun had not yet reached its highest point in the sky when they came to a large forest. David-Michael looked around at his men to assess how they were holding up. They had left the main enclave only one month earlier. They would visit more enclaves over the next week, before heading back to the Main Enclave for some rest, and a little time to spend with their families.

David-Michael and his men were traveling through the woods and approaching a clearing, when they saw them. The Clansmen stopped at exactly the same time, each instantly recognizing the threat; in the distance, just beyond the clearing, stood a large gathering of urba. David-Michael estimated there were easily a thousand men or more in the gathering. At least half of them were on horseback, and all of them were well armed.

"We should get out of here before we are spotted," he told the clansmen. They were turning around to leave when he heard it.

"Well...Well...Well...What do we have here, clansmen? And so far from home...?"

Hundreds of men were closing in on them from the surrounding woods. In the middle of the closest group was the man who had spoken to them. He was a big man, well over six feet, with a nasty scar over his right eye. While he had never met him, David-Michael certainly knew of him. For the first time in a long time, David-Michael felt fear, not for himself, but for his mission. He turned around to see that the larger assembly of a thousand men in the clearing was closing in from behind. David-Michael and his men were surrounded and hopelessly outnumbered. He turned back to face the big man.

"You must be Kraken," he said, in a low voice.

Kraken looked around at his men and then back at David-Michael, pleased with himself that someone from the Warrior Clan had recognized him.

"Well, I am honored," he said, with a mock bow toward the clansmen.

"What do you want, Kraken?" asked David-Michael with a commanding voice.

"And who are you?" the big man asked.

"I am David-Michael, of the Warrior Clan. I ask you again, what do you want?"

"Well, straight to business, I like that! You are a man after my own heart, David-Michael! Okay then, I will tell you what I want. I want to know where the Oracle is, and I want to know now. I want the knowledge of the Ancients for myself. It follows that since I am already all-powerful, that I should be all-knowing as well. Now tell me, clansman, where is this Oracle."

David-Michael looked at Kraken, showing none of the fear that he felt inside.

"I don't know what you are talking about, and even if I did, why would I tell you anything?"

"Oh I don't know, maybe because if you don't, I will have to convince you."

"I am a clansman, Kraken. I do not fear death."

"Who said anything about death? No, I have no plans for killing you clansman, at least not for a while. I have never had the opportunity to torture anyone from the Warrior Clan before. No, I expect that it will take some time to break you. Something I expect I will enjoy, very much," Kraken said, smiling from ear-to-ear. Kraken's men moved in. Many of them died at the hands of the mighty clansmen, but with such overwhelming numbers, there could be only one outcome.

Chapter 25
The Fifth Map

Qua Democracy Eram Prognatus (Where Democracy Was Born)

The man looked out through the window over the waterway at a flock of pelicans flying back toward the land, returning to their nests with meals to feed their hungry young. Brother Wayne held a special place in his heart for that particular species of bird, which had served as a metaphor for the love of Christ for well over two-thousand years. Just as pelicans puncture their own flesh if necessary in order to provide a meal for their little ones when food is scarce, so too Jesus shed his blood for his children, in order that they might live. Certainly, the Lord is good!

Wayne, along with Norris and the other clansmen, waited in the small cabin by the waterway, while the man everyone knew only as "Foghorn," walked back over to the rest of their group, and offered them another round of wine. As handsomely as the clansmen were paying him for passage on his ship, he would gladly have given them all of the wine, and about anything else that they asked for, on the house. They had brought three wagons full of food, and two wagons full of other goods of great value, along with them to trade for the passage to and from their destination. Nevertheless, he wasn't constantly offering them the wine only because of their generous payment. The truth was they were beginning to get restless, having waited over a week for a ship that was supposed to have sailed two days earlier. While not as unpleasant to do business with as some of his other customers, like Kraken's men, clansmen were certainly every bit as dangerous, if not more so. He preferred the clansmen as customers however, because Foghorn knew that while there were no more ferocious or better-trained fighters than the clansmen anywhere in the world, the clansmen were also much more disciplined, and much less likely to start trouble than were Kraken's men. It was the total depravity of Kraken and his followers, along with their swelling number, that men had grown to fear. While a clansman would kill someone quickly enough, they tended to do so swiftly and mercifully, whereas when Kraken's men killed someone, they did it slowly, taking the time to enjoy every perverse minute of it.

"May I offer you more wine, sir?" he asked, walking over to Clansman Norris.

"Foghorn, we have been waiting here patiently for over a week now. We must soon be underway as our business is most pressing, and our time is short. If your ship is not here by nightfall, we will be forced to leave here and find another ship, taking our payment with us."

"Don't you worry clansman, sir! That ship will be here today, you have my word!"

An agitated Norris simply answered, "It had better be."

Norris looked around at all of the other clansmen sitting idly about and soon decided that the men needed some training to pass the time.

"Men! Gather outside and prepare for training." The men rose from the table and rushed to the door. "Your men may have a tough time training, given how much wine they have consumed, are you certain it is wise, Clansman Norris?" asked Wayne.

"Most of them have taken some wine, but that makes little difference to a clansman, for we were trained as young men to fight under any and all circumstances."

"I have always been interested in learning more about how members of the Warrior Clan have developed such keen fighting abilities. May I watch?"

"But Brother Wayne," replied Norris, "I thought priests were interested only in peace."

"We are interested in peace, Clansman Norris, but we are still men!"

Norris looked at Wayne for a moment, before turning and looking over the waiting clansmen for a moment. "Clansman Thompson!"

A younger man from the second row answered. "Yes, Lord Norris!"

"Please warm the men up for me, while I take a moment to educate our priest about warrior training."

"Yes, sir."

Norris gestured to some chairs and a table sitting outside of the cabin. The two men sat down to enjoy some wine as Thompson led the men in their training.

"Training in the Warrior Clan, Brother Wayne, involves both unarmed and armed defense. Clansmen are required to carry multiple weapons, typically a long sword, a short sword, a knife, and in some cases, a firearm."

"Firearm, you mean like revolvers? But there haven't been any of them around since the Golden Age!"

"While they are relatively rare outside of the Clan, Brother, they do still exist, though few outside of the Clan know that we possess firearms. Most of the world forgot about such weapons centuries ago. While weapons leftover from the Golden Age are still in use outside of the clan, to the best of our knowledge, no one has manufactured new firearms, or ammunition for them, since the Golden Age; no one that is, except for us. For five centuries, the knowledge of how to create and maintain firearms has been carefully preserved and protected by the clan as a closely guarded secret. Sharing information related to the manufacture of firearms with anyone outside of the Clan is absolutely forbidden, under penalty of death."

"Fascinating," remarked the priest.

Both men turned back to watch the clansmen continue to train. Thompson had already warmed them up and was now leading them from their hand exercises into their kicking drills.

"What about unarmed fighting, Clansman Norris?"

"For the clansman, every blow, whether it is a kick or a punch, is a killing technique," he answered. "Many years of studying human vital points, coupled with intense physical training, enable us to kill with a single strike. It requires many years of rigorous and disciplined training, honing our timing, our distance, and our power. An unarmed clansman can easily defeat five or more armed men. When a clansman wields a weapon, however, he can kill fifty men."

"It has made your people the stuff of legend," said the priest.

"Perhaps," Norris responded."

Brother Wayne watched as the clansmen practiced various unarmed weapon defense techniques.

"What are they doing now, Clansman Norris?" asked Wayne.

"While certainly not something to be desired, losing one's weapon in a battle is always a possibility, one that we must prepare for. During these drills, one man attacks with a knife or a sword. The defender moves off to one side while blocking the attacking arm, followed by an immediate counter attack to a vital point, perhaps the throat or the groin. The defender might also choose to attack at the exact same time the attacker did, foregoing any block, electing to allow the offensive attack to serve as both defense and offense. On these occasions, the attack is the defense. The men also practice various knife and sword attacks, slashing attacks, attacks from overhead, and stabbing attacks with the knives and the swords. Most often, we prefer to stay to the outside of the attacker's arm."

When they had finished their sword and knife defense, the men moved on to unarmed firearm defense, something that they had rarely ever had to use, but given the approaching battle with Kraken, they practiced it with intensity unlike anything Wayne had ever witnessed before. They practiced defending firearms pointed at their heads, their torsos, and their backs, always moving off at an angle, always leaving room for the bullets to miss their bodies, sometimes by fractions of an inch.

"Now Brother Wayne, during the next training exercise, the men will fight with various combinations of weapon-to-weapon attacks. In some cases, one will have a knife and the other a firearm; in others, each man would have a knife, or each a sword. They will practice firearm-to-firearm, knife and sword, sword and firearm, and so forth."

"Pretty much any combination imaginable," said Wayne.

"Exactly."

"Such devotion and discipline, it truly is remarkable," said Wayne.

"Each man must demonstrate tremendous discipline and determination," Norris told him. "Each man strives to perfect each and every move in his defense or his attack. They spend hours a day working on controlling their timing, controlling their distance, and controlling their accuracy. Each man is a scientist, a tactician, and a master of his craft. Yet each man will never permit himself to be satisfied with the level he has attained, when his timing improves, he must work tirelessly to make it even better. When his distance improves, he works to make it even better."

As Wayne watched the men in action, the term "self-discipline" began to take on an entirely new meaning for him.

"Regardless of what the clansman is working on," continued Norris, "whether he is working with a sword, a knife, or a firearm, whether he is practicing unarmed defense or a simple stance, a breathing exercise or meditation, he will study and work on each and every single detail of that technique, no matter how minute, until he has mastered it."

The two men sat quietly for some time, watching as the clansmen continued in their training. When the group paused to rest, Wayne turned back to Norris.

"For many years I have listened to stories of the clansmen, and their prowess in battle," Wayne remarked. "Most often, I attributed the stories to exaggeration or embellishment. Now, having seen your men train for only a few hours, I truly understand why clansmen are the most feared warriors of the Dark Age; you have earned it. You have my respect sir."

"Thank you, Brother."

Norris stood up and was about to start working with the men on some advanced training when the cry suddenly came out from some distance away, further down the shoreline.

"Foghorn, it's here! The ship is coming into port!"

Norris stoically faced his men, bowed, and dismissed them, instructing them to prepare to leave as he walked over to Foghorn.

"We need to leave immediately; will you be ready to go?"

"Of course, of course, we will get you on your way, sir! We need just a few minutes to get stores onto the ship and we should be on our way."

Norris walked over to Wayne. "Brother, are you ready to leave?"

"I am, Norris, thank you."

Norris nodded and went to look for the ship. He walked over and stood next to Foghorn, looking out over the waters. Foghorn pointed toward the ship, which was still in the distance.

"There," said Foghorn, pointing to the tops of the sails, now visible over some large rocks that blocked most of the ship from view. "Can you see her sails sticking out there? She is beautiful isn't she?"

The clansman ignored his questions.

"We board as soon as she is docked, sir," Foghorn told him.

"Her captain knows how to take us where we want to go?" asked Norris, determined to waste no more time now that the ship was in view.

"Indeed, yes sir, he does. He probably ran into some nasty weather sailing back down the coast, I'm sure it was the only reason for the delay."

***

It took only a few hours for Norris and his men to finish loading the ship with supplies for the long journey ahead. Soon after everyone was on board, the ship set sail.

Night was falling as the ship pulled away from the shore, and with a strong tailwind behind them, they were making good time. A clansman came up from below deck to enjoy some of the fresh air. He could smell the ocean as the ship cut through the water, and the light of a full moon reflected brightly off the dark waters. He turned and looked up at the

181

moon, which seemed to glow brighter than he could remember ever seeing it. There were so many stars out that he could easily make out the constellations.

"Are you out enjoying some of the refreshing night air, my son?" asked Brother Wayne, walking up beside the clansman.

"Yes, Brother."

"Is this your first time out on the water?" enquired the priest.

"Oh, no. The village where I was born was near the ocean," answered Clansman Gibson. "My father was a fisherman; he would often take my brothers and me out on the water with him early in the morning."

"I would imagine that this brings back some fond memories for you then."

"Yes, yes sir, it does."

The priest looked up in the sky, admiring the beautiful panorama above him. Suddenly, he found himself searching for something, something that seemed to be missing.

"Tell me, my son, does anything up there look different to you?"

Gibson looked up at the sky and studied it for several moments. "Why yes, something does look different now that you mention it Brother, but I'm not sure what it is."

They both stood side by side, staring into the night sky, when it suddenly dawned on Wayne what troubled him.

"I need to speak with Norris, as quickly as possible."

A few minutes later, Gibson emerged again from below deck with Norris.

"Yes Brother, what is it, what's wrong?" asked Norris.

"We need to make a stop before we arrive at our destination."

"Where, Brother? You understand the urgency of our mission. What could be so important that we should detour from our destination?"

"Rome. We must go to Rome. I must speak with the Holy Father as quickly as possible."

As they discussed the details and reasons behind their detour, no one seemed to notice the faint outline of another ship far off in the distance.

Chapter 26
The Effect

In the blink of an eye, he saw the entire planet stretched out before him, and what a beautiful world it was! In place of the ruins and squalor he had known during the Dark Age, he saw a world transformed, filled with magnificent, beautiful cities that sparkled in the morning sun. Great metropolises spread out over the countryside as far as the eye could see, covering the landscape like a royal robe of splendor. Signs of advanced technology were present everywhere, on the ground, in the water, and in the air. It was a world of plenty, a world of peace, a far different world than the one in which he had lived his entire life. The ruins of the ancient meros were gone, replaced by new, fabulous structures made of steel, a strange and exotic glass, and composite materials the likes of which he had never seen before, that reached for and touched the bright-blue morning sky. Men, women, and children walked down the beautiful streets in bright, attractive apparel. Food and water were available in great abundance everywhere.

There were incredible machines and gadgets of every sort scattered throughout the brave, new world. Some of them he recognized from ancient books dating back to the Golden Age, others he had never seen before. Elegant machines of every kind moved people about on land, on the sea, and in the air. The ruins of the ancient meros, which had once been all but deserted, inhabited by violent urba and wild animals, were now vibrant, wonderful, and alive. There was peace, and plenty for all. The darkness had lifted at last, revealing a new and glorious age.

As he stood in awe at the wondrous images, a brilliant flash of light suddenly appeared, and the scenery of the dream took an unexpected and distressing turn. The marvelous technology, the impressive architecture of the buildings, the food, the people, and the smiles of happy families and the expressions of peace and contentment mysteriously vanished. To his horror, the vision took a cruel and oppressive turn. Instead of laughing children strolling freely and peacefully along the sparkling streets of the cities, there were slaves, suffering under the cruel whip of their oppressive masters; suffering under the cruel whip of their people dying for want of food and water, suffering from cruelty, torture, and oppression at every turn. There was anguish, pain, and misery everywhere he looked. At the center of the great suffering, he saw a large man with a scar over his right eye, sitting on a throne of marble, ruling with cruelty and without mercy.

Henry heard a voice say to him, "The time has come, the prophecy is fulfilled. Behold, and remember!"

Then he awoke. Another dream, it was all just another dream.

Pope John Paul V climbed out of bed and poured himself a glass of wine. He decided to take a casual stroll around the balcony, as was his custom following a restless night's sleep. What did it all mean, the time has come, and the prophecy is fulfilled?

The pope looked up at the host of celestial bodies that dotted the night sky. The full moon was out shining brightly against the backdrop of ebony, and the stars shown brilliantly in the darkness. He enjoyed taking long walks in the early morning hours, when the day was still fresh and young, when it was still quiet and dew sat on the grass. It was always a peaceful time for him, an opportunity to meditate and to hear his own thoughts.

As he continued walking about on his balcony admiring the night sky, he noticed the missing heavenly light, and try as he might, he could not find it anywhere in the sky. The Effect was gone. Could it be the sign? After searching the sky for over half an hour, he stopped looking. It was gone. The Effect, the remnant from The Pulse, the horrific catastrophe that had wiped out civilization five-hundred years earlier, and had caused the Great Collapse, was gone.

The pontiff pondered what it all meant. He knew that it must be the sign foretold during the time of the Great Collapse, the sign that the time had come to seek the map, and to find it. This occurrence, foretold ages ago, was the long-awaited sign from God that the time had finally arrived for the Church to seek out The Great Oracle. If indeed there were any people left with enough faith and courage to seek it out, the Oracle would, for the first time in five centuries, yield up all of the knowledge of the Ancients, all of the knowledge that was lost during the Great Collapse. God had promised mankind an opportunity to rise from the darkness, and the chance to rekindle civilization. The Dark Age was about to end.

The man struggled with the meaning of the vision he had seen earlier. In his mind's eye, he played back the imagery of the vision in his mind, searching for its meaning. Was the vision similar to the one Joseph interpreted for Pharaoh in Ancient Egypt, with years of plenty followed by years of famine, or did it represent instead, a choice? That had to be it; a choice what he had seen in his vision. The man known as Pope John Paul V, the man once known only as Henry, a lowly, unassuming priest, believed in his heart that he now understood both the vision and the prophecy, and realized that they had precious little time. If they did not find the book and the Great Oracle soon, before Kraken, the evil and ruthless barbarian would claim its power as his own, plunging the world into a perpetual blackness, a world void of hope, and light, and civilization. Kraken would use its power to conquer the rest of the world, with no one, not even the clan, able to stand in his way. With the power of the Oracle at his disposal, he would become unstoppable, and any hope of a re-emergence of a new Golden Age would be crushed into powder, lost for millennia.

The man of God considered what to do next. What could he do? He had already dispatched Darius and Sebastian to the Enclave, to Sarkoth, to seek his assistance and to search for the maps. After additional consideration, he decided that he would send a message to the Council, requesting that that they hurriedly seek the Oracle as soon as they had procured the map. He would also ask them to pray, to pray for the light over the darkness, to pray for faith, and to ask for a hope that could overcome the growing despair. The outcome would be, as it always had been, in God's hands.

Pope John Paul V would call upon all of the priests and all of the congregants with him in Rome and abroad, to fast, and to pray. He would call a special service, petitioning the Lord for the success of their mission. Perhaps God will be merciful, and will spare his people from the age of evil. After all, was that not the purpose of the visions?

The pope pondered these things as he continued walking his balcony. After a few minutes, he walked back into his chamber, got down on his knees, prostrated himself before God, and prayed. After two solid hours of prayer, the Holy Father rose from prayer, crawled back into his bed, and after some time, fell into a deep and restful sleep.

***

"Please pardon the interruption your Holiness." The pope slowly opened his eyes to see the face of his dear friend, Cardinal Daniels. "I beg your forgiveness for disturbing your rest, your Holiness."

He sat up in bed and looked at Cardinal Daniels, trying to shake off the grogginess long enough to focus on what the cardinal wanted to say. He looked outside and estimated by the location of the sun in the sky, that it was already late morning.

"That is quite alright, old friend."

"Did you have trouble sleeping again last night?" the cardinal asked him.

"Yes I did, a little. I had a dream Eric, a vision. I believe the Lord revealed to me that the Dark Age is ending, and that we must seek the Oracle with all haste. We are racing against time now, old friend." The pope's face took on a somber appearance. "Eric, listen to me. If we do not succeed in this quest, in finding the Oracle, the world will be plunged into despair for a thousand years. We must not allow the Oracle to fall into the hands of someone like this urba, Kraken. If he is not defeated, we may have to destroy it."

"I agree, your Holiness, we will destroy it if we must."

The pope nodded, climbed out of bed, and rose to his feet.

"So what news have you brought me this morning?"

Cardinal Daniels had nearly forgotten. "Forgive me, your Holiness. A ship pulled into port this morning. Brother Wayne and Clansman Norris from the Warrior Clan were on-board. They wish to speak with you as soon as possible."

The pope climbed hurriedly out of bed and began getting dressed.

"Praise our Lord and Savior, Jesus Christ, this is wonderful news! By all means, please tell them that I will be right out."

"Yes, your Holiness," replied Daniels.

Pope John Paul V finished dressing and hurried out to the Reception Hall to meet with Brother Wayne and Clansman Norris, and found them waiting when he arrived. Both were sporting full beards, and each man looked a bit worn from the long journey. The Clansman looked like a young and powerful warrior, with a serious demeanor. He had forgotten how fearless they could be.

"Welcome, Gentlemen! Brother Wayne, it is good to see you again. I guess that you must be Clansman Norris?"

"I am. Greetings, your Holiness," answered Norris, bowing his head in respect.

The pope smiled, remembering well how the clansmen valued respect and honor so highly. Perhaps, he reflected, if everyone valued self-discipline, respect, and honor as highly as the Warrior Clan, the world would be a better place.

"So what brings you here, Brother Wayne, and how have things been progressing? Please, take a seat," he said, gesturing for them to sit down on the sofa in the Reception Hall, hoping to make the Clansman more comfortable.

"As to our progress, Your Holiness, Brother Darius, Brother Sebastian, and all of the other priests have met with Lord Sarkoth at the Main Enclave, as you directed, for the First Council. During the meeting of the council, we learned that the book had already been located just prior to the meeting. The book mentioned a map, which will lead us to the Great Oracle of Knowledge. The map was divided into seven pieces during the Great Collapse. We believe that one of these pieces is located in Athens. While on our way to Greece, I looked up in the night sky, and realized that the Effect had disappeared! Since I knew we would pass so near to here, I thought we should come to you, tell you of our progress, about the disappearance of the Effect, and to seek your guidance as to how to proceed."

"Praise the Almighty and Merciful Lord!" exclaimed Pope John Paul V, clasping his hands in prayer, offering thanks. "The Lord gave me a vision just last night. It seems that we have been given a choice, succeed and civilization will once again thrive, or fail, and the world will endure a suffering such as it has never seen." He could see the dejected look on the faces of those present and decided to change the subject. "So, tell me what you have learned from the book that was discovered at last."

"This map was developed by a group that formed immediately following the Great Collapse, consisting of a group of clergy and scientists. They called themselves The Unity. The Unity knew of the Oracle's existence, created the map, divided it into seven pieces, and scattered them at seven monasteries throughout the world. We believe that our brothers from that time each took a piece of the map back with them to these seven monasteries, and hid them there, waiting for the time to come when God would give us a sign. We were on our way to an ancient monastery in Greece when we stopped here."

"I now understand, Brother Wayne, thank you for bringing this news to me. The Lord has shown me that the urba known as Kraken seeks the Oracle as well, even as we do. If he finds it, and gains control over it, all is lost. The suffering we have endured during the Dark Age will be nothing compared to what future generations will be forced to endure under the tyranny of this evil man and his offspring. We must not allow that to happen!"

"Do not worry your Holiness," said Norris, speaking at last. "Even as we speak my people are preparing to launch a major attack against Kraken and his so-called army, even while the search for the Oracle continues."

"Can the Clan defeat Kraken, Clansman Norris?" asked the pope.

"My people are extremely skilled warriors, Your Holiness. Yes, we can defeat him; I believe in short order, if we strike soon. Some of our men have already been dispatched to our more distant enclaves scattered throughout the Outlands, rounding up as many warriors as they can to fight against Kraken."

"Then I will pray for your victory, Clansman Norris," the pope told him. "If you are unable to defeat him, we may need to destroy the pieces of the map that we have, just to keep them out of the hands of Kraken."

"Yes, your Holiness," Norris replied.

"Now, please come with me. You must both take some food, and some rest, before resuming your journey. Perhaps we can share some stories of the Clan, eh Clansman Norris? Tell me please, how is Lord Sarkoth? You probably do not know of this, but he and I were close friends once, many years ago, and indeed, we still are to this day." The three men walked out of the Reception Hall and into the Dining Hall, sharing stories of the Clansmen, and the Outlands.

That evening, after sharing dinner together, Brother Wayne and Clansman Norris took their leave from the Holy Father and re-boarded their ship, resuming their voyage to Athens. Norris, who had enjoyed being back on land, now looked forward to arriving at their destination. He had finally found his sea legs, but he had soon grown tired of the confining ship. Raised in the Outlands, he was accustomed to roaming freely through the woods and fields, sometimes traveling many miles throughout the countryside surrounding the enclave in a single day. The Captain told him that they had only a few days remaining until they reached the land called Greece; Norris would be glad when they arrived.

Chapter 27
The Sixth Map

Valde Urbs of Crocus Vir (Great City of the Yellow Man)

"Unbelievable! We have been at sea for months, and now this!" the captain exclaimed. The aged captain tugged absent-mindedly at his gray beard, exasperated and fearful for his ship, her passengers, and her crew. He had done everything he could to avoid the storm, but despite his efforts and that of the first mate, they were now smack in the middle of it. The storm had been delivering relentless punishment to the ship and its crew all day, belting the deck of the ship with wave after wave. The captain felt compelled to take whatever swift and drastic action necessary to see them safely to shore.

"If I didn't know better, I would say that something, or someone, is doing everything they can to stop us from making it to our destination! If we don't do something soon, we will not survive this journey!"

He called out to his first mate. "Go down below and bring that priest up here." The first mate complied and hurried down below. A few minutes later, he returned with the priest in tow.

"Brother Dan, would you please do something about this weather? How can I get you where you want to go with the weather constantly working against us so?"

"There is nothing I can do Captain Mays. It is in the Lord's hands, not mine."

"Then how about asking Him to do something about this storm, and soon, before my ship and my passengers are torn apart!"

"Well, I will see what I can do," the priest replied.

The priest knelt down on one knee while holding onto a rail, so that the tossing ship did not throw him into a bulkhead while he offered a prayer.

"Holy Father, Merciful Lord…we have undertaken this mission with the hope of finding the means to bring peace and civilization back to the world, with the hope of being able to carry your light once more to all people. We ask now that you prosper our way, oh Lord. Please, merciful Father, cause this storm to cease, the waters to calm, the sun to break through, and please oh Lord, speed us on our journey, so that your name will be glorified in the presence of all aboard this vessel. We ask this in the name of our Lord Jesus Christ, amen."

"Thank you, Brother," said Mays, looking around expectantly. He doubted it would do any good, yet because he was desperate; he was willing to try anything.

Just moments after Brother Dan concluded his prayer; the waves began to diminish, the howling wind slowed to a whimpering breeze, and the rain stopped. A few minutes later, the sun broke through and the clouds began to dissipate.

Captain Mays gazed up in utter disbelief at the sky as the sun broke through the parting clouds. He looked down at the ocean that was now as calm as he had ever seen it, and then he cast a bewildered glance at the priest. Finally, he looked over at his First Mate and said, "Go down below and tell everyone to get up here on the double, and have the crew come on deck as well; they must see this!"

Moments later the first mate returned, trailed by the clansmen and the rest of the crew. "As all of you know, only minutes ago we were under assault by a most vicious, terrible storm. My first mate here can bear witness that in an act of complete desperation, I requested that the priest, Brother Dan here, petition his God to calm the storm enough that we might survive this journey. Brother Dan was gracious enough to do as I requested. He got down on his knees, and offered a humble prayer to his God, asking for the storm to cease, and for a safe journey for the remainder of our voyage.

Within moments, and I mean within moments, the winds died down, the waves calmed, the rain stopped, and now, look around you, the sun is shining. Not even five minutes ago, I feared for the safety, for the very lives, of all the souls on board. Now, I ask you to take a moment and look around at the weather. I'm not sure about a lot of things in my life, but one thing I know for certain; Brother Dan's God had something to do with this."

Looking at the priest, Mays said almost tearfully, "Brother Dan, I confess that I know little about your God, and I certainly cannot speak for these others here, but please tell me, what I must do to follow your God, for I am a wretched man!"

Clearly moved himself, the priest gently replied, "In the Holy Bible, the Lord Jesus says that we should have faith, that we should believe that he is the Son of God, that he died for our sins, and that if we love him, he will save us from our sins and give us eternal life with him in Heaven. Will you trust and believe in him, with confidence, that he, who calms the storms of our lives can do this for you?"

"Brother, I don't know much, but I do know that I have spent over twenty years on the ocean, and I have never seen anything even resembling what I saw happen today. Given what I have just witnessed, yes, I believe if he said these things, then they are so."

Brother Dan called for some water and after blessing it, and after he had Mays kneel on the deck, he poured some on the captain's head and making the sign of the cross, he said, "Captain Mays, I baptize you now in the name of the Father, and of the Son, and of the Holy Spirit. Welcome into the Lord's family." Mays rose and looking up at the sky, and then at the passengers and crew, smiled broadly. He then looked at the crew, and said," Now then, what are you looking at you salty pirates? Let's get this ship back on course, we have some passengers who are counting on us to get them where they want to go!" The crew grinned at the old man before scattering to attend to their assigned tasks.

That night at dinner, there was a small celebration with some feasting and merriment, as they celebrated Mays' experience, and their survival. They were so delighted that they never noticed the wreckage from another ship, floating in the sea some distance behind them.

***

With the timely aid of another strong tailwind, the ship soon arrived in the body of water once known as the Sea of China. As they pulled into an ancient yet still functional seaport, the crew and passengers had little idea what to expect. In a land so far away, how could they? They had only been able to find their way using ancient maps that had remained in the possession of either the Church or the Clan. Using these maps, they had been able to navigate a great distance, far greater than anyone else had for nearly five-hundred years.

All of the clansmen were clothed in armor from head to toe, fully prepared for anything they might face, or at least as prepared as they could be. The chief clansman, Manasa, walked over to Brother Dan.

"Brother, do you have any idea how far the monastery is from here?" he asked the priest? Brother Dan fumbled through his pack and pulled out an ancient map.

"Well, according to this map, we should only have to go inland about five miles." Dan moved his index finger along a road on the map. "It looks like we need to go this way."

"Brother, this is an extremely large mero. Do you have any idea how far five miles inside a mero of this size is? Who knows what kind of beasts and urba we may find?"

"I did not mean to suggest that it was going to be easy, Clansman Manasa."

"Forgive me Brother; I guess we are all still a little exhausted from the long journey."

He turned and spoke with one of his men. "Carlos, take some men and bring out the horses and the supplies. Tell everyone to stay alert, we have no idea what to expect here."

"Yes, Lord Manasa," replied Carlos.

They brought the horses off the ship and began their journey inside the mero. While in some ways the mero looked similar to other meros they had been in before, there were differences, particularly in the architecture and the writing, still apparent even after centuries of disrepair. As he looked around, Manasa wondered why the lettering looked so different from what he had seen back home. Although the clansmen had received some limited education inside of the Main Enclave, for the most part their studies had been more on practical subjects, so he had little knowledge of foreign languages.

"You may have noticed that the writing here is different from what you learned back home," said the priest. "The people of this land were once called Chinese. They spoke and wrote in a completely different language, hence the different characters on all of the buildings." The priest was about to continue when he noticed a look of alarm on the faces of the clansmen. When he turned and saw what had alarmed the usually stone cold clansmen, he understood the reason for their concern. A giant animal, an enormous, orange, and black cat of some kind, was slowly walking toward them.

"Brother, get behind us, quickly," Manasa told him.

Clansmen leapt ahead and beside him, surrounding the priest to protect him.

"What is that thing?" asked Carlos.

"It looks like some kind of a cat," answered Manasa, "a big, orange cat."

"I believe it may be a tiger," said Brother Dan, "a powerful member of the big cat family, a distant cousin to the lions we see in some of the meros at home. I have never seen one in person, until now, but I have heard stories." The men and the tiger stood staring at each other for some time, until the fierce feline finally thought better of it, determining that the creatures before it were not going to be easy prey, and moved on, leaving the men to themselves.

"That was one of the most remarkable creatures I have ever laid eyes on," remarked Carlos, as they moved away. Everyone breathed a sigh of relief.

The group rode on for some time through the deserted mero, looking for the monastery. The map, which was not very detailed to begin with, was made even more difficult to follow by the fact that after five-hundred years, things looked different in person from what they did on the map. Manasa led them as best he could through the ruins of the mero, casting an occasional casual glance toward the western sky, where the sun was already sitting low on the horizon. They were running out of daylight.

"Brother, we need to make a decision soon," said Manasa. "Do we make camp here or do we continue?"

"Well, I believe we are fairly close now. Can we safely continue just a little while longer?"

"That is fine with me, Brother, but I believe we should camp indoors. If this mero is anything like the ones back home, the beasts will hunt at night. It would be far safer if we spend our nights inside."

The group continued until they happened upon an ancient building that Dan thought vaguely resembled monasteries he had seen before.

"Let's take a look at this building ahead. I think this could be it."

The men walked up to the door of the building, where a sign sat above the door, now faded and worn down by centuries of neglect. Written in Chinese and English, were the words, Trappist Haven Monastery.

"This is it!" exclaimed the priest. "If my brothers and I were correct, the map will be inside somewhere. This is another of the ancient monasteries that dates back before the time of the Golden Age. One of our brothers from here could certainly have been one of those included in the number of The Unity."

Three of the clansmen took point, ensuring the way would be clear for the priest to continue inside the monastery. Moments later, they returned and after giving the all clear, the group proceeded inside.

Based on the conditions inside the monastery, Brother Dan surmised the building had been abandoned long ago, likely hundreds of years earlier. They began looking around inside of the monastery, searching everywhere for a clue that would lead them to the map. The priest was impressed when he saw books and documents covered in dust, written in Chinese as well as English and Latin, scattered throughout the various rooms.

"Manasa, Brother Dan, over here. I've found what looks to be a library." They followed Carlos' voice into a large, lined with bookshelves. The bookshelves looked mostly empty, though some books remained.

"Very good Carlos, very good indeed!" said Manasa.

The men began looking through the books that remained on the shelves. As the others continued looking through the books, Brother Dan felt himself strangely drawn to a small statue that sat on the mantle over an ancient fireplace. The statue was covered in the dust and grime that inevitably comes with centuries of neglect. It was in poor condition, with scorch marks that suggested it had survived a fire at some point in the distant past. Dan walked over to the figurine, and knocked off some of the dust. With some of the dust and grime gone, the priest could tell that the statuette was of a monk reading a book. "I don't believe it! This is it; this is what we are looking for!"

"What? That is only a statue," exclaimed Manasa. "I thought we were looking for a map!" Brother Dan took the figurine from the mantle and began searching for the map.

"Indeed we are, but do you recognize the book that this monk is reading?" he asked.

"I do not see–wait, isn't that the same symbol as the book we saw at the enclave?

"Indeed, it is!" Dan continued examining the statue. "Nevertheless, I cannot seem to locate a map. What a beautiful piece, however!" the priest remarked. "Splendid craftsmanship!"

Monasa walked over to Brother Dan and held out his hand.

"May I examine it, Brother?"

"Of course," he answered, handing over the figure to Manasa, who took the statue and smashed it against the mantle.

"Why did you do that? That was a beautiful work of art!" protested the priest.

"Tell me now, was it worth it?" asked Manasa, holding out a piece of well-preserved cloth, that was clearly a piece of the map. He handed the cloth to the priest.

"Brother?" asked Manasa. Brother Dan took the cloth and studied it for a few moments.

"Yes, this is it, definitely, this is it!"

"Alright then, we will stay here tonight," said Manasa.

Brother Dan secured the map, stowing it safely in his bag. They celebrated finding the map by breaking out some wine and some bread. After some dinner and some relaxing conversation, the jubilant group set a watch, and settled down to sleep, planning to head back to the ship at first light. The priest and the clansmen, fatigued from their long journey and the day's tiring trek through the mero, soon fell asleep.

Hours later, Dan awoke to one of the clansmen sounding an alarm during the middle of the night. "Clansmen, to arms! We are under attack!"

Manasa leapt to his feet, his sword already drawn. "Protect the priest!" he commanded.

Five of the clansmen immediately formed a protective circle around Brother Dan, who was clutching his pack. Two-dozen urba had poured into the monastery and attacked the group while they were still sleeping. They surrounded the clansmen like a swarm of locusts. The clansmen fought furiously to protect the priest. At one point, each clansman was fighting two or more urba at the same time. Manasa noted that the swords seemed far superior to what they encountered before.

"Clansmen, these urba seem more skilled than those we have fought in the Outlands. Be on your guard!" he said.

The urba pressed their fierce attack. While they were no match for the clansmen man to man, their superior numbers made it a more evenly matched battle than what the clansmen were accustomed to. The Warrior Clan rarely encountered warriors of such skill. Manasa knew what would happen if the furious battle continued much longer. The superior numbers of the urba afforded them a critical luxury that the clansmen lacked; rest. The clansmen would soon grow tired while the urbas exchanged places. They had to end the battle soon, or all would be lost. Manasa took the lead, with his short sword in the left hand and the long sword in his right hand. With two attackers coming at him at once, Manasa blocked with his long sword and countered with the short. He

195

used the body of the first attacker to take the attack of the second attacker's sword, as he sliced with the long sword and thrust with the short.

In a room next to where Manasa had begun to rally, Carlos suddenly found himself surrounded by three men. Feigning an attack at the middle urba, he actually launched an attack to the rear instead, kicking the urba back five feet and, driving him through the back wall behind him. He sliced at the leg of the urba to his left, followed by a final cut at the remaining attacker who had been facing him. After another few minutes of fighting, the urba suddenly and inexplicably began disappearing into the darkness from which they had appeared. As quickly as it had started, the altercation was suddenly over.

Manasa quickly glanced around the common area of the monastery, where they had camped out. He took a quick count of the clansmen before realizing that the priest was missing.

"The priest, find the priest!"

The clansmen fanned out across the monastery looking for Dan. After several minutes of searching, Manasa found him lying unconscious on the floor near the rear entrance to the monastery, with a cut on his wrist and a wound on his head that was still bleeding. Manasa was kneeling on the floor next to the injured priest, feeling for a pulse, when the injured clergyman began moving and groaning.

"Brother Dan, are you okay?" he asked. "What happened?"

"Oh, what?" Opening his eyes, the priest started looking around the room. "They– took my bag. I tried to stop them, I tried to take it back, but they cut my arm, and something struck me from behind," he said, placing his hand over the wound on the back of his head.

"I knew it! I thought something was wrong with the way the Urba took off. Don't worry, Brother, we'll find them, and the map." He then stood back up and yelled to the other clansmen. "The priest's bag, everyone start looking for the priest's bag!"

After searching the building for thirty minutes, Manasa abandoned the search.

"Oh, no," Carlos suddenly exclaimed, "they're gone!"

"What is it, Carlos, what did you find?" asked Manasa.

"Outside, the horses, they're gone!" answered Carlos, pointing outside.

"What do you mean?" asked Manasa, rushing for the door. Manasa raced past Carlos and out the front entrance. The horses were gone, taken by the urba. "It looks like we're on foot then," remarked Mansa.

He turned back to Dan. "Don't worry, Brother Dan. We will not leave here until we have found that map."

Jeff. W. Horton

Chapter 28
The Final Map

Urbs of Silicis - Vir in Gero
(The City of the Rock-Man in the Bear)

The men were still celebrating the retrieval of the map. There had been no loss of life, and there had been no incidents. As surprising as it had been, they had seen no urba since arriving at the Baltic Sea port in St. Petersburg. Now that they had the map, they were happily preparing for their return journey back to the Main Clan Enclave. The men were still several miles from the ship when their moment of levity was interrupted.

"BOOM! BOOM! BOOM!"

Brother Benedict had never heard such a sound, except during a thunderstorm. He looked up but the sky was clear, and the sun shining brightly. Though the noise was unfamiliar to the priest, the clansmen recognized it, however, though it was much louder than what they were accustomed to hearing.

"That sounds like some kind of gunfire, Brother!" said Yoshi.

"It sounds like it's coming from the ship, sir," said one of the men.

Yoshi looked at two of the men and said to them, "Stay with the priest!"

He and the rest of his men broke into a run and made for the ship. With most of the Clansmen sent to retrieve the map, only a few had stayed behind to guard the ship. It was a risk, but given the choice of the mission or the ship, the choice had seemed obvious. The ship was their only way home, however, and Yoshi now began to question the wisdom of that decision. If the ship were under attack, their help would be sorely needed.

He arrived at the dock only to find a second vessel attempting to pull up next to theirs. It had fired its canons only as warning shots, as a precursor to boarding it. Yoshi and his men had arrived just in time, as men from the attacking ship were already starting to board theirs. He and his fellow clansmen ran up the gangplank to meet and engage the enemy. Though greatly outnumbered, the clansmen held back the onslaught of men from the other ship, making short work of the majority of them. After losing all of their men in the first wave of boarders, the attackers began retreating to their ship. Just as Yoshi and the others began to relax, the attackers suddenly stopped their retreat, and parted to make way for someone or something that had emerged from down below on the enemy ship. From the moment he stepped onto their ship, it was clear to Yoshi, and the others, that there was something different about him; a difference in his mannerisms, his movements, even in the way he walked. He had an air of arrogance about him that stood out among the others. The way the attackers moved aside to let him pass conveyed to Yoshi that the men held him in high regard, or feared him. Most likely, an expert swordsman.

Much to Yoshi's surprise, he cleared through two of the clansmen in fairly short order, killing the highly trained men of the Warrior Clan handily, something Yoshi had never before seen. After recovering from the initial shock, he rushed over to deal with the intruder himself.

After smiling at Yoshi, the enemy attacked him with a downward stroke, which Yoshi blocked before counter-attacking with his short sword. The enemy aptly defended, responding with a straight thrust to Yoshi's heart, which once again, Yoshi parried, but only barely. There was no longer any doubt about it, the attacker was highly skilled, and Yoshi had his hands full. The epic battle went on for some time, with neither of the two men gaining any ground nor giving any quarter. It went on until the two swordsmen were both exhausted. During the few seconds it took them to catch their breath, Yoshi noticed that his brothers had already dispatched the remainder of the enemy. A few of them made movements toward the master swordsman that Yoshi had been fighting, but he waived them off. While he made it appear that he wanted the man for himself, the truth was he was afraid they would be killed. Yoshi was by far the most skilled swordsman in the group, and the intruder was a challenge, even for him. Besides, Yoshi rarely encountered such skill outside of the Clan, so it was an opportunity for him to test himself.

As the enemy came closer for his final attack, Yoshi drew from a method of fighting taken from one of the best swordsman that ever lived, an ancient warrior named Miyamoto Mushashi. Yoshi was well versed in the fighting arts, particularly swordplay, and he had paid particularly close attention to Mushashi's teachings, as detailed in the Book of Five Rings, an ancient book dating back to well before the Golden Age. The Clan had several copies at the Main Enclave, and Yoshi had read the book many times over, studying the techniques in detail, and putting them into practice until he had come to master them.

Yoshi chose to use Mushashi's second method of forestalling an enemy, the Tai No Sen Method, in dealing with the master swordsman before him. As the enemy attacked, Yoshi feigned weakness when the enemy reached him, acting as if he planned to jump aside. This gave the enemy a moment's pause, a split second where he relaxed for just a moment. Following the Tai No Sen Method, it was during this split-second that Yoshi dashed in, attacking strongly. He plunged his short sword into his enemy's torso, followed by a fatal cut with the long sword, ending the fight with the decisive blow. Once Yoshi was certain that the fight was over, he became aware of his brothers cheering his victory over the enemy. They knew, as did Yoshi, that had he not defeated this superior enemy swordsman, many of them would have perished and perhaps, the mission itself would have ended in failure.

Yoshi took half of the men over with him to the enemy ship and dispatched all the urba aboard, giving them the option of jumping into the ocean or facing the fearless clansmen. Only the captain of the ship and the crew were left untouched. After the fighting was over and the threat eliminated, Yoshi walked over to Brother Benedict, who had been brought onboard.

"Please give me just a few minutes, Clansman Yoshi, so that I may say a few words for our dead."

"Very well. Thank you, Brother Benedict."

When the priest had finished, he went with Yoshi to meet with Captain Harris.

"It's a good thing you arrived when you did, Clansman Yoshi. We were outgunned and outnumbered! So what do you plan to do with the enemy ship?" Harris asked them.

"The way I see it, we have two choices, we can sink it or we can sail it back home," Yoshi answered. "I spared the lives of its captain and its crew. What do you think, Captain?"

"Well, it isn't easy to come by ships these days," said the captain. "And while I don't know what all of this is about exactly, I suspect that it would benefit the Clan, and the Church as well for that matter, to have another vessel at their disposal."

201

Yoshi looked at Brother Benedict. "Brother?" he asked. The priest nodded his head.

"I must agree with Captain Harris. The Church-Clan Alliance will certainly need ships if we are successful."

"Very well then, it's settled. I will select a few men and have their things taken over to the enemy ship to keep the ship's captain and crew company. First, however, I would like to have a few words with the captain."

"Clansman Yoshi, may I come with you?" asked Brother Benedict.

"I don't know Brother; it might get a little ugly. Perhaps you should stay here."

"I appreciate your concern. If you need me to leave, you have only to ask."

"Very well then, Brother. We should get over there now, as we need to be heading back soon."

Yoshi spoke with several of his men. They gathered their things and went over to relieve their brothers, who had been keeping an eye on the captain and crew.

"What is your name?" asked Yoshi.

"I am Captain Abihu, and this is my Ship, the Nemesis."

"Who are you working for, and why did you attack our ship?"

The captain sat and said nothing for a minute, pondering how he should respond to the questioning, if at all.

"You will answer me," warned Yohsi. "My men have been attacked, and some have lost their lives, because of you. Do not test my patience!"

"Answer a question for me first, and then I will happily answer yours."

"Ask your question," said Yoshi, snarling.

"Are you clansmen?"

"We are."

"Then if you promise me protection, I will answer all of your questions. Otherwise, you might as well kill me now, because I would rather die at your hands, than his. I have seen him in action, and he enjoys killing, finding great pleasure in finding new and more painful ways to kill a man."

"So, you are working for Kraken then? That is not really a shock, though I am surprised that he has ships, and that he would send someone so far just for our benefit. Very well, you have my word that we will protect you, until we are no longer able to, or until he is dead, whichever comes first."

"Thank you. To be honest with you, I despised working for that lunatic. What choice did I have though? We were sent here to recover whatever it is that you were seeking, after you found it. While I don't know exactly know what that is, he wants it, badly."

"So, if he sent these men this far from home, we must assume that he has sent men after the other expeditions as well," said Brother Benedict.

"Undoubtedly," answered Yoshi, "and Kraken's power and his reach have obviously grown much more than we were led to believe. We must hurry back with all speed to warn the council, and prepare a preemptive attack against Kraken and his army, and soon," said Yoshi.

"Captain Abihu, would you be willing to sail this ship back home, with some of my men accompanying you, of course?"

"I would," he answered, "if you follow through on your promise to provide me sanctuary. Kraken will not only kill me, he will make my death unbelievably slow and painful," he added.

"Then you will follow us and our ship all the way back. If for any reason you fail to fulfill your part of the bargain, believe me when I say that you will have nothing to worry about anymore, for you will no longer be alive. Am I clear?" asked Yoshi.

"You are clear," the captain responded.

Yoshi and Brother Benedict moved back over to the other ship, and after burying their dead, they began the long journey home.

Jeff. W. Horton

Chapter 29
Breaking Point

He was shaking uncontrollably again, and this time he was in agonizing pain as well. A lesser man would have already broken, and told his captors everything he knew. No matter how tough someone is though, no matter how hardened or how well trained, every man reaches the point where he can be broken, and David-Michael was rapidly approaching his. He knew it would take only one more round of torture, two at the most, before he would break, and gladly tell Kraken everything he knew. The clansman was thankful that he had passed out when he did during the last round of torment; because he had felt himself weaken to the point that he was nearly ready to do anything to stop the misery. They were keeping him alive for the moment, but he was beginning to sense that if he did not give them something soon however, they would end up torturing him to death. Either way, the clansman knew that regardless of what he told them, he would soon be dead. David-Michael knew this was one of the peculiar things about torture; that even when a man knows he will die whether he talks or not, he still does anything and everything he can to end the suffering. Only the day before, they had stretched him out on a rack, tied him with ropes, and turned the wheels until he felt his arms and his legs being ripped from his torso. He had been held captive in Kraken's dungeon for only a month; but to David-Michael, it might have been an eternity. Soon he would tell them everything they wanted to know, so he had to come up with a plan and he had to do it soon, before he betrayed the Clan, and their cause.

He had been searching for a means of escape since he arrived, but he was now too weak and dehydrated, and he suspected that he was probably sick with fever as well. Pain had been his constant companion throughout the ordeal, so he also had trouble sleeping. Despite all of this, he fought through the pain, constantly seeking a way out.

In between torture sessions, his thoughts had frequently turned toward his men. While he suspected they were already dead, he held out hope that some might yet be alive. But alive or dead, if the opportunity came for him to escape, he was resolved that he would do so without stopping for his men. The intimate knowledge he possessed about the Main Enclave, knowledge of its weaknesses; secret entrances, guard changes, and many other details, left him no choice, as such knowledge could easily give Kraken the advantage when he attacked the Main Enclave. Even more importantly, David-Michael knew details around the search for the map that could lead Kraken to the Great Oracle, including the routes of all of the expeditions returning from their respective destinations. He must act, and soon, before it was too late.

Day after day and night after night, he struggled to find other options, running each scenario through his mind, how he might kill Kraken, and end the threat. Regardless of how desperately he wanted it however, any outright attack against Kraken in his weakened state would only end in his re-capture. His poor physical condition aside, Kraken was always surrounded by his elite personal guard. David-Michael knew he had to find another way.

His thoughts turned back to escape. They would be coming for him again soon, hauling him back in front of Kraken, and then back to one of the torture chambers, or the rack, where after yet another day of unending agony, he feared he would tell all. Despite his frail physical condition, he must attempt to overpower the guards and escape. He began gathering all of the concentration he could muster, and focused it on making a mental map in his mind. He would be taken out of the dungeon, up the stairs, past the main entrance near the torture room, and then into the throne room, where Kraken would be waiting. Then, he would be brought back to his cell until the Master Torturer was ready for him. For the past week, he had questioned David-Michael in a newer building that stood apart from the rest of the fortress. The Master Torturer had a greater variety of options for extracting information from the clansman there and seemed to prefer it. The clansman tried desperately to remember what the area outside of the fortress looked like. His chances of escape were extraordinarily slim and he knew it, but he must try. He would make his move when he was between buildings on the way to be tortured, where he would either escape, or die trying. Either way, the problem would soon be resolved, and the threat to his clansmen brothers eliminated. With a vague outline of a plan in place, the clansman finally permitted the exhaustion he had been keeping at bay for some time, to overtake him, causing him slip into a much-needed, merciful sleep.

David-Michael awoke a few hours later to the sound of the door at the top of the stairs being unlocked and opened. The metal door screeched and strained, as if complaining at being forced to open against its will. Two guards came down the stairs.

"Well, well, well, we certainly hope that you have been comfortable down here, Mr. Fancy-Pants Clansman. Is there anything that we can do to improve your stay with us?"

The two men laughed together while one of them opened the door.

"Come along then, Mr. Clansman, sir. Lord Kraken would like to have another little chat with you." The two men laughed again. David-Michael attempted to stand up, before falling helplessly back to the ground.

"What's the matter then, been enjoying your stay with us a little too much? Well then, we will have to have a word with the chief torturer, see if we can make your time on the rack a little less comfortable next time! For now however, you will have to come with us. Lenny, give me a hand." Looking back at David-Michael, he told him, "I am warning you now tough guy, no funny business, or we'll run you through!"

The two men hauled him back up the stairs and took him to stand in front of Kraken. They had to carry him into the throne room, dragging his feet as they did so.

"Well now, looks like you have not had the best day today, my friend," Kraken said, laughing. "I thought you clansmen were supposed to be a tough lot. Hah! It looks like your reputation has been greatly exaggerated if you ask me."

David-Michael looked up and cast a defiant look at Kraken. It was for show, but it was convincing. Perhaps Kraken would tire of the game and kill him before he revealed any damaging information that could endanger his brothers and sisters at the Main Enclave.

As he looked up at Kraken, sitting arrogantly on his throne, the warrior was also surprised to see a beautiful young woman sitting next to him, a woman he had never seen before. How could a lovely creature like this be with a monster like Kraken?

The latter must have noticed that David-Michael's glance rested just a little too long on the young woman.

"Ah, you like my new girl Jessica, do you clansman? Well, why don't you tell me what I want to know and maybe I'll see what I can do for you!" he said laughing, grabbing the girl, and pulling her over to sit with him.

The guards carried David-Michael over to a chair and sat him down. He was still in great pain and barely able to move. He recognized that Kraken seemed exceptionally pleased by this revelation, but the girl clearly was not. Did Kraken's girlfriend, Jessica, grimace at my suffering? It seems out-of-place for any friend of Kraken's, be it a girl or otherwise.

Kraken smiled, chuckling for a few moments, before letting his face harden into granite. "Now then clansman, tell me what I wish to know. Tell me more of this book that was found, tell me of this so-called Oracle, and tell me more about the fortifications at this enclave of yours."

"As I have already said many times before," David-Michael answered weakly, "I am only a simple guard. I know nothing of these matters."

"You will tell me what I want to know!" roared Kraken. "I plan to attack your precious Main Enclave soon. I will attack and destroy everyone and everything inside it, every man, woman, and child. I will know everything I need to know then." He paused, studying David-Michael intensely for several moments. "I know "clanss–man," he said mockingly, "that you were traveling to different enclaves. I know that you were trying to gather your people together at your Main Enclave, and I know that you found the book, and that you are looking for something called the Oracle. Now tell me more, or I promise you I will make you suffer unimaginable pain.

"I am only a simple clansman…," he repeated.

"Very well, simple clansman."

"Take him back to his cell," he said to the guards, "until the master torturer returns. He will see to all of your needs clanss–man," he said. Kraken looked over at the guards.

"Get this pathetic piece of garbage out of here. Tell the master torturer that if the clansman doesn't give up some useful information this time that I said to kill him, and to take his time doing it. I don't have any more time to waste on him. I have other sources!"

The men picked up David-Michael and began carrying him back to the dungeon, expecting no trouble at all from the beaten-down-clansman. They dragged him down the stairs and placed him back in chains, until the Master Torturer returned to complete his preparations for their final session together.

He was astonished when, after he had been in his cell no more than fifteen minutes, he heard the door open once more. It seemed too soon for them to be taking him to the Master Torturer. He was surprised yet again when instead of the two guards, he saw a beautiful face before him. It was the woman he had seen with Kraken, his girlfriend, Jessica.

"You are a clansman, from the Warrior Clan?" she asked him, with a compassionate and concerned look on her face.

"I am," he answered.

"My name is Jessica, and I've come to help you."

"Why would you help me," asked David-Michael. "Kraken sent you to win my trust, didn't he? You're his woman," he said quickly.

"No, my lord, he did not send me, and I am most certainly not his woman. That monster cares for no one but himself. That filthy animal took and ripped me away from my home, away from my family. Believe me or don't believe me, it's your choice, but either way, we must get out of here–now," she said as she began to untie the ropes that bound him. "Kraken is growing tired of waiting for you to give him information. He has given instructions to the Master Torturer, who has just returned, to end your life should you not tell him what he wants to know. They will be here shortly to take you to the torture chamber. If they find us like this, we will both die a slow and excruciatingly painful death. Kraken hates the Warrior Clan."

"Why? We have done him no harm, at least not yet?"

"Because the Warrior Clan is the only thing he fears, and the only thing that stands between him and his dream of ruling the world.

"Then leave me and go. I am prepared to die."

"I will not. The people in my village have heard of the Warrior Clan, and I must admit that based on what I have seen of you, the stories do not tell the half of it. Yours is a brave and courageous people, David-Michael. You are a noble man, and I would rather die myself than to let that madman kill you."

Jessica continued working at the ropes until at last he was free. She grabbed one of his hands and pulled his arm across her shoulder.

"You are still weak, my lord. Let me help you." The woman led him out a different door from the one she had entered. "Kraken made sure he had a back way out of this stronghold, in the event it was ever threatened. Come with me, through this door."

It seemed all too easy to David-Michael.

"I cannot allow you to come with me to the Enclave, it is forbidden," said David-Michael, as they made their way out of the stronghold and past the guards standing just outside.

"Then blindfold me," she said determinedly, as they made their way through the woods surrounding the compound.

"You know he will kill you, if he discovers your betrayal."

"I should be so lucky," she said dryly. "He would probably let me live, taking great care to keep me alive as long as possible, in order to prolong my suffering. Even I cannot imagine the suffering I would endure. Oh, how I despise that creature."

"Why didn't you try to escape sooner?" he asked the girl, who turned to him with a flash of anger.

"And just where exactly was I supposed to go? You don't know Kraken the way I do. I told you, the only thing he is afraid of is the Warrior Clan." She stopped when she noticed that David-Michael was breathing heavily. "We should stop here so you can rest a moment." They sat for a moment on the ground next to a large tree. "There is a stable where he keeps the horses just on the other side of these woods. We can find some horses there." She grabbed hold of a piece of her clothing and tore off a strip of cloth. "Here, you can use this as a blindfold."

David-Michael took the cloth and looked at her. He had been suspicious of her and perhaps, he still should be. Despite himself however, he was beginning to like this Jessie, and he was beginning to consider that perhaps, she was telling the truth.

"If you come to live with us at the enclave, you will never be permitted to leave," he told her. "It is our way."

"You mean I cannot leave, even to warn my village that Kraken may come looking for me?"

"There is no need. We will be taking care of Kraken very soon." He looked around, trying to determine where they were. "We need those horses. I need to warn my brothers of the coming attack. They must make ready to do battle with Kraken."

"Okay, follow me," she said.

When the guards came for him some hours later, they arrived at his cell, only to find it empty.

"We must let Lord Kraken know what happened, immediately!" one of them exclaimed.

"What in the world are you talking about?" the other asked. "What do you think will happen if we tell him that the clansman has escaped?

210

I'll tell you what will happen; we will be tortured to death in the Clansman's place. Look, if we simply tell Kraken that the clansman died in his cell, we'll be in the clear. As long as Kraken doesn't ask to see the body, he'll never know!"

"I don't know," said the other guard. "What if he finds out?"

"And what if he doesn't?" asked the first. After some discussion, they agreed. They would tell Kraken the prisoner was dead.

Chapter 30
Bokra

"Well at least we have four," said Sarkoth. "We must hope and pray to the Lord of Heaven and Earth that the other three will be here soon."

Sarkoth addressed the Council, including a gathering of the elders from all of the remote enclaves contacted by David-Michael and his men.

"But Lord Sarkoth, it's been nearly a year. Surely if they were going to return, they would have been here by now," said Sanjo. "Should we not move against Kraken now, before his strength grows anymore?"

"Brothers, I believe my brother Sanjo is correct." Ferrell stood to address the assembled council. "We should prepare now. Kraken's grows stronger daily and his army swells. It is only a matter of time before he works up the courage to come against us anyway. I propose that we move against him now."

Brother Darius rose to address the council. "Clansmen, if I may speak. Should we not hold off on moving against Kraken until all of the pieces of the map are here? If we act now, what are the chances that our brothers will make it back to the enclave without being intercepted by Kraken?"

Lord Sarkoth rose to speak. "You are correct Brother Darius, in that we must ensure that the way to this enclave remains open. We will not make our stand here; instead, we will take the fight to Kraken, away from the Enclave. We must wait though until the time is right, to ensure that we have the high ground against our enemy."

"We know, Lord Sarkoth," continued Darius, "that Kraken sent men to follow and intercept each of our expeditions once we had the map. It is only logical to assume that he has done the same to our brothers who sailed the great waters to the monasteries in distant lands. It may be that Kraken's men fared better than our brothers did. What should we do if he now has the remaining three pieces to the map?"

"If Kraken has obtained pieces of the map, we must retrieve them. Remember the importance of finding the Oracle," said Brother Francis. "We believe that if we do not find the Oracle, the opportunity to bring about a new Golden Age will be lost."

"Brothers, brothers all, I have a special request," said Brother O'Reilly. "I would ask that we all take a moment to pray for God's guidance in this entire affair. Remember that without his help, all is lost anyway, for we can do nothing without him."

"Thank you Brother O'Reilly. Clansmen, let us join our brothers in a moment of prayer. Brother O'Reilly, would you please lead us?"

"Of course, Lord Sarkoth, I would be honored." O'Reilly cleared his throat and began.

"Our Father, who art in Heaven, Hallowed be Thy Name,
Thy kingdom come, Thy will be done,
On Earth, as it is in Heaven.
Give us this day our daily bread,
And forgive us our trespasses, as we forgive those who trespass against us,
And lead us not into temptation, but deliver us from evil,
For Thine is the Kingdom, the power, and the Glory forever,
Amen."

He continued, "Please Lord, deliver us from the great evil that has spread across these lands. Help us, and guide us as we navigate these uncertain waters. Give us clarity of thought and determination in action. Give us victory over this wicked evil enemy. For we ask in the name of our Lord and Savior Jesus Christ.

Amen."

"Thank you, Brother O'Reilly," said Lord Sarkoth.

After the prayer, a woman came in and delivered a message to Lord Sarkoth. After taking a few minutes to read the message he said, "I move that we adjourn for the evening and continue this important discussion first thing in the morning." With that, Lord Sarkoth rose, and without saying anything further, left the Main Gathering Room.

***

The following morning the council, after sharing a short meal, reconvened in the Main Gathering Room. Once again, Lord Sarkoth, sitting at the head of the table, opened the meeting.

"My Christian and Clansmen brothers, we have news regarding Kraken". He motioned to one of the guards, and they brought in Bokra, bound.

"It is with great sadness that I must inform you that we have been betrayed by former Clansman Bokra. He went to Kraken after our last Council Meeting. We do not yet know for certain what information he passed along to Kraken." He looked over at Bokra. "What we do know, however, is that this is how Kraken learned of our expeditions to find the maps. Fortunately, he has not yet been successful in obtaining any of the pieces to the map, at least not any that we are aware of. The traitor is scheduled to be executed later today." Bokra bowed his head in shame.

"I'm curious Lord Sarkoth, how did you learn of his treachery?" asked Brother Sebastian.

"He came forth with the information himself," the Clan elder replied.

"You mean he voluntarily came in himself and confessed?" he asked.

"That is correct." Sarkoth looked coldly back at Bokra. "Tell us now while you still have a chance; tell us what other information you gave to our vile enemy. If you have any honor left within you, tell us all!"

Bokra lifted his head and looked sheepishly at Lord Sarkoth. "I have told you all, my lord, I swear it. I told him only about the Christian expeditions to find the map, and that is all. I told him nothing else."

The priest studied Bokra for a few moments before turning back to Sarkoth. "I wonder, Lord Sarkoth, whether he might be more useful to our cause if he lived."

"What do you mean, Brother?"

"Perhaps, he could act as a spy for us as he did for Kraken. If you believe he has a sincere desire to redeem himself, he could yet prove useful."

Now Sarkoth turned to study Bokra. "Well Bokra, what say you? Do you have a desire to redeem yourself, and your honor?"

"I do, my Lord. I had no idea what this barbarian was like. Had I known the truth of it, I would never have betrayed you, or the Clan." Sarkoth looked at Bokra for a few moments.

"I believe him. Perhaps we can safely make use of the traitor." As he finished speaking, a guard unexpectedly entered the room and waited at the back to be recognized. Sarkoth motioned to him and the man came forward and spoke quietly with Sarkoth for a moment, before leaving the room. Sarkoth smiled and sat down. "It seems we have some unexpected visitors."

The guard returned a short time later with David-Michael, accompanied by a strange woman that no one seemed to recognize.

Everyone in the room fell silent for several moments upon the arrival of the man they all thought dead. He was in bad shape, but he was alive. The room seemed to come alive with excitement at the resurrection of the beloved warrior and teacher. Several clansmen jumped up and walked over to David-Michael to embrace him.

Lord Sarkoth spoke first. "As you all know, our brother, David-Michael, was intercepted by Kraken as he journeyed to the remote enclaves, recruiting our brothers in our fight against the vile man and his growing army. David-Michael endured torture and great suffering at the hands of our enemy, and faced certain death, were it not for the intervention of this beautiful young woman, Jessica Medina, who herself was taken prisoner by Kraken some time ago." Sarkoth turned to face Jessica.

"Thank you, my dear Miss Medina, for returning our brother, our friend, back to us, and thank you, David-Michael, for all that you have endured on our behalf!" The room exploded in applause. After several minutes, Sarkoth held up his hand and the room quieted down. "Now, our brother has endured great suffering and needs time to recuperate. First however, I believe he brings news of great importance."

Sarkoth turned and looked at David-Michael.

"Clansman David-Michael, would you like to tell us what you have learned?" David-Michael coughed, winced in pain, and walked over to address the gathering.

"Brothers, as Lord Sarkoth has said, I was captured by Kraken and his men some weeks ago, and I learned a few things while spending time in his stronghold, which I feel I must share with you now. First of all, Kraken has already mobilized his army, which he plans to use in a surprise attack against this enclave at any moment." Once again, a buzz of excitement filled the room at the revelation of the unforeseen development. David-Michael continued. "He plans to make war on the entire Clan. He sees us as a threat, perhaps the only threat, to his complete domination, not only of these lands but also of the whole world. He has acquired ships, which means that our brothers traveling to the distant lands are in great danger."

"You say that he is on his way here, now?" asked Sarkoth.

"I do not know when it will begin, my lord, but I know that he is preparing to move at any moment, so I believe the attack is imminent. He has also learned of the Oracle, and desires it for himself."

216

"We must send out scouts immediately to look for movement," said Sarkoth. "David-Michael, can you tell us where this stronghold is located?"

"Yes, my lord."

Sarkoth looked over at the senior guard. "Bring Cyrus to me immediately."

"Yes, Lord Sarkoth," the guard answered.

Sarkoth turned toward Jessica.

"Miss Medina, do you have anything that you would care to offer? I don't mean to put you in a situation that compromises your relationship with Kraken," he added.

"Relationship with Kraken, my lord?" David-Michael shook his head, anticipating what was coming. "My only relationship with Kraken is my desire to see him dead! He murdered my parents, kidnapped me along with half of my village, and made me do things...no my lord, there is no relationship between me and that, animal."

Sarkoth grimaced and shook his head.

"Please forgive me, my dear; I had no idea. I did not fully appreciate the nature of your relationship with him. Is there any information that you can share with us that may aid us in dealing with him?"

"I know only that he fears you, Lord Sarkoth, and the rest of the Warrior Clan. Despite his bravado and his rhetoric, he is deathly afraid of you; even more so after the way David-Michael so bravely endured such punishing torture at the hands of Kraken's master torturer."

Sarkoth did not miss the way she looked at David-Michael when she said that. Curious.

"He believes that you clansmen are the only thing that can stop him from conquering the world," she continued, "He is a vicious and profoundly cruel man, my lord. If he succeeds, I am afraid of what will become of the people in my village, and of the people in all of the other villages in the Outlands. I may be able to provide you with some details about his stronghold, some of his top military leaders, and the like. Perhaps you will find some of it useful. Please, Lord Sarkoth, you must stop him."

"We will certainly do what we can, my dear, and thank you."

About that time, the guard returned with a lean, weathered, and hard-looking man. His name was Cyrus, chief of the Clansman Scouts.

"You summoned me, Lord Sarkoth?"

"Yes. Please, take a seat, Cyrus. Did you bring a map?"

"Of course, my lord." He reached into his cloak and extracted a map, which he placed on the table before the Council.

"Clansman David-Michael, can you show us approximately where Kraken's compound is located?"

"Yes, my lord," answered David-Michael. "It is only a three day ride from here, riding west, away from the Great Waters." He pointed to a location on the map. "His stronghold is located near this mountain, with mountains behind and West of the compound. A river is to the East, leaving only one way in and one way out."

"He is an exceptional strategist, it would appear," said Sarkoth. "Very well. Cyrus, I would like you to send men immediately in the general direction of his stronghold. It appears that Kraken plans to attack us any day now. We need patrols looking for troop movements, and most importantly, we need to know the moment his armies are on the move."

"Yes, my Lord, it will be done."

Sarkoth turned toward Ferrell. "Ferrell, I would like for you to lead our men into battle. Will you do this?"

"Of course, Lord Sarkoth, I would be honored."

"Where do you think we should meet him in battle?" asked Sarkoth.

"I believe that we should take the fight to him. We should meet him in the field, preferably soon after he leaves his stronghold."

"I know of just the place, Ferrell," said David-Michael. "There was a valley between two mountains that I passed through on my way back here. I believe this would be the perfect place to meet him."

"Then we should prepare. As for you, my old friend and teacher, you must try and get some rest. We will need you," said Ferrell.

"I will, but Kraken has made it personal for me now, so I want in."

"Then you shall be in, David-Michael," said Sarkoth. "Your knowledge of Kraken's stronghold will prove invaluable, as will your considerable knowledge of military strategies."

"Lord Sarkoth, what about the expeditions from the distant lands, have we heard anything from them?" asked Darius.

"There were some ships spotted by some of our scouts along the Great Waters a few days ago. It is possible one of our expeditions was among them. If so, we should be seeing them soon, possibly today or tomorrow. In all likelihood the more distant meros will take longer, possibly as much as another month, assuming that that they have already found the map, and are able to make it back," he said grimly.

"Have we been able to determine anything about the location of the Oracle based on the four pieces of the map that we have?" asked Sarkoth.

"No, I am afraid not," Sebastian responded. "We believe that the Oracle may be somewhere in these lands, based on what we have seen of the four maps, but without the rest of the map we cannot be certain even of that. It appears our brothers in The Unity did a very good job at making it next to impossible to discern the location of the Oracle without all seven pieces."

"Then we must wait until we have the remaining pieces," said Sarkoth, "and hope that our brothers have been able to find and keep them from Kraken."

Chapter 31
The Assault

"Collins! Mansa, tell Collins to report to me immediately!" Kraken was not happy. He was ready to move, and he had no additional information from Bokra.

"Yes, Lord Kraken," answered Mansa, just before disappearing out the door.

"If that worm, Bokra, doesn't deliver some useful intelligence to me, and soon, I will enjoy delivering a slow and painful death to him!" Kraken growled to the other generals in the room.

Mansa returned a few minutes later.

"Collins will be here momentarily, Lord Kraken."

"He'd better be." Kraken turned his head back and forth, noticeably agitated.

"We must move against the Clan immediately, Mansa. The clansmen have been making contact with enclaves throughout the Outlands, and beyond. We must not allow them to succeed in gathering the majority of the enclaves together. They are the only thing keeping me from fulfilling my destiny to rule all of the Known Lands. We must accelerate our timing for attacking their enclave. By attacking them now, before they are ready for us, we can inflict the greatest damage on their people. We will use catapults and other siege works that we built for use in the Mero Wars. We will lay waste not only to their warriors, but to their women and children as well. They will be forced to hide behind their precious walls, while we destroy their precious enclave piece by piece. It will be a damaging psychological blow to my greatest enemy."

"Yes, Lord Kraken," replied Mansa.

The conversation was cut short when General Collins entered the room. Mansa backed away and left.

"Yes, Lord Kraken. I understand that you wanted to see me?"

"I want a status on the battle plan. Where is it? You were supposed to have it to me this morning!" Kraken roared.

"It is nearly finished, my lord," he answered, cringing a bit, as he did so.

"Nearly finished? Nearly finished, you say. General Collins, are you begging me for the chance to test out my latest torture rack? Nearly is not good enough, I want it today, by day's end."

"But my lord, it is not that easy. These are not mere urba packs that we are dealing with this time but clansmen. The Warrior Clan has studied and mastered the art of war and combat for hundreds of years. They have devoted themselves to it, and they are extremely disciplined."

Kraken got up from his throne, pulled out a short sword, and before the general could even flinch, he cut off his left ear. The general screamed in pain, holding a hand to where his ear had been before, in an attempt to slow the bleeding.

"My dear general, I don't want to hear about their devotion, about their skills in combat, I want to hear about mine! The next time that you give me excuses, it will not be an ear that I separate from your head, it will be your head that I will separate from your body."

"Yes, Lord Kraken. I will have the assault plan ready for you by tonight," replied Collins, as blood trickled down his neck and dripped onto the floor."

"Now, stop bleeding all over my floor and get that plan finished and to me by nightfall. And send in Mansa…"

"Yes, my lord," he answered, as he bowed and left the throne room.

Kraken looked on the board at the position of his army. He had divided his army into three groups, over fifty-thousand men in each one. Two groups would attack the enclave in a frontal assault; using the catapults to weaken their defenses and ladders to scale the walls. The third group would stand ready in reserve and would catch any stragglers as they tried to escape from the fierce onslaught. Many of the specifics would be in the battle plan that Collins was supposed to have already finished.

These are not mere urba packs that we are dealing with this time but clansmen. "How dare he," Kraken mumbled to himself, "the clansmen are mere men, while I am Kraken the Terrible, Kraken the Mighty, and Kraken the Great! I cannot be defeated! It is my destiny to rule the world of the Dark Age. People everywhere will tremble in fear at the mere mention of my name for a thousand years. I will crush the Clan first, and then the pathetic Christian Church that I so despise. I will leave no hope alive for those who think to defy me." The doors to the throne room opened and Mansa walked in.

"Yes, my lord?"

"Tell me, have we any word from our spy in the Clan, that worm–Bokra?"

"None, my lord," replied Mansa.

"What do you think happened? Maybe they found out he was working for us, and had him executed?"

"I do not think so, my Lord," he said. "Certainly it is possible, but we were careful after he made contact with us, to take precautions that he would not be discovered."

"What about that clansman in the dungeon? Do we have any new information from him? Has he broken yet?"

"I am sorry, Lord Kraken, but the guards reported that he refused to reveal anything before he died in his cell from his injuries."

"Incompetence! I am surrounded by incompetence! Execute the guards, at once."

"Yes, Lord Kraken," answered Mansa. He was not about to remind Kraken that it was his order to push the torture either until the prisoner surrendered the information or until he died.

"What do we know about the Clan's recent activity?" asked Kraken. "Have they found the Oracle? Where are the men we sent to follow their expeditions, and why haven't any of them reported back yet?"

"As to the recent activity, Lord Kraken, we believe that some of the expeditions have returned and made it back to the Clan. We know that several groups of clansmen have recently been spotted entering the enclave. While these may well be clansmen that have come in from the remote enclaves, we have no way of knowing for certain. We know little else of recent activity at the Main Enclave. As to the Oracle, we have no reason to assume that they have found it as of yet. I suspect that they are still waiting to hear from some of their expeditions."

"And what about the men that we sent to follow their expeditions?" barked Kraken.

"We have no word from them, my lord. Perhaps they were successful and a few of the clansmen escaped and made it back to the enclave," suggested Mansa, unwilling to state his true suspicion, that the clansmen had killed their men.

"I tire of this waiting game. Whether I have a battle plan or not, whether General Collins is alive or not, we will leave tomorrow to attack the Clan's Main Enclave. Tell General Smythe to have the other generals get their men ready. We leave tomorrow for the enclave, no matter what. We will destroy these miserable clansmen, once and for all. They have been an irritating thorn in my side for far too long. I will crush them like the insects they are."

"Yes, my lord," he said, bowing as he backed away and left the room.

Mansa left the throne room and went to look for General Smythe. As he walked down the main hallway, he was suddenly grabbed and pulled into a side hallway by General Collins.

"Mansa, this is madness. I need weeks, possibly months to plan for a proper assault against the Clan. You must say something to him."

"Why should I do that, General?" he replied. "Do you think I want to end up like you, missing an ear, or worse?"

"I'm telling you Mansa, there is no way anyone could have an effective battle plan ready by this evening!"

"Then perhaps I should go ahead and tell him that, so he can schedule your subsequent torture and execution?"

"No, no, please don't do that. I will find a way, somehow."

"I suggest you do just that, and I would make it quick. The sun is already low in the sky. You have only a few hours left before sundown. Battle plan or not, he intends to leave tomorrow. He is growing increasingly impatient waiting to take action. He did not get where he is by constantly waiting."

"That may be," whispered Collins, "but he has never attacked men that have devoted themselves to perfecting their killing art either, has he now?"

Mansa smiled. "That may be Collins, but as I said, if I were you, I would have that plan ready, by nightfall."

Mansa continued down the main hallway to look for General Smythe, as Collins left for his quarters to work on the battle plan. As he slinked away, Collins had a sinking feeling that no matter what happened, he was certain to be dead within a few days, at the hands of the Clan, or Kraken.

***

Mansa was having a difficult time locating Smythe. He decided to walk outside and to the large field where many of the men were lined up. Mansa knew that General Smythe was not like Collins, or the other leaders. He was an exceptional general, one who cared more for his men then he did about himself, not the type Mansa would expect to be working for Kraken. He sometimes wondered why Smythe even served

Kraken. Perhaps he thought it somehow served some greater good, or more likely Kraken held his family somewhere and would have them tortured and put to death if he refused. As he walked over to the field, Mansa began to think about what Collins had said. He was right; they did need more time to prepare for an effective assault against an enemy like the Warrior Clan. Across the field, he saw a man standing, pacing back and forth, as the men practiced some of their drills.

"General Smythe?" The general finished what he was saying to one of his men, and came over to speak with Mansa.

"Yes, Mansa, what can I do for you?"

"Lord Kraken wanted me to relay to you that he expects you to have your men ready to leave tomorrow morning for an assault against the Clan."

"What? Tomorrow morning? Is this some kind of a sick joke, Mansa?"

"General Smythe, you are certainly welcome to go ask Lord Kraken that question yourself if you like. As for me, I'll take a pass on that."

All the general offered in reply was a muted, "Hmm, good point. Tell Lord Kraken that I'll try to have the men ready in the morning."

Mansa just stared and smiled at the general, who threw his hands up in the air, shook his head, and said, "Uh, what I meant to say was that the men will be ready in the morning."

"That's what I thought," Mansa replied, as he turned and walked away.

Mansa walked back to the stronghold, pondering the course of events.

If I survive this, maybe I'll just find me a nice village in the Outlands somewhere to settle down in.

Chapter 32
Two Armies

Ferrell was leaving the barracks on his way to meet with the men when he was abruptly grabbed from behind.

"Do you have to go?" asked Ariel, her hand still on his shoulder. Behind her stood his sister, Tara.

"Yes, Ariel, you know I do, I must go. If we don't stop him, Kraken will capture the Oracle, enslave everyone, and plunge the world into an age of unbearable darkness and misery."

"Before you go then, I want you to know something; I want you to know that I care about you, that ...I ...mean... I care deeply about what happens to you."

Ferrell looked at her and said, "Ariel, I..."

"You be careful then, Ferrell Young, you hear me!" she said as she wrapped her arms around him, kissed him, and ran back inside.

"She's in love with you, brother, you do know that don't you?" Tara remarked.

"Yes, Tara, I know."

"Did you know that she plans to come with me, to help with caring for the wounded on the battlefield?"

"No, she cannot go, she is no warrior!" said Ferrell, with a concerned look on his face. "She's had no training!"

"You try stopping her then, big brother. I tried telling her that it was too dangerous, but she wouldn't listen. She figures that everyone else is risking their lives to stop Kraken, and that she should do the same." Tara watched as Ariel disappeared back into the barracks. "She has a strong spirit, Ferrell, she's a good woman."

"I know, Tara, I know," he said quietly, clearly concerned for her safety.

"Looks like you feel the same way she does," said Tara, smiling at her brother.

Ferrell just looked at his sister, slightly annoyed.

Sanjo suddenly appeared, running from the direction of the Great Hall, where the clansmen were gathering.

"Lord Ferrell, please come quickly."

Ferrell hesitated, looking after Ariel with great longing, fearful he might never see her again.

When Tara noticed the look, her heart went out to her brother. She walked over to Ferrell, and placing her hand on his shoulder she said, "Don't worry big brother. I'll do my best to protect her. I know how much she means to you."

Ferrell looked down at Tara, and felt a great surge of brotherly love for her. "Thank you, Tara. I have another favor to ask you, something that is very important to me."

"Sure, no problem, Ferrell, anything."

Ferrell placed one hand on each of her shoulders, and looking into her eyes, he said, "I want you to take care of yourself as well. I love you, Tara, and I don't want anything to happen to either of you. Be careful out there, promise?"

"Promise. Don't worry about us, big brother; you need to focus on the battle. Just come back to us, okay?"

"I will, I promise," he said, before turning to join Sanjo and the others.

***

They hurried to the Great Hall, where Sanjo led him to the Gathering Room. Lord Sarkoth was talking with one of the scouts when he saw Sanjo and Ferrell.

"Tell him," said Lord Sarkoth. The man looked at Ferrell, still breathing heavily from running to bring news. Ferrell recognized him as Franklin, one of the Clan's best scouts.

"We saw a large army gathering near Kraken's compound. It looked as if they were preparing to march. From the looks of it, they should be ready to leave by tomorrow, the day after tomorrow at the latest."

Sarkoth looked at Ferrell with a question in his eyes.

"Do not worry, my lord," Ferrell said to Sarkoth. "The men have trained long and hard; they are ready."

"What of our plan? Are we prepared to implement our plan?" he asked Ferrell.

"We are as prepared as we can be, my lord."

Ferrell looked at Sanjo. "Will you please spread the word to the other commanders? We must be prepared to leave at first light. We don't know for certain how much time we have, and it is important that we have the best terrain for the battle."

"Of course, Lord Ferrell."

After Sanjo left to carry the message to the commanders, Ferrell looked at Sarkoth, who still wore a look of concern, and said again, "They are ready, my lord."

"Very well," said Sarkoth, shaking off his concern."I will let our Christian Brothers know what is happening. Perhaps they will pray for us, and their God will go with us into this battle, whose outcome will determine the future of the entire world for a thousand years," he said soberly.

As Sarkoth left to meet with Sebastian, Darius, and the other priests, Ferrell left for the open area where the Clan army was conducting training exercises.

When he arrived, he walked along the front of the field, and viewed the men. When the commanders saw Ferrell, they had the men form companies, and lined them up in front of him. As he looked on them, he thought of the coming battle with Kraken. He and Sarkoth had been discussing the strategy for the battle for several weeks. While the clansmen were warriors whose skills were unmatched anywhere in the world, and while they well educated in war strategies, they had little large-scale combat experience. The Clan policy of avoiding contact with the outside for so long had made it largely unnecessary. That, coupled with the fact that there had been no wars for centuries, meant that the enemy had no real experience either, other than the recent Mero Wars. Ferrell and Sarkoth had agreed that Kraken's skirmishes against unskilled urba packs and their merciless assaults against small villages would prove of little value against the Clan army. Nevertheless, unlike Kraken, the Clan valued the lives of their clansmen, and did not want to lose any more then they had to in the coming battle.

Ferrell had recommended dividing the army into seven divisions. He thought it poetic that it matched the number of pieces that made up the map to the Oracle. Four of the division commanders had led the expeditions to retrieve the map. His friend and mentor, David-Michael, would lead one of the three remaining divisions. Josiah and Isaac, two of their top military leaders, would fill the remaining two. While the clan had been nearly as successful as the Church at holding on to some of the knowledge from the Golden Age, they mostly possessed information related to military strategy and the fighting arts. All of the battalion commanders also had at least some knowledge of the "Art of War," a book on military strategy written by Sun Tzu well before the beginning of the Golden Age. Ferrell himself was well versed with the many strategies contained in it. He would strive to employ some of those strategies in the coming battle. From all reports, they would be greatly outnumbered by the enemy, but the Warrior Clan had trained for battle since the Great Collapse.

The battalion commanders had all of their men ready. The cavalry stood out front, followed by the infantry, then the archers. Ferrell prepared to address the men.

"We have just learned that Kraken has been preparing his army of barbarians to lead an assault against the Main Enclave, against us, the Warrior Clan, and our families. They seek to destroy the last remaining hope for restoring civilization to this dark world, to destroy or enslave everyone we know and care about, and to spread fear and chaos across all lands. We are all that stands in the way. Tomorrow, we leave to meet them in the field of battle. Tomorrow, we will teach them the meaning of fear, when they meet fifty-thousand warriors from the Warrior Clan in battle. Then, they will know the meaning of fear!"

"Who are we?"

"Clansmen!" the men replied with one voice.

"Who are we?"

"Clansmen!"

"Who are we?" he asked the third time.

"Clansmen!"

"Yes, we are clansmen. We are the Warrior Clan. We march against an enemy that we must defeat. We march against an enemy that seeks to plunge the world into a time of even greater suffering than it already knows. We march against an enemy that seeks to enslave the world. We fight for ourselves, we fight for our families, we fight for the Church, and we fight for the Clan! Who are we?"

"Clansmen! Clansmen! Clansmen!"

"Yes, we are clansmen. Get plenty of rest my brothers, for tomorrow, we go to war!"

Chapter 33
Rallying the Troops

The sun was barely peaking over the horizon when Mansa returned from checking on the status of the army. As he approached the door, he thought, if only for a moment, about how easy it would be to keep on walking past, instead of walking into, the stronghold. Unfortunately, he suffered from an ailment common to most men; Mansa craved power, and the rewards that came with it. As Kraken's top lieutenant, he had the most to gain should anything "unfortunate" ever happen to his master. Of course, no one would care if Kraken were killed in battle, because no matter how much they enjoyed the power he gave them, most of them feared and despised him even more. No, while Mansa might fantasize about leaving Kraken's service, he already knew he would go inside and bring Kraken the report on the readiness of the men; he was already addicted to the power that came with being Kraken's top man. He entered the stronghold and proceeded to the bedroom, where his master was still asleep. Mansa hated waking Kraken; he really hated waking Kraken.

When Mansa knocked on the door, there was no answer. He knocked a second time but there was still no answer. Kraken had made a late night of it the evening before, as he always did. Mansa wondered why, the night before they faced their most powerful enemy in a battle to the end, it should be any different for Kraken. His arrogance made him both the best and the worst leader at the same time.

Mansa opened the door. "Lord Kraken?" There was still no answer. "Lord Kraken," he repeated.

"What is it you fool, why are you disturbing me again?" Kraken asked from beneath his covers. "Come here so that I can silence that tongue of yours for good."

"I just wanted to let you know that the army is assembled and ready to attack the Clan, my lord."

"Attack the Clan you say? Oh, that's right! Today is the day isn't it?" he asked, sitting up in bed with a smile on his face. "Well, in that case, you may keep your tongue Mansa, at least for another day. Well then, let's get moving. Tell my personal guard to bring my armor, and let us prepare to attack these pathetic clansmen, take their precious map, and be off to find this so-called Oracle then, shall we?"

Mansa summoned the guard and instructed them to bring Kraken's armor and weapons.

"This is a great day, Mansa," Kraken said, as his guards brought in his weapons and armor. "The day I have dreamed of for many years. Once we crush these so-called warriors, there will be nothing, and no one, left that could possibly stand in our way. Once we have crushed their army, we will burn their enclave to the ground. I will personally enjoy squeezing the life out of Sarkoth with my own bare hands!"

As his servants dressed him in his armor, Kraken continued, "Mansa, are the generals prepared to implement the plan that Collins came up with last night?

"They are, Lord Kraken. He and the other generals were up late discussing it."

"Marvelous," he said as the last piece of armor was fastened in place.

Kraken admired himself in the mirror. Unlike the armor worn by the Clan, Kraken and his generals wore armor that was much cruder, made from pieces of light scrap metal they were able to find. They melted the metal and fashioned it into a sort of scale-like armor. While looking ridiculous, the armor was actually quite effective. The only major downside was that scraps of metal were hard to come by, and difficult to work with. Therefore, only Kraken, his generals, and a few of his officers wore armor, the rest wore nothing. A few minutes later, Kraken was fully clad and ready for battle.

"Alright Mansa, let's go outside and say good morning to my army!"

The two walked outside and to the field where the army was gathered. Kraken wanted to give a speech that would so inspire his men that they would charge into the battle and mow right over the clansmen.

As he approached the vast number of men that stood before him, many urbas pressed into service, others conscripts from villages in the Outlands, and some who voluntarily followed Kraken because of his fierce reputation, he grew flush with power over the hundreds of thousands of lives that he now controlled.

As they saw him, many began shouting, "Lord Kraken! Lord Kraken! Lord Kraken!" After this had gone on for fifteen minutes or so, Kraken finally motioned for them to quiet down so he could speak.

"Greetings, men! This morning, we have gathered for a very special occasion. We gather now to destroy our hated enemies, to conquer and squash those that dare to defy us, and to take our rightful place as the masters of these lands. When we are done, we will rule in absolute fear, and all will cower in a land where my word is law, a land where we will plunder and crush all those who dare stand in our way. We will make them our slaves or we will destroy them. What we see that we like, we will take; anything we see that we do not like, we will destroy. I will become ruler of all lands, everywhere. I will command the land and the sea; I will be the absolute ruler over all! No one will stand in our way!"

The chanting resumed. "Lord Kraken! Lord Kraken! Lord Kraken!"

Kraken held his hands back up in the air, gesturing for silence.

"Now there are those that do not want this to happen. They want to stand in our way, between us, and between dreams of uniting these lands. What should we do about this? Should we allow this to happen, or should we crush them underfoot, like the insects that they are!"

"Crush them! Crush them! Crush them! Crush them!"

"Yes, my friends, yes, and we will crush them. The clansmen think they can defeat us, but they are mistaken! We are the Kraken Empire. No one can defeat us; we are unstoppable, we are invincible, we are the Kraken Empire! Now, we go to crush these clansmen insects!"

Kraken and his generals led the men out of the field and toward the Clan's Main Enclave, his army chanting, "Kraken! Kraken! Kraken!"

Chapter 34
The Deciding Strategy

Kraken's commanding general, General Collins, was no fool. While he would never have shared the truth with anyone, other then perhaps Smythe, and especially not with Kraken, he knew all too well that if the Clan was successful in recruiting men from only a modest number of their enclaves, that the battle would be perhaps, evenly matched at best. His hope rested in several factors. First was the sheer size of their army, which was considerably larger than anything the Clan would be able to pull together. Second, he hoped that the Clan would be unable to muster enough clansmen from the remote enclaves in time to meet them on the battlefield. With the capture of David-Michael, that effort had largely ended, and they had no more reports of anyone recruiting clansmen from other enclaves. Of course, the recruitment effort by the Clan likely continued by word of mouth, even after David-Michael had been permanently silenced. Third, they would catch the Clan off-guard with a surprise attack, leaving Sarkoth and his clansmen off-balance, and un-prepared for an assault. Collins knew well that the Clan might learn that they were marching in their general direction before the massive army arrived at the enclave, but he hoped that without enough advance warning, there would be little they could do.

He did not like marching with so little intelligence regarding the enemy. While he had advised Kraken that they needed Bokra's assistance, and he had listened to the sage advice at first, there would be no stopping Kraken's foul temper, which had discouraged Bokra from ever returning. This, along with the unfortunate death of David-Michael while being tortured, had dealt them a crippling blow. Intelligence was often the key to winning decisive battles, and Collins knew it. With both Bokra and David-Michael gone however, Kraken and his men had very little of it; they were going blindly into battle.

Kraken's army consisted mostly of conscripted men, who had no choice but to join or die. His arsenal of siege works included catapults, trebuchets, and a few siege towers. His military units consisted mostly of archers, cavalry, and infantry, armed with bows and arrows, swords, and in some cases, firearms. General Collins was one of the rare individuals alive during the Dark Age, outside of the Clan and the Church, who knew how to read and write. He had spent considerable time learning about warfare from the few books about battle that he had been fortunate to come across in the meros. It was Collins who had built up Kraken's army, had ordered the building of the catapults and the siege towers, the stockpiling of arrows, and the forging of swords.

While Kraken would never acknowledge that he had anyone but himself to thank for his dramatic success and his rapid rise to power, it was not so, for he owed a great debt of gratitude to Collins. Kraken credited his ingenuity in taking Collins wife and daughter prisoner, and locking them away in the dungeon, with helping motivate Collins to work for him. Collins still shuddered at the thought of what Kraken would do to his family should he ever refuse to serve him.

As they traveled the road that led out of the Stronghold and toward the Clan's Main Enclave, he mentally reviewed his battle plan. The cavalry units would ride up front, doubling as scouts, followed by the infantry, followed by the archers, followed lastly by the catapults, trebuchets, and siege towers. Once at the enclave, the siege engines would pound and eventually weaken the fortified defenses at the Enclave, while the archers provided cover for at least some of the infantry. While the Enclave was under the bombardment from the catapults, trebuchets, and the constant volley from the archers, Kraken's infantry would take the battering ram and assault the front gate, what Collins had surmised was probably the weakest link in the protective wall around the enclave. Once the gate gave way, either the Clan's army would pour out, or Kraken's army would pour in. At that point, while Kraken's army would undoubtedly sustain a ridiculously high number of casualties, there could be only one outcome. It was a simple strategy, true, but it was the best that he had been able to develop with such short notice, and a missing ear.

A natural and brilliant strategist, had he been afforded more time, General Collins would have developed a much more thorough and elaborate battle plan. His enemy was considerably more skilled and dangerous than Kraken's men, so he would have thoroughly prepared for various scenarios, and developed strategic and tactical plans for dealing with the clansmen if they found the Clan waiting for Kraken's army to arrive, but he had not had time. As night began to fall, Collins leaned over to Kraken, who was riding next to him.

"My lord, perhaps we should stop and make camp for the night. We need the men to be well rested at first light, so they will be ready to crush our enemy completely."

Kraken looked at Collins as if to say something, but then simply stopped and agreed. As soon as they dismounted from their horses, one of their cavalrymen returned from patrol with a prisoner.

The man quickly dismounted his horse and ran over to the two men, looking at Collins first and then at Kraken.

"Lord Kraken. We intercepted this man and some clansmen attempting to make it back to the Enclave. Fortunately, we had them greatly outnumbered, and unprepared for us; we caught them completely by surprise. They killed most of my men, but we were able to capture this man before we made our escape.

Kraken looked at the man and asked, "Who are you?" The man said nothing.

Collins responding said, "My lord, perhaps this man is from one of their expeditions to the distant meros! Look at his garments. Though they are completely worn out, you can clearly see this man is a priest of the Church!"

Kraken looked at the man once more and screaming, he repeated, "Tell me who you are, priest!" He smacked the man, knocking him to the ground. Mansa walked over, began searching the man's belongings, and found a pack. He looked inside the pack and then, looking at Kraken, he broke into a large grin that stretched from ear to ear.

"Well, well, well, look what we have here! What do you think this might be, Lord Kraken?" he asked, as he held up a piece of cloth with a drawing and some scribbling on it.

Kraken smiled back and said, "Well I am not sure now mind you, but it looks like a map to me!" he roared, holding both hands up in triumph. "General Collins, I want you to triple this man's rations for a day," he said, pointing toward the cavalryman. "He's made me a happy man! I think this calls for a celebration!" Kraken pulled out his firearm and fired five shots in the air, terrifying most of his men and all of his horses, which, startled by the noise, tried desperately to escape, but could not.

Meanwhile, as Brother Wayne lay in the grass bleeding, a tear merged with the blood as it trickled down his face.

Chapter 35
The Day Before

The clansman stood still as if he were made of rock. The sound was faint at first, but soon grew louder, into a dull roar. He quickly turned the reins and the horse obeyed. He led the steed off the main road and behind some trees. He then forced his horse to lie down as the sounds approached, and he did the same. There were horses, many horses, and the voices of many men talking. They seemed excited. The voices grew more distinct as they drew closer. They were near, very near. He looked out and saw them coming around the same bend of road that he had been on earlier, before he first heard them coming. As he lay with the horse concealed behind a small hill and some trees, he observed a man, a prisoner, walking beside one of the lead horses, dressed like one of the priests back at the enclave. He surmised that the enemy had captured him on his way back to the enclave. The clansman decided he would try to discover what was causing all of the commotion.

"We have it Mansa, we have a map!" gloated Kraken.

"Yes, Lord Kraken, but we only have one of the seven pieces."

"Well, we will just have to get the other six pieces when we arrive at the enclave tomorrow, eh Mansa?"

"At least we now know what they were so busy looking for. They can never find the Oracle without it, my lord."

"So true, so true."

The clansman slowly and carefully let his horse stand back up, and walked it on a path that was perpendicular to the road Kraken's army was on. He considered making a dash for the map, but decided if he failed to retrieve it, none of the clansmen would ever know that Kraken had it, nor would they know he was coming with such a large army. He thought better of the idea, and decided to head back to tell Ferrell.

Once well clear of the advancing army, the clansman scout quickly went from a trot to a full gallop. He took several small paths that were shortcuts, big enough for a single rider but far too small for an advancing army. He finally joined up with the other clansmen about two hours later, just as they were stopping to make camp for the night. They immediately took him to Ferrell.

"Lord Ferrell, I have urgent news."

"What is it my brother, tell me."

"It is Kraken, my lord; he has captured a priest, and one of the pieces of the map that leads to the Oracle. He must have intercepted one of the expeditions as they returned from the foreign land."

Ferrell sat for several minutes, contemplating a course of action. "Listen, take this news back to Lord Sarkoth immediately, and tell him that I suggested he send Bokra... he will understand."

"Yes sir!"

"Now make haste boy, there are many lives riding on this information. You must hurry, and be certain that you are not discovered by Kraken's men!"

"Yes, my lord," he replied, as the young warrior scout mounted his horse once more, and made for the enclave.

"Ride like the wind, clansman!" Ferrell yelled after the scout as he rode out of camp.

***

The scout and the horse were both exhausted when they arrived at the enclave a short time later. It took a few minutes for him to catch his breath enough for him to be able to say to one of the guards. "I have some important information, and a message for Lord Sarkoth from Lord Ferrell. I must speak to him at once, it is urgent."

A few minutes later Lord Sarkoth appeared. "What is it, young rider?" he asked.

He relayed the story about the priest and the map, as well as Ferrell's message, to Sarkoth, who appeared discouraged upon hearing the news about the map, and perplexed about the reference to Bokra, but only for a few moments. "Ahhh, I see. Excellent idea, Ferrell," he said to himself, as he looked over at one of the guards. "Bring Bokra to me, at once!"

Bokra walked into the receiving area where Sarkoth was seated. "Yes my lord?"

"Bokra?" began Sarkoth. "I want to offer you a choice, and a chance to redeem yourself, are you interested?"

"I am, my lord."

"I must warn you; that in all likelihood, you will not survive this mission."

"Lord Sarkoth, I am a clansman, taught to not fear death. Besides, I deserve to die for my betrayal. This is my doing. Had I not gone to Kraken, he would not have known about the map; I would welcome an opportunity to make amends. Besides, I would prefer to die with honor, especially if my death means that others may live, rather than living out the rest of my life in shame."

"If you fail, it will mean an end to the hopes and dreams that our people have had for almost five-hundred years, do you understand?"

"Yes, Lord Sarkoth. I am honored that you are willing to trust me, especially after what I've done. I will not fail you."

"Good. Then you must travel to Kraken's camp under pretense of bringing him important new information. You must save the priest, and bring back the map he was carrying when he was captured by Kraken. Can you can do this?"

"Yes, Lord Sarkoth, or I will die trying."

"Then go, and may the Christian God be with you."

***

After getting more details from the scout in regards to the location of Kraken's camp, Bokra took a horse and made for Kraken's camp. Though it was dark when he arrived, Bokra could not help but gasp in horror at the mere size of Kraken's army. Campfires lit up the countryside as far as the eye could see, like a forest full of fireflies. He was stopped around a half-mile up the road from the camp.

"You there, where do you think you're going?"

"I am here to see Lord Kraken, my name is Bokra, and I have valuable information for him." The man left for a few minutes and returned with Mansa.

"Well, Bokra. We really didn't expect to see you again. Your timing is fortuitous, what information do you have for us?"

"I need to speak with Kraken in person," said Bokra.

"Well, that may be a while as he is preoccupied at the moment."

"I can wait," answered Bokra.

Bokra walked around the camp, looking for the priest, and the map. As he approached Kraken's tent, he heard screams of pain, the screams of a man being tortured. Bokra concluded that the priest and the map were likely in Kraken's tent.

"Lord Kraken," said Mansa, sticking his head in the tent.

Jeff. W. Horton

"What is it this time, Mansa, you fool?" roared Kraken. "Why must you always disturb me when I am having fun? This old man will tell me what I want to know, now won't you old man?" he asked, slicing into the priest's flesh on his arm and pulling back another layer of skin. The priest, who was unable to endure any more pain, mercifully passed out.

"Now Mansa, tell me what is so important that you disturb me yet again?" he growled.

"The clansman traitor Bokra is here my lord. He claims that he has some important information to share with you, information he says that you will want to hear immediately."

"Well then, send the traitorous dog in. And tell him this had better be good." Mansa led Bokra in to see Kraken. When Bokra saw the condition of the priest, he felt an intense urge to vomit, for the priest barely even resembled a man anymore. Bokra doubted the priest would live to see another day.

Kraken sat on a makeshift throne, apparently now in a better mood. It occurred to Bokra that torture seemed to bring Kraken great pleasure. What a monster.

"Well Bokra, you worm, where have you been? Mansa tells me you have news. Now, tell me what you have for me quickly, before I put a swift end to your miserable life." Bokra casually glanced around the tent as he approached Kraken. He saw what he thought was a map sitting out on a table on the far side of the tent.

"Lord Kraken, forgive me if I seemed in anyway disrespectful when last we met." He was biding for time, trying to find a way to get the priest and the map out. The priest was in terrible condition. He doubted the priest would make it much longer without his help.

"Is that the information that you considered so important that you came here to tell me and interrupt my fun?"

"No, of course not, my lord," answered Bokra.

"Then tell me what you have for me, now," roared Kraken, "or this miserable priest will not be the only one I play with this night!"

"Most of the expeditions sent out by the Clan and the Church have recently returned, all except for two. I assume that this may be one of them?" he asked, motioning toward the priest.

"It is. This is good information that you bring then Bokra, for tomorrow, we will attack your miserable "Warrior Clan." We will be prying the other maps from Sarkoth's cold, dead, fingers by this time tomorrow. So one expedition has yet to return?"

"Yes, my lord. It sailed to one of the more distant lands."

Kraken looked at the priest, still passed out on the floor.

"I believe this old fool will die before he translates what is on the map for me."

"Maybe I could help, my lord?" asked Bokra. Kraken looked at Bokra, trying to discern his intentions.

"What do you mean? Exactly how do you intend to do that?" asked Kraken.

"The priest does not know that I have betrayed the Church and the Clan. Perhaps, if I was able to gain his confidence, I could get him to tell me what you want to know."

Kraken looked a little disappointed.

"But then afterwards, you could do whatever you wanted to with him," added Bokra.

Kraken then smiled. "What is your plan?"

"Let me talk with him. I will tell him that I am here to rescue him and the map. I will tell him that he needs to tell me what it says, just in case something should happen to him and the map on the way back to the enclave."

"Perhaps you are here to rescue him and the map," said Kraken with a cold stare.

"You said it yourself, Lord Kraken, the last time we met. If Sarkoth finds out that I have betrayed him, he will have me killed himself. Besides, you and your men can wait just outside the tent. We will make as if we are escaping, but as soon as he tells us what he knows, you can have him seized and um…finish what you started earlier."

Kraken started laughing. "Bokra, I find you more interesting each time I see you. Your people are usually so…boring. You are considerable more colorful then your brethren." After studying Bokra for several moments, Kraken stood up. "Very well, we will do as you suggested Bokra. But make no mistake about it, if it looks like you are up to something, I will kill you myself, understood?"

"Of course, my lord."

"Very well, I will leave before the old fool wakes up. Find out what I want to know quickly Bokra, my patience is thin and I have a war to fight."

Kraken left the tent, leaving Bokra alone with the priest and the map. Bokra made for the map, folded it up, and placed it inside his cloak. He then walked over to Brother Wayne, and holding his head up with one hand, he gently patted him on the cheek, trying to wake him.

"Priest, priest, wake up!" he whispered. Brother Wayne opened his eyes briefly before passing back out. Bokra walked over to a table and brought back a cup of water, splashed a little on his face, and offered it to the priest, once he was able to rouse him for more than a few moments. Gradually, some light came back into the priest's eyes, and he groaned in pain.

"Who are you? Have you come to torture me too?"

"No, Brother, I am a clansman, my name is Bokra. Do you not remember me from the Council meeting, before you left out to retrieve the map?"

"No, I...yes, I do remember you. Bokra you say. That's right, I remember you, I am Brother Wayne."

"Brother Wayne, I need for you to tell me what the map says."

"No, no, we need to get out of here, now!" exclaimed Brother Wayne, still in shock from the torture. "We must find some horses and escape!"

"Brother, if I find us some horses, then will you tell me what the map says? You should tell me in case something happens to you and the map, so we can still find the Oracle!"

"Okay my son, find us some horses, and I will read what is on the map."

"Okay, I'll see what I can do. You wait here and I will be back in a moment."

"No, no, do not leave me here!" Bokra looked at the priest and was almost overwhelmed with pity, and guilt. The priest would have readily sacrificed himself if it meant not betraying the Church and the Clan; at least, he would have been willing to give up his life. Doubtless, he would eventually break under the torture, unless he died first.

Bokra walked over to the tent opening and looked out, feigning as if he was checking to see if the coast was clear. He was in fact looking to see that Kraken and his men had heard what was said. It soon became evident that they had been listening, as one of them brought a horse close to the tent and tied it off next to Bokra's, before clearing the area.

"Okay Brother Wayne, it is clear now. Please, come with me." The priest limped over to Bokra, who helped him onto the horse. Bokra then spoke quietly but loudly enough that he felt the others would overhear. "Here climb up on the horse and then tell me what the map says." The priest climbed on the horse and just as he was starting to speak, Bokra leapt up on his own horse and started galloping away, with Wayne leading the way. Kraken and his men soon realized what was happening, and having prepared for such a betrayal, the archers fired at them from behind. Trailing far behind the priest, Bokra took great pains to make his horse weave back and forth, creating a more difficult harder target for the archers, one of them got lucky as his arrow found its target, striking and piercing Bokra's shoulder from behind. The clansman then pushed his steed hard, until he was able to reach Wayne. Bokra reached into his cloak, pulled out the map, and handed it over to the priest.

"Brother Wayne, here is the map. Our camp is just an hour's ride down this road between these two mountains. I will hold them off for as long as I can. You must hurry Brother, or they will catch and kill you."

"I understand."

"Forgive me, Brother Wayne," he said, before turning to block the road, preventing Kraken's men from catching the fleeing priest. Bokra was a clansman once more as he fought furiously, killing Kraken's men one after another. This was his chance to right a wrong, the chance to redeem his honor and his name. He was like the whirlwind, his blade flashing as it reflected the light of the moon, allowing no one to pass. Bokra fought on for close to an hour, before eventually, succumbing to exhaustion and his injury, he fell off his horse and onto the ground, satisfied he had redeemed himself by giving their mission a chance at succeeding.

***

Brother Wayne looked for a moment at the mighty clansman, who fought so courageously to give him a chance to escape with the map, and after making the sign of the cross he turned, and made haste for the Clan's camp. Brother Wayne rode furiously for what seemed like an eternity, calling upon what little remained of his strength just to stay on the horse. Though he saw no one as he looked back, he knew that riders would be following hard after him along the long, winding mountain road once Bokra fell, so he rode on, praying for the strength to hold on until he reached the clansmen's camp.

***

They rode on as hard and fast as they could, knowing the suffering they would endure if they failed to catch the miserable priest. He was almost an hour's ride ahead of them, but he was weak and severely injured from being tortured by Kraken. There would be no excuses if they failed. They travelled for quite some time until they saw lights up ahead and slowed to investigate the source. Campfires dotted the landscape below them as far as the eye could see. Tying their horses out of site, from the edge of a large drop-off they looked down at the large

245

gathering of clansmen at the camp. They had not expected to see clansmen this close, especially so many. Terror gripped them before they quickly turned tail, and made for their own camp. As they sped away, they began to fear that they would not survive the coming battle.

***

"What? What are you talking about?" He grabbed one of the men, smacked him, and threw him to the ground. "You saw what?"

"An army of clansmen, Lord Kraken."

Kraken yelled for Mansa who quickly responded.

"Yes, my lord?"

"Bring me General Collins, now!" After a few minutes, Mansa returned with General Collins.

"Collins, this man says there is an army of clansmen no more then two hour's ride down this road. How is this possible, and what are you going to do about it?" General Collins looked at the man on the ground and knelt down on the ground beside him.

"How many would you say there were, ten-thousand, twenty-thousand, more? Tell me what you saw."

The man answered, "After the clansman fell, we followed the priest for another two hours at a full gallop. As we started closing in, we saw lights in the distance in a large open field. There were tents everywhere. There must have been at least fifty thousand men there, as far as the eye could see. We left in a hurry, so we could come back and tell you what we had seen."

"Yes, of course," said General Collins.

"Well?" barked Kraken.

Collins shrugged his shoulders. "We knew this was a possibility, Lord Kraken. Somehow, they must have learned that we were preparing to march, and decided to intercept us in the field, where they felt they would have the advantage. Of course, it's possible that they were preparing to fight us anyway."

"Well, what do you intend to do about this, Collins?"

"There is not a lot we can do about this my lord, had you given me more time to prepare..."

Kraken lunged at General Collins and pulled his blade with blinding speed, so fast in fact that Collins did not have a chance to react before Kraken landed on top of him, pinning him to the ground, with his knife at Collins' throat.

"Were it not for us going to battle tomorrow, I would most surely have killed you just now," he said with a snarl.

"My lord," said General Collins, gasping for air under the weight of Kraken's considerable frame, "We can proceed as planned. We have far superior numbers. There is little chance of help coming to their aid from the remote enclaves at this point."

"Listen Collins," he said, "if the battle goes badly tomorrow, guess whose family will rot to death in the dungeons of my stronghold? Guess which in your family will die first?"

Kraken got up and told them all to get out. It was late and his war would likely start the first thing in the morning.

Chapter 36
The Night Before

Norris was still on his knees when Brother Sebastian kneeled down and performed Last Rites for Brother Wayne. He brought out the anointing oil, and began placing it on his head and on his hands.

"I'm so sorry Brother Wayne! I failed you, and the Clan, and by doing so, I have endangered the entire mission! By failing to protect you when you needed me the most, I allowed them to capture and kill you. Please forgive me!"

Wayne struggled to open his eyes and look at Norris, whose eyes were beginning to well up with tears. "There is nothing to forgive, my friend! There were far too many, there was nothing you could have done. "

"I will avenge you, Brother, with my last breath I will avenge you, I promise!"

Sebastian, who had stopped the Last Rites to give the men a chance to talk, continued.

"Through this holy anointing may the Lord in his love and mercy help you with the grace of the Holy Spirit," and on his hands "May the Lord who frees you from sin save you and raise you up. " Sebastian sat down next to Norris and waited for the end.

Not long after Sebastian finished administering the rites, Brother Wayne died. Soon after his passing, and after collecting Bokra's body, the priests and the clansmen all gathered for the funerals of Brother Wayne and Clansman Bokra. Sebastian walked up front and faced the gathering.

"Brothers, clergy and clansman alike, let us remember today the courage and bravery shown by these two men, Brother Wayne and Clansman Bokra.

"I knew Brother Wayne for a long time, having served with him long ago in a distant land. I remember on one occasion, there was a family that lived near our church. They were farmers, with a number of animals around the farm. One day, as we were walking back after visiting with this family, Brother Wayne stepped into a little something left behind by one of those animals that lived on the farm. Brother Wayne let out some words that would make an urba blush!" Brother Sebastian started laughing and continued, "I said to him, 'now Brother Wayne that is not becoming of a young priest!' He answered me, 'That may be true Sebastian, but if the Lord has no room for the occasional lapse of the tongue, he should never have permitted men to become farmers!'" The priests and clansmen smiled.

Sebastian continued, "I know that most of you now know of the death of our brother Bokra, as well. He died trying to save Brother Wayne and the map, giving him time to get away with one of the seven pieces of the map that had also fallen into Kraken's hands. I know that some of you are also aware that Bokra had betrayed us by carrying news of the expeditions to find the maps to Kraken in the first place, and that some lives were lost because of his betrayal. Nevertheless, our Lord and Savior Jesus Christ taught his disciples long ago, 'No greater love has any man than this; that a man lays down his life, for a friend.' Bokra sinned when he betrayed us all by going to Kraken. In the end, however, he repented of his sin, and greatly regretted what he had done. He asked Lord Sarkoth only that he might redeem himself by retrieving the map, and Brother Wayne."

Sebastian paused, looking around at the clansmen gathered around him. "I know that some of you are Christian, and that some of you are not. It is certainly my prayer that tonight, all of you will come to know the Lord Jesus Christ as the Son of God, that you will acknowledge him as your savior, and that you will be baptized, before going into battle tomorrow. Would any of you like to do this now?"

One man stood, and walked over to Sebastian, followed by another man, and then another, and then another. So many came that the priest had to ask for more water several times. When the last person had been baptized, the priest said, "Now brothers, tomorrow you go into battle. Let us now go to the Lord in prayer with one accord. Please bow your heads now as we pray.

"Most Holy Father God, we ask that you go with us tomorrow as we fight against your enemies, as these brave men go to fight with Kraken and his enormous horde; we ask that you fight for us Lord. We ask that you strike down our enemy in battle, oh Lord. We ask that we may fulfill your will, and restore civilization once more to this world.

Now Oh Lord, we ask once again that you will bless us, not only in tomorrow's battle, but also in our quest to retrieve the remaining piece of the map, and to find the Oracle."

Sebastian then raised his hands and said, "And now brothers, please receive the benediction. May the Lord bless you and keep you. May the Lord make his face to shine upon you. May the Lord lift up his countenance upon you, and give you peace."

Immediately following the funeral, Ferrell, David-Michael, and Sarkoth met together in the main tent, discussing the strategy for the coming battle.

"It sounds as if we will be heavily outnumbered," said David-Michael. "What can we do to level the playing field?"

Lord Sarkoth sat with his chin buried in his chest, lost in deep thought, for several moments before looking up.

"Though much history was lost during the Great Collapse," he began,"the Clan has been able to hold onto some knowledge of ancient battles. There was one battle in particular that I have been struggling to recall the details of, something about the ancient Greeks, when they were heavily outnumbered, ahh–now I remember. Do either of you remember hearing of the Battle of Thermopylae, in Ancient Greece, when three-hundred Spartans battled a horde of ancient Persians? During this ancient battle, it was said that three-hundred men blocked a pass that the vastly larger Persian army would use to invade their land. This small group of men was able to successfully hold the vastly large number of Persians at bay."

Ferrell looked at David-Michael, who shrugged his shoulders, and then back at Sarkoth. "What do you have in mind, Lord Sarkoth?" he asked. Sarkoth pointed to a location of the map sketched on the cloth before him.

"I propose that we meet his army here, at this narrow valley," Sarkoth replied. He pointed to a point on the map where a large open area led to two large hills with a narrow passage in between. "His men must pass through this passage on their way to the enclave. We will need to leave just before first light in order to arrive there before Kraken and his men. We can setup an ambush here, before they arrive. If we are fortunate enough to have Kraken leading the way, we will cut off the head so that the serpent dies. If he is not in front, he will still be forced to funnel his men through this narrow pass in order to get here."

"We will have leveled the playing field by eliminating his advantage, his superior numbers," finished Ferrell. "Very clever, Lord

Sarkoth, clever indeed! Should we bring our heavier weapons as well Lord Sarkoth, along with our firearms?"

"We can bring in our heavy weapons, like the cannons, but we will leave the revolvers here. Men who have little or no training with the sword could too easily use them against us in battle. No, we will face these men armed with our swords, our martial skill, and with our courage."

Sarkoth sat back down and frowned.

"What is it Lord Sarkoth?" asked Ferrell, a bit concerned by the Elder's look of consternation.

"I fear that this battle could last for a long time, my brothers, and that many lives will be lost. They still hold superior numbers, though we have the superior fighting skill. If only there were a way that we could shorten the battle, end it more quickly, and decisively."

David-Michael studied the map for a few moments and said, "Lord Sarkoth, I just thought of something that might help end this battle in a timely and decisive manner."

Chapter 37
Preparations

All around him, the world was already buzzing with activity that would usher in a new day. A radiant sun was just starting to peek over the horizon, and Ferrell thought he spotted a couple of young bucks in the woods up ahead. A misty fog hovered just above the field they were passing through, as well as over a large lake just ahead and to the left of them. Fish were jumping as he and the other clansmen passed by the lake on horseback, adding to the chorus of cicadas that still sang loudly, while birds began chirping, joining in nature's symphony.

As they approached the woods, Ferrell's thoughts drifted back to Tara and Ariel, and their conversation the night before.

"Ferrell, do you have a moment?" Tara asked, sticking her head in his tent.

"Of course, Tara, come in," said Ferrell.

Tara walked in, followed unexpectedly by Ariel.

"We both wanted to say good luck tomorrow," Tara said, before wrapping her arms around him. "I love you so much, brother; I just wanted to make sure you knew that!"

"I know that, Sis," he said, gently patting her on the back," and I love you too. Don't worry, I'll be okay."

Ariel moved close to Ferrell as Tara stepped aside. Ariel leapt into his arms and kissed him passionately, so much it made Tara blush.

"I know you're busy Ferrell, but I had to see you. I had to make sure you know how much I love you, that I've loved you from the moment I first laid eyes on you many years ago. Please be careful tomorrow, I won't be able to bear it if something happens to you now, just as we are getting to really know one another!"

"I will do my best, Ariel, I promise. I've wanted to talk with you as well. Listen, I'm not the most pleasant fellow to be around at times, in

253

fact, I'm certain that I can be most disagreeable when I set my mind to it. But ever since I met you, I mean, since we began spending more time together, well, I've felt more alive than I ever thought possible. What I'm trying to say Ariel, is that once this is all over, well, maybe we could talk about what the future might hold?"

"Oh, Ferrell!" She kissed him again, before pulling him close into an intimate embrace. Finally, Ferrell pulled back slightly and gently placed his hands on her slight shoulders.

"You should probably leave now, Ariel. We are going to have a long day tomorrow and will be leaving early, and there is still some more planning to do. Thank you, both of you, for coming, I can't tell you how much it means to know you care," he said, reaching for his sister's hand while still embracing Ariel. The three of them embraced for several minutes, before preparing to leave.

"We will be there with you tomorrow, Ferrell, though we will be in the rear, tending to the wounded," said Tara.

Ferrell turned to Ariel. "Ariel, I would try to talk you out of going, but I suspect it would be pointless." Ariel just smiled in affirmation. "Tara has had martial training and is a formidable warrior."

"Thank you, brother!" interrupted Tara, beaming with pride.

Ferrell continued,"Please listen to everything Tara tells you tomorrow, Ariel. It could save your life, and that means everything to me." Ferrell looked deeply into her eyes, and found himself longing to spend more time there with her. "Please be careful tomorrow," he told her. "I have a lot of catching up to do when this is all over, with both of you."

"We will–and Ferrell?"

"Yes?"

"I lo…" Ferrell put his hand over her mouth.

"Wait and tell me after this is all over, okay?"

"But I…," she started again.

"After, okay?" Ferrell asked, looking at her warmly.

"Okay," she finally agreed, "when this is all over."

***

Ferrell turned his attention back to the present, and noticed that the sun was rising and the darkness quickly fading. The men proceeded quietly as instructed, lest an enemy scout should hear them and alert Kraken's army to the waiting ambush. They had to keep the element of surprise on their side; it was a crucial element of their strategy.

"The pass is just ahead my lord, through these woods," said Julius, in a low, hushed voice.

Ferrell nodded. "Have any of the scouts reported back yet? I need to know where they are, and we need to get our cannons and archers in place as quickly as possible."

"No, my lord, none have reported back as of yet." Just as he had finished speaking these words, a lone rider appeared from the woods. He came up and pulled up next to Ferrell.

"My lord."

"What news do you have? Did you find them?" he asked.

"Yes, they have not broken camp yet. They are still several miles on the other side of the pass. It looked like some of the leaders were standing over a map talking, but most of the men were still asleep."

"How many men would you estimate there were?" asked Ferrell.

"I saw as many men as you might see blades of grass in the field, my lord. I would say there were easily a hundred thousand men, probably more, and that is a conservative estimate."

Ferrell just nodded his head. "That is just about what we expected to find, isn't it Ferrell?" asked David-Michael, who came up beside him on the other side.

"Yes it is, but I had hoped that we were mistaken."

Ferrell and the others led the men through the woods, relieved that they were going to have time to position their men before Kraken and his men arrived. They had gambled that traveling in the darkness and then through the woods would help serve as cover in the event Kraken had any advance scouts out on the main roads, which he almost certainly would. Once the clansmen were in position, no scouts would be able to get back through the pass to warn Kraken but until then, they must be extremely careful.

They would soon be approaching their position at the Western Pass, in front of where Kraken's army would emerge. It was the only way through the mountains for many miles. On either side of the pass were large fields, which would play an important strategic role in the coming battle. As they began to emerge from the woods, the other commanders came up beside Ferrell.

"David-Michael, I'd like for you take the cannons and the archers and get them into position. Remember the plan; wait for the signal then hit them with everything you've got, before dropping back to provide cover for the infantry."

"Consider it done," said David-Michael.

"Julius, go ahead and send a company of men to guard the pass in case any scouts try to make it back through. Then, get the cavalry into position. I need you to divide their ranks, Julius, don't let me down!"

"I will not, Lord Ferrell."

Suddenly a lone rider took off across the open field, making for the pass.

"A scout, trying to make it back to warn Kraken," said Ferrell. "He must not make it through that pass!"

"Do not worry, Lord Ferrell," said Sanjo confidently, "he won't!" Sanjo took a bow and quiver from one of the archers and taking his time, placed the arrow on the bow, timing the pace the scout was making across the field, and getting just the right angle.

"Sanjo!" exclaimed Ferrell.

"Do not worry, my lord Ferrell, I will not miss!" he said confidently, just before letting the arrow fly. They all watched as the arrow sailed through the morning sky. Just when it looked as if the rider would make it through the pass, they breathed a collective sigh of relief when they saw the rider suddenly fall from his horse. The relief lasted but a moment however, as they watched the horse continue making its way through the pass and out of sight.

"Do you think they will find the horse, question what happened to its rider, and send more scouts to investigate?" asked Julius.

"No, I don't think so. Even if they do suspect something, I don't believe that Kraken would wait another hour to launch his attack, much less another day. From what I'm told, he is as impatient as he is brutal."

"I'll see to the cannons and archers now, Ferrell," said David-Michael.

"And I'll get those men guarding the pass," said Julius, before turning and disappearing amongst the men.

David-Michael worked to get the cannons and the archers ready, positioning the canons in the front and the archers behind them at strategic locations along either side of the pass, careful to ensure they were at proper angles for crossfire. He placed the cannons while Julius positioned men on either side of the pass; tree lines on both sides would enable the warriors to remain out of view until Kraken's men had passed through.

Sanjo stood next to Ferrell as they watched the infantry form companies on the battlefield. Every clansman wore full armor and was heavily armed, leaving only his firearm behind.

"Remember, Sanjo, our strategy is to take advantage of the narrow pass, where Kraken's army will be forced to pass through in smaller numbers. Once half of his army has made it through, we will begin bombarding them with cannons and arrows, in waves. We will then send in the cavalry in a wedge formation, breaking through their ranks, and throwing their men into disarray, before separating into smaller regiments, with three regiments guarding the pass and blocking off retreat. Another will accompany the infantry, protecting them as they progress. The plan is to divide the infantry as well, into two regiments, one in the front, and one in the rear. The one in the rear will rest while the one in the front will fight. As they tire, the two groups of warriors will swap places, allowing fresh warriors to replace weary ones. Archers and cannons will be in position at an angle behind both groups, continually assaulting Kraken's army as it comes through the pass."

"It is a sound strategy, Lord Ferrell," said Sanjo.

"Having the high ground will be a deciding factor as well," added Ferrell. He then turned to face Sanjo. "Sanjo, I want you to find Norris, take your infantry regiments; and get them into position. First however, I want you to find Sergei, and send him to me immediately." Sanjo turned to leave when Ferrell yelled after him.

"And Sanjo, please remind the men about what they are fighting for, the very survival of the Clan, and their families!"

"Yes, Lord Ferrell." Sanjo dashed off in search of Sergei, finding him a short while later near the front of the gathering on the field, with Yoshi, near the entrance to the Western Pass, where Kraken would soon pass through. They were each sharpening their swords.

"Clansman Sergei, Lord Ferrell wants you to report to him immediately."

"Thank you, Sanjo. Do you know what he wants, I don't want to miss anything," he said, smiling at Yoshi with a peculiar mixture of solemnity and humor.

"He didn't say, he only said immediately." Sanjo turned to leave before stopping and turning around. "Have either of you seen Norris?"

Sergei and Yoshi shook their heads, before Sergei took off at a fast trot toward Ferrell's tent. Sanjo then turned and disappeared into the mass of clansmen.

Sergei found Ferrell waiting for him outside of the tent, already dressed in full battle armor. Yoshi could see the weight of responsibility weighing heavily on his friend's shoulders.

"Lord Ferrell, you wished to see me?"

"Yes Sergei. We don't have much time so I will make it quick. I have a…favor to ask of you."

"Anything, Lord Ferrell, name it."

"You know my sister, Tara?"

"I do indeed, my lord. She is one of the fiercest, and loveliest, fighters I have ever seen! She is a lioness, Lord Ferrell."

"I hope so Sergei, because she will be on the field of battle today, tending to our wounded."

"I see," answered Sergei, an expression of concern on his face.

"She will not be alone either. There is another…woman…that I care deeply for; she will be working alongside Tara, caring for our wounded. She has no training, Sergei, I fear for her safety."

"Then fear no more, my lord, I will stay close to both of them until this is all over. I will gladly lay down my life for them, Lord Ferrell."

"Thank you Sergei. Clearly, our priority has to be stopping Kraken, so I don't expect you to stay with them the entire time, just check on them from time to time, as you are able, if you would."

"I will do it, my lord, do not worry," said Sergei.

"Thank you, my dear friend, I am greatly in your debt," Ferrell told him, placing his hand on Sergei's shoulder. Sergei, in turn, placed his hand on Ferrell's.

"No, Lord Ferrell, it is I who am in your debt. I missed you, those years you were gone. It's good to have you back, old friend."

Ferrell took a deep breath, holding back the intense emotion that one finds only amongst friends that have faced death together, and said simply, "It's good to be back, Sergei."

Seeking to lighten the moment, Sergei adeptly changed the subject. "So, how are we doing?"

"Well, while having a larger army can certainly be a decisive advantage during a battle, it can also be a decisive disadvantage when an army needs to move quickly. By dividing our smaller number into even smaller divisions, we were able to move our men over much longer distances than we would have been able to do with a single, much larger army. It's enabled us to arrive here ahead of Kraken, and prepare for the battle, allowing us to choose the location, as well as taking the high ground. I'd say we are doing okay, so far."

"Do you think we can win this thing?" Sergei asked, with an expression of hope written all over his face.

"I know we can, Sergei, I have no doubts whatsoever."

"Then let's do it!" said Sergei. "Don't worry about your family, I will look after them."

"I never said the other woman was a member of my family."

"I know what you said, Lord Ferrell, I know," Sergei said, smiling, as he made his way back with the others.

Ferrell looked out over the Clansman Army, which was spread out before him. He and Sarkoth had divided the Clan Army into three divisions; heavy artillery/archers, cavalry, and infantry. Julius led the cavalry, David-Michael the heavy artillery, with Sanjo and Norris leading the infantry. Altogether over fifty-thousand soldiers of the Warrior Clan stood ready and determined to defeat a vile and merciless enemy.

An hour later, everything was in place and the men were ready. By the time they had finished deployment, the sun was already high in the sky. The five men met together on horseback in the middle of the field before assuming their respective positions.

"It will not be long now," said Julius.

"I believe you're right," replied Ferrell. "Kraken's generals will want to move quickly, hoping to strike early and catch us unprepared."

"Do you think he knows we are here?" asked Sanjo.

"He may be aware of some troop movements, but I doubt he suspects we are here waiting for him," answered Ferrell.

"No matter the outcome, Lord Ferrell, it is a great honor to serve under you once again," Norris said to Ferrell, bowing his head in respect.

"I agree. I can think of no one that I would rather fight beside, Clansman Ferrell," echoed David-Michael.

"Nor I," said Julius.

"The honor is all mine," said Ferrell, managing a slight smile." He surveyed the field and noted the sun's position in the sky. "They should be here any minute. Tell the men to make ready."

Chapter 38
The Final Battle

Ferrell had arrived back at his position at the top of an opposing hill no more than five minutes when a scout on horseback came galloping into camp.

"Lord Ferrell, they are coming!"

He looked at the pass and while he could not yet see them, he thought he heard the wind carrying the faint sound of tens of thousands of footsteps, off in the distance. As they drew closer, voices joined the drumbeat of the march of a hundred-thousand men. To Ferrell, they sounded more like belligerent barbarians then they did an army. Looking down from above, Ferrell watched as Kraken's men slowly began trickling through the pass, while the clansmen stayed hidden, out of the enemy's field of view. Ferrell motioned to the scout to come closer.

"Did you see Kraken?" he asked him.

"No, my lord, I did not."

Ferrell grimaced as he took the flag in his right hand, looking toward the pass and then toward David-Michael, who stood ready with the cannons and archers. Patience. Patience. Ferrell raised the red flag high, signaling David-Michael and the archers to stand ready.

It was hard to tell how many men had already come through the passage, but when it seemed close to fifty-thousand men, he dropped the flag, pointing it toward David-Michael.

"Now!" yelled David-Michael to the archers and the cannons.

The archers let loose with a volley of arrows on Kraken's horde, as the cannons, creating a deafening thunder, hurled devastating cannonballs into Kraken's men, who began scattering throughout the valley below. Some of Kraken's men were able to use shields with some success against the onslaught of arrows, but no shield could protect them from the powerful Clan cannons, which blasted significant holes in the enemy lines. When Kraken's men regrouped, the clansmen let loose with a second volley of arrows and cannonballs, slaughtering many under the constant hail of artillery, causing the urban army to begin a hasty retreat. The clansmen however, permitted no quarter. While the onslaught drove the enemy back toward the pass, Julius led the three regiments of cavalry positioned near the Western Pass as they attacked from the rear and from the sides, effectively cutting off any retreat, all while David-Michael continually bombarded the main body of Kraken's army as they came through the pass. While the four divisions attacked from the front, the three other cavalry divisions, equipped to travel lightly and quickly, had circled around Kraken's army, positioning themselves between Kraken and his stronghold. This meant that Kraken's men found themselves attacked on four fronts. With cannons, archers, and infantry in the front, and cavalry in the rear and the sides, and lines of infantrymen in the front, the rear, and the sides, Kraken watched his army being devastated by the Clansmen from all around.

Kraken had sent most of his cavalry and about half of his infantry ahead of him, leaving him and his Generals in the center of the massive army. They had been riding out front, leading the army's march toward the Main Enclave for most of the journey from the stronghold. General Collins however, recognizing the potential for an ambush at the pass, had finally convinced Kraken that they should move away from the front.

Seeing the Clan's devastating attack from all four sides, however, he raised his hands in a battle cry and suddenly charged forward, ignoring the protests of his generals. He soon reached the front line, where his infantry had already engaged the Clan's infantry. Kraken pulled his sword and began ferociously hacking his way through the clansmen infantry. Seeing their leader charging forward through their enemy then caused Kraken's men to rally. Slowly, the tide began to change, as the clansmen began to buckle under the sheer number of Kraken's infantry. Kraken himself continued dispatching clansmen one at a time. Kraken had always been an exceptional fighter on the ground, but he was even more so when he was on horseback. When one of the clansmen would attack, he would use his horse to block the attack and knock the clansman to the ground. Kraken would then grab his spear, and thrust through his enemy through, pinning him to the ground where he lay. For some time, the clansmen advance began to give way against Kraken's charge, and they were forced to retreat. Just when it began to look as if Kraken and his men might actually break through the Clan lines however, Ferrell appeared in the midst of the clansmen, slowly yet methodically making his way through Kraken's men, before being joined by Yoshi, Norris, and Sanjo. As more and more of Kraken's men fell before Ferrell and his commanders, their enemy once more began losing hope, as more and more of their comrades fell before the blades of the Master Clansmen. At the same time, the clansmen infantry also began to fight with a renewed vigor, inspired by their leader, who proved his right to lead where it counted the most, on the field of battle.

***

The wounded were coming in faster than they were able to treat them now. While she never regretted her decision to help Tara with tending to the wounded, she wondered on more than one occasion whether she was in over her head. It was very apparent to Ariel that Tara knew what she was doing; clearly, she was very familiar with the field dressings that each of the clansmen carried with him.

"Ariel, can you come here for a minute, please?" asked Tara.

"Sure, let me finish wrapping this dressing and I'll be right there."

Moments later, Ariel joined Tara next to a clansman that had been seriously wounded.

"Do you see where this man was stabbed?" Ariel nodded. "Can you hear that sound?" Once more Ariel nodded. "His lung has been punctured. We have to close that wound so he can breathe again."

"What can I do?" Ariel asked her. Tara handed her a special bandage that looked different from the others. Beeswax?

"I just need you to take this and hold it over the hole in his chest while I wrap the bandage around it. This will enable him to breathe until we can do a proper job of sewing up his wound."

Ariel did as she was instructed; fighting back the ever-present urge to vomit at the sight of the sucking chest wound. Tara finished wrapping the bandage and looked up at Ariel.

"You're doing well Ariel, especially in light of the fact that you have never done anything like this before." She smiled thoughtfully at Ariel before turning to the next injured clansmen.

Ariel paused to look around the camp; women moved back and forth, busily attending to the wounded. A few minutes later, Sergei appeared with another clansman, carrying yet another wounded man to the medical tent where Tara and Ariel were working. Ariel looked to see who it was.

"Tara, it's Ferrell!" yelled Ariel.

"Ferrell? What happened?" she asked Sergei and the other man as they laid him on an open bed.

"One of the canons fired on a position near where he was fighting," answered Sergei.

Tara took a couple of minutes to look her brother over carefully, taking time to check his vitals and listen to his breathing.

"Tara, is he okay?" asked Ariel, distraught to see Ferrell lying unconscious, with no idea whether he would ever wake again.

"I think so," answered his sister. "His pulse is strong and his breathing sounds okay. I see no visible wounds or any slash or stab marks, except for this scar on his shoulder, but it looks several months old."

"I was with him when he got that injury, Tara. He was shot with an arrow in our village, fighting off bandits," Ariel told her.

She spent several more minutes examining her brother. After a while, she finished her examination and looked up at Ariel and Sergei. "I believe he's going to be okay, it looks like he was just knocked unconscious."

Ariel walked over to Ferrell's side and held his hand. Tara walked over to where Sergei was standing.

"Sergei, we certainly have been seeing a lot of you today. Don't get me wrong, I have no objection," Tara said, smiling warmly at him.

"What can I say? I guess I'm a popular guy!" said Sergei, grinning back. Tara stopped for a moment, long enough to cast a suspicious glance toward one of her brother's oldest friends.

"Sergei, did Ferrell tell you to keep an eye on us? Is that why we keep seeing your handsome face in here time and time again?" Ariel thought she noticed Sergei, a man with no small reputation as a lady's man, blush for a moment.

"Why, I..."

"Well, next time you just tell my big brother that I can take care of myself. Now get yourself back out there. They need you more than we do!"

"Okay," he said, smiling, anxious to rejoin his brothers in the battle. "You'll keep me posted on how Ferrell's doing?" he asked.

"Of, course," answered Tara.

"Then ladies, please excuse me!" he said, before disappearing in the masses.

"What an interesting man!" Ariel remarked.

"Oh, he's the best kind of man," said Tara, smiling in a way Ariel had never seen her do before. *She likes him.*

The moment of levity soon came to an abrupt end however, as six of Kraken's men, suddenly rushed into the tent.

"I told you he was in here!" one of the men exclaimed.

They looked around inside before rushing toward Ferrell with their swords.

"Die, you clansman scum!" yelled the leader, as he reached the table where Ferrell was.

He brought his sword down toward Ferrell's neck. He was surprised however, by the sound the blade made as it reached the neck of the warrior. Instead of the sound of his sword cutting through flesh and bone, it made a loud, clanging sound.

"Hello, urba scum," Tara said, in a calm, steady voice, filled with controlled fury. She left her long sword in place to protect the injured clansman, while bringing her smaller sword around to the neck of the urba invader. He collapsed in a heap at her feet. Soon, another two stood on either side of her, waiting for the right moment to attack. She waited until one of Kraken's men stabbed at her. She sidestepped the attack, causing the blade to enter the torso of his compatriot. Tara then turned, plunging her sword into the urba in front of her. Suddenly, a scream caused Tara to turn her head, where she saw Ariel being harassed by the remaining three urbas. She was moving to help Ariel when another urba suddenly came up from behind Tara, wrapping his arm around her neck and cutting off her air supply, to the point that she began losing unconscious. Suddenly, the man relaxed his grip and dropped to the floor like a sack of potatoes. Sergei withdrew his short sword from the back of the urba, even as he sliced at the second, then the third urba. With all of them dead, Sergei stopped to check on Tara and Ariel.

"Are you both okay?" asked Sergei, spending slightly more time looking over Tara than he was Ariel.

"I believe we're both fine, if a bit shaken up, Sergei," said Ariel.

"Thanks, Sergei!" said Tara, smiling at the warrior.

Ariel turned back to one of the injured men she had been tending to, intending to give them a moment's privacy. Tara's scream sent chills down her spine.

"Tara, what is it..." she stopped short of completing her question because it would be unnecessary. An arrow protruded from Sergei's chest. A short distance behind him stood one of Kraken's archers, who had recognized an opportunity to take out one of the clansmen warriors with an easy shot. He reached back to pull another arrow from his quiver, an arrow that he would never have the opportunity to use. With blinding speed, Tara reached for a double-edged knife she carried in her boot and with one smooth movement, threw it twenty feet, where it lodged in the neck of the urba that had shot Sergei in the back. After the archer collapsed, the two women quickly set to work to attempt something that Tara feared would prove hopeless, to save Sergei's life.

Ferrell awoke a short time later to find Sergei wrapped in bandages, lying on a table next to him.

"Sergei!"

"Lord Ferrell, you're awake!"

"I am, I guess. What happened?"

"One of the cannons, my lord. It fired near your position and you were knocked unconscious. Are you okay?"

"Yes, I believe I am, old friend" Ferrell answered, sitting up and climbing off the table.

"What about you, what happened?" he asked.

"You know me, Lord Ferrell; I'll do anything to get out of a battle!"

"Ferrell!" Ariel rushed over to Ferrell, wrapped her arms around him, and kissed him for a very long time. "Are you okay?" she asked.

"Yes, Ariel," he said, blushing as he looked around the tent at his men, "I'm fine. I must go now, the battle is still hot."

"Please be careful, Ferrell, and come back to me!" she said as he walked away. Ferrell looked at her, nodded, and smiled, before looking back at Sergei.

"Stay here Sergei, until this is over. You're no good to me dead."

"Yes, my lord. I'll look after these two while I'm resting," he said with a smile.

***

When Ferrell re-entered the fight a short time later, he did so with a renewed vigor. Once more, the enemy was driven back, and Kraken, seeing that the tide was decisively turning in favor of the clansmen, rode over to where Ferrell stood fighting two urba infantrymen at the same time, and attacked, hoping to kill his enemy while he was preoccupied. Once again, he tried the same technique that had proven so successful for him throughout the day, but for the first time, the technique failed him. He was now fighting against a master clansman, and Ferrell anticipated the move and easily dodged out of the way, striking back with his sword. Kraken barely avoided the counterattack, with just enough time that the blade barely missed his neck, slicing through his shoulder instead. Kraken screamed out in pain, and glaring at Ferrell, jumped off his horse to meet him on the ground. Ferrell struck the wooden portion of the spear with his sword, cutting the spear in half. Drawing his short sword with his other hand, he parried a sword strike, and struck Kraken with a front-kick to the groin. Screaming in pain a second time, the urba leader repeatedly swung his sword at Ferrell in vain, attempting to decapitate the clansman. This went on for some time, until Ferrell changed tactics, and instead of blocking the attack, he simply moved slightly backward, so that the blade of the sword missed him fractions of an inch. He followed up with another slice at Kraken, this time to his mid-section. As before Kraken, a seasoned fighter and extremely fast and graceful for such a big man, dodged the fatal blow at the last second. Instead of losing his life, he took an ugly cut on his arm instead. Screaming for a third time and seemingly in agony, Kraken fell to the ground and while holding his bleeding arm , he reached into his cloak and pulled out a revolver, out of Ferrell's field of vision. Kraken had been in many battles and had survived for two reasons; he was a ruthless killer and he was always prepared. Ferrell advanced for a final attack and as he drew closer, Kraken rolled over and revolver in hand, turned toward Ferrell, who saw the firearm at the last second. Kraken pulled the trigger just as Ferrell was moving off-center to avoid being fatally struck by the bullet. Despite the attempt however, he was struck in his shoulder and knocked to the ground. Ferrell felt a searing pain where the ancient bullet passed through his shoulder. Doing his best to ignore the pain, Ferrell came right back at Kraken, striking at the arm that held the firearm, severing Kraken's hand which then fell to the ground. Just as Ferrell moved in to finish him off, a number of Kraken's men moved in and attacked Ferrell, buying Kraken just enough time to get back on his horse. As he did so, he looked at Ferrell and vowed, "You and I will meet again clansman, I promise you!" With that, he turned the horse and rode away, back toward the Western Pass.

Collins watched as the wounded urba leader left the battlefield, and questioned whether he should continue the hopeless fight or surrender. He thought about his men, whose lives were in his hands, and about his family, and what Kraken would do to them if he learned Collins surrendered. If he surrendered to the Clan, Kraken would have him and his family killed. If he returned to the stronghold, the men Kraken left in charge would not permit his family to leave until Kraken returned, only to order Collins' family executed. After going back and forth in his mind,

Collins decided not to surrender, at least not yet. If the fight continued going against them, then he would reconsider.

***

Kraken was approaching the rear of his army, when he was surprised to find them under attack as well. It appeared that his army was under attack from all sides. He looked down at the bloody stump at the end of his right arm. He was losing a lot of blood and would have to do something soon before it was too late. He looked around the field of battle, looking for an escape route. To his left was a small wooded area that extended along the leftmost field where the battle was taking place. It was too small to move troops but there would be enough room for a single rider. Just as he approached the wooded area on his way to freedom, a lone rider suddenly appeared, blocking his path.

"Well, well, well, what do we have here? It looks like you ran into a bit of trouble back there," the rider said, pointing to Kraken's hand. "Now I know that you weren't planning to go somewhere and miss out on all of the fun were you?"

Kraken looked at the clansman and said, "Don't I know you from somewhere? I know I've seen you somewhere before. Wait, I remember now, aren't you supposed to be dead, clansman?"

"That's right, I'm so sorry to disappoint you," said David-Michael, gritting his teeth and visibly hostile. "You killed my men, kept me prisoner, and tortured me for months. Perhaps now I can repay you for your kindness," he said, drawing his sword.

Kraken looked him in the eye and said, "Of course. May I draw my sword first, or will you kill an unarmed man?"

"Go ahead you urba scum. Unlike you, we clansmen still value honor, and do not kill unarmed men. I will permit you to draw your sword before I kill you."

He reached into his cloak and drew his hand back out, but instead of a sword, it held a revolver, which Kraken used to shoot David-Michael in the chest, knocking him off his horse.

"You clansmen, and your pathetic honor!" he laughed. As David-Michael lay in the grass bleeding, Kraken rode off into the woods, roaring with laughter as he went. One of the clansmen, who had seen David-Michael fall from a distance, rushed to his side.

"Lord David-Michael?" the wounded clansman looked up at his clansman brother, struggling for each breath.

"Kraken has escaped," he gasped, "you must find and kill him, or this is all for nothing." They were the last words David-Michael said before he died.

***

Once he was safely clear of the battle, Kraken tore off part of his shirt and wrapped it around his wrist, tying it into a tourniquet. He would go back to the stronghold; where there would be someone to tend to his wound and keep him from bleeding to death. He would not stay there, however. The battle was lost, and the clan was sure to defeat his army, he was certain of that now. He had killed so many enemies, conquered so many meros, and destroyed so many villages! Besides the considerable pain he was in, Kraken was beside himself with anger. He was infuriated that everything he had planned for, worked so hard for, the empire he had built from nothing, all lost in a single day!

Perhaps not all is lost. There is still a possibility I can get back all I have lost, and then some! Kraken rode hard to make the stronghold before he passed out. One way or another, despite the loss, Kraken would still have his empire.

Ferrell looked on as Yoshi and Wilijah led their men from the rear, and Sanjo and Norris led their men from the front. The clansmen advanced on the urbas from all directions, and were nearly at the point where they would meet in the middle. The entire battlefield was littered with dead and injured. The battle was all but over, however, as the last of Kraken's men fled into the surrounding woods. Ferrell saw that all of his commanders remained alive, but David-Michael was missing, as was Kraken. Had Kraken escaped? He was still surveying the battlefield when one of the men called out, "Lord Ferrell, come quickly!"

Ferrell rode over to where the clansman was kneeling down next to a dead clansman lying on the ground. He then saw David-Michael, his former teacher and mentor, his friend, lying dead on the ground by the clansman.

"Teacher," he whispered, kneeling down next to his old friend. After several minutes, Ferrell looked at the clansman that had called him over. "Do you know how it happened? Did you see him fall?"

"I did, Lord Ferrell. It was Kraken, my lord, he has escaped."

"Kraken," he said quietly, gritting his teeth. Ferrell looked around at all of the dead that lay stretched out all over the battlefield. "This is all his doing. This will not be over until Kraken is dead. He is sure to rebuild his former empire if he can, and he will not rest until he has the Oracle.

"Send for Sanjo, and have him report to me as quickly as possible."

"Yes, my lord."

The man hurried away and returned a short while later with Sanjo.

"My lord, I am sorry for your loss. I know that he was your mentor, and a dear friend."

"Thank you Sanjo. Listen, I need you to form details to bury the dead, starting with prisoners. Also, please find as many of the priests as you can, and ask them if they would please say a few words over our fallen brothers."

"Yes, my lord, it will be done," answered Sanjo.

Ferrell stood looking down at the body of his old friend, as Sanjo left out to carry out Ferrell's orders. "And Sanjo..."

"Yes, my lord?"

"Please also find the other commanders, and send them to me."

Chapter 39
The Stronghold

A thousand men accompanied him to Kraken's stronghold. Though it was unlikely that most of them would be necessary, Ferrell would not risk Kraken's escape. While most of his defeated army lay dead all over the battlefield, the enemy that survived the epic battle had escaped by fleeing in all directions into the surrounding woods, and Ferrell and the other clansmen had no way of knowing how many remained loyal to Kraken, nor how many might rally back at the Stronghold.

As they neared the compound, Ferrell dispatched several scouts to determine what kind of resistance they might encounter, and to determine how best to surround the compound. A short time later, the scouts finally returned and reported to Ferrell.

"Lord Ferrell, we saw only small groups of men, mostly scattered throughout the woods. As you instructed however, we did not enter the stronghold, but we could see no guards standing outside when we arrived."

Ferrell thanked them for their reports as the battalion of men continued their march toward the stronghold. A few hours later, they arrived at what had once been Kraken's seat of power. Ferrell ordered the men to approach quietly and to encircle the compound, to block off any chance of escape.

As they prepared to dismount from their horses, Ferrell addressed his men. "Now the chances are small that Kraken is here, but be careful not to let your guard down. He, or some of his men, may still be inside. Should you come across him, do not attempt to take him alone. He is an exceptional fighter… I know, I faced him in battle today myself."

When they entered the compound, they found it abandoned. There were no guards posted, nor were they able to find any of Kraken's men anywhere on the grounds. Next, they moved into the stronghold itself.

Upon entering the darkened structure, even the most hardened of the clansmen were disgusted by what they saw. Cages filled the large room just inside the main entrance. Many contained corpses, a few contained people that were still alive, if only by a thread. A few of the clansmen quickly began releasing the poor souls still alive in the cages, offering them water and treating their wounds.

The clansmen began going from room to room, looking for the enemy, and for other survivors of the depraved tyrant's cruelty. In an adjoining room, they found racks, and all manner of torture devices, with bloodstains throughout. Everywhere, evidence of the brutality, inhumanity, and evil, portended what would have happened had Kraken been successful and defeated the Clan. Ferrell truly regretted that he had not finished what he started on the battlefield, when he had the opportunity to destroy Kraken, and failed.

"Lord Ferrell, we found something you should see," one of the clansmen called out. "We're down here, sir."

Ferrell and the others found the stairs and followed the voice. "Here, sir."

He was able to resist the sudden urge to vomit when the stench reached his nostrils, but just barely. In one of the rooms, they found a man lying on the floor, alive but unconscious, stabbed in the lower abdomen by a dull knife. In the same room, there was another cage, where a woman and a little girl sat huddled in a corner, barely aware of the clansmen, hovering close to death. The clansmen opened the cage and very gently and tenderly tended to the woman and child.

"Give them some water, and then some food, but treat them very gently. Give them whatever they need," Ferrell instructed, with a furrowed brow. He looked over at the man, who was still unconscious and bleeding profusely from his wound. Julius kneeled down and checked the man's condition.

"This wound cannot be more than a few hours old, my lord. It also appears this man may have been one of Kraken's generals," he said.

"Why, what makes you think that?" Julius pulled out a map from the man's cloak.

"It looks like a rough map of the area, and a drawing of our Enclave." Ferrell looked at the map.

"Try to bring him around." They splashed a little water on the man to see if they could bring him to. The man started groaning in pain and opened his eyes.

"Who are you?" he asked Ferrell.

"I am Ferrell Young, of the Warrior Clan. Who are you?"

"Clansman? Thank God! My name is Collins. I am...rather I was one of Kraken's generals. To think I ever served that monster!"

"Why did you serve him then? The woman and the girl, they are yours?"

"My wife and daughter," replied Collins. "Kraken had them kidnapped and tortured, until I agreed to help him build his empire. Then he held them captive to ensure my cooperation."

"What happened to you?" asked Ferrell, pointing to his injury.

"When the battle started to go badly for our army, and I saw Kraken run away, I decided to come back here, to try to rescue my family. I arrived here only to find the compound deserted. I searched for my wife and daughter, and..." A round of vigorous coughing interrupted Collins' recounting of events. One of the clansmen offered him some water, and began tending to his wound. "I finally found them down here," he continued, "I was trying to find a way to release them when Kraken found me. He cursed me for leaving the battlefield, and when I accused him of the same, he did this to me. He said he would just leave me to die here with my family." He began coughing up blood when he tried to speak some more.

"My wife and my daughter, are they...?"

"They should be fine," replied Julius, having finished a cursory examination of the woman and her daughter. "They need food and water, but they should recover."

"Please, take care of them. I never wanted to fight the Clan, I had no choice, he forced me to. Please, do not punish them for what I did!" He coughed up more blood and groaned in pain.

"We do not punish the innocent for the acts of the guilty, General Collins. Neither will harm come to your wife or your daughter, at least from us," said Ferrell, "I promise."

"Thank you," said Collins.

"I have a question for you, Collins. It is clear that you are dying, will you tell us where Kraken went. Surely he boasted where he was going before he left you to die."

Collins struggled to speak. It appeared that he was already beginning to fade.

"I don't know where he is going. He only said...something...about going to get something...said he would have it for himself...Oracle...?"

Ferrell never had an opportunity to ask another question before Collins died. He reached down and closed his eyes.

273

"What do you think about what he said? Does Kraken have part of the map?" asked Julius.

"Maybe he is attacking the Main Enclave even as we speak? We have to get back there, now!" said Sanjo.

"Listen, calm down, everyone. First, there is no way he could get into the enclave. Remember, Lord Sarkoth commanded that we leave a division of men there at the Enclave to protect the map. In addition, since we know we have six pieces of the map, the most he could possibly have is one piece, and we don't even know if he has that. After all, Monasa and Brother Dan went further than any of the others, so it is likely that they have not even returned yet."

"We need to search the rest of this compound for more survivors. Then, we will burn it to the ground, agreed?" Everyone nodded in agreement.

After searching the rest of the enclave and finding no one else alive, the clansmen took Collins' wife and daughter, along with the rest of the survivors, and left Kraken's stronghold. As soon as they were all out, Ferrell took a torch and set the stronghold on fire. They stood for a few minutes watching it burn, before leaving and taking the survivors to the Main Enclave.

Chapter 40
The Map

They rode side-by-side down the long path leading into the Outlands. Each man was exhausted and looked forward to a long rest at the Main Enclave. After months at sea, they were relieved to be off the ship, and back on dry land after such a long voyage. The men were elated at the prospect of arriving back at the Main Enclave, despite their heavy hearts and the dreadful news they carried with them. Their journey after making landfall had been a mostly quiet one, as the men dealt with the disappointment in their own way.

It was still early morning but the fog had already lifted, and the sun was shining brightly. They had travelled a long way, barely saying a word, mindful of the consequences they would all soon have to face. Manasa ended the silence.

"It looks like the start of a beautiful day, Brother Dan."

"Indeed Manasa, it certainly does."

"I had a question I was hoping you could answer, Brother. You mentioned several weeks ago that you thought the disappearance of the Effect in the night sky would usher in a new Golden Age, what did you mean?"

"Well, since the time of the Great Collapse, the Church has held that the disappearance of the Effect could be the sign from the Lord that the Dark Age would soon end. It was also prophesied that the Oracle would remain hidden until the sign from God appeared in the night sky."

"So when the Effect disappeared a few months ago, it means the Oracle will be found soon, despite what happened to us?"

"Actually, the prophecy was that the disappearance of the Effect could usher in a new Golden Age, not that it would. It may be that the Oracle will never be found, despite everyone's efforts."

"And the Oracle, Brother, tell me again, what is it?"

"Well, we don't really know. The prophecy doesn't reveal exactly what the Oracle is, only that it contains the knowledge and wisdom of the Ancients, and that when the sign appeared, the Oracle would give up its knowledge to the one that was wise enough to find it, along with the key to unlocking its mysteries."

"Is that all you know about it?"

"Yes. It's possible that at one time the Church knew more about the Oracle than it does today. With the chaos following the Great Collapse, however, and the five-hundred years of the Dark Age since, everything else has been lost to us. Of course, it's possible the Ancients intentionally left everything else about the Oracle secret, until it was discovered."

"It has been said that it was the arrogance of the Ancients that led to the Great Collapse, and then the Dark Age," said Manasa. "If that's true, how do we know that we will we will be able to do any better then they did, given all of the knowledge they possessed? That is assuming, of course, that we are even able to find this Oracle now, given what happened," said Manasa.

"I suppose we don't know that we can do any better, Manasa," answered Brother Dan. "I just pray that we have the opportunity find out one day. Maybe it turns out that we can do no better than the Ancients, but then again, perhaps we can!"

Manasa burst into laughter. "Brother Dan, always the eternal optimist!"

"It's in the job description, my friend!"

***

By mid-afternoon, the priest and the clansmen saw the Clan enclave coming into sight. As the group approached, the word began to spread quickly among everyone at the enclave that the last expedition had returned. The priest heard a loud sound, like a brass instrument but much louder and deeper, coming from somewhere inside the gates of the Main Enclave.

"What is that sound?" asked Brother Dan.

"That is the Clanshorn, he answered. "It is used only during times of emergency, and times of great celebration," answered Manasa.

"They sound it because they believe we have the map?" he asked.

"I believe so, yes," answered Manasa.

The gates to the Main Enclave opened on their arrival and they walked into the enclave. Lord Sarkoth himself met them just inside the gate. Upon seeing Lord Sarkoth, the men dismounted, bowing in respect to the aged elder.

"Lord Sarkoth," said Manasa.

"Welcome home, clansmen, and to you as well, Brother Dan."

"Thank you, Lord Sarkoth."

Sarkoth smiled. "They sound the Clanshorn in celebration of your arrival. For yours is the seventh and final piece of the map!"

"You mean the others have already returned, and they were all successful?" asked Brother Dan.

"Indeed, Brother Dan, they were. We have been concerned about you, especially the last few weeks, ever since we defeated Kraken's army in a great battle."

"Defeated Kraken's army? That is good news indeed, my lord," said Manasa.

"We defeated his army yes, but Kraken himself still lives. We had started to worry you might be dead as well, and that Kraken had the seventh piece of the map. Enough talk for now, however. You have had a long journey."

"But, Lord Sarkoth, we…"

"Come. Join us as we gather in the Gathering Hall to place your seventh piece of the map together with the others, and we will learn the location of the Oracle together! Afterwards, you must take some rest, while we prepare a great feast of celebration for the safe arrival of our brothers, and the seventh piece of the map." Manasa and Dan stared at one another, each feeling the same sinking feeling in the pit of his stomach.

Several clansmen youths came and took the horses to the stables, while Dan and Manasa joined Lord Sarkoth in the Gathering Hall. The room erupted with great applause, as all of seven expedition teams met together again for the first time since the search for the seven pieces of the map had begun. Brother Dan and Manasa looked at each other as if to say, I cannot believe this is happening.

Brother Sebastian started with the invocation. When he had finished, Lord Sarkoth thanked the priest and started the meeting.

"Brothers of the Church and Clansmen brothers, truly we live in historic times! Consider that for the first time in five-hundred years, the Warrior Clan and the Holy Christian Church have joined forces, just as the sign prophesied long ago to signal the end of the Dark Age has appeared. We have defeated a powerful, common enemy in battle in recent days, and last, but not least, we now have the seventh and final piece of the map that, if legend and prophecy are true, will lead us to the location of the Oracle."

The room erupted in applause and celebration. He then turned toward Manasa and Brother Dan. "Clansman Manasa, Brother Dan, would you please hand me the seventh piece of the map?"

Manasa and Dan hung their heads before looking up at Sarkoth and the others.

"Lord Sarkoth, we..."

Brother Dan started to speak but Manasa cut him off.

"It is my fault, my lord," Manasa said quietly.

"What is your fault, Manasa?" Sarkoth's smile faded before disappearing altogether, replaced with an expression of distress. "Do you mean to say that...?"

"Yes, Lord Sarkoth. We do not have the seventh piece. I have failed you, the Clan, and the Church." He rose from the table and fell on his knees before Lord Sarkoth. "Please forgive me, my lord!"

Once the initial shock of the pronouncement had worn off, Sarkoth looked down and smiled warmly at the distraught warrior.

"Nonsense. Rise, Clansman Manasa, and tell us what happened."

"Yes, Lord Sarkoth." Manasa rose and looked at Brother Dan, who started to rise until Manasa shook his head. Brother Dan smiled warmly and sat back down. Manasa sat back down at the table and addressed Sarkoth.

"We found the map at the monastery. We then setup camp inside to rest overnight, before starting for the ship in the morning. We were surprised, however, by a full urba pack in the middle of the night. These were not like urba we had ever encountered before, and they were highly skilled in martial fighting. We fought for some time, killing many of them in the process. Just when we started to tire however, giving the urba the advantage, they suddenly disappeared. We found Brother Dan a short while later lying on the floor unconscious, and the map gone."

Sarkoth began stroking his chin. He looked at Manasa and Brother Dan.

"You think these were Kraken's men?"

"We think they were hired by Kraken, my Lord. We searched all over the mero looking for the map. Some distance from the monastery, we found Brother Dan's bag, but not the map. It had been tossed to the side with everything still in it, except for the map.

"I see."

Sarkoth looked at Ferrell.

"Please have the other six pieces of the map brought in," he said.

"Yes, my lord" answered Ferrell, who then left the room.

He reappeared soon after with the remaining pieces of the map, and laid them on the table before Sarkoth and the others. On each piece, there was writing, along with drawings, references to geographical landmarks, including mountains, rivers, and oceans.

The group spent hours trying to determine how to make all of the pieces fit together correctly. It was Darius that finally unraveled the puzzle.

"Brothers, do you see these symbols? On each piece, there is this symbol; each one contains a color that is slightly different from the rest. The symbols at first glance appear to be part of the topography of the map, representing part of the landscape. But I believe that together they make up a different kind of symbol, this symbol in fact," he said, pointing to the symbol of the Unity on the front of the book with the same name.

Sebastian walked over to his fellow priest, placed his hands on his shoulders, smiled, and said, "Brother Darius, though considerably younger, your wisdom far exceeds my own."

Brother Sebastian took the pieces, aligning each symbol as Darius had said, until they formed the symbol of The Unity.

"Here is your map gentleman!" he said with a big grin on his face.

The six pieces fit together perfectly, with the missing piece being conspicuously absent. Everyone in the Gathering Hall studied the map in some detail, looking for rivers, mountains, or any other landmark they could discern.

"Like the book entitled The Unity, the names on this map are also written in Latin," said Francis. "This river, it was once called, The Potomac."

Alex, who had been studying the map for a while but had said nothing, finally joined in.

"I believe I recognize this river, as well as these mountains here. But I do not see the word "oraculum" or "oracle" anywhere on the map."

Brother Sebastian grimaced when he realized the impact of the missing piece.

"It looks to me as if the missing piece is the one with the exact location of the Oracle on it," he said. "Alex, do you concur?"

Alex sat studying the map for another minute. "Yes, Brother Sebastian, I believe you are correct. Worse yet, I believe that we are talking about a large geographic area here. If it's as big as I think it is our chances of finding the Oracle without the missing piece are slim to none. We could search for years and years and never even come close."

The clergy and clansmen, some of the brightest minds of the Dark Age, spent the remainder of the day searching for ways to find the Oracle without the missing piece, but at the end of the day, the collective effort proved fruitless.

Lord Sarkoth stood. "Does anyone have any other ideas, any ideas at all? Surely we have not exhausted every possible option?"

"Perhaps we should begin searching in the missing area?" suggested Sebastian.

The priest's suggestion was met only with silence, however.

"Brother Sebastian," started Alex, "we cannot possibly find the Oracle without the remaining piece, it's hopeless. If it had been one of the other six pieces, then yes, maybe. Without this particular piece, however, there's just no way."

"We have to do something, Alex, we cannot have come this far, only to fail now!"

***

Alex just looked at his old friend, shrugged his shoulders, and sighed, empathizing with Sebastian's understandable surprise and anguish at having come so close, only to be thwarted at the last minute.

"We always knew it was a long shot, Brother Sebastian. Finding the book, finding the monasteries, finding the map, and returning safely back home. Frankly, I'm surprised we made it this far. I believe we can..."

"What's wrong, Alex?" asked Brother Sebastian, wondering why his longtime friend had stopped in mid-sentence and grown suddenly quiet. Alex sat at the table, staring at the missing area on the map and saying nothing. Something about it troubled him, something pertinent, and very important. Was it the shape?

"Oh, I'm sorry," he said after a long silence, "it's nothing brother. I thought for a moment I was on to something. Never mind though, I guess it was nothing."

"Brother Sebastian how would you like to proceed?" asked Sarkoth.

Sebastian scratched his head, still visibly stunned by the unexpected turn of events.

"I honestly don't know, Lord Sarkoth. I suggest we sleep on it overnight, and reconvene tomorrow morning?"

"I believe that is a good idea, Brother. It will give us all a chance to get some rest and clear our minds Very well. If there are no objections, we will reconvene after breakfast tomorrow morning."

Chapter 41
The Founders

Five-hundred years earlier, during the time of The Great Collapse...

The two men were stopped as they approached the camp by several guards standing in front of the large wooden gate. All four guards were armed with assault rifles. One of them stepped forward to address the visitors.

"May I help you, gentlemen?" he asked.

"Sure. I'm Commander Chris Anthony, U.S. Navy Seals. My friend here is Sergeant Jack Carter, Green Berets. We just wrapped up a mission for the President of the United States. We were told that Colonel Simmons was setting up a camp here, and that we would likely be welcomed."

"Wait here just a moment, Commander, I'll be right back."

Anthony nodded his head, walked over, and sat on a large rock located just outside of the fence that surrounded the compound. His companion joined him a few moments later.

"Do you think he will let us in?" Carter asked.

"It's hard to say. From what the president and Dr. White said, he's a great guy. He's also a former ranger so yeah, I think he will."

Several minutes later, another man appeared at the gate's entrance. He looked like military as well, and had an intensity in his eyes that caused Anthony to draw an immediate conclusion.

"Colonel Simmons! My name is Commander Chris Anthony, Navy Seal."

"Nice to meet you Commander. As you guessed, I am Colonel Conrad Simmons, Army Rangers. Who is your friend here?"

"Sergeant Jack Carter, Green Berets, Colonel."

"President Michaels and Dr. James White told me that you might allow us to join your community here, once we completed the mission," offered Anthony. Well, Sir, we just wrapped it up, so here we are, hoping that we can join you."

The two men shook hands with Simmons.

"It's nice to meet you both. So what was your mission?" asked Simmons.

"Well sir, let's just say that it had something to do with saving the future," he said with a grin.

"That's good enough for me, Commander, welcome to our camp. Now then, if you would please come with me, I'll take you to your quarters."

As the two men walked inside the gates, Anthony noticed the flurry of activity going on all around him. Several new structures were under construction, and he could see men and women in multiple locations digging new wells.

"So how are President Michaels, and Dr. White?" Conrad asked with a smile.

"Well sir, they both seemed to be doing fine the last time we saw them. They were supposed to sail for Seattle about the same time we sailed for China late last year. We just pulled back into port a month or so ago in Norfolk, before setting out to find this place."

"Looks like a lot of activity going on, Colonel," Carter remarked, looking all around the busy camp.

"That's right Sergeant, there is," Simmons replied. "We are digging new wells, improving the walls in several sections, putting up new buildings, and growing new crops. We plan to build several new farms here over the next year or so. Either of you gentlemen interested in farming?"

"Yes sir, that, or whatever else we need to do to contribute, Colonel. You just put us to work wherever you need to."

"What are your areas of interest, gentlemen?" asked Simmons.

"Well, aside from my military training, I like to paint, sir," said Anthony. "I know it's not a very useful skill when you're trying to survive the biggest catastrophe in human history. As a Seal, I was involved in a lot of special recon and unconventional warfare; I found painting to be effective at relieving some of the stress."

Conrad nodded. "I understand that, Commander."

"Anyway, it helped me focus, wind down after sticky missions."

"How good of an artist are you, Anthony?" asked Simmons.

"I'm pretty good, sir. I took it up as a child, seems I had a knack for it. Let's just say that at one time, I probably could have taught art classes at most any university in the country."

"Excellent," said Simmons.

"I was also trained in unconventional warfare by the Army, Colonel," said Carter. "I can also play a mean guitar sir, if you have one lying around."

"To be honest with you gentlemen, I suspect that music, art, and unconventional warfare are all skills that will come in useful here. But for now, believe it or not, I'd like to ask if you would be willing to do a painting for us, Commander."

"A painting, Colonel, of what?"

"Of this!" said Simmons, waving his arms around the compound. "I would like to try to capture the spirit of everything we are doing here in a painting for future generations to see, just as it is now, just after the world fell apart. Perhaps future generations will come to appreciate it. What do you say, Anthony, are you interested?" Anthony looked at Simmons for a minute, trying to get a read.

"Sure, Colonel," he said with a smile. "I guess I am. One problem, however. I don't have any supplies."

"No worries, Commander," said Simmons. "I've already taken care of that. Can you start to work on it tomorrow?"

"Um, sure, Colonel."

"Wonderful. For now, why don't we get you two settled into one of the cabins, and I'll get you both something to eat. What do you say?"

"Sounds good, Colonel, thanks."

The two men followed Simmons into one of the cabins and set their things down on some bunks setup in a corner. The beds were a little Spartan, but clean and functional.

"Here you go, gentlemen. This will be where you bunk. Go ahead, get settled in, and meet me over at the mess hall afterward. It's the building in the center of the camp. It's not much yet, but it's coming along just fine. I will introduce you to the others at dinner, in about an hour. Sound good?"

"Yes sir," said Anthony. "It sounds very good, thanks."

"Alright then, I'll see you at dinner."

"See you there." Simmons left and the two men sat on their respective bunks and breathed a sigh of relief.

"This is really something here, Chris, don't you think?" Carter asked.

Anthony pulled out a piece of paper and looked it over.

"Yeah, it really is incredible, especially given the circumstances." Carter walked over to look at the paper his friend was holding in his hands. His eyes grew wide when he saw what was on it.

"What are you doing with that, Chris?" he asked. "You know you're not supposed to have it! It's too risky!"

"Don't worry, Jack, it's not the original, just a copy. I was bored on the voyage back so I drew it from memory. I'm not going to share it with anyone, I promise. It's just a memento, that's all." Anthony flipped the piece of paper around in his hand.

Then, an idea popped into his head, and he smiled.

***

Five-hundred years later, in the Dark Age...

Alex continued tossing and turning in bed, much as he had done all night as he slept. It was the same dream in which he was once again being escorted on a tour of the main enclave. Then, he suddenly found himself back in the small galleria of the Great Hall, standing in front of the painting of the founders. There was something there, in the painting, something important, something urgent. In his dream, he was carefully examining the painting. One of the founders stood looking over a set of building plans spread out on a large table, pointing to something on the plan. Alex then found himself standing in some woods near a large lake, looking at some ancient buildings. The sequence repeated three times, and then he awoke.

Alex sat up in bed in a cold sweat. There was something about the dream that he couldn't get out of his head, something that continued nagging at him, something about recent events, something about that painting. In his mind, he continued going over the dream repeatedly, trying to discover what it was that he kept missing. Finally, it came to him as if a bolt of lightning struck him. He quickly dressed and left his quarters, walking down the long hallway to where a clansman stood guard.

"I need to speak with Lord Sarkoth, please, it's urgent."

"I'm sorry, sir. Lord Sarkoth left a few minutes ago with Brother Sebastian."

"How about Clansman Ferrell, is he still here?"

"I haven't seen him yet this morning. He's probably still sleeping, sir."

"Could you please wake him? Tell him it's Alex, and that this is important."

"Yes, sir." The guard left and returned a short while later with Ferrell, who still looked half-asleep.

"What is it Alex, is everything okay?"

"I'm sorry to disturb you, Clansman Ferrell. Something's been bothering me since yesterday, something that I believe may be very important. I have an unusual request to make."

"Certainly. What do you need?"

"When we first arrived here, Lord Sarkoth took me on a tour of the enclave. On that tour, he showed me a special room, where a painting of the Clan Founders hangs on a wall. You know the room of which I speak?"

"Of course," answered Ferrell.

"Could you please take me to the painting?"

"Now?"

"Yes, please. As I said, I believe it may be important."

"Of course, come with me."

Ferrell escorted Alex into a deeper, much older section of the Great Hall, to a special room, where someone always stood guard. The clansman guard stepped aside and allowed Ferrell and Alex to proceed into the small room.

"There it is, Alex, the painting of Conrad Simmons, and the other founders of the Warrior Clan."

Alex studied the painting.

"Why did he show you the painting, Alex?" Ferrell asked, obviously curious.

"When Lord Sarkoth learned what it is that I do, searching and finding artifacts, and my keen interest in art and history, he offered me a short tour of the Main Enclave, particularly around the Great Hall, where the Clan keeps various paintings, period pieces including swords, armor, and so forth, that have been preserved over the centuries. This painting was the one he identified as holding the most meaning to clansmen."

"So what is it that we are looking for now?"

"I'm not sure, exactly. There is something about it, something that I have seen somewhere before." Alex scrutinized the painting, making an effort to take in every detail. After he had stared at the painting fifteen minutes, he could tell that Ferrell was starting to get impatient. Maybe it was just my imagination. He started to turn away and leave, when he noticed something in the painting.

"Ferrell, what is that on the table in the painting, the document that Conrad Simmons is pointing at?"

"I've always assumed it was just a plan for the enclave," answered Ferrell.

Both men studied the document stretched across the table in the painting.

Alex abruptly turned and looked at Ferrell and started to grin. He clapped his hands together.

"What is it, did you find something?" asked Ferrell.

"You tell me, Ferrell. Look at the plans on the table in the painting. Do you see what Conrad is pointing at?"

"You mean that document?" asked Ferrell.

"Yes. Does it look familiar? Focus on the outline."

"No, I don't, like I said I...wait, it does look vaguely familiar, but I can't place it."

"Do you know who painted this?"

"I don't know, let's see." Ferrell put his hand on his head. "It seems like he was one of the Ancient warriors, like Conrad Simmons and many of the others. It is said that he had just returned from some kind of important mission, not long before this was done."

"Perfect. I suspect then that he was doing work for the Unity. Now, take another look at the document on the table."

Ferrell looked back at the painting. Suddenly, his eyes opened wide.

"That's it! The map, it's the same shape as the missing piece of the map!"

"Yes, it is, isn't it?" Alex asked, barely able to contain his exuberance. Ferrell turned and grabbed Alex by both shoulders. While Alex knew it was intended as a gesture of endearment, both shoulders erupted in pain. Clearly Ferrell was just as excited by the discovery as Alex was, perhaps a little too excited. He suddenly felt a great sense of relief that the clansman was on his side during the conflict with Kraken.

"Great job, Alex, great job! Just when we started to fear everything was lost. We must tell Lord Sarkoth, immediately!" said Ferrell, as he ushered Alex out of the room and out the door, searching for Sarkoth.

Several hours later, everyone reconvened back in the Great Hall. Alex took the missing piece of the map that he had re-created based on the document in the painting, and placed it with the pieces of the map they had in their possession.

"Look at that!" exclaimed Brother Sebastian. It fits perfectly, incredible! May God richly bless you Alex, you have saved the day!"

"The man that did the painting must have had firsthand knowledge of the map, probably having it in his possession at some point. Then, for whatever reason, he decided to include it this picture," Alex told them.

"Praise God for that!" added Darius.

The room grew deathly quiet as the group began studying the map, this time with the missing piece of information. Sebastian's face took on a troubled look as he looked down on the missing piece.

"I still do not see the word "oraculum" or "oracle" anywhere on the map," said Sebastian.

"I believe that I know the reason for that, Brother," said Dan. "Manasa and I were talking on the way back about how it was the knowledge of the Ancients that led to the Great Collapse and the beginning of the Dark Age. The question came up whether we were likely to do any better this time around. I believe that for this reason, our brothers in The Unity may have appropriately chosen this word 'sapientia' instead of the words 'oraculum' or 'scientia' on the map."

"What does the word 'sapientia' mean?" Alex asked.

"It means wisdom," Sebastian answered, smiling. "The wisdom to use the knowledge of the Oracle wisely, perhaps? Excellent work Brother Dan!"

"If we do find the Oracle, we should try to learn from their mistakes," said Dan. "We must do our best to take steps to ensure that we do a better job with the knowledge than the Ancients did." Dan looked up at Manasa, who nodded his head in affirmation. Dan continued, "What little we know of the Ancients that was passed down to us through the centuries, many of them worshipped their knowledge and technology rather than God."

"Maybe we should take steps to encourage everyone to remember our Maker this time around," said Darius.

"Perhaps we will, Brother," said Sarkoth.

"First however, we have to find the Oracle," said Alex. "I've been looking at this map and I think I might know where this is," Alex said. "If I'm right, and I think I am, it should be about a week's ride from here, maybe two, if we follow the ancient roads. I made a journey to the area once, a long time ago, looking for artefacts. I believe I might be able to find my way again."

Chapter 42
Making Plans

"Okay Yoshi, my turn."

Yoshi attacked Sanjo with the stick, missing the other clansman by less than an inch, a blow that would have seriously injured or even killed him had it landed. Sanjo's timing was impeccable, however. He moved in quickly toward Yoshi, stopped the downward attack by meeting his stick while it was still near the twelve o'clock position, and counter-attacked with a mock strike to Yoshi's face with his own stick, followed by another strike to Yoshi's temple, and then another with the end of the stick to his solar plexus. He followed the stick attacks with a roundhouse kick to the mid-section, knocking Yoshi back several steps and then landing him on the floor.

"Hey, watch it!" Yoshi yelled at Sanjo, who was smiling, laughing, and having a great time with Yoshi's unfortunate landing on his backside.

"Sorry about that, Yoshi." About that time, they noticed that Ferrell was standing in the corner.

"Lord Ferrell!" exclaimed Yoshi, as he jumped to his feet and bowed to Ferrell.

"Relax Yoshi, Sanjo. I was just checking to see whether you and your men are ready to make the trip to the South Lands."

"My men and I are ready whenever you give the order, Lord Ferrell," answered Sanjo."

"As are mine, my lord. Just give us the word," said Yoshi.

"We need to find the Oracle as soon as possible," he told them. "We will be taking nearly a thousand men, leaving around five-hundred men there when we are done, along with enough supplies to establish a new enclave close to or even at the site of the Oracle. The trip will take at least twice as long to get there as it normally would, given all the supplies we will need to take with us. Sanjo, I would like for you to lead an advance scouting party, along with Alex and me."

"I would be honored, Lord Ferrell."

"Yoshi, I would like for you to stay with the priests and ensure that they are well protected. We still do not know where Kraken is or even whether he is still alive. If he is, you can bet he will not stop until he has the Oracle."

"Yes, Lord Ferrell, I will guard them with my life," said Yoshi.

***

After additional preparations for the trip had been finalized, Ferrell went to see Sarkoth, who happened to be walking with Sebastian when he found him in the Courtyard. Not wanting to disturb the Clan leader, he turned to leave.

"Clansman Ferrell, won't you please join us?" Sarkoth asked him.

"I am sorry for disturbing you, Lord Sarkoth. I wanted to let you know that we are ready to leave, my lord, just give us the word."

"That is good to hear, Ferrell, thank you. The word is given, so you may leave at your convenience. You are taking enough men to guard the Oracle once you find it, as well as enough to establish a new enclave near the Oracle?"

"Yes, my lord. We are taking over a thousand of our best men. We will leave around five-hundred, well-armed clansmen at the Oracle, while the other five-hundred will start the new enclave. We will also be taking enough supplies for both."

Sarkoth was pleased. "Excellent, Clansman Ferrell." Ferrell was turning to leave when Sarkoth stopped him. "Before you leave, there is one more thing I would like to discuss, with you, Ferrell. Would you please sit with us, just for a few minutes?"

"Of course," answered Ferrell.

Sarkoth looked at Brother Sebastian, and then back at Ferrell. "Brother Sebastian and I were just discussing what might happen after we find and activate the Oracle. We have been so focused on finding the map, and on fighting Kraken, that we have had little time to do anything else."

Ferrell suspected he knew where the conversation was going as Sarkoth continued."As you know, for the hundreds of years since the Great Collapse, the Church and the Clan have independently pursued the common goal of preserving as much knowledge from the Golden Age as possible, with the hope of one-day restoring civilization to the world. As you also know, my friend Henry will be arriving here from

Rome soon, to see the Oracle for himself, assuming we find it of course, and to help determine how we use it. I am wondering whether you have any thoughts on this Ferrell."

"I am certain that you and the Christian pope will chart the best course of action, my lord."

"But I want to know your thoughts, Ferrell."

Ferrell considered what Sarkoth had said and after a minute or two, said, "Certainly we must protect the Oracle and its power from the likes of Kraken. Then, I believe we must determine what the Ancients did wrong, learn from their mistakes, and do what we can to avoid repeating them. Perhaps the Oracle can help us understand what happened to the Ancients. Then, we can try and build a better civilization than they did."

"Excellent, Ferrell. Now do you have any ideas now how we might do that?"

"Perhaps we could start by building enclaves in distant lands, to help establish a means of spreading civilization. Perhaps working with our Christian brothers, we could set up a church at each enclave. The priests would have protection and could help spread civilization in these lands. I think it would be important that we maintain the laws we have today, and allow the clansmen to choose whether to become Christians or not."

Sarkoth smiled at Ferrell, looked at Sebastian, and said, "This is why I have such great faith in him, Brother Sebastian. He is an excellent warrior, a brilliant strategist, and a wise leader as well. It is one of the reasons I have selected him as my successor when I die."

The shock on Ferrell's face was apparent. "Clansman Ferrell, are you well?" asked Sebastian. Ferrell looked at Sebastian, back at Sarkoth, and then back at Sebastian.

"I am fine Brother, thank you. Lord Sarkoth, I am flattered that you would choose me as your successor, and I am greatly in your debt but..."

"But you are not certain whether you want to be my successor?" asked Sarkoth, who appeared a bit perplexed by Ferrell's response.

"Well, as you know my lord, I was gone from the Clan for quite a while. It was during my time away that I began thinking that I might want to settle down and have a family some day."

"So why would that stand in the way of you becoming my successor?"

"But, I thought that..."

291

"Nonsense," Sarkoth answered. "While it is true that it has been a custom for the last hundred years or so that the High Elder has not married, that was not the case for the first hundred years after the founding of the Clan. What is required and expected, however, is that the Clan's leader will choose his successor based upon what is truly best for the Clan. Leadership of the Warrior Clan is not a birthright, do you understand this?" Sarkoth asked him.

"I do, my lord. Again, I am honored, thank you Lord Sarkoth." Ferrell bowed deeply, demonstrating his deep honor and respect for Sarkoth.

While the significance of the moment was not lost on Sebastian, he thought he would introduce a moment of levity.

"So Clansman Ferrell, I was wondering, do you have a particular young lady in mind that you might want to start this family of yours with?" The priest was not sure but he was almost certain that he saw Ferrell blush. Sebastian looked over at Sarkoth, who he assumed must have been wondering the same thing. They both burst into laughter, enjoying the moment, even if it was at Ferrell's expense.

Ferrell stood, obviously embarrassed, and bowed to Sarkoth.

"With your permission, Lord Sarkoth, I would like to check with Alex to make sure that he is ready to go."

Sarkoth nodded. "Of course, Clansman Ferrell. Be certain to send a messenger as soon as you have located the Oracle."

"It will be done, Lord Sarkoth."

As Ferrell stood to leave Sebastian said to him, "May God go with you, Clansman Ferrell."

"Thank you, Brother," he answered, before leaving the room.

Chapter 43
Following the Map

"Dad, please! I want to go too, maybe I can help!"

"No! It is simply too dangerous, Hannah, I cannot allow you to go. You are all that I have left in this world, and I have put you at way too much risk over the years. I cannot, and I will not, place your life in anymore."

"But Dad, I want to spend time with you! If you go and you find the Oracle, you might be gone for a long time. Who knows how long you would be gone!"

"You will be safe here with the Clan, Hannah," insisted her father.

"But that is not the point Dad; I want to be with you!"

"I just don't know what to expect."

"How dangerous could it be, with a thousand clansmen with us? Besides, think about what an opportunity it would be for me to learn, I mean, we're talking about the Oracle of Knowledge!"

"I don't know, Hannah, I just don't think so."

"Dad, finding the Oracle will change the world! Don't you want me with you when that happens?"

"Okay, okay. Wow, when did you become such a tough negotiator?"

"You mean I can go with you?"

"Yes, yes, okay, come with me. Besides, you're right. It will be a historic moment and as you said, we will have over a thousand clansmen with us as well. I can't imagine how that would not be safe."

Hannah wrapped her arms around her father and squeezed him tightly.

There was a knock, and when Alex opened the door, he found Ferrell standing there.

"Good morning Alex," said the clansman. "I just wanted to make certain that you are ready to go. We will be leaving shortly."

"I am ready Ferrell, thanks." Ferrell looked down at Hannah and then back at Ferrell.

"Are you planning to take her with us?"

"I was going to ask you if it would be alright, she really wants to go. Do you think it will be safe?" he asked.

"I will personally guarantee her safety, Alex. She will be surrounded by a thousand clansmen."

"Thank you, Clansman Ferrell!" said Hannah, running over to the hardened warrior. She jumped in his arms and hugged him, before giving him a kiss on the cheek. For the second time Ferrell blushed.

"You are welcome, Hannah Montgomery," he said, as he grunted, and walked away.

It was mid-afternoon and the sun was already dropping lower in the sky when they mounted their horses to depart the Clan's Main Enclave. The enormous contingent of clansmen and priests passed through the massive gates and protective walls of the enclave on the long journey to find the Oracle.

Sanjo led an advance scouting party of ten men. With only light provisions, they were able to move quickly, looking for trouble ahead, and ensuring the way was clear for the expedition.

A group of elite clansmen consisting of fifty warriors rode with Ferrell and Ariel. Hundreds of clansmen rode behind the group of elite warriors, followed by Alex, Hannah, the priests, and Yoshi, who Ferrell had assigned to protect them. Behind them was the remainder of the expedition, consisting of over five-hundred clansmen.

They rode for days through the woods and through the fields, looking for the ancient road that would lead them all the way to the land of the Oracle. It was nearly nightfall of the third day by the time they finally found it. The long caravan of clansmen and priests began making their way along the ancient road, now crumbled, with grass and trees now growing through much of it. They had been traveling for days, so Ariel was getting fidgety.

"Do you think we will be able to find the Great Oracle Ferrell? Does it really exist? I heard about the Oracle growing up in the village, but I always thought it was just a fable."

"We have every reason to believe it does exist and yes, I believe we will find it," Ferrell answered.

"Just try to imagine it, Ferrell, all of the wisdom of the Ancients, knowledge that has been lost for five hundred years!" Ariel said, bubbling over with excitement at the prospect. "Thank you so much for bringing me with you Ferrell!"

Ferrell looked at Ariel and smiled. He cared for her, and enjoyed her company more with each passing day. His only hesitation in bringing her had been his concern for her safety. If anything were ever to happen to her because of him, he would never forgive himself; he had almost lost someone close to him when he nearly killed David-Michael, and he doubted whether he could live with himself if something happened to her. On this trip, however, there was no reason to expect there would be any trouble.

"You're welcome, Ariel." He looked at her and smiled. "Did I ever really have a choice?"

Ariel smiled back. "No, now that you mention it, you didn't!" she said, smiling playfully back at him.

"I thought you might enjoy it, making a historic journey that will be talked about for untold generations. Besides, I expect it should be safe enough." He watched as she adjusted her position in the saddle and started to laugh."

"What's so funny?" she asked, looking at him indignantly.

"How are you holding up?" he asked. "I know you've been doing a lot of riding these last few weeks, you must be getting...a little uncomfortable," he said with another chuckle.

"Go ahead and say it, saddle sores. Yes, I've got saddle sores, now leave me alone!" Ferrell burst out laughing. "I'm sorry for the fast pace, Ariel, but we have to move swiftly. Lord Sarkoth wants to locate the Oracle as soon as possible. He's worried about Kraken, and he just learned from Darius that his old friend, Henry, the Christian pope, is on his way here from Rome. Lord Sarkoth would like to locate and have access to the Oracle by the time he arrives."

"Pope John Paul V is coming here? Wow."

Further back in the procession, Hannah kept looking around as they traveled, taking in all of the wondrous sights and sounds of the trip. With the exception of her time at the Clan's Main Enclave, she had never been out of the area around her village. She watched as deer ran through the woods, listened to the birds singing in the trees all around her, and she looked around in awe at the many ancient ruins and relics that she saw along the way. Ferrell had told them that they would bypass the meros as much as possible in order to avoid placing Alex and the priests in unnecessary danger. Still, there were many ancient artifacts and ruins to see along the way. There were strange looking beasts made of metal that came in many colors and shapes, resting on almost all of the ancient roads that they came across. She saw the remains of giant metal birds, her father called them airplanes, covered with underbrush, and incredibly tall buildings that reached into the sky. She tried to imagine what the world looked like during the Golden Age, the tall, beautiful, glittering structures, the ancient roadways, and the giant metal birds soaring through the sky. Brother Sebastian had said they once carried people over the lands and Great Waters to destinations both near and far. Hannah looked over at her father.

"Dad, can I ask you a question?"

"Of course, honey. We have a long trip ahead of us and plenty of time, so ask away."

"What do you think will happen after we find the Oracle? Do you think the world will look like it did during the Golden Age?"

"That's a great question, sweetheart, but I don't really know. From what I have learned on my expeditions, especially over this past year, it took thousands of years for man to develop the technology of the Golden Age. If we do find the Oracle, and the stories are true, we will have access to the same knowledge that they had during the Golden Age. The question is, what will we do with that knowledge, how will we use it? I don't know the answer to that honey. I imagine that some things will look the same, while others will look very different." Hannah wondered at the possibilities. She thought about finding the Oracle, about the future, about a new Golden Age.

While Hannah daydreamed about the Oracle, Ferrell was wondering about other things. Why did Sarkoth choose him to succeed him as the next High Elder of the Clan? A year ago, it would have been easy to imagine what it might be like, but now? If they found the Oracle, the world would undergo a dramatic metamorphosis. The Clan itself had already changed. After five-hundred years, their isolation from the world outside was no more. They had collaborated with the Christian Church; they had fought a war against Kraken and his men. No, all Ferrell could say for certain was that the world was going to be a far different place after they found the Oracle. There would be many difficult decisions facing them, and he was not certain how much longer Lord Sarkoth would be alive. While he was in extremely good health for someone of his advanced age, he was a very old man, and there was no telling how much longer he had.

"You seem to have a lot on your mind, my friend," said Sebastian, who had pulled up next to Ferrell and was now riding beside him.

Ferrell grunted.

"Thinking about what Lord Sarkoth told you?" asked the priest.

Ferrell looked at him with a perplexed look.

"It wasn't difficult to guess, Clansman Ferrell. We have spent considerable time together, and I have watched as you planned complex battle strategies. Having only recently discovered that you will lead the Clan upon the death of Lord Sarkoth, well, I naturally assumed it might weigh heavily on your mind; it would be a lot for anyone to take in. How are you holding up?"

"Only a year ago, I doubted I would ever see the Main Enclave or Lord Sarkoth again. Now he wants me to take over when he dies. Yes, it is a lot to think about."

"Well, I for one cannot think of anyone more qualified to follow a man as respectable and honorable as Lord Sarkoth."

"I am not worthy."

"Ferrell, I have seen you lead these men into battle, and I have seen the way they follow you, the tremendous respect that they have for you. They hold you in very high regard. I doubt anyone but Sarkoth himself comes close to the respect that you command."

"Thank you, Brother Sebastian."

Wilijah stopped ahead, and pulled alongside Ferrell as he approached.

"Lord Ferrell?"

"Yes, Wilijah, what is it?"

"One of the scouts has returned. It appears that our path ahead is blocked."

Ferrell turned and rode back next to Alex.

"Alex, do you have any idea how close we are to the ancient road that you spoke of? It appears that our way is blocked up ahead. We may need to find another way around."

"I would guess maybe another hour's ride, maybe two," answered Alex.

"Do you know of another way other than the path we are on?"

"I am sorry Ferrell, I don't."

"Thank you, Alex."

Ferrell looked over to Wilijah.

"Tell the scout that we need to find another way around. Have them look for a path. If they cannot find one, have them take some extra men to clear the way. Remember, we need to move a thousand men!" said Ferrell.

"Yes, my lord."

As they approached where the path was blocked, the scouts had not yet returned. Ferrell looked at the sky and saw that the sun was now low in the sky.

"Wilijah, we will make camp up ahead, please pass the word along to the rest of the men."

"Yes, Lord Ferrell."

They stopped for the night in a field between two wooded areas, just off the main road. As darkness crept in, they set up camp and began preparing dinner. As everyone sat down to eat a short time later, Alex walked over to where Ferrell, Sebastian, and Darius were eating.

"May I join you?" he asked.

"Please do, Alex," answered Sebastian. Alex walked over and sat next to his friend. "Something on your mind?" asked the priest.

"I've been wondering about something," said Alex. "Does anyone have any idea what the Oracle is, and how we are supposed to activate it? I understand it is supposed to hold the knowledge of the Ancients, but what exactly does that mean? Is the Oracle a statue? Is it a library of books? Is it some mystical device? How will we even know when we find it?"

"Those are excellent questions, Alex, and we are all hoping that you will be able to help us find the answers."

Alex looked at both priests and asked them, "Can either of you tell me anything else related to the Oracle that you have not already mentioned, anything passed along over the years, anything, even if it seems trivial, or unimportant."

"Well, let me see," said Brother Sebastian. "The Oracle is said to contain all the knowledge of the Ancients. We know that we were supposed to wait until the sign appeared in the sky, signifying that the time to seek the Oracle had come. It seems there was something else....let's see, oh, yes, there was a children's rhyme, something about the Oracle being a sleeping giant that lives underground, but of course, there is no mention of this in the documented information about the Oracle that was passed down from the Ancients. You said to mention anything, even something as trivial as a children's story."

"I heard that rhyme as a child, my mother used to sing it to me," said Darius. Perhaps there is some truth to it?"

"Sometimes stories are passed down, even as rhymes, that contain some elements of fact," answered Alex.

"I don't know if there is anything to it Alex. As I said, it was only a rhyme," Sebastian reminded him.

"Is there anything else that you can think of?" he asked.

"Nothing I can think of," answered Darius.

"Nor I, Alex," said Sebastian.

Alex looked over at Ferrell. "What about you Ferrell? Perhaps there was something that was passed along through the Clan regarding the Oracle?"

"I cannot think of anything Alex, I'm sorry. Perhaps something will come to mind over the next few days."

Wilijah suddenly emerged from the woods and approached Ferrell.

"Lord Ferrell, they have cleared the path. We should be clear to proceed at first light."

"Thank you, Wilijah. Please, sit down and join us."

Chapter 44
The Lake

They rode for two more weeks before coming at last to the area on the map that indicated the location of the Oracle. The area was isolated, far from the closest meros. While there were some structures scattered around the general area, mostly they saw woods, some clearings, and structures that had long ago surrendered to undergrowth and trees.

"Well, this looks like the location shown on the map. Now what? I don't see anything," said Ferrell.

"Are you sure this is the right position on the map, Alex?" asked Darius.

"Well, it's hard to say for certain, there are no specific marks on the map. We must have everyone search the entire area, look for anything that might look out of place. The location on the map is labeled Research Triangle Park; perhaps there is an ancient sign visible somewhere. We should split up so we can cover more ground. Let's meet back here around noon, when the sun is the highest in the sky."

"Very good. I will spread the word to the men," said Ferrell.

They searched for miles in all directions for the location marked on the map as the location for the Oracle.

"It's like we are looking for a needle in a stack of needles!" Alex remarked to his daughter, who was riding beside him. "We don't even know what we are looking for. We must be missing something." Finally, Alex stopped and got down off his horse. He pulled out a reproduction of the map, walked over to a stump and sat down. "What could we possibly be missing?" he asked, going over the map yet once again.

"Can I help, Dad?" asked Hannah.

"Sure honey, I need all of the help I can get."

Hannah sat down next to her father and they looked over the map together.

"On this map are geographic markings such as rivers, creeks, and a few of the ancient roads. The location marked on the map for the Oracle is at the north end of a large lake. We've searched for hours all around the north end of the only lake in the area however, and we've found nothing. Actually, we've searched around all of it, and found nothing.

"Dad?"

"Yes Hannah, what is it?"

"Didn't you tell me once that some years it rains more than others?"

"Yes baby, that's right."

"And didn't you also say that you read somewhere once that the weather can change significantly, over long periods of time?"

"Yes Hannah, that's right. Why are you asking me about this now?"

"Well...I was just wondering. If the map says that the Oracle is located near the north end of the lake, and the level of the lake rises or drops based on the amount of rainfall, isn't it possible that the lake is not as full now as it once was, say, hundreds of years ago?" Alex took the map, looked at Hannah, and gave her hug.

"Hannah, you are brilliant!"

Alex saw Sebastian and Darius examining an old structure nearby.

"We think that we're onto something!" The priests left what they were doing and joined the father and daughter. The four of them started walking north.

"I'm beginning to think that it could take us months, perhaps years, to find the Oracle, even with the map," said Darius.

"Maybe," said Alex. "If we made the mistake we think we made, it should not be so hard to find. It looks like we just need to try looking farther north. We need to imagine the lake being much larger, as it may have been five-hundred years ago. If I am right, the Oracle should be no more than a few miles from here."

As they walked at a brisk pace to the north, Alex saw a group of men standing idly by a hundred yards away in the woods.

Alex walked over to where the men were standing.

"We believe we know the approximate location where the Oracle is. Can you please come and give us a hand?" asked Alex.

"Yes, sir, of course," one of the men said, eager to help.

They walked several miles north of the lake. Eventually, they happened upon a number of smaller, unassuming buildings.

"Are we getting close, Dad?" asked Hannah.

"I'm not sure, Hannah, but I think we are. It's possible we misread the map, and that the Oracle is really hundreds, perhaps even thousands of miles from here, but I don't think we did. I believe we're very close to the Oracle now." He looked around the area, assessing its qualifications as a location for the Oracle. "Let's stop for a bit and rest." After a few minutes, Alex was able to catch his breath and began looking around. The area was littered with small buildings all around them.

"This should be about right, I would think. Let's start here. We'll have to begin searching these structures one by one. Look for anything that might have the Unity Symbol, or other markings that could identify the location of the Oracle, maybe something similar to these symbols on the map."

"Dad, do you think that people once lived here?" Hannah had wandered over next to him and sat down without him even noticing.

"I don't see any wells, or homes, or anything indicating people lived here. It's strange, in some ways, this area is like the Outlands, in other ways it's more like a mero. Mostly, there's just a lot of buildings with letters all over them."

"What do these words mean?" she asked.

Alex evaluated some of the buildings, amazed that any of the lettering was still visible. On some of them, the letters were raised, making them easily legible, while on others, the lettering had faded long ago.

"They say different things, names mostly. Like parts of most meros I've been in, I suspect that people probably used to work in these structures. It doesn't look like people ever lived here, or at least not since well before the Golden Age."

They searched several of the smaller buildings in the area but found nothing. In some of them, he was able to find books that were preserved well enough that he was still able to read them. Alex wondered what kind of work people had done there. Did they buy and sell? Did they make something? While Alex was able to read some of the books, he did not understand the meaning or context of many of them. The people must have known much about advanced ancient knowledge.

Eventually, his eyes came to rest on one of the smaller buildings. It was an unassuming, ordinary looking building. It also had the raised lettering, like some of the other structures in the area. The letters were almost completely faded, worn down by weather and time, but remained legible. The words "Dfficial Besearch And Collaborative Library of the Earth." He decided to investigate the building further and as he approached it, found that he had misread some of the letters. It actually spelled "Official Research And Collaborative Library of the

Earth." He stood for a few moments, staring at the lettering. It reminded him of his experience with the painting. There was something there, but what? Finally, he saw it: Official Research And Collaborative Library of the Earth-ORACLE."

Could this be it? It must be. He looked over the sign and the building, looking for something else. When his eyes came to rest on the front door, he noticed something etched faintly into the door. If he had not been looking for it, he would never have noticed the sign of the Unity.

"Hey," Alex yelled to the others, "I believe we have found it, the location of the Oracle!"

Chapter 45
Into the Darkness

"Over here!" Alex yelled to the others. Hannah came running and was soon joined by the others.

"The door is locked. We have to find a way inside, this has to be it!" Alex told them.

The big man gave it a good hard kick and the ancient door flew open.

"Wait," said Alex, "we will need torches."

They found six sticks, tore up some clothing, and wrapped the clothing around the sticks tightly. One of the clansmen then pulled out a flint and using the back of his knife and some dry leaves, started a small fire to light a couple of torches.

"These should last a while at least. The sun is still high in the sky so we should be able to see some inside without them. Let's wait to light the rest until we need them," he said.

Alex led the way as they looked around inside the front entrance. There were a number of windows just inside the door, allowing enough light inside so that they were able to see. In the perfectly preserved room, they saw chairs, various books, and other ancient artifacts common to most of the ancient meros he had been in. The contents of the room had remained virtually undisturbed except for the dust. "It is doubtful that anyone has been inside this building since the Great Collapse," Alex remarked, as he looked through drawers in a desk. Finding nothing of interest, Alex suggested they move on.

As they walked deeper into the structure, the light from the windows grew dim and they were forced to light the remaining torches they had brought inside with them. After walking through a number of rooms and finding much the same thing, they soon came to a door, and then some stairs.

"How far down do these go, Dad?" asked Hannah.

"I don't know honey, I would guess they go down at least several floors, but it's hard to tell without more light."

"Is it safe?" she asked.

"I believe it should be fine, sweetheart, and these stairs certainly seem study enough. They're made of some kind of metal and rock, so we should be fine."

After they had gone down another level, they searched the next floor, finding mostly the same thing they had on the first. Finding nothing else, they continued going floor-to-floor, looking for something, anything, that might be connected to the Oracle mentioned in the prophecy. By the time they reached the tenth and bottom floor, Alex had nearly given up hope, beginning to suspect that the stories had been just that, nothing but stories. Upon reaching the last floor, however, they found that things looked substantially different from the rest. The air was much thinner and the torches struggled at times to stay lit.

There was a metal door, with the words, "RESTRICTED AREA", and below that the words "HIGH VOLTAGE." The door opened with a blast of old, stale, air. Inside, it was pitch black. Even with the torches, it was hard to see, with visibility no more than ten feet, but Alex had a sense that they were in the middle of a very large room.

Suddenly, a shrill scream came from across the room.

"Hannah, what is it? Are you okay!" yelled Alex.

"I'm okay, Dad. I'm over here!"

Alex followed the sound of her voice until he could make her out in the faint light. He held the torch down next to where Hannah was standing. There was a skeleton sitting in a chair, clutching a book in its hands.

"Brother Sebastian, Brother Darius! Look!"

Alex held the torch in one hand, and pointed to the book in the skeleton's hands with the other. On the cover of the book was a now familiar symbol.

"It is the sign of The Unity," said Sebastian.

"What is The Unity?" asked one of the men. Brother Darius noted that he was a large man, much bigger than all of the others."

"Why, the ones that wrote the book, the ones that told us about the Oracle, of course!"

"Oh yes, of course," he answered.

Alex took the book, opened it, and thumbed through it. "Wow, this is great stuff, listen to this...

'Friend,

If you are reading this, unfortunately, we must have been correct in our prediction, civilization has long ago fallen apart, and the world plunged into perpetual darkness.

Since you have made it this far, you must have correctly interpreted the clues we left behind, and you have collected all seven pieces of the map. We can only hope that the remnant of The Pulse, which has been clearly visible in the sky, what we call, The Effect, has dissipated by now.

We regret all of the trouble and danger that you likely went through in order for you to find this place, but we felt we had to take extraordinary measures to ensure that the Oracle did not fall into the wrong hands. Since you have made it this far, we felt that it was only fitting that we provide you with some background about the Oracle, about us, and about what has happened, that you may find useful.

We learned of the Oracle from one of the greatest computer scientists our civilization ever produced, Dr. Bjorn Yvornsky, who happened to be among our number at the Unity conference. Dr. Yvornsky worked as part of a special project called The Official Research And Collaborative Library of the Earth, or Oracle.

The Great Oracle is by far the most advanced supercomputer ever built. The Oracle, built with a revolutionary new crystal technology, has a virtually unlimited capacity for the storage of information. The Oracle also includes the world's most advanced artificial intelligence, complete with a complex, extremely advanced, interactive voice-recognition and holographic interface.

Dr. Yvornsky, and the rest of his team, working with scientists from across the planet, have placed into the Oracle all of the world's available knowledge, accumulated over seven-thousand years.

Because the power requirements of the Oracle and all of its associated systems were enormous, a completely self-contained, fusion-powered, nuclear reactor was installed within this facility to power the system.

Once the Oracle has been activated, you will be able to ask it virtually any question imaginable, and it will formulate an answer using all of the information contained within its core. It will also be able to tell you everything you need to know in order to maintain and repair it.

Had it been operating when the Pulse occurred, the Oracle would have been destroyed along with everything else. We believe that two critical factors should have worked together to protect the Oracle; first, the unique design of the Oracle's crystalline technology, which was also used in the fusion reactor, as long as it was not active when the Pulse struck, or while the Effect is still visible. Second, the fact that it was not yet fully connected when the Pulse struck. If Dr. Yvornsky is successful in reaching the Oracle, and completing the steps necessary to connect it to the reactor, it should be ready for activation by the time you read this. Unfortunately, with The Effect still very active in the sky above us, we are unable to test it to be certain, so we leave that final step to you.

Here are the instructions for activating the Oracle. At one end of this room, there is a panel marked HIGH VOLTAGE. Inside this panel, there is a master power switch. You can identify the master power switch by its black-and-yellow striped handle. Flip the handle up, and that should activate the reactor and turn the power on. You will need to wait fifteen minutes. If the reactor is operational, the power will come online and the lights should come on. The entire building was designed to be powered by the reactor.

At the other end of the room is a console. The white console will rise out of the floor. On the console, you will see a green button. If the power is on, the button should be flashing green. Insert the key, turn it clockwise, and press the green button. Within five minutes, the system should start coming online.

If what Dr. Yvornsky said is accurate and if everything is still intact, all that you should have to do is flip the power switch, press the button, and the Oracle itself will help with the rest.

If it is God's will, the Oracle will come online, and should be a tremendous assistance in re-building, and restoring civilization to our darkened planet. We hope and pray for your sake, and for all future generations, that it works.

Lastly, a final warning. Do not attempt to activate the Oracle if the Effect is still visible in the night sky. The moment that you do, whatever you have activated will stop working, and all of your efforts to this point will have been in vain.

In many ways, we envy you. You stand in the doorway to a bright new world full of discovery and wonder beyond your dreams. If you take advantage of this opportunity, and learn from our mistakes, God willing you can build a new and better world than we have ever known. Avoid becoming so dazzled by and dependent on technology that you begin worshipping the work of your own hands rather than God, the way we did. Instead, we hope you will build a world in which faith and technology work together in a synergistic bond, combining the love of God and the morals and ethics of Christianity, with the limitless power of technology. It is our fervent hope and desire that the brave, new world that we have envisioned for you comes to pass. The future is now in your hands, my friend; may you fare better with your world than we did with ours.

May God bless you all in your brave new world,

Signed,

The Unity'"

Chapter 46
An Old Acquaintance

"Okay everyone, look for some kind of panel, or box. It might be on the wall or on the floor. It should have a sign with some lettering on it, similar to what we found on the door when we came in."

"You mean like this one?" asked one of the men.

Alex dashed over to see what he had found. A dejected look fell over his face.

"No, that isn't it," he said.

"Alex, over here!" Darius was at the end of the room nearest the back wall. He held a torch over a grayish colored metal box. On the outside was a label that read:

"WARNING. HIGH VOLTAGE-HANDLE WITH CARE"

"Yes, this is it!" exclaimed Alex.

Alex lifted the door covering the panel and found the yellow-and-black stripped handle

"Okay, everyone," said Alex, "I have absolutely no idea what is going to happen next, if anything. Does anyone want to leave before I lift this switch up?"

Alex looked down at Hannah. "Listen honey, maybe you should go up and get some air. I'm sure one of these fine men would be happy to escort you." Hannah looked stubbornly at her father. "Oh, I know that look. Okay, okay, I will go ahead and flip the switch. Here we go." Alex raised the lever to the "On" position, but nothing happened. He waited for several minutes and still, nothing. Finally, he let out a heavy sigh.

"Well, I guess it's been too long, or else it was damaged when the Pulse struck after all," said Alex.

"Wait, listen!" yelled Hannah.

Just as they had all started to lose hope, they began hearing strange and unfamiliar sounds. It started with a slow, whirring noise, and some clicking and popping, followed by clanking sounds. After the imperfect symphony had continued for several minutes, the room was suddenly filled with a blinding white light and the room came alive with bizarre lights and sounds.

At first, everyone found it difficult to keep their eyes open. The artificial light was much brighter then any of them had ever seen outside of the sun, and their eyes had not yet had time to adjust from the faint glow of the torches to such blinding light. In addition to illumination, the air also suddenly grew cooler and it became much easier to breathe. After a couple of minutes, everyone's eyes had adjusted; Hannah was the first to comment. "Yippee!"

The room filled with excitement and wonder as they celebrated the moment, barely able to contain their enthusiasm. Darius could see that everyone wore large smiles across their faces, everyone except for the big man and his companions. It had been hard to see them clearly, after they had started descending the stairs. Before that, all of them had been in a hurry to locate the building, and caught up in the excitement of the moment. Now, under the illumination of the bright lights in the strange room they were in, he could see everyone clearly. For the first time, he noticed the unusual scar above the right eye of the big man.

Looking at him, he leaned over to Brother Sebastian and asked, "Brother Sebastian, where did Alex find these men? Do you remember seeing any of them on the trip from the Clan Enclave?"

Brother Sebastian looked over the men and said, "No, Darius, now that you mention it, I cannot say that I recall seeing any of them on the way here. But really, you know, there were so many, and I am no longer a young man!" Darius stared at the big man just a few seconds too long because this time, he noticed Darius's interest.

"Brother Sebastian," he whispered to the elder priest, "do you recall on our ride down here, when Ferrell was describing his battle with Kraken, didn't he describe him as a really big man, with a scar over his right eye?"

They both looked on with fear as the big man walked across the room over to where they were standing.

"Well, well, this is great isn't it? Looks like we have found the Great Oracle of Knowledge! Now, we can bring civilization back to the world and end the Dark Age. Exciting isn't it!"

Darius started backing away as he started to say, "You, you....you are Kr–aaagghh." Darius was never able to finish his sentence. His voice trailed off as the big knife entered his mid-section, penetrating his heart, and ending his life. The unusual cross that hung around his neck made a loud noise as his lifeless body slammed onto the hard floor.

Brother Sebastian yelled at Kraken. "You...you...you beast! You, you animal! You murderer!" Kraken began laughing as his men moved to position themselves around Alex, Sebastian, and the rest.

"Ah.....music to my ears, priest!" he exclaimed, barely able to contain his amusement. "And you want to know what the funniest part of all of this is! You invited us down here! Imagine, how ironic it was, that you invited us here! Ha...ha....ha..." Kraken's laughter went on for some time, terrorizing his captives. Eventually it subsided and he began looking around the room. "Well, I was getting a bit bored with all of this pretending anyway, eh?"

Sebastian noticed that Kraken was missing his right hand. Whether he had done a good job at keeping his severed limb hidden or whether it was just the poor lighting that had kept them from discovering the deception earlier, he could not tell. Either way, Kraken soon noticed Sebastian staring at his hand.

"Oh yes, this! One of your little clansmen friends did this to me. I am looking forward to seeing him again!"

"Lord Kraken." One of his men had walked over to Kraken and whispered something so the others would not hear.

"We're too far underground, it's not possible." Then after a few moments, he said to the man, "Go ahead and check though, just to be on the safe side." The metal door slammed just behind where Kraken was standing, as he continued, "Oh, don't worry, no one heard your little friend scream. No one that far up can hear anything down here with us being so far underground, not to mention this heavy, metal door, behind me. But let's just say that with several hundred of your pals running around up above, I would like to have a little peace of mind."

"Well you better get all of the peace of mind while you can. Because you can rest assured, you monster, that you will have no rest in Hell!" said Sebastian, still distraught at the cold-blooded murder of his young friend, and fellow priest.

"You know, that is just one reason why I don't like you priests. All of your talk about a life after this one, about some miserable carpenter that died and then rose from the dead... what was his name again? Oh yes, Jesus? That other priest, your Brother Ramos, used to pray to this Jesus day and night, even while I was torturing him, even as he died! You priests really should worry a little more about what happens in this life!"

Kraken started moving toward Sebastian when Alex, attempting to distract him said, "So tell me something, Kraken is it?"

"Eh?" Kraken turned his head to look at Alex. "What…who are you anyway? You're not a priest, and you're not a clansman, so what are you even doing here anyway?"

"My name is Alex; I do some work for the Church sometimes. I was helping them find the book that eventually led us here."

"Alex, don't get involved!" exclaimed Brother Sebastian. "You don't need to worry about me, after all, I'm just an old priest, an old man, and I know where I will wake up when I fall asleep here. "

Kraken turned back to Sebastian for a moment. "Don't worry priest, I haven't forgotten about you. You and I will get better acquainted in just a few moments. But for now, I am interested in Alex." He looked back at Alex. "So, you are the one that found the book, the one that found the map, and now the one that found this place? Impressive, I must say. I might be able to use a man like you when I re-build my empire."

"So how did you end up here?" asked Alex. "We heard that you left the battle when you were injured, when you lost your hand!" said Alex.

"After I got this fixed," he said, pointing to his stump with his good hand, "I waited for the fools to leave their enclave and followed them here. The stupid clansmen moved slowly because of their number, and because you and the priests were with them, along with your charming…" Alex's blood froze as he saw that Kraken was looking at Hannah who was standing across the room, "…daughter," he continued. "My, my, my, what a beautiful daughter you are, too!" Kraken began walking toward Hannah, smiling as he did so.

"You stay away from her!" yelled Alex, before being grabbed from behind by one of the men. Kraken ignored Alex and continued walking slowly toward his daughter.

"Perhaps we should get better acquainted, my dear!" The door suddenly opened behind him as he began getting close to Hannah. "Was everything clear?" he asked, pausing but not bothering to turn around.

"No…" was the reply, just as Kraken felt a sharp, searing pain as a long steel blade suddenly emerged from his chest, that cut upward for a moment, and withdrew. Kraken dropped down to his knees. "…everything was not clear," finished Ferrell, as the door opened again and the room filled with clansmen. The men who had followed Kraken offered only a brief resistance, which did not last long.

Hannah ran over to her father and held onto him tightly. Ferrell cleaned his sword on Kraken's shoulder. The former urba leader, now on his knees, looked up at Ferrell and opened his eyes wide.

"You!" exclaimed Kraken,

"You were right," said Ferrell. "You did see me again…" and with that, Kraken fell to the floor, dead.

Ferrell looked around the room and said, "Is everyone okay?" He saw Sebastian on the floor next to Darius, kneeling down next to his dead friend's body, weeping. Ferrell shook his head sadly, hung his head low, looked at Sebastian, and said, "Brother Sebastian, I am sorry for the loss of your friend, he was a good man."

"Yes, he was a good man, Ferrell," Sebastian replied, wiping tears from his eyes. Sebastian turned and said to the clansman, "Thank you Clansman Ferrell. I grieve for myself, and for my loss, but not for him. I know that my friend, my brother, is with our Lord now, the same Lord Jesus that led us to find this place."

"Ferrell?" The clansman turned to Alex.

"Yes, Alex?"

"How did you find us? I mean, we are ten floors underground."

"Yes, we are. We had been searching for you and had eventually picked up your tracks, which led us here. We were just preparing to enter the building when one of Kraken's men emerged from the doorway. He was wearing our clothing, no doubt taken from some of our fallen brothers on the battlefield, but we knew he was not one of us."

Alex walked over next to the console that would activate the Oracle. He was looking down at the console as some of the clansmen prepared to pick up Darius' body, and carry it back up the stairs for burial. Alex noticed a hole with a strange pattern in the console. They were going to need a key.

"Oh no, how could I have missed that?" Everyone stopped what they were doing, and looked at Alex. Several of the clansmen put their hands on their swords.

"What's the matter Alex?" asked Sebastian. "What is it?"

"It was in the book. We were so focused on the map, that we forgot the book mentioned a key, we need it to activate the Oracle."

The priest walked over and looked at the console. "Is this where the key goes?" he asked Alex.

"Yes, I believe so."

"Hmmm, I believe I have seen this pattern somewhere before." He thought about it for a moment, he still had a tear on his cheek when he remembered. He walked over to the clansmen that were carrying Darius' body out the door.

"Wait one second please, dear brothers!" He made the sign of the Cross and said to his fallen friend and said, "Please forgive me, Brother Darius." He removed the cross from around his neck and nodded at the men, letting them know it was okay for them to carry him on out.

"I knew I had seen this somewhere before. Brother Darius had brought this back with him from Rome. The Holy Father wore it around his neck for many years. Darius told me that Pope John Paul V had requested that he wear it when he sent Darius here. He told Darius that it was important, but he never said why. He had the key around his neck the entire time, and he didn't even know it," muttered Sebastian. "The cross is the key. I suppose His Holiness knew, perhaps it was something that had been passed down from pope to pope since the time of the Great Collapse."

Sebastian offered the key to Alex, who took it and inserted it into the console. The archaeologist took a final look around the room as he prepared to press the green button, which was now flashing green.

Chapter 47
The Great Oracle

Alex stared at the flashing green button for several moments before turning to look at Hannah.

"Should I push it, Hannah?" he asked her, with a mock look of worry on his face.

"Dad, please! Push the button!"

"No, I'm afraid I can't,"he answered, with a mischievous grin, "but you can!"

"Me?" she asked, thrilled at the prospect.

"Come on, press it!"

Hannah walked over to the console and after pausing a moment, looked at her father, cracked a big smile, and pressed the flashing green button, which stopped flashing immediately after she had pressed it. Everyone looked around the room, wondering what would happen next. Lights dimmed all around them, leaving only a very faint light that they could barely see by, while bright colored lights shone all around, and various clicking noises filled the large room. Suddenly, a palpable silence filled the room when all of the noises stopped.

"Look, there, something is there!" yelled one of the clansmen, as he and several others drew their swords.

Terror gripped them as a faint golden glow slowly materialized in the middle of the room, seemingly out of nothingness. It began as a pale, white, and yellow glow, which slowly grew brighter in both intensity and clarity. What began as a vague shape of color slowly formed into a tall staircase that seemed to extend well above the ceiling. Clouds hovered around the top of the stairs, where what appeared to be an exotic, beautiful young woman stood. She slowly began descending the stairs.

317

Alex had never seen such a beautiful woman before. He and everyone else in the room stood transfixed until she reached the bottom of the stairs. She stood approximately 5'8, with long, flowing black hair. She wore a stunning blue gown that nearly matched her brilliant blue eyes. Everyone in the room wore the same startled expression. Suddenly, she began to speak.

"Bonjour." "Hello." "Ciao." "Алло." "Hola." "Guten,"

The young woman paused between words just a few moments, before continuing to say "hello' in another set of six languages. "Oh, my," exclaimed Sebastian, dumbfounded as he looked upon the stairs, and the woman, that had appeared out of thin air.

"Language identified-English" she said.

"Greetings, I am Pythia, an avatar, or human interface for the "Grid-Based Real-Time Exabyte-Capacity Avatar Terminal Official Research And Collaborative Library of the Earth," also referred to as the GREAT ORACLE. How may I help you?"

"Fascinating," said Sebastian.

"Who, or what, are you?" asked Alex.

The woman turned to face Alex. "My name is Pythia. I am a computer-generated, holographic interface for the Great Oracle, an advanced supercomputer serving as the repository of all human knowledge. The Oracle is a completely interactive, supercomputer system, equipped with a revolutionary form of artificial intelligence, and a holographic, highly-advanced voice-recognition human-interactive interface, called Pythia."

"Are you, alive?" asked Hannah.

"I am not what you would call alive, though I am a highly-advanced computer with a form of artificial intelligence. I suppose you might consider me a kind of artificial life form. I am unlike any computer ever before built by human beings."

"What is a computer?" asked Hannah.

"A computer is a machine that manipulates data according to a list of instructions."

"What is a machine?" she asked.

"A machine is any mechanical or electrical device that transmits or modifies energy to perform or assist in the performance of human tasks."

"And what human tasks do you assist with?" asked Alex.

"I assist with learning, teaching, with storing and providing information to people, and I can assist with nearly any task stored within my data crystals."

An image of the insides of the Oracle suddenly appeared just as Pythia had. Alex tried to touch the image, but his hand passed right through. The same thing happened when he tried to touch Pythia. Alex was so surprised that he jerked back in shock.

She's not real!

"I was built to contain all of the vast knowledge that humanity has accumulated over the past seven thousand years. Stored within my core is all of the available knowledge possessed by mankind at the time I was built."

"And when were you built?" asked Hannah.

"My construction was completed in the year 2025, though I have never been activated, until now."

"Pythia, I have a question. Centuries ago, civilization collapsed, following an event we know only as, The Pulse. We understand that you can help us re-build our world, restore civilization, is this true?" asked Sebastian.

"Of course. Stored in my core is all accumulated human knowledge, everything from how to build an airplane or a house, to how to plant crops and cure many diseases."

"Pythia," asked Alex, "can you tell us what happened five-hundred years ago? What caused The Pulse and the Effect?"

"I have no record of any event happening after the year 2025. I do not have enough information to form a sound hypothesis. Nevertheless, I could offer a possible answer to your question."

"Please do, "said Alex.

"A catastrophic event called The Pulse that occurred five-hundred years ago and suddenly ended civilization, could refer to an electro-magnetic pulse, though there is none on record powerful enough to disable electronics across the entire planet. If you provide me with as much information as you can, I will provide the best hypothesis possible to explain what has happened."

Sebastian motioned to Alex. "Alex, if you will permit me, perhaps I can help here."

"Of course, Brother."

"Pythia," began Sebastian, "approximately five hundred years ago something happened. It was a single, unexpected, unanticipated event, that we still call, The Pulse. It so disrupted human society that it brought about the Great Collapse of civilization, and caused the beginning of what we call The Dark Age. According to legend, The Pulse somehow caused The Effect, a mysterious ribbon of light that appeared in the night sky around the same time of the Great Collapse. The Effect was something we never really thought much about until now. It disappeared a few months ago. The Church has long held that The Effect was somehow related to the Great Collapse, and the beginning of the Dark Age. Lastly, we recently found a book written during The Great Collapse, which suggests that people alive at that time believed that The Pulse would last for a hundred years. Please tell us everything you can about what happened?"

"Do you presently have electricity? Do you have any machines that use electricity, any which functioned during the Dark Age, before The Effect disappeared?" asked the Oracle.

"I have no idea what electricity is," answered Sebastian. He looked around the room. Everyone either shrugged their shoulders or shook their heads.

"I now have enough information to provide a working hypothesis. It is as follows:

"Sometime, in or around the year, 2025, some kind of Electromagnetic Pulse, or EMP occurred. This could have been a man-made event, or it could have been a natural phenomenon, perhaps a massive solar flare discharged by the Sun, interacting in some manner with the Earth's magnetic field. This would explain the aurora borealis you described in the night sky. If an event did occur, whether natural, created by man, or both, it would have to have been enormous to affect civilization on a global scale. Had this been a normal EMP blast, like those associated with nuclear blasts, then the impact would not have been global. Even if the EMP were large enough to impact the entire planet, then civilization would still have been able to recover within a decade or two. Something about this event must have been significantly different from a nuclear-induced EMP. This enormous EMP blast may have been trapped somehow by the Earth's magnetic field, creating what you call The Effect. It is likely that this Effect is what prevented civilization from recovering from the event.

"An EMP can damage electrical components like computers, electronics, and communications equipment. By the year 2025, the world relied heavily on electronics to support nearly every aspect of people's lives. Most of the world's critical infrastructure relied on electrical components; everything from the power grids, power plants, communications, heating, air-conditioning, food, water, and transportation, to weapons, recreation, medical care, even education depended on electricity in some form or fashion.

"If an EMP event was trapped in the earth's magnetic field, it follows that after such an event, with no way to rebuild electrical systems that civilization depended on, society soon began to unravel. Businesses that relied on electricity to cool, to heat, for water, for food, and for communication, abruptly came to a screeching halt. Homes that relied on electricity for heating and cooling were no longer inhabitable. Governments that were unable to communicate both internally and externally soon ceased to function altogether. Military, police, and emergency responders that depended on electricity to operate soon fell apart.

"Given the rapid expansion of the world's human population by the year 2025, there was a growing dependency on machines to support and fuel that growth, which undoubtedly exacerbated the impact of the event, especially in metropolitan areas. People that lived in the urban, metropolitan centers relied on electricity to survive. When the electricity failed, the large urban areas became incapable of sustaining life within months, possibly even weeks. People living in these urban areas were soon faced with deadly competition for food, water, and supplies. Anarchy quickly followed as people began dying in high numbers from dehydration, starvation, disease, and violence. As seasons progressed from autumn into winter, people living in the cities were forced to burn any materials that they could find to stay warm and survive. Some of the most readily available items were derived from wood; items such as papers, furniture, and books. Within a decade, most of the books were probably burned for fuel. The growing scarcity of books, combined with the increased time spent focused on survival, eventually led to a growing problem with illiteracy. Gradually, most of humanity's accumulated knowledge faded from the face of the earth. This scenario, while only a hypothesis, would account for what you call The Great Collapse, the complete collapse of human civilization.

"With no electricity, humanity's technological progress was set back a thousand years. With the world plunged into conditions reminiscent of medieval times, people once again came to rely on primitive weapons such as bows arrows, and swords. Like the Dark Ages that followed the collapse of the ancient Roman Empire, so too conditions deteriorated and civilization once again descended into darkness."

Pythia fell quiet, standing motionless in the center of the large room. After a few minutes, Alex spoke up.

"Pythia, civilizations were around before electricity was invented, weren't they?"

"Yes, they were."

"Then why was civilization set so far back?"

"Because the electro magnetic pulse did not stop everything gradually, it stopped everything instantly. Mass confusion ran rampant as food and water disappeared, and people began to die in large numbers. I estimate mortality to be around seventy to eighty-percent within the first five years alone. The estimated population remaining alive on the earth after ten years is five-hundred million people. The estimated population after twenty years is one-hundred million.

"Civilizations existed for thousands of years before electricity because cultures had gradually devised ways of dealing with their environment without electricity. For example, food was prepared and preserved in a far different manner before electricity, and houses built before electricity had extra-high ceilings in order that the house could stay cool in the hot summer months. They had fireplaces to burn wood in to stay warm during the winter months, and cities were built near rivers and streams so they could find water and wash clothes. Farming required only seeds, a strong man, a horse, and a plow. By the time I was built however, the knowledge of such ancient practices had long since faded from the collective human memory. The Pulse, coupled with The Effect, caused the delicate fabric of society to unravel. It would take some time for the world to find a new balance, and for stability to be restored."

During Pythia's response, the Oracle had displayed numerous holographic image; computer graphics that simulated an EMP, machines stopping, and people dying from starvation, violence, or from disease. Some of the images were so horrific that tears flowed freely from many in the room, but no more so than from Brother Sebastian, who felt overwhelmed with sadness, and compassion, for the great number that had died.

Sebastian made the sign of the cross and with his voice trembling said, "So many people dead. So many lives lost. How awful and how very sad." Alex wrapped his arm around the shaken priest.

"Pythia, what is an electromagnetic pulse?" asked Hannah.

"An electromagnetic pulse (EMP) is a quick, powerful blast of electromagnetic energy that ranges across a significant portion of the electromagnetic spectrum. In short, it disrupts anything that uses electricity."

"Including a computer?"

"Especially a computer."

"Then why didn't it affect you?" Hannah asked, scratching her head.

"I was most likely spared because of the revolutionary design of the crystalline circuitry that I and the fusion reactor were built with. In addition, I was not yet activated, nor was I connected to any outside electrical system at the time of the pulse."

"Oh," replied Hannah, uncertain whether she knew any more than she did before she asked the question.

"Are there any more computers like you?" asked Alex.

"Unknown. There were none in existence at the time of my creation that I am aware of."

"Can you please show us what the world was like during the height of the Golden Age?" asked Ferrell, who, fascinated by what he had seen, had walked up to stand beside Sebastian and Alex.

"Certainly."

The entire room was once again filled with images, this time of busy streets, trains, automobiles, city lights, baseball games, and much more, as the Oracle provided what was requested, a representation of what the world was like at the height of the Golden Age.

"Pythia, how do we restore civilization?" asked Alex.

"That is for you to decide. As an artificial life form, I was not programmed to decide the course of human development."

"Can you give us some suggestions where to start?"

"I can."

"Please do."

"I suggest you start with education."

"But how?"

"By utilizing holographic images, I can efficiently educate many human beings at the same time. Fifty people could attend training for six months on a given subject. For example, I could teach fifty how to read and write. When those fifty have completed their training, they can leave and teach another fifty, who in turn teach another fifty. Since I require no rest, this can continue around the clock. Each group can attend for four hours, which means I can teach six groups each day. This means twelve groups of fifty or six-hundred people the first year will learn how to read and write at each location. With seven locations, four-thousand-two hundred people would be literate the first year, with each of those teaching another fifty, four-hundred and twenty-thousand people would be taught the second year alone, one-hundred and forty-two million the third year, and so on.

"What did you mean by 'other locations'?"

"I am connected via fiber optic cabling to seven locations all over the world. Washington, New York, Chicago, Arlington, VA, Athens, Greece, St. Petersburg, Russia, and Hong Kong China. All of these locations have nodes that connect to my systems here, and like me, the nodes at these locations were never active so they should also function when activated. Video streaming and holographic systems are available there as well, enabling me to interact with people there at the same time as I interact with people here."

"These are the same seven locations where the pieces of the map were located!" whispered Sebastian.

"We have been looking for you for a long time Oracle," said Hannah.

'Well now you have found me, and as long as my nuclear fusion power source continues operating properly, I will be here for a long time."

Suddenly, the door swung open and Ariel burst into the room. She had been running and was out of breath.

"They tried to stop me Ferrell, but I was determined to see if you were okay. What are you doing down here? Did you see the lights inside this building, it's incredible! It's like being outside, where is it coming from? It is like the Sun! Why did...." She froze as she noticed the beautiful woman that really was not a woman, standing in the middle of the extremely large room."

"Ferrell Young, care to explain who she is?"

"Why that Ariel, is the um...the Oracle," answered Ferrell.

Chapter 48
After the Darkness

Less than a year after the discovery of the Great Oracle, High Elder Lord Sarkoth, the revered leader of the great Warrior Clan, died peacefully in his sleep of old age. There was great mourning everywhere as news of his death spread. The man who had successfully led the Warrior Clan for well over fifty years, a man that was revered and respected by many inside and outside of the Clan alike, left behind a great legacy; the slow return of civilization to a darkened planet. Nearly one-hundred thousand clansmen, and one thousand priests of the Holy Christian Church, including the pope himself, attended his funeral.

It was widely known throughout the enclaves scattered throughout the Outlands, that Clansman Ferrell had been carefully chosen by Sarkoth to succeed him as High Lord Elder. Most everyone realized that the clan he would lead would be far different from the Clan they knew. The Clan that had cut itself off from the world for hundreds of years to preserve life had become forever engaged with the outside world. They would be needed to protect the Oracle, and preserve the peace, until civilization had once again taken root. Ferrell realized that eventually, perhaps within a hundred years, the Clan, as it had been for centuries, would no longer be needed. It would begin to fade away, slowly at first, then faster as governments formed and civilization was re-established. It was the way of things.

Ferrell had been greatly moved by what he had seen during the time spent with the Christian priests. They had impressed him with their courage, their dedication, and their willingness to die for others. In their own way, they were very much like the clansmen in their bravery, and their dedication to the principles they lived by. He finally came to understand what Sarkoth had seen in them, and why he had such great affection for his friend, Henry.

After a number of discussions with Ariel and Sebastian, Ferrell surprised everyone, Ariel most of all, when he decided to become a Christian himself. Ariel had been persistent, trying since before they were married to convince him that he should follow Christ. While he had always questioned the existence of the Christian God, there was no denying that by preserving the Oracle, and leading them to it, they had been given a great gift. For all of its knowledge and power, the Oracle was just something man-made, a computer, a machine. There was some other force at work that had been ordering events. The pope and Lord Sarkoth, crossing paths as young men, and the alliance that was later forged between the Church and the Clan; Alex finding the book; the discovery of all seven pieces of the map; the sign; the discovery of the Oracle, which still worked after five-hundred years; these were no accidents, and Ferrell knew it.

Lost in his thoughts, Ferrell barely heard the knock on the door.

"Lord Ferrell, may I come in?" asked Sanjo, who now served as Ferrell's personal guard. He smiled as he said, "You have visitors, my lord." Ferrell stood as Ariel walked in with their son, David.

"Hello Ferrell, how are things going today?"

He picked up his son and gave him a hug.

"It's been a busy day. I just don't know whether I'm cut out for this. I really don't know why Lord Sarkoth picked me to lead the Clan. What do I know about leading so many? I should be back in the village, helping with some of the work being done there!"

"Now you know that's not true Ferrell. You are right where you are supposed to be, you must believe that! Lord Sarkoth knew how you cared for the Clan, and about doing what was right. He knew that you were the right man, a man of integrity."

"What is going to happen now?" Ferrell asked his wife. "All over the Outlands, you can find people who have learned how to read and write. Urbas are leaving the meros in order to learn. Everything is changing so fast. What will the world look like when David grows up? Will he even remember the old ways?"

"He will do like his father has always told him to do; he will learn and adapt to the new ways, while also learning and respecting the old." She walked behind him and put her arms on his shoulder. "Mind if I change the subject?" she asked.

Ferrell grunted.

"Did you hear the news?" she asked.

"What news?"

"The news about Brother Sebastian?"

"No I haven't. Is he okay?"

"Well, you know that he has been overseeing much of the education process taking place at the Oracle."

"Yes, I know this."

"Well, it looks like he got news today that the pope wants him to come back to Rome, to succeed him when he dies, just as you succeeded Lord Sarkoth when he died.

"Well, Brother Sebastian is a good man; the world needs a lot more like him. Yes, I think he will make a fine pope, too," he said.

"I understand that Alex has taken on a new role," said Ariel.

"Yes, he has finally decided to settle down. He plans to leave teaching in order to lay down the groundwork for a new government. It seems he's learned a good bit about the people who founded the government that once ruled this land."

"What was this land called during the Golden Age?" asked his wife.

"According to the Oracle, it was once called the United States of America. From what Alex told me, it was the greatest civilization that had ever existed. "

"Well, perhaps Alex can help ensure that when we rebuild, we build a better world than the Ancients," said Ariel.

Ferrell looked down at his young son, pulled him close, and wrapped his arms around him.

"Perhaps he can," Ferrell repeated quietly, holding his son and looking out the window and up at the beautiful blue sky.

As he considered what was to come, Ferrell peered into the future, and found the unknown smiling back at him.

Epilogue

The rain continued to fall outside of the window, sometimes in heavy sheets that sounded like an assembly of snare drums as it beat against the building. She was oblivious to the sound outside her room however; instead, she was listening to the beating of the drums as she watched the battle from a safe distance, her father standing by her side. The sound of a hundred-thousand swords clanging, echoing across the mountains and valleys that surrounded them. She looked up at her father, her face a mixture of fear and awe at the excitement all around. He smiled back at her, but she knew that it was a front, because she knew he was afraid, perhaps even more than she was, though she didn't understand why. The Clan was invincible; the outcome of the fierce battle was inevitable, so she failed to understand her father's concern. She turned back to watch the battle. Both armies fought fiercely, but none as bravely and as confidently as Ferrell. She had seen how he had plowed through Kraken's army. Kraken. She had seen him at various points throughout the entire fight; his big frame on a big horse caused him to stand out easily amongst the masses. She was beginning to wonder where he was, she couldn't find him anywhere on the field of battle. Suddenly she felt her father grasp her hand so tightly that it hurt her. She looked up to protest when instead of her father, she found herself staring in horror into Kraken's face. "My, my, what a beautiful daughter you are too!"

She opened her eyes as she heard the door to her room close. She looked around and saw her great-granddaughter Jessica, her husband Ben, and her great-great-grand children, standing around her.

"Well, well, look who's here!" the ancient woman said to the children as they ran to be by her side.

"Great-Great Grandma!" they screamed in unison, laying their heads on her tired frame as they did so. Jessica walked over to the bed, as her daughter moved over to give her room to get in close enough to give the woman a hug.

"Great-Grandma," she said tearfully, laying her head gently on the old woman's shoulder. "We just heard a few hours ago. What are we going to do when you're gone?" she asked, as tears began flowing freely.

"Nonsense, Jessica, my dear, you'll do just fine. Just look at these beautiful children. Besides, don't write me off yet. Remember, I've been around for a long time."

"Almost a hundred years now, not bad!" said Ben as he walked over to the bed, where he stood across the bed from his wife. "Hello, Hannah, how are you? Are you doing okay? Are you in a lot of pain?"

"No, no, I'm fine. The doctors came around this morning and gave me something for the pain. I'll be fine."

"Great-Great-Grandma, tell us again, please?" the little girl asked expectantly.

"Yes, please, please!" pleaded the little boy.

Hannah looked up at Jessica and Ben and smiled, pulled herself up in bed, making enough room that the children could climb up and join her.

"And so," she began, "during the years immediately following the discovery of the Great Oracle, as had been foretold, a fabulous new Golden Age was born. As you all know, it was the discovery of the Great Oracle that provided our ancestors with access to the lost knowledge of the Ancients. The disappearance of the Effect, and the discovery of the Oracle, quickly lifted the world up and out of the Dark Age, ushering in a new era of enlightenment, and prosperity." The aged woman began coughing. Ben rushed over to pour her some water, before handing it to her. She thanked him, sipped at the water, and swallowed hard before continuing.

"Now, I was there when some very great men accomplished the very heroic feats, which made it all possible, men like your great-great-great-grandfather, Archaeologist Alex Montgomery, Ferrell Young of the Warrior Clan, Brother Sebastian of the Holy Christian Church, and so many others. Had they not succeeded in finding the Great Oracle, and fulfilling the prophecy, our world, our generation, along with our descendants, would still be enduring great suffering and misery under the wicked Kraken.

"As I look back now, back to the end of the Dark Age, I still remember how we lived in crude villages, with little more than bows and arrows, with no electricity, without any of the conveniences we enjoy today. Considering the living conditions we were forced to endure then, I am truly amazed at how far we have come in such a short time, a testament to the brave and heroic actions of the many, not the few, who dared to have such faith and courage during a time of great despair! I am thankful to God Almighty, for the incredible civilization that we continue building on this planet." She stopped to sip some more water. Jessica motioned for the children, but Hannah shook her head and waved her hand. "Please Jessica, I'm fine, let them stay. " Jessica smiled and stepped back.

"Would you like me to recount some of what has taken place since that historic moment so long ago?"

"Yes, Grandma Hannah, yes!" they both pleaded.

"Okay then. Less than a year following the discovery of the Oracle, entire populations were already learning to read and to write. The following year, brand-new printing presses began mass-producing the written word on newly made paper for a whole new generation. This in turn led to a means for communicating thoughts, ideas, theology, ideology, science, mathematics, chemistry, between one another.

"Meanwhile, ancient farming methods learned from the Oracle produced crops on a scale large enough to allow the populaces to spend more and more time focusing on education. New medicines were soon developed, too, allowing new doctors to help new patients live longer, and lead much more productive lives. Knowledge filled a deprived world the way air fills a vacuum. Within only three years, technologies that had been unknown for five-hundred years suddenly began re-appearing.

Even during those early years, when the new civilization was still in its infancy, a number of people sought to take steps to ensure what had happened to the Ancients did not happen again. With access to the vast accumulation of knowledge contained in the Oracle, and under the guidance of the Church and the Clan, a unified humanity sought to chart a new course. It took quite a while, but the efforts to build a unified government paid off. With the Oracle to educate us, the children of the New Golden Age carefully studied various forms of governments, seeking to understand what was right and what was wrong with earlier forms of government. Taking great pains to ensure a complex system of checks and balances, the new world would have the chance to build something new, something better, something that had never existed. With the network nodes located across the globe, the world grew as one. The accelerated growth in knowledge aided by the Oracle, and the lack of war, allowed civilization to grow at a phenomenal pace across the globe."

She stopped the narrative for a few moments, pausing to sip some of the refreshing water, which served to moisten her parched lips and dry throat.

"Grandma Hannah is not feeling well, kids, we need to let her rest."

"No, I'm fine. I'll have plenty of rest where I'm going soon, dear." Hannah looked back at the children. "Now where was I? Oh, yes, accelerated growth. Within five years, bicycles and electricity reappeared. Within fifteen years, electric cars and electronic communications reappeared, within twenty years plastics, composite materials; even planes could once more be seen in the sky. Cities were often torn down in order to build new ones. New schools, hospitals, churches, roads, and homes, were being built where they had never existed before.

"It took only seventy-five years for civilization to meet and even exceed the level of technology that existed during the Golden Age. Like the phoenix that rose from its own ashes, civilization rose out of the ashes of the Great Collapse, giving birth to a second and even grander age. It's a brave new world now children, with a bright and shining future, on an uncertain and uncharted course. Humanity has been re-building civilization on top of the ashes of the last one, with the knowledge gained over seven thousand years right at our disposal, twenty-four hours a day, seven days a week, three-hundred and sixty-five days a year, year in and year out. The wonderful, blessed New Golden Age that we live in, offers us the chance to learn from our past, enabling us to avoid making the same mistakes our ancient ancestors made. Maybe, just maybe, this time, we will build a better world, a world where our future takes us to the stars. Only time will tell."

Hannah's smile slowly began to fade. As her weary eyes grew tired and began to close, she turned, groaning in pain for a moment before laying her head back down to rest. The little girl laid her head back on Hannah's chest.

"I love you very much, Grandma Hannah," she said.

"Me, too!" said the little boy, doing the same.

"And I love you children more than you'll ever know! And I love you, all of you," she added, looking at Jessica and Ben, "so very much!"

The elderly Hannah's eyelids began growing heavy, so very heavy, until they peacefully and gently began to close. She tried fighting it, but the effort was futile. She felt herself slowly drifting away, as the sounds in the room slowly faded; she opened her eyes to find herself once again among old friends and familiar faces, speaking kindly to her, welcoming her. None warmed her heart more however, than the bright, smiling face of her beloved father Alex, who embraced her, as they walked together into the warm and glowing light.

Jeff W. Horton

Jeff Horton was born in North Dakota, the youngest son of a career Air Force Master sergeant, where he spent the first four years of his life before moving to North Carolina. A somewhat voracious reader growing up, he read everything from comic books to The Bible, including stories by many popular authors such as Sir Arthur Conan Doyle, H. G. Wells, Jules Verne, Edgar Rice Burroughs, Michael Crichton, Tom Clancy, C. S. Lewis, and J. R. R. Tolkien.

Jeff Horton's novel, The Great Collapse, a story about the coming of the pulse and the end of civilization, was published in 2010. He is a member of the North Carolina Writers Network.

When he's not penning his next novel, he enjoys reading, going to church, and spending time with his family.